# ANCESTORS

Paul Croo... ...ty.ie ...ball
Stadium an... ...for his
African sl... ...ued subject to the ... ...s not possible
and it has ta... t be returned ... ...rch to trace them.
*Ancestors* is his h... stamped

# ANCESTORS

## Paul Crooks

BLACKAMBER BOOKS

Published by BlackAmber Books Limited
PO Box 10812, London SW7 4ZG

First published 2002

Copyright © Paul Crooks 2002

Typeset by RefineCatch Limited, Bungay, Suffolk

Printed and bound in Finland by WS Bookwell

ISBN 1–901969–07–X

To my wife and daughter
with love

We Are Who We Were

If the following narrative does not appear sufficiently interesting to engage general attention, let my motive be some excuse for its publication. I am not so foolishly vain as to expect from it either immortality or literary reputation. If it affords any satisfaction to my numerous friends at whose request this has been written, or in the smallest degree promotes the interest of humanity, the ends for which it was undertaken will be fully attained, and every wish of my heart gratified. Let it therefore be remembered that in wishing to avoid censure, I do not aspire to praise.

Olaudah Equiano, *The African* (1789)

# CONTENTS

# FOREWORD

*Ancestors* is the result of a thirteen-year quest for my African forebears. As a child, I often wondered whether it was possible for anyone to trace his or her roots, but the thought of raiding archive after archive, with no guarantee of success, was not something that appealed. When I embarked on this quest, I was an administrator working for the National Health Service. I had no resources, no contacts, no knowledge of research methods and techniques, no knowledge of what was possible; nevertheless, I was determined to go ahead.

Jamaica was important to the development of the British Empire during the seventeenth and eighteenth centuries. Yet it surprised me to find that the British Colonial Office kept extremely good records of those who inhabited the British West Indies. The wealth of stored information about neglected historical events astonished me. Documents in archives and repositories in London and Jamaica revealed one of my great-great-great-great-grandmothers (Ami Djaba) and one of my great-great-great-grandfathers (John Alexander Crooks). Both were born in Africa, I discovered, but laboured on a Jamaican sugar plantation almost two hundred years ago.

They lived at a time when slaves in a normally sedate Jamaican parish erupted into civil unrest. It became known as the Baptist War, and it precipitated the ending of slavery in the British West Indies. When it was over, John Alexander Crooks uprooted his family and headed for the hills to begin a new life. I wanted to find out why.

So I set about piecing together a chronology, using the fragmentary information I had collected: names, dates and places. There were other fragments, too, gathered from the slave registers of 1817 to 1833. I identified blood relationships, and overlaid this information with what I learnt about the undercurrent of social and economic discontent that swept through slave communities in the British West Indies before emancipation. Some of the anecdotes gave me intriguing insights into plantation society; I also came across documented conversations between slave and master. This animated my understanding of the frustration my forebears must have felt about the social injustice of their time, and of people's courageous efforts to overcome the mundanity of their existence. Some of this I have woven into my narrative.

*Ancestors* is my attempt to reconstruct my family's pre-emancipation history in a way that aims to be both informative and enjoyable. But I pray that the spirits of my ancestors, and others, whose experience of the slave holocaust has been documented and handed down to us, will forgive me for the occasional fictional liberties.

This book would not have been possible but for Richard Hart's two-volume *Slaves Who Abolished Slavery* (1980–85), which provided me with the historical backcloth against which my plot is set. I was thrilled to meet Richard at his home a few miles away from mine in London, when he was still documenting the struggles of the people of the West Indies. Richard, I am grateful to you.

Other books which helped me develop the historical and cultural background are listed in the Bibliography.

I also acknowledge my gratitude to the staff of the Public Record Office, the British Library, the Family History Centre and the British Library Newspaper Library, all in London; and in Jamaica to the staff of the Hanover Museum, Hanover, the National Library of Jamaica,

Kingston (Eppie Edwards, in particular), and the Institute of Jamaica Social and Economic Research Department.

My thanks to Marcie Williams, Janet Shearer, Evangeline Claire, Mr Dudley Heslop, and Ami Dede Djaba – people I met on the road to discovery.

Special thanks to Mum, Dad and my brothers, Lloyd and Mark, for a lifetime of encouragement and support; and to the rest of my family – large in number. I love you all.

# Chapter 1

# August 1798

THE BOY DREAMT that he was suffocating. He feared he would die if he did not wake up. His eyes flew open and were met by the darkness that filled the ship below deck. The close air was stifling. He could almost taste the stench of vomit, putrid excrement and urine. He gasped; he was still short of breath. His teeth chattered and a shiver shot through his body. His head twitched, then jerked up from the wooden plank. Undigested food erupted from his mouth and washed over his belly.

He heard a soft voice say, 'Boy, Boy, it's all right. It's all right.' It sounded distant and vague. He did not respond. He wept. A hand gently touched his brow, wiping sweat away. It was the last thing he remembered before losing consciousness.

Some hours later Boy awoke again. He found himself staring up through a gap in the hold-cover three feet above him. He gazed beyond the grid hatch to the sky. The gratings admitted only a few determined rays of light, by which he could just make out the enormous post standing in the middle of the ship. This, he realised, was the post that was met by the criss-crossed ropes up which shipmates climbed, while vast bloated white sheets captured the wind; the post on top of which a man occupied a nest looking out to sea. Splashes spotted curved planks holding the structure together, like ribs. He felt as if he were caged within the belly of a large beast, an elephant perhaps. When the hatch went up he could see beyond the post down the aisle toward the stern. Down there the roof

1

covered a cramped space from which he had often heard groans, the groans of many more Africans – men. The planks of wood were uniformly flat, with no joins, and ran the length of the ship. What tools carved these planks? Sea breezes rushed into the ship's portholes, bouncing off the sides and rattling metal chains. The noise was like wailing. Boy thought it sounded like the eerie cry of lost souls, of ancestral spirits promising him a life. He raised his head, inhaled and thanked the spirits for their mercy as he thought of the night that had just passed. He tried to remember how many sunrises had come and gone since he was made to board the vessel. A hundred and seven? A hundred and nine?

A fly tickled Boy as it landed on his nose. He tried to raise his arm to swat it away, but the heavy iron shackles and his lack of determination derided his efforts. It was the first time for several hours that he had moved at all, and he had no feeling from one side of his buttocks down to his toes. He shifted slightly, and screamed in pain. The sting of open sores against the rough wooden surface brought tears to his eyes.

'It hurts, Ami,' he cried. 'Oooh.'

She moved slightly, to allow Boy lateral movement, which gave him a small measure of comfort.

'Are you all right?' she asked.

Boy just groaned. When the stinging cooled, his mind turned again to the fly. It occurred to him that he had not seen any insects for a long time, not since the ship hit the wide-open seas. He looked for more, and saw two weaving in and out of the light in pursuit of each other. We must be close to land, he thought. The man lying on the other side of Boy had sometimes robbed him of food but had begun refusing food recently, which was a relief. For the last nine sunrises, the shipmates had been making the man suffer terribly for his decision. He had been taken on deck each day after feeding, and flogged; blood from the last

2

whipping had caked on Boy's left shoulder. Boy made no movement that would disturb him.

Another interminable hour passed. Boy turned his head towards the man, who was staring up at the hold, lying like a log, his mouth ajar and making no sound. Boy stole a closer look; with a pang of horror, he realised that the man was dead. Boy moved his elbow, putting space between him and the body; the width of a hand was all. It was not good to touch the dead. Boy prayed that the pale-faced men would soon appear, to remove the body and dispose of it in the Atlantic graveyard benignly named the Middle Passage: the vast ocean between West Africa and the West Indies. He even thought of rejoicing for the man's sake, but could not bring himself to do so. He wondered how many captives were left to tell the grim tales of those lost. The schooner *James* had started her voyage with a cargo of almost three hundred black men and women. Less than two hundred survived when she ambled into a bay on the Jamaican coast. He felt a soreness in his throat whenever he thought about all those who had died and been flung overboard.

These thoughts led Boy to wonder why Ami had never asked him his name. To her, he was just Boy. She had befriended him on the day they were placed together, side by side, in the hold. During the voyage, she had taken time to teach him the tongue of the Krobo people, and he was now fully conversant in the language she called Ga-Dangme. She often spoke of her home, which was two sunrises from the coast, and of her people, who fished in the rivers dissecting the plains of Accra. She told him one day that she had always hated the local slave market. Her father had often cursed and sworn at the powerful slave merchants at the Salaga market. At Korle-bu, beyond the Korle lagoon, freed slaves had settled on land abutting the sea; her father had helped many escaped slaves to get there and obtain their freedom. Boy listened carefully to Ami. She talked about her life, the lives of friends and family, her homeland – anything that came into her mind. He spoke only when spoken to.

'Did you hear the heavy rain last night?' asked Ami.

'No,' replied Boy.

'When I heard *nyon-gbo*, I wished for it to flow down and engulf you. I wanted it to take away your sickness. I wanted it to strengthen you.'

'It didn't come to me.'

'Don't worry. Later I will pray to the ancestors to protect you. I will ask them to make you grow stronger. Have faith, little one.'

Boy always found Ami's voice soothing, at times a comforting distraction from what was happening around him. When she spoke of her homeland, he imagined it as if it were his own: an enchanted forest, with an abundance of yawning gullies. The weather was mostly warm and dry, producing sanguine evening skies, though there were times when clouds gathered and unleashed torrential rain for days on end. Her people, the Krobo, made beautiful body adornments by stringing together deep-sea blue Koli beads, like coral but ground from stone. Boy and Ami had shared a brief moment of pleasure when he recognised the beads as those his people called Kori. He thought of his father, a village elder, a man of high status, and a judge. He recollected the day when his father banished a thief to a nearby village, there to become a slave.

'Boy,' said Ami, 'you say nothing. What are you thinking?'

'My village,' he said.

He closed his eyes and imagined looking out at the village from within the dark thatched hut that was his home. He thought of a sun-lashed day outside, of the men gathering weapons to go hunting in the forest that surrounded the village, and of women talking while forming Kori beads on grinding-stones, to be sold to neighbouring

4

villages and passing travellers. The memory brought back a vague yet vividly smiling image of his mother. Tears began to swell, and streamed down his face. The last time he saw her, she was spinning cotton outside their hut; she had golden trinkets about her arms and legs.

She vanished and the dark faces of his kidnappers appeared. He tried to banish that memory, concentrating instead on the constant murmuring of men lying on shelves in the hold below, completing tired accounts of their capture. Many of the stories were about Africans, young men, women and children, the strongest, fittest and wisest of the towns and villages, who had disappeared, never to be heard of again. Most of the stories began with the outbreak of war between two nations carrying century-old grudges or with a betrayal; they ended with people falling prey to pale-skinned men like those on deck. The men talked as if they were rehearsing their epitaphs before greeting the creator.

One man began an account of how his village had been invaded. Boy wondered why the man was telling his tale: he seemed to address no one in particular, just anyone still breathing the fetid, steamy air. He said the invaders had come from a nearby village with which his people had been at war for many years. He had been sold to the Ashanti king and made a slave. When the king tired of him, he was handed on to a pale-faced man, in payment for guns. He said it was so that the Ashanti kingdom could maintain its strength and expand further outward from Kumase, reaching the coast two hundred miles to the south, the Volta River in the east, Sehwi to the west and the Mossi kingdom over two hundred miles to the north. They had conquered these areas over five generations. A sudden bout of coughing made the man cut his story short.

Although this was the first time Boy had heard of anyone being sold for guns, some aspects of the story reminded him of his own capture. He translated man's tale from Twi into Ga for Ami, and for the first time she asked what bad luck had befallen Boy. How was it that he had been separated from his parents?

'Did they take anybody else from your village?' she asked. 'Or were you the only one?'

'I am by myself.'

'How did it happen?'

'Bandits,' he said. 'On big, big horses ... soldier-bandits.'

Ami coaxed him to tell her more. He told her that his father had been preparing him for a rite of passage in the swamps in a serene valley on the Benue River, the long, chief tributary of the Niger. He woke early one morning to the smell of forest freshness. The air was cooler than it had been for many days, the result of a downpour the night before. He and his father were not far from their home, in a village within the kingdom of Oyo, where neighbour waged war against neighbour.

The bandits pounced from a thicket of trees and shrubs. They grabbed Boy first. A short man leapt on his father's back, knocking him to the ground. His father rose like an elephant, showing the strength of a man half his age. Holding him round the neck with one hand and raining down blows with the other, the man shouted, 'Quick! Grab his legs!' Boy's father was cut down again as he fought furiously against the onslaught of six men. 'Leave my son! Please don't harm my son!' his father cried, refusing to surrender. The men clubbed him into submission. After ten minutes of struggle, the men had Boy and his father subdued, and tied their hands behind their backs. Later that day, a woman and a boy from a nearby village joined them. By the time six sunrises had elapsed, they were part of a caravan of ten with nooses round their necks.

They were marched, in line, across land for many days. Some Yoruba men attacked the bandits as they followed the river south, but were easily repelled. Boy travelled for many weeks, and through many towns and villages, suffering hunger and thirst until the caravan – less two who had been sold as slaves – arrived in the Ashanti kingdom. He was separated from his father and traded to an Akan emissary, who gave him as a present to a high-ranking official in the Ashanti army. Boy had spent almost a year travelling. When he reached the coast, he was sold to white slavers and secured with padlocks to other dark men. 'They took all my clothes off and burnt my skin.'

There was a long silence. Eventually Ami asked tentatively, 'Before the men took you away, did you ever tell your mother and father that you loved them?'

Boy sniffed a couple of times and admitted, in a single syllable, that he had not. He fell silent again, listening to the deep African voices close by; they were solemn and hushed.

A heavy metal object sliding slowly off a shelf and thudding to the floor broke the quiet. It made Ami jump, and she hit her head against the post that had been her companion throughout the voyage. Boy heard her chains rattle as she vigorously rubbed her forehead. The ship slowed and came to a halt. Boy watched as Ami listened to – or for – something. Through the sluggish murmuring of captives who had been delirious for the last three sunrises, there seemed to be a realisation that the survivors' lives were about to change direction. A man began a slow and rhythmical chant. A woman joined in, in Akan. Another man followed suit, then another, until there was a sizeable ensemble. The men's voices, as deep as they were sombre, seemed to vibrate along wooden planks. Some people beat their hands and chains against timber – Boy assumed that they did not know the language.

'Why are they chanting?' he asked.

'I do not know,' Ami replied, 'but listen.'

A woman further along the hold started a similar chant.

Ami turned her body awkwardly, crying out, 'Oh my beloved people, we will be one with our ancestors!'

7

She broke into prayer. Boy reached out towards her face, his hand alighting on her cheek, to feel her tears, to mop them. But he was weak and his arm tired quickly. His limp hand slid off her face, smothering her tears.

'I'm scared,' he said.

'Listen, there is movement up above!' called a voice from the shelf below; it was the man who had given the account of his capture. 'Can everyone hear it?'

'Something is happening,' Ami said. 'People running, cheering as well, as I have never heard before. Boy, can you see anything?'

Neither Boy nor Ami had a good view; their fellow captives seemed equally at a loss.

The grid hatch was wrenched open by a shipmate. Boy grabbed Ami's hand and held it tight. He saw three pale men hurtle pass the man who had opened the hatch. They leapt down the stairs. One of them missed a step in the rush and slid down the last few, crash-landing to the floor. Zealously they occupied a separate aisle each and began unshackling the captives a few at a time. The chains clanged viciously as they were tugged through the runners, ricocheting off them in a circle of metal pegs. Many of the weaker slaves were pulled from the shelves by their ankles.

One of the shipmates wore the grin of a madman, and seemed impervious to the suffering below deck. He released Boy from the hold. Boy did his best to help himself out of his chains and away from the spot where he had lived so uncomfortably for so long. He gritted his teeth and used every muscle in his body to haul himself up. As he slid to the floor, he could feel something slimy under his feet: vomit. At least two captives close by had been sick the day before, and the vomit must have been there ever since, like an adhesive to ensure that the cargo stayed put.

He hadn't yet adjusted to standing upright, and fought to keep his balance as the ship dipped, rose and swayed gently. The movement was gentler: the ship must have anchored. He longed for the fresh smell of the wind skimming the pale blue sea. It was the time of day when the captives were made to jump up and down. 'I will soon breathe again,' he thought.

He moved towards the hatch, carefully avoiding a particular shipmate who always used his rifle-butt mercilessly against the bare backs or limbs of defenceless men, women and children.

The shipmate with the mad grin ushered him towards the steps. At the same time he dragged off the shelf the corpse that had lain next to Boy and added it to a pile of bodies at the end of the row, to be thrown overboard later.

Ami nudged Boy. 'Look at him,' she said. 'That one is so ugly, much uglier than the rest of them. He thinks he's strong, but he's not. He tries to scare us but really he is the one who is consumed by fear.' Boy watched the first contingent of Africans being frog-marched up the steps to the top deck. He noticed the luminous blue eyes of another shipmate, who wore a look of glazed concentration; he was listening intently, alert to every cough and groan, to every clank of chain. Boy dipped his head the instant he met the shipmate's eyes and ducked behind some tall men, trying to make himself invisible, trying to avoid triggering the shipmate's wrath.

Boy realised he was losing track. In all the unfamiliar movement, he did not know where Ami was. At that moment he heard a woman cry out. Two tall men in front of him formed a barrier. He poked his head between their thighs and saw one of the shipmates brandishing a whip, about to lash a woman cowering before him. When the whip landed it was Ami's head that reared up, her scream so shrill and full of pain that the rats infesting the lower deck scattered to find the darkest holes of the hull. The shipmate hadn't singled her out for any particular reason; he didn't even look at her when he hit her. Boy had seen

9

this man administer lashes at jump-times, rage burning in his eyes.

It was Ami's turn to go through the hatch. Boy tried to help steady her as a shipmate moved on. Slowly she put her right foot forwards, the chains weighing on her ankles. She lost her balance, lurched forward and grabbed the first thing that would support her. It was the shoulder of another shipmate. His look of horror betrayed his fright at being manhandled in this way. Ami's ebony hand reached over his right shoulder, gripping him just under his left armpit. Boy tugged at her arm, realising the danger.

'Ahhhhh!' the shipmate cried. He broke free from Ami, grabbed Boy and tossed him aside, then turned on Ami, punching and kicking her as if fighting for his life. Ami keeled backwards and fell to the floor. Boy instinctively pushed against a tall African man, who responded and helped Ami to her feet. The man gestured to the shipmate with an outstretched arm, as if to say, 'She cannot harm you.' Boy's heart was bashing so hard he could hear it. He was sure the man would be made to suffer for his bravery. His own terror broke loose in tears and shivers. The shipmate appeared to compose himself by gripping Ami's jaw and pushing her forward. The brown man stretched his arm out to catch Ami whenever her strength threatened to desert her. She made yet another tired attempt at steadying herself.

'Thank you,' she managed to say.

The man responded with a few words that Ami did not understand. She dipped her head in grateful acknowledgement.

'He is Hausa,' Boy recognised. 'He said that these ugly people prey on the weak and you must look strong . . . always.'

Ami raised her head and offered a little smile.

The shipmate had a long chain draped round his neck. He held some keys, which every now and then he tossed from one hand to the other; the noise appeared to be associated with the chain. Was he going to beat Ami with the chain or – worse – wrap it round her neck and strangle her? The shipmate grabbed the chain tight with his grubby right hand, and winked at Boy. Cutting a craggy smile, he chained the Hausa man and Ami together by the ankles. He shoved them towards six other Africans, similarly paired, who were being sent up on deck.

# Chapter 2

# The Scramble

WHEN BOY REACHED the main deck, he saw ten men standing on guard, their guns cocked, while their Chief leant himself against the door of his cabin. The Chief's eyebrows came down close to the bridge of his nose and his upper lip turned upward, almost touching the tip of his nose. Putting down his gun, the Chief poured himself a glass of what Boy took to be the blood of Africans.

In astonishment and terror, Boy screamed, 'Mwene Puto! Mwene Puto!'

The other captives retreated a couple of paces, echoing his cry. Boy feared that all the shipmates might be followers of Mwene Puto, who ground the bones of kidnapped Africans to make gunpowder. 'The Chief, he is the Lord of Death,' he thought. The Chief had only to taste the red liquid in his glass and his intention to eat all the dark-skinned people on the deck would be proved. But the Chief merely waved his hand, signalling his men to relax. One of the shipmates took up a position behind a swivel-gun and trained it down on the shackled men and women crowded on deck amidships.

'Do you think they will kill us and eat us now?' Boy asked Ami in a strange, high pitch of bewilderment.

'No. If they were planning to do that, they would have done so by now. They give us a meal every day, sometimes two. Yam. Rice. Corn. You must ask yourself, why?'

The sun was high in the sky, and the day was hot and humid. Between the groups of captives, Boy could see land. He felt a great rush of relief, and stooped as low as he could,

12

to see if he could get a better view. Between him and the shore was the mysterious sea inviting him to jump in; the rails of the schooner stood high and wide, a menacing reminder that there was no escape. Through the criss-cross of ropes he could see emerald patches of shallow rock, smothered in sea-urchins. Although his neck ached with stiffness, he couldn't keep still. He twisted from side to side, checking and rechecking, trying to get a sense of this new place.

The ship was anchored at the mouth of a deep bay, and he saw a number of boats – sizeable, but much smaller than the ship – coming out of the port towards them. He scanned the shore for any signs that would give a clue as to where next he would be heading. The land-smells carried on the breeze reminded him of the shores he had embarked from. He indulged the thought that he had returned, but to a point further along. It would soon be time to get off; it would soon be time to go home.

The land sloped gradually until it was lost behind the sea-line, and at this point it became the eye of the bay. He kept turning, tracking the sea along the merging horizon over to the other point, where the land crept up from behind the sea-line. Three hundred paces inland from the beach, the land soared spectacularly into the sky, where scavenging birds – John Crow, he thought – were circling the hills. The coating of rich, deep-green forest covered the hills like a canopy. At the sight of the forest, Boy felt another rush of relief: surely the spirits of his ancestors would continue to watch over him.

The boats were drawing near, and he could see people waving, hear them shouting at the tops of their voices. The boats vanished from sight when they reached the side of the ship. Boy's relief vanished, too, and he began to feel sick.

With the Hausa man shackled to her, Ami began edging towards the side of the ship where the boats were gathering. When she reached it, she could not help herself: she vomited the contents of the last feed on to the people below. Fists waved and there was much cursing. Amid the chaos, the shipmates shouted excitedly at the people at the tail of the convoy hurrying towards the ship.

A large hand suddenly appeared in Boy's face and clamped round it, like an octopus round a stone. He felt a sharp tug, which made his neck snap back. When the hand let go, Boy found himself at the back of a cluster of captives watching the spectators. He could no longer see Ami.

Some of the shipmates started pushing the spectators – a showman's attempt to get some semblance of order. Boy saw an opening and clutched the lower rail. A shipmate made a lacklustre attempt to prise him away, but the Chief tapped the shipmate on the shoulder and the shipmate stopped tugging and stepped aside. The Chief lashed Boy with his whip, hard. Boy yelped, his pain was mingled not only with terror but with rage. The Chief raised a clenched fist, ready to hit Boy, but thought better of it as a low, angry murmur of protest ran through the captives. He wiped sweat from his forehead, then snatched a shipmate's pistol and fired two shots in the air. The captives hushed and the shipmates' control was absolute again.

The Chief went to the side of the ship and beckoned the people on the boats to climb aboard the ship. Amid much yelling and cursing, they began to do so. Boy moved decisively away from the ship's side. His head was bent so that he could see where he was treading, and he collided with Ami. She was propelled backwards to the length of the chain attaching her to the Hausa man.

'Run! Run!' came a cry from behind.

Boy reacted instantly, bolting towards the stern. He ran twenty yards, brushing through a storm of fleeing captives. Panic made him breathless. Fright made him wheeze. He forgot that Ami and the Hausa man, with fetters on their ankles, could not match his speed. Men, women and children rushed recklessly, wildly swarming around him.

14

Boy raced to the side of the vessel and pulled himself up to catch a glimpse of his only escape route. Tears sprang to his eyes when he saw captives who had jumped for freedom being recaptured and hauled aboard the small boats by the shipmates. A young woman, still shackled by the wrists, was in the sea, struggling to keep her head above the waves. Sucking in salt water, she gasped for air, choked and spat. With a last gasp, she disappeared behind a great rolling wave. The wave crashed against the hull, splintered, then turned into the indistinguishable vastness of the sea. The woman was gone, her identity lost.

Boy ran to the other side of the ship, where a few captives were huddled. He clambered over their backs and dived for the sea, for the freedom he craved. As his feet left the deck, someone grabbed the chain between his manacles. He felt himself take a circular path through the air, and braced himself as he hurtled towards the outside of the hull. His hip crashed into it, and pain shot through him. He dangled there, exhausted. He shut his eyes and could think of nothing. He felt weak and light-headed. 'I am to become a spirit, at last,' he thought. But what would it feel like to drown? What would it be like to breathe water and to feel life ebbing away? When the water filled his lungs, would it hurt? If it did, would he claw his way back to the surface, to beg for life? And if he drowned, if he died and couldn't find his ancestors, who would he turn to, to beg for life?

Boy opened his eyes. The waves were reaching for his feet: the rulers of the sea had come to take him as an offering. He kicked out wildly at the thought. Then, with astonishment, he realised that someone was holding on to him.

'Ami!'

The two searched each other's eyes; a few seconds were enough to recapture what they had been through together. Ami gritted her teeth and began painfully hauling him

15

back on board. He fell into her arms and she collapsed on to the deck, taking him down with her. He laid his head in her lap and sobbed. She cradled him in her arms and stroked his hair.

The gentle moment was short-lived. A group of fifteen or so captives were being lanced and forced backwards. Although the Hausa man immediately pressed forwards with all his weight, he could not prevent the captives tripping on Ami and falling, threatening to crush all three of them. Ami let go of Boy in an effort to shield herself. Boy felt his ankle twist as a woman fell on his leg. He did his utmost not only to push her off but also to protect Ami. Suddenly he felt someone grab him round the waist. Then he was wrenched away and thrown, spinning, towards the Chief's cabin door. He hit his head and lay dazed on the floor, while fleeing captives leapt over his legs. He crawled to a sheltered part of the deck and hauled himself up into a crouch; he stalled, gathering his senses. His head pounded, and he feared the worst for Ami. Once again he was alone. He must find somewhere to shelter, but where? And how could he escape?

He felt a ghostly shadow, as of a bad spirit, and spun round, the inside of his nostrils hot with a sudden rush of blood. A white man stood there, staring down at him with deep blue eyes, their pupils dilated. The man was over six feet tall. His age was difficult to tell: he might be approaching his thirties, although the wrinkles carved in his forehead suggested that he might be older. The man's penetrating look reached out at Boy's soul. Boy shifted one way and the man moved simultaneously; it was as if the man were listening to his thoughts. He sensed his destiny had finally confronted him. In one hand the man held a rope to which six captives were tethered. Boy knew he must escape the man's glare. There was nowhere to hide. He looked up at the ship's sails, and for a moment considered climbing the rigging to get away. The man seemed to have read his thoughts and the blue eyes dared Boy to do it. Boy accepted the dare, but as he leapt for the rigging the man's arm shot up; he caught Boy's ankle and hauled him back down to the deck. Boy's hands were afire as the ropes dragged through them, but he refused to let go until he landed in an undignified heap on the deck. Even then he pressed upwards, but the man's boot bore down on his back, trapping him, forcing him to stay still. It was no good, Boy thought; there was no escape; he would have to accept the inevitable.

Holding Boy firmly by the arm, the man shoved his other captives to the side of the schooner. And when all were firmly secured, their captor jostled them on to the boats to be taken ashore.

# Chapter 3

# Lucea

WHEN THEY REACHED land, the captives were taken to a market settlement and herded into a wood-railed, dirt-floored pen with a tattered cloth canopy for a roof. Boy heard a man with skin as dark as the night sky saying that they were in a place called Lucea, on the north-western coast of the island of Jamaica, many moons away from their homeland. The man said that the only way to get back was on the ship, but that no ship ever returned captives to the homeland.

Boy was too exhausted to understand what that meant. He simply listened, leaning against one of the wooden posts that supported the canopy. He was still shackled to his six companions – three women, two men and a girl who he thought was two years younger than him, which would make her about nine. He stared at the ground, his mind blank.

When consciousness next visited him, he was still standing, his head hanging low on his thin chest. His vision was blurred, so he focused on some tiny holes in the ground from which came a steady flow of red ants. His bottom lip hung low, as if in a stalemated tug-of-war with the force of gravity. The pain of the last few months overwhelmed him. Physically broken and malnourished, he had changed from a podgy, happy-go-lucky child to a shrivelled shadow of his former self. He was in such distress that he was slow to realise that the ants swarming over his feet were biting him. He squashed as many of them as he could, then rubbed his feet hard; the bites stung with a vengeance.

He slowly raised his head; his neck ached from over three months of being unable to stand straight. He moved his head from side to side, backwards then forwards, gaining some relief. He twitched his face a little and his skin felt tight – a mixture of dirt and dried tears. His scrawny legs ached terribly, and he felt a tingling shoot up and down them. He dropped into a squat, knees drawn up to his chin and pressed as near to his shoulders as possible, and eased his head gently back against the post. His lips were cut and swollen, a throbbing reminder of recent events. He closed his eyes and thought of Ami, praying quietly.

After a few minutes, it was borne in on him that the iron rings round his ankles were older and rustier than those he had worn before. They dug into him, and the chafing had rubbed away his skin; the resultant wounds were a weeping mess. Boy looked out at the market where their pen stood. He was reminded of market day at home: this place was similarly noisy, with people everywhere, hustling and bustling and shouting at one another in a language whose rhythms seemed familiar. A fat woman was haggling over the price of maize.

Bewildered, Boy stared. The people looked like his own people, except that these were dowdily dressed. There was no richly coloured Kente cloth, no beads or earrings meticulously carved from wood. And there appeared to be no ceremony in the way they dressed. Some walked around with nothing on from the waist up, no adornment at all; their skin was their clothing. There were horses, too, though smaller than the ones back home. The buildings held a strange appeal: unlike the huts at home, these had rooms built one on top of the other.

Every so often the sounds of the marketplace were punctuated by screams from a big tent about fifty paces away. Boy peered through the crowds, trying to see what was going on. To his alarm, he glimpsed the face of a grown

African man screaming like a child scalded by boiling water. Yet more cries, more pain, more anguish.

Across the crowded market he saw another crude canopy and, under it, a white man brandishing a piece of glowing red iron. Boy was fairly certain he knew what the man was doing, and the next scream left him in no doubt whatsoever. The man put down the piece of metal and picked another from the fire, fixing his eyes on the left shoulder of an African woman who had been forced to her knees before him. Boy stared in horror as the man, with a deft movement of his hand, planted the hot iron on her back and held it there briefly. Writhing in pain, she was led away. That particular branding was over.

In front of the branding-man there was a long line of Africans, some of whom Boy recognised from the ship. In terror, he realised that his own turn would not be long in coming.

The blue-eyed man who had captured Boy suddenly appeared, sucking the deep orange pulp from the stone of a mango. He looked his captives up and down, then yanked the chain that joined them, and dragged them across the market towards the branding-place. He made them sit down by one of the canopy poles, and looked them over once more. He smiled as he peered down at Boy. Boy did not dare return the look, instead fixing his stare on a lizard which had appeared from nowhere: it had run down one of the poles, and stopped when it reached halfway. There was not even a twitch; it was as still as a wooden carving and stared straight ahead. Boy wanted to keep as still as the tiny creature, in the hope of diverting his captor's attention from him. It worked, at least for the time being. The captor stopped smiling, turned away, and grabbed the strongest-looking captive, a man with tribal scarification marks on his face.

Tall and straight-backed, hands chained behind his back, the African sat cross-legged at the man's feet. The pair of them exchanged fixed glares, the African's full of hatred, as if he wished to kill the other man. The captor looked back, apparently unperturbed, but through stern gestures indicated that the African should refrain from such expressions: it was not good to look a wild beast in the eye. The captor began circling the African, and suddenly flung him on his back. Two other white men grabbed him and rolled him over. One of them sat on his back while the branding-man burnt a C into his right shoulder. The African, determined not to show pain, gritted his teeth. The veins stood out from his neck and his eyes bulged as his back was burnt. When it was done he collapsed, urine flowing down his legs. The branding-man's helper rolled the African over, grinning when he saw the wet patch of earth. The captor stood by as the African was branded again, this time on his face. Boy could see the raw red mark on the man's shoulder, and the smell of burning flesh made him feel sick. He took deep breaths, filling his lungs to try and stave off nausea. He closed his eyes and wished hard for it not to happen. It worked.

Boy's turn had come. The branding-man looked at him, sizing up where to put the mark, then reached for him. Boy pushed the hand away. The branding-man snarled, as if eager for a fight, and Boy backed away – into the clutches of one of the helpers. The branding-man picked the roasted tong from the fire. A helper grabbed Boy's wrist and twisted it, forcing him to his knees. The branding-man clamped his large hand round Boy's neck, and the helper's grip tightened each time Boy struggled. When the iron was pressed against Boy's shoulder, he screamed in agony. His back was on fire and he felt a rush of blood to his nose and his ears. He bit his tongue. The helper released him. Boy writhed around the floor in a wild attempt to smother the pain. The branding-man put the irons in a vat of water, and they sizzled loudly.

The captor mumbled something incomprehensible, and

a sly smile broke as he slapped the helper on the back. The branding-man was pointing to something unexpected in the marketplace.

A man in strange black clothes was marching towards them. Although he was stooped, the eyes peering over his half-rimmed glasses were intense and purposeful, and they were fixed on the men in the branding-place. He carved his way through the crowded market, pushing, shoving and bumping many black folk with the carelessness of the wind through trees. Many seemed ready to challenge him until they realised he was white; then they just carried on about their business. As he came nearer, Boy saw that he had blue eyes and mustard-coloured hair. He was short, clean-shaven and slight of frame. His black coat and white collar, and the big leather-bound book he held in his hand, marked him out from all the other white people.

As soon as he reached the branding-place, presenting himself within a touch of Boy's captor, he began shouting and waving his hands, as if telling him off. There was no response from the captor – at first. Boy noted the new-comer's thunderous expression. He saw also that the captor acknowledged his presence only by the occasional glance from the corner of his eye.

The captor snarled. He had a chain in his hand, which he threw to the ground. He clenched his huge fist and looked as if he might punch the man.

The captor was the larger and more dominant of the two. Boy took a couple of chopped steps backwards, thinking that the two men would now fight, but the captor's wild look gave way to a forced grin and he laughed harshly, then spat at the other man's feet. Some of the phlegm caught his chin and he wiped it away with his sleeve. His opponent did no more than look mortified. In silence, the captor rounded up his slaves and led them to a mule-cart on to which they were loaded with the help of a couple of men from the branding-place. Boy was again struck by the contrast between the aggressive captor and the strange black-clad man, who stood rigid and pale.

As the cart drew away, Boy peered back over his shoulder. The strange man's blank, faraway expression evoked thoughts of Ami. How frightened she had looked when she faced a cocked gun ready to spray her in all directions. His thoughts of her intensified as a black woman in the increasingly distant marketplace brushed by the black-clad man, almost knocking him off balance. For a lightning moment Boy thought she was Ami. He tried to jump to his feet, but fell backwards as the cart bounced over a pothole. He landed on top of a dark, slim man with high cheekbones and slightly protruding teeth. Irritated, the man kissed his teeth: the sound of saliva swishing through his molars was a bit like the sea, but sharper. Then he smiled and good-naturedly eased Boy off him and helped him to kneel up. Boy peered back again, searching for the woman, but she was lost in the crowd. Sitting back on his heels, Boy pondered Ami's fate. Would he ever see her again?

The cart rumbled on and on. Boy was half asleep when he noticed the African who had invited the wrath of the captor. He was feeling around the letter C branded on his face, tearing away bits of dead flesh and flicking them over the side. Boy looked away when the African registered his stare. As he closed his eyes again, Boy was startled by a heavy hand on his shoulder – to his relief, it was not the hand of any of his pale-faced tormentors. He sat up, offering a polite smile in the hope of establishing a friendly connection. But a smaller man in the cart stole everyone's attention away from Boy, introducing himself quietly.

'Muhammad al-Hakim,' he said, pointing to his chest.

'Mensah,' the strong man replied, mimicking the action.

The two men were plainly ready and willing to communicate. Boy shifted his position, eager to follow the conversation. He was also thankful for Muhammad's

23

intervention, because he had feared that Mensah might impose his will.

'Ashanti,' said Mensah, thumping his chest.

'Dagomba,' said Muhammad, smiling.

Mensah sneered at him, making Boy feel nervous.

'These people, they are so ignorant,' said Muhammad leaning back. 'You understood what I just said, didn't you, boy?' Boy nodded. 'You know the language of the North, don't you?'

Boy dipped his head and began scratching on the wooden floor of the cart. 'Yes,' he said.

'Oh?'

'I know Twi, I know Ga, and I know his.' Boy pointed to Mensah.

'So what language does he speak?' Muhammad asked.

'Akan,' Boy replied confidently. He had begun scratching pictures on the wood of the cart floor – the sun, the moon and a hut, his home.

'You know much for one so young. It is good that you like to know things.'

As they progressed through a wooded area, Muhammad introduced himself to one of the sad-looking young women on the cart, but he did not understand her reply. Boy did, though, and he said, 'Her name is Abena. She speaks Akan.' Then he went back to his pictures.

'Very good. I can see you will be of great use to me, boy. What shall I call you?'

'Boy. That is what the woman Ami calls me. Everyone calls me Boy. You can keep calling me Boy, if you want to.'

'I will do that, Boy.'

Next, Muhammad eyed the youngest girl, who was snuggled up asleep beside Abena.

'Her name is Oyoe,' said Abena, wiping droplets of sweat from the girl's face.

This time Muhammad did not look to Boy for an interpretation; he seemed to know what had been said. Abena twisted loose strands of Oyoe's thick entangled hair, making little locks stand up. The girl slept with her mouth open, her lower jaw bouncing slightly as the cart jolted along. Abena swatted at the mosquitoes that hovered near her mouth.

Boy was still keen to observe the potential connection between Mensah and Muhammad. He sensed that Muhammad was a man of great wisdom and learning: that was apparent from the way he held his chin high, as if to communicate with the sky, the clouds, the sun and trees. He might be a stargazer, and if he were he would know many things mystical and scientific. He succeeded in catching Muhammad's attention and led Muhammad's eyes towards Mensah.

Muhammad smiled assuredly at Boy. 'I was taught in Gobir at a place called Degel. I spent many years there. Did anyone ever tell you of such a place?'

Boy shook his head.

'I know much about the Ashanti,' Muhammad went on. 'They are a proud nation, and conquerors in their own right, stately – and, yes, too arrogant to be loved. They respect people who possess knowledge. And so I believe this man and I have much we can talk about.'

Boy pulled back as Muhammad leant towards him and said, 'You have nothing to fear. You should know that a man should resign himself to his fate with patience and courage.' After a pause he added, 'I want you to tell that man what I have just said.'

Boy's translation made Mensah growl.

'Did I say something bad?' Boy asked.

'No, you didn't,' Muhammad replied. He went on sturdily, 'Tell him this: the possession of life or anything material without enjoying it is not worth having. It is no good for me and neither is it good for you!' He snorted, punched his left hand with his right fist, then sat back. 'Go on, tell him.'

Muhammad had got Mensah's attention, and he was not finished yet. Boy moved closer to Muhammad, and again passed on the translation. Addressing Mensah directly, and pausing only to let Boy translate, Muhammad recited a familiar story, told in different versions by many generations of the peoples of the African west coast. He told of a boy who was in danger of being burnt while playing with fire. 'Seeing his father coming, the boy called out to him for help; but his father started to tell him how he had erred. "Help me now," cried the boy. "You can tell me about this later on when I am safe."' Muhammad explained that Mensah was about to enter the fire and that his words would be unable to protect him from whatever dangers he might later face. He told Mensah that he should heed these words before it was too late. Boy was glad that the Ashanti did not attack Muhammad, as he thought he might. For a brief moment he believed Muhammad had gained the upper hand.

Mensah sat pensively for a few moments. Then, unexpectedly, stubbornness showed once more. 'Ashanti kotoko!' he announced.

'What did he say?' Muhammad asked Boy eagerly.

Boy was bemused. 'He said, "Kill thousands and thousands more will come."'

Muhammad quickly countered, 'It is always dangerous to choose the wrong time for doing a thing.'

It was Boy's last translation: the talking stopped. Mensah curled up in his corner of the cart, facing the sun, slipping back into silent despondency.

Time passed. Boy noticed that Muhammad had become increasingly restless since he had last spoken. Although the conversation between Mensah and Muhammad troubled him, there was something Boy liked about Muhammad. The precision of Muhammad's speech reminded Boy of his own father.

'Doesn't he like us?' Boy asked tentatively.

Muhammad looked across at Mensah, who was snoring. He gave Boy a knowing smile, then answered, 'He dwells on the past, on one that is talked about only in stories told by mothers' mothers to children's children.' Muhammad told Boy that the Ashanti had tried to overpower Dagomba on the battlefield one dry season over thirty years ago. It was said that the Ashanti launched an invasion which brought them into direct conflict with the Southern Mossi kingdom. The Ashanti warriors were armed with long-barrelled shouldered guns and thought they would bore through Dagomba and press further North. But they couldn't overcome the Dagomba, hard though they tried. They were on foot, whereas the Dagomba were on horse-back and could move very quickly, although every time they charged their horses reared, afraid of the sound of the guns. The Ashanti decided after the first unsuccessful battle to use horses, thinking that they would then be equal and more. But they knew nothing about horses or riding, and they failed and had to retreat, shamed by the stalemate. But emissaries from Dagomba offered overlord-ship to the Ashanti, rather than fight them again. They knew the Ashanti were strong and determined and would keep coming; each attack would be stronger than the last.

Muhammad eventually reached the end of his story: 'It wasn't so long ago that King Osei Mensah achieved the changes to the law necessary to bring Dagomba fully within Ashanti reaches of government. Men like our friend here did not like it – they would have preferred to fight my people to the end.'

# Chapter 4

# Crooks' Cove

THE SOUND OF a bell ringing outside woke Boy. A smile crossed his face as he sat up, stretching his arms as high as he could, believing that he was at home. He yawned massively, then laid his head on the floor again, ready to go back to sleep. The bell clanged again, and Boy's eyes flashed wide open in panic; raising himself once more, he rubbed them vigorously, remembering the truth. He tried to recall how he had got off the cart. Seeing the faint imprint of his head in the dust reminded him of the shock of being dropped on to the ground from a considerable height. Then he had a recollection of drawing his knees up towards his chest – that was all he could remember about his arrival. Who had carried him inside? Mensah, he supposed. Those few hours of sleep on the floor were the best sleep he had had since the ship sailed from Africa.

He looked around. It was still dark, but through a crack in the hut's wooden wall he could discern the pattern of the landscape against the breaking dawn. Cockerels were crowing, and there was a distant, comforting chorus of birdsong. He wiped the sleep from his eyes and scratched his skinny thighs, feeling the effects of too many days without a proper wash.

The gentle sounds of other Africans beginning to stir were disrupted by the sound of men approaching. Boy sat up.

The door was unlocked and flung open. Two silhouettes materialised in the doorway, one of them holding a gun. The shape of the man in front looked vaguely familiar. A third came in with a lamp held low, followed by the unmistakable figure of the captor. He counted the Africans, to make sure that all were present, then rounded them up and put chains round their necks. Linking them in one line, he hustled them outside.

With his chains dragging along the ground, Boy looked towards the horizon and the start of the sunrise. He wondered whether this was the same sun that lit the grasslands of his homeland. If so, was his father gazing upon it from the other side, seeing what Boy could see? Or was this a different sun? No, it must be the same one, for he had checked it every day for over three months. It invariably rose and went down in the expected place, and it had been his companion all the way on the ship, just as it had at home.

Watching the Africans emerging from the huts around him, he was struck by how badly they held themselves: their feet dragged, their shoulders were hunched. They looked starved of any dignity, which they must surely have possessed at some time in their lives. The majority of the men wore little more than coarse linen trousers tied at the waist. Women wore long linen garments and covered their heads with a twisted handkerchief or two. How long could these Africans have lived here?

After fifteen minutes' laborious walking, Boy and the other captives reached the foot of a hill. At the top was a house more enormous than he'd ever seen. He peered up at the magnificent brown stone structure and the cleared ground around it; it must be the Chief's house. They made their way up a wide dust track cut through the trees. When they were within a few yards of the house, Boy glanced back over his shoulder and he marvelled at how big the Chief's lands were: cane fields surrounded workhouses from whose chimneys smoke was billowing; cattle grazed in pastures near the pens, and the hills beyond the pens were covered in trees. Beyond the hills was the sea. He could make out a stream flowing westward towards the coast, cutting through the work complex. The blue ocean sweeping in from the west into the cove capped its beauty.

Boy scrutinised the house, which stood like a fortress against a wooded backdrop. It was raised off the ground by masonry built not much higher than he was himself. Boy noticed two slits in the masonry, each about the length of his arm and half a handspan wide, with a space the length of three men between them. He imagined people peeping out, spying on other people walking by. Six stone steps led up to the veranda. In the centre of the veranda, outside the fortified door, was a large padded chair. There were four mahogany chairs neatly placed around an oval table. Boy counted six windows on either side of the main door, each with strips of wood across it to keep out the light and insects.

A child lay on his back on the veranda watching the party approach.

'Pickny, go and get your master,' commanded the captor.

The child obediently went indoors. Within five minutes an imposing if rather awkward white man was standing at the doorway. He had slanted, opaque eyes, a jolly smile, unexpected folds in his forehead and a roundly jutting belly. Having greeted the captor with a friendly pat on the back, he suddenly swung round and shouted down the hill, his voice loud and hollow. Almost at once an African woman came into view, stepping quickly round the last bend before the house. Another, much older woman followed, leaning on an attractively carved dark-wood staff. She seemed to be out of tune with the urgency that Boy had picked up from the man's call. The man stamped his foot and shouted angrily at her, both hands beckoning her to hurry.

The younger woman accelerated from a stroll to a trot. The old one was left virtually at a standstill, tapping earnestly at the ground with her staff. She swayed her thickset frame from side to side, unable to manage any appreciable increase in speed. While waiting for her to arrive, he tutted and tapped his feet impatiently. She eventually greeted him with an enormous smile and nodded politely to Boy. Suddenly, a fraught exchange ensued between her and the man. She collapsed at his feet, clutching his trousers at the ankles. Boy held his breath and tensed his stomach at what might happen next. He looked towards his captor for a possible reaction, but there was none. After a merciless tongue-lashing from the man, the old woman rose to her feet, using her stick for support.

Boy looked straight at the man, whose belly seemed to edge out a few more impossible inches as he tilted backwards, pointing to Boy. Drawing breath, he said something to the captor for whom Boy still kept a watchful eye. The captor scratched his chin. The fat man gripped Boy's head, vice-like.

'August!' he proclaimed. Then he let go. Boy could feel still the impression of those fat fingers on his head.

The fat man took a more exasperated look at Mensah, then seized Mensah's jaw and shouted, 'Samson!'

He snatched Muhammad's arm. 'Allick!'

Pointing to Abena he pronounced, 'Beneba.' Then he was finished. It was as if he had had enough. Oyoe had been ignored in this unceremonious renaming.

Boy, now August, did not see the fat man again for two weeks, because on the day of the renaming he was taken by the older woman to live with her in the slave village. She fed him every day, made sure he washed every morning and insisted he do daily chores. Her name was Franky, and she made August know straight away that he had ruined everything for her. It was a girl she wanted, not a boy – Massa had promised her a little girl. Massa chose her to take August because they spoke the same tongue, and also because she was old. She told him she wished he would go away.

Boy was confused about how grateful he should be to Franky, especially since she slapped him up the side of his head when he spoke for the first time, asking who Big Belly Man was. She said, 'Massa John, his name is Massa John, and watch out for me, and you, if I should ever hear you call him Big Belly Man again.' She slapped him again, and then one more time, so that he wouldn't forget. Yet she reminded him strongly of his mother's mother: strict – almost inhumanly strict – but somehow also kind. And with each day that passed he felt this strange bond grow stronger.

August followed Franky around the slave quarters; he was never more than a step behind. On their eighteenth day together, down in one of the plantation walks, his foot caught on the root of a naseberry tree and he stumbled. Instinctively he caught Franky's hand. Her mouth became twisted and her eyes chilled.

'What's wrong with you, Boy,' she barked.

August's eyes locked on hers for a few uneasy moments. He dropped his eyes humbly, reassured by the fact that, despite her occasional harshness, Franky had not cast his hand away. She had made sure he didn't fall.

She loosened her grip, slightly. 'Come,' she said, towing him.

After that, Franky began to talk to August more freely than before. She told him about the seasons, her tired body, how chickens like to foul the place and how dogs barked in the mornings, that crickets kept her awake at night with chattering legs – a whole host of odd things. She warned him to watch himself when he was around his captor, whom she called Massa Frazer. She interrupted her flow only to introduce August to the village folk.

August enjoyed being with Franky and learnt not to give her too much bother. He would follow her as she knocked on doors and rounded up a posse of elders to meet in her hut in the slave quarters. There the Africans indulged themselves in the old ways. August was made to sing children's songs and tell the stories that had been passed on to him in his motherland. He enjoyed making the elders happy; he liked the attention – even status – they gave him. They, for their part, wanted only to be reminded of home. No creole children were allowed anywhere near Franky's hut when all this was going on; creoles were born in Jamaica and could offer the Africans nothing of the distant memories they held dear.

Every morning, August rose to the sound of the clanging of the bell. He put on the standard clothes Franky had laid out for him, clean clothes made of Osenburgh linen, and set off on a walk around the estate. On one of his first walks, he counted fifty or so huts that formed the slave village, scattered on each side of the path. They were alike: most were constructed from timber and thatch with windows either side of the door. They were not particularly sturdy, and many looked ravaged by the elements. Some had a hardwood frame, with interstices well plastered. Each hut was surrounded by its own garden. He favoured the rosebushes.

Franky took him to visit the houses where the drivers and other people of such status lived. They visited Sis Bell, one of the young field workers, who invited them in. Her house was, like Franky's, about fifteen feet long and divided into two rooms. When she went in or out, Sis Bell had to stoop so that she did not bang her head on the beam across the door. The floor was dry earth, in one room neatly layered with coconut-tree leaves.

On their way home, Franky pointed out the coconut trees, the mangoes, the breadfruit and the pawpaw among all the other trees. Every time she reached a landmark she drew attention to it: 'See coconuts tree ova there, see the banana tree there, too.' August repeated everything she

33

said in the way that she said it. From the road, the village appeared obscure, the trees providing heavy seclusion for the slave community, blocking the sunlight and spreading cool shade everywhere. Tall shrubs provided cover for the slaves' covert domestic activities.

One morning, Franky stood with August at the back of the cabin, looking down on the half-acre of kitchen garden. It was cultivated, filled with oranges, shaddock, cocoas and peppers, a profusion of yams and ackee; like most families, Frankie also kept hogs and poultry. Franky put her hands on his shoulders and told him that one day he alone would live off her land; her cabin, too, would belong to him. She raised her beautifully crafted staff and pointed to a spot in the middle where nothing grew. The grass was reclaiming a dusty rectangular spot which she had kept bare for many years.

'Mi spirit will never rest if yuh put anyt'ing over that piece of land,' she said.

'Why?' August was puzzled.

'Don't ask why. Dem say fool love check what wise man shun. Remember dat. Oh,' she added, 'everyt'ing me have dat was good, dem tek it away. Dis is all mi have, it was given to me and mi will never have anyt'ing more.' She bored her stick into the dust about a thumb-length. 'Mi heart is sick. I here today but tomorrow I might be spirited away. With dese t'ings yuh just don't know.' Franky gently gathered his shirt in a fist. 'When mi gone, mi spirit will watch over yuh, and this piece of land. Yuh understand?'

'Yes, Nanny,' he replied.

As the days turned into weeks, August's command of the local language improved. Children in the village laughed at him whenever they heard him speak the tongues of the motherland. He found that many of the old people spoke Akan or Ga.

One day he ventured out to the edge of the village to view the fieldhands at work in the cane pieces. He went to the creek running between the workhouses; as he crouched down, he spied some large black mudfish wriggling by the stone embankment. Wanting to touch one, he bent further forward to dip his hand in the water. An unexpected splash almost knocked him back as a tubby boy rushed through the water. He was carrying a spear whose shaft was slim, its steel head not flattened but round with a sharp point. He was trying to ambush a rat, but the rat sensed danger and bolted into the cane piece twenty yards away, the boy in hot pursuit. August picked himself up and ran after them, his curiosity ignited. The rat vanished, the boy came to a standstill, and August caught up with him.

'What are you doing?' he asked.

'Catching rats,' came the reply.

August felt joy. The boy was about the same height as he, perhaps a shade shorter, and they were about the same age – it was a long time since he had played with anybody his own age. Play they did, splashing around in the creek, before even exchanging names. Eventually, August discovered that the boy was called John Hope, with Hopey as his pet name. August asked what a pet name was. Hopey said he didn't really know but guessed it was like a dog's name, because Massa kept plenty of lazy dogs running around, serving no purpose other than messing in his yard – Massa called black people 'lazy dogs' all the time.

August said, 'I don't like Massa call after me, like me is a dawg.'

'Den yuh can be di bird – a guineabird,' laughed Hopey, playing on the name by which creoles sometimes referred to Africans transported there.

An hour passed as the boys carried on getting to know each other, talking and playing all the while. Hopey invited August to go with him back to his cabin. On the way August noticed the strangely dressed man he had seen in the market shouting at Massa Frazer. Hopey told him the man's name was Reverend Rose, that Massa John called him Daniel, and that Frazer called him all sorts of rude names, though only when black people were around. He explained that the Reverend was a man who talked of nothing but spirits, magic, fear and death, that he talked to black folk about a ghost or a duppy, a Massa that none had ever seen. If August behaved himself, this invisible Massa would take him to a beautiful faraway place in the sky, where he would be united with his ancestors. Hopey said that the Reverend was going to the house to pour water on two of the villagers.

That night, in bed, August thought of what Hopey had told him about duppies, and getting away from the plantation to that faraway place.

He rose late the next morning, to the calling of a girl who had appeared at the door to the hut.

'Mamma Franky,' August called, 'someone wants to see you.'

'Is who?'

'I don't know.'

'Den ask dem what dem want.'

August looked the girl up and down a couple of times. Her dress was two sizes too big, dusty and torn in places, presumably hand-me-downs. He stared into her hollow, begging eyes.

'Does Madda Franky have any food she can give me?' she asked, proffering her empty calabash bowl.

'She wants to know if you have any food you can give her,' August called.

'Oh, dat mus' be Quashiba. Give her some food for mi, August. Mi in the garden, and mi hands dirty.'

Holding out his hand, August asked Quashiba to pass him the calabash. Franky always welcomed children who appeared at her home, hands cupped or carrying a pot. Their mothers could not always see to feeding them because they toiled elsewhere day and night, and spent their rest days trying to recuperate. Franky never asked for an explanation. Some children used their hands to take a dollop of food out of her large faded Dutch pot, which held enough rice and peas to feed the whole village, or so it seemed. Others would stay and eat, confident of another generous helping before long.

August filled the calabash to the brim with rice and peas, topped it off with pieces of jerked pork, and handed it back to Quashiba. Within an instant there was a fly on a piece of pork, and she waved it off. August found a plate for her to cover the food on the way home. She thanked him and walked away; he noticed how thin her legs were.

August's thoughts turned to Franky's unbridled generosity. She was mother to all mothers in the village. It wasn't a role she revelled in; she just accepted the responsibility as if it had been given her by fate. Everyone knew her well and everyone used her well. And when Franky hadn't been there Quashiba's eyes had fallen on him as if he had Franky's powers. He felt known, and chose not to dwell on how he might be used with the passing of time.

# Chapter 5

# Franky

THE NEXT DAY August and Franky strolled out to the fields and passed the small provision grounds outside the village. Some of the older slaves had plots there and grew crops to sell at market.

'See dat piece of land, right over dere?' Franky asked, pointing to a vegetable patch in the middle of the home grounds, where peas, maize and potatoes grew. 'Dat is also my land. Dat is what I call my dinner-time groun. Say it, boy din-na . . . time . . . groun.'

'Din-na-time gron.'

'No. Groun . . . *groun*,' she emphasised.

'Groun.'

'Very good,' she said encouragingly, like an overseer; he slipped his arm through hers.

She said August could share her plot for now, but when he was older he would have to go up into the hills into the woodland with the other villagers to cultivate his own. She explained that Massa planted sugar cane all over his land, which meant there was no place for the slaves to grow their own food. August wondered what it would be like to work as a fieldhand; Franky still hadn't told him.

After a few minutes, they reached the edge of the cane fields, which stretched far. Franky told him it was about a mile from where they stood to where the fields met the woodland, out to the north. To the south, the fields were interrupted by pastures where cattle and mules grazed. As the breeze skimmed off the ocean out to the east, the lush green cane shoots parted and waved like ocean waves.

August wanted to dive in head first and run free through them.

They continued walking away from the village. There were scores of black, yellow- and brown-skinned people working hard, slaving – cutting sugar cane, gathering it in bundles and loading the bundles on to carts. August tugged gently at Franky's arm, and they stopped to listen to women singing songs to the rhythm of the hoeing and chopping.

> If me want for go in a Ebo
> Me can't go there.
> Since them tief me from Guinea
> Me can't go there.
>
> If me want for go in a Congo,
> Me can't go there.
> Since them tief me from my tatta
> Me can't go there.

A driver started to run, a whip clenched in his hand; he stopped and stood over a black man, and they heard the driver cursing. Judgement was passed: three lashes on the back. The crime: to be caught sitting down, resting with his head between his knees.

'Jesus have mercy! It's my cutlass I was cleaning!' the black man cried, but the sentence was coldly executed and the whip tore pieces of flesh out of his back, bloodying his shirt. Frazer was overseeing the workers. He ordered the slave to be taken away and put in the stocks until the next day.

August moved closer to Franky, trying to hide from Frazer. 'Why did Massa Frazer do that?' he whispered.

'August, if yu want to avoid beatin', yu mus' learn some t'ings about the buckra's god. Buckra doesn't like to hear negroes say bad words about him god.'

She put an arm round his neck, nestling his chin in the safety of her hand. He listened intently as she told him that Frazer wanted black people to like the white people's god, because he feared our way. 'Dat is why yu will never catch mi prayin' with dem.'

'Franky!' called Frazer. 'Where on this earth do you think you're going with the new guineabird?'

Franky turned quickly and waved to Frazer. 'I am jus' showin' him around, Massa,'

Frazer motioned her towards him. 'I want this boy up at the crack of dawn and in this cane field working besides all the others, do you hear me?' he bellowed. Franky nodded. 'Tomorrow. Understood?'

'Yes, Massa, tomorrow. Mi will mek sure of dat.'

'And another thing.' Frazer was about to launch into a tirade but caught sight of another slave slacking. 'Quaco, just go and touch that blasted dog over there for me. Do you see him?'

'Yes, Massa, me can see.' Quaco was a hardy creole whose grin stretched from one ear to the other. He rushed off to administer a whipping, which he did admirably, making Frazer smile.

'Where was I now? Can't remember. You can go.' Frazer emphasised the dismissal with his thumb.

Franky quickly ushered August away to another cane field, where women were cutting cane, clearing openings and digging holes. Some were heavily pregnant; others had their babies wrapped in linen on their backs. The women worked as hard as the men, and it was obvious from the sweat and lines etched on their faces that the work taxed them to the limits of their endurance. Many had white handkerchiefs wrapped round their heads, which Franky said served them in the way turbans did back home, keeping their heads cool. All the women wore aprons.

Franky and August walked further out into the fields, and Franky said she would show him how cane holes were dug. She took a rusty hoe from a black man and began poking at the ground, but she soon tired and handed the hoe to August. Eager to impress, and prove himself a humble and able student, he attacked the ground vigorously.

'Slow down, bwoy,' the man said. 'Yu goin' work yourself into the dirt in Franky's kitchen garden, if yu don't slow down.'

'Mind your own business, massa,' Franky muttered, but she tapped August on the shoulder to tell him to dig more slowly.

Franky called to Sis Bell and asked for her bill. She wanted to show August how he should use it when required to help clear land for cultivation. She grabbed the cane and swiped downward, connecting at an angle about six inches from the ground. She demonstrated four more times, stopping short of making a mark. Her exuberance drew the gaze of some men passing by with baskets on their heads. 'Harder. You haffi chop harder,' they laughed. One limped up and saluted her. He was a young man, not much taller than she was. He had a tray in one hand and balanced a basket of manure on his head.

'Brother Sam McFarlane,' said Franky, 'where yu t'ink yu going with dat?'

McFarlane smiled awkwardly. 'Busha tell mi fi bring manure.' He was referring to Frazer as the head white worker on the plantation.

Gesturing to August, she begged, 'Oh, show dis boy what fi do with it.'

McFarlane placed the basket and tray on the ground, and scooped some of the manure on to the tray. He helped August to balance the tray on his head. Franky retreated to a shady tree on the edge of the cane piece, while August and McFarlane delivered the quotas to the women close by. August took his to Sis Bell and helped her fill two holes. He spent the next half-hour digging cane holes with her.

41

Sis Bell told him that her mother had taught her to speak Ga. As they worked, she asked many questions. Where did he come from? What did he miss most about home? How did he find the villagers? When asked whether any of the Africans that he had met on the ship had arrived at Crooks' Cove with him, he spoke only of Allick.

August enjoyed Sis Bell's gentle gaze and soft voice. An hour had passed by the time he had dug the tenth and final hole. She congratulated him, which was refreshingly different from the streams of abuse he had often heard, especially recently. He wanted to be in her favour for ever.

Although he was still puffing from his efforts, he asked, 'Can I help you dig one more hole?'

'Of course. But then yu mus' go. Mother Franky look like she ready to move on.'

He scratched at the surface and then paused and shyly asked an important question: 'Who should I talk to, if mi want to find out about somebody on another property?'

'Talk to Nancy.'

August had been afraid she might say that. Nancy was Massa's house slave. When she came down from the house it was usually to talk to the skilled workers, or, if not them, to the coloured people. Rarely did she have fun with the children. Everyone was courteous to her, including the white workers. When she was done, she strode straight back to the house; no dawdling along the way; August never saw her sitting reflecting on a wall somewhere. Engaging her in idle chat before asking his question seemed impossible. His impulse was to stay away from Nancy until he could work up enough courage.

As they moved on, Franky drew August's attention to Edmund, the white bookkeeper. No one knew for sure what 'bookkeeper' meant. To the villagers, he was the man who drove the slave-drivers who drove the slaves. But what did that have to do with books? Edmund kept no book. He simply stood in the cane fields ordering slave-drivers such as the foolish Quaco to 'touch up' the slaves here and there. He was a pinkish rose colour, tinged with flaming orange on his forehead because he spent most of his day out in the fields, often without a hat.

A coloured boy suddenly looked as if he were about to faint: he reeled, and his eyes rolled up until only the whites could be seen. Edmund noticed at once, and wasted no time in signalling Charles, one of the two drivers, to take action. Charles ran over to the boy, and said sharply, 'Pickny, get yu'self back to work!' The clip round the ear that accompanied the words brought the boy back to life.

Franky, seeing that the incident made August shudder, led him away. They followed a procession of black folk who were carrying cane from the field towards the mill house. She explained that they would add it to a stack before returning to the fields to cut more.

'Is that how they will treat me tomorrow?' August asked, hoping the answer would not be the one he expected.

Franky tried to reassure him with a gentle smile, and said, 'Quaco is de worst of de worst. Him is one of dem field slaves who, if yu give dem a whip, it go straight to dem head. One time him was a humble nega bwoy. But since him turn man him turn fool. But Charles don't worry about him. Charles is a lovely man, really. Him will treat you good – mi will see to that. Him only do enough to keep Massa happy, him won't do more than him have to, to keep de slaves dem working. Him is a good man. Yu see him jus' save dat bwoy's life. If him did drop to the ground, Massa would sure kill him. De trouble with Charles is dat him love buckra god. Buckra's god works for buckra only. Poor Charles, him blind. Him can't see what's going on.'

The following morning, Franky took August to see the hothouse, a hut about twice the size of her small shack. August peered in through the one and only window. What he saw was pitiful: a boy about five years old, lying on a bed, showing no movement, no emotion. He had been in the sugar mill, crushing cane, when his hand got caught between the grudgeons. He had cried so much that his tear ducts were dry. He kept his arm still, just moaning feverishly now and again when the throbbing peaked. Medical help had been sought as soon as the accident happened, but the doctor was on his way to see the sick daughter of some well-to-do white folk, and after that he planned to visit friends in the parish of St Anne's.

A young woman sat in a chair by the bed, bent over a pail of water. She was nursing the boy as best she could. Franky signalled to August, who was still peering through the window, to go inside. Once in, he moved to the farthest corner away from the boy and stood unnerved, staring at the disfigured hand.

'Diana, call to one of the boys outside. Mek dem go over to Sister Bell and ask fi some Bay rum. Mi want rub some on de child chest fi get rid of the fever.'

Diana obeyed, then returned to her chair by the bed. Franky sat at the foot of the bed and began rocking to and fro, humming a mournful tune. She pointed to a spot in the middle of the room. Something about August and the accident triggered memories of her past: she told them of her son's death, all of forty years ago.

His name was Quamino; he was seven, raven black, and on the small side for his age. His right leg was shorter than the left, but despite this he always wore a smile, and was as independent as he was gay. His father, Joseph, loved him dearly and took him everywhere, and showed him everything. Franky used to go down by the creek and find them fishing, using only their hands. Joseph was tall, dark, had tight curls and not a blemish on his skin. He loved women – that was what men folk did – but Franky was his pearl. Joseph taught Quamino to carve, and together they made a staff out of cedar wood. Over time they added carvings and more carvings to it until there was no room for more. The handle was cut in the shape of a king's bearded head, with two smaller heads, for ears. The largest face was symbolic of Quamino's father – majestic. One of the smaller heads had Franky's serene face – like an African queen's. The smallest face was Quamino's.

Quamino decided one day during the rainy season that he had had enough of labouring in the fields. It was hard and he could barely cope. Most children of his age were assigned either to working in the great house or to looking after the fowls out by the pens. He just wasn't cut out for the fields, and the busha men knew it.

One day Massa John's favourite uncle, Alexander Crooks, took it upon himself as overseer to chase Quamino around the field, whipping him with a cat-o'-nine-tails. The injuries were not severe, but they were enough for Quamino to realise that life could not be taken for granted. He mentioned this to another boy in the field before he went home and changed his clothes. He said nothing to his parents about what had happened, but early the next morning, while everyone slept, he took some fruit – only a couple of mangoes and a green-skinned orange – crept out of his mother's hut and went away. The news that the boy had run reached Massa Alexander's a few hours later. It made the Massa sneer; he promptly visited Franky and chided her for not raising her boy properly.

Massa Alexander, his eyes pinched, pointed out a trail of small holes stabbed into the soft ground. 'The piccaninny can't have gone far,' he said. 'He's lame. He'll have one hand on his staff, and he has a bag in the other hand. He ran from here. I would bet a few hundred that those marks show which way he went.' He glared at Franky. 'Your boy has done a very bad thing and I will not tolerate it.'

Massa Alexander sent his bookkeepers and the dogs out to retrieve the boy. One of the dogs was a Cuban dog called Roughian.

Within two hours the boy was caught. Franky recalled the sight of him draped over one of the bookkeeper's mules. Torn to shreds, he breathed irregularly, and was slipping in and out of consciousness. There was blood running down from his back and dampening the mule's hind leg.

The men said they had found him sleeping just over the hill under a bush by the creek. He was heading towards the Thorpe property, but he wouldn't have known it. They set Roughian on him to wake him up. They said it was a long time since they had seen what the dog could do. They said that after seeing the way it threw the boy about, they tried to get it off, but it wasn't easy – getting the dog off, that is.

Franky said the bookkeeper kept sniggering as he told his story. He slid the boy off the mule and Quamino dropped to the ground like a lump of meat. Franky picked her son up in her arms and ran to the hospital. As she laid him on the ground, he died. Franky just cradled his mangled and motionless body. Her grief was silent, yet tangible.

Joseph came, touched the boy and left immediately, uttering not one word. Franky learnt later that the man who had fathered her son returned to his hut, lay down on his four-poster bedstead, curled up, closed his eyes, and remained thus until he was buried with his son in the kitchen garden.

When Franky finished her tale, all eyes were riveted on the staff lying on the ground beside her.

'That is very sad, Miss Franky,' said Diana, stuttering slightly with emotion, 'but I never knew you did have a likkle boy.'

'It was long ago. Before you were born.'

August respectfully reached over and picked up the staff. He ran his fingers from bottom to top, blew dust out of the crevices of the bearded figure, and stripped off a shaving that stuck out, so that Franky wouldn't get a splinter. The staff was worn at the handle but many of the impressions were still as magnificent as the day they were carved. He helped Franky to her feet. Again, it was time to move on.

As they returned home, August noticed a set of buildings which Franky seemed to ignore. He asked what they were.

'Yu don't need worry about dem. Dem is de trash house. It's where dem put de cane when dem done with it. It easy to ketch fire so don't let me ketch you over dere.'

Back at Franky's hut, they spent a couple of hours doing some gardening and picking plantain for their evening meal.

At two o'clock Franky took August to the borders of the Estate to see the neighbouring plantations of Haughton Tower in the east and the Spring Estate to the south. As they walked eastward, she explained more about the way things were on Crooks' Cove sugar plantation, stopping every now and again to check that August understood the new tongue. She enjoyed shifting from time to time back into Ga, whenever he didn't understand the Jamaican patois. August was learning fast.

'If yuh repeat anyt'ing mi tell you, mi going Obeah 'pon you,' Franky quietly insisted every time she told August something sacred. She described an incident twenty-two years ago, in 1776, when the powers that ruled Jamaica had helped a mother country at war with Americans. 'De Americans wanted to be free from de mother country when dem realise dat dem was mighty as a nation. De ocean dat Africans cross when buckra bring them come is de same dat divide America and England. Dat's why America decide to break free.' A number of slaves, both creole and African, decided to attack Fort Charlotte while the island was depleted of many white workers. The plan was to rise up and overthrow buckra. 'But,' said Franky sadly, 'it never work out.' Her voice trembled when she told August that thirty or so men and women had been sentenced to death.

Massa John found out that one of his slaves – Cuffee, a

47

carpenter – had been implicated, and was so appalled that he decided to execute him, on the grounds of the plantation, at a central point within the slave village. He made his drivers pour tar all over Cuffee and set him alight. Cuffee looked Massa in the eye and in supreme defiance made not one sound as his skin took flame. The fire worked its way up Cuffee's body and blazed until nothing was left but charred, smoking remains. When it was over the Massa bowed his head, turned and strode towards the refuge of the great house.

Franky was almost inaudible when she ended her story. 'Bwoy, let mi tell yu: if yu want somet'ing in dis life, yu have to pay for it. Everyt'ing in dis world cost somet'ing, and it's not money you have to always take and pay. I hope you understand what mi trying to say?'

'Yes,' he replied, but he didn't. He did, though, now understand why there was always sadness in her eyes, at odds with the happiness she tried to convey to Massa. She went to great lengths to conceal the pain she still felt at losing those she had loved.

# Chapter 6

# Nancy

AUGUST STOOD AT the bottom of the hill looking up at Bardanage. He had stalled, wondering whether he should visit Nancy to ask her about Ami. It was a long time since Sis Bell had advised him to.

Feeling his armpits, he picked gently at short, fine strands of pubescent hair. Hopey had been taunting him about his lack of hair, telling him he was still a 'bwoy' and showing off his own thick growth. This infuriated August, especially because Hopey's voice had deepened whereas his remained childishly high-pitched. Hopey had hair sprouting from his chin and August had none. But August had spurted in height. At least there wasn't a woman in the village taller than him, he always retorted.

August saw Nancy appear on the veranda, leaning on the railings and peering across the estate. He had never spoken with her at any length, though whenever she came down into the village he would offer a glance of greeting in her direction. He had been trying to catch Nancy's eye whenever he saw her, say good morning, or good afternoon. She usually said hello to him and asked how he and Franky were, but that was all. But that evening he began climbing the hill towards her. He looked around, checking that the overseers were not lurking nearby.

Nancy called to him when he got close. 'Boy, what do you want? Didn't Franky tell you that you shouldn't come up here? Nega boy, go away,' she urged, pointing him back towards the village. She looked around to see who might be within earshot.

'I come to talk. I must see you. Please don't tell Massa,' August begged in a low voice.

Nancy checked again, then went to the door of the great house and closed it. 'All right, but don't get me into trouble. What do you want? Quick.'

August went closer and leant against the banister. He felt tense.

Nancy stood with her hands on her hips, and August noticed her stomach bulging beneath her dress. 'Is a baby you're having?' he asked softly.

'Who tell you? Franky?'

'Yes. But I can tell.'

'My belly is not that big, is it? I only find out the other day, you know.'

'That is good.'

'What makes you say so?' She sounded abrupt, which surprised August.

'I don't know,' he replied.

August wasn't sure whether he could put into words the joy he thought a woman should feel about creating a new life.

'Hmm,' she said, swinging round and turning her back on him, as if to assert her superiority as a house slave. 'I was jus' now thinking of the name. My two children think it's going to be a baby boy. But the baby is going to be a girl, I know, I am always right. Anansi they want to call it. But I will call her Annie.'

From what Franky had said, August knew Nancy despised Africans for spending too much time telling stories to children – especially her own children, twins, John and Catherine – even though the villagers sometimes went out of their way to be friendly. Nancy felt they were jeopardising everything she had worked for. She lived to please Massa, and she hoped that one day he would free her and her black-white children. Massa saw only the blackness in them, and black people on his plantation were slaves.

Nevertheless, Nancy took great pains to make sure her children knew how different they were from the negroes. She referred to the Africans, guineabirds or salt-water slaves, as low-class, the men as negas. She saw them as slaves lacking in 'etiquette' – unlike domestic and professional slaves.

Having heard about Nancy, August was confused by her inconsistency. He often saw her mixing with Africans, but then she would argue, rather unconvincingly, that she was teaching guineabirds to learn Jamaican ways. She seemed to be on a mission to civilise them so that they, too, could make something of themselves. Nancy recalled how Brother Charles Crooks used to be an ignorant guinea, but he was prepared to learn how to work on Crooks' Cove Estate. He was an example of how a slave could climb to great heights simply by being obedient – always.

Charles was a head driver and was receiving religious instruction so he could be an even better negro. He was important enough to be given authority over his slave gang of more than sixty field workers, and he made sure there was no slacking when the gang went about their work. How did he manage it? Simple: he let the whip do his talking. He had authority to use it how he pleased in taming the negroes' natural instinct to be lazy – that's what Massa had told Charles the day he promoted him. Nancy remembered vividly how angry Massa had been with Charles at first, neglecting to thank Massa on being handed a brand new cat-o'-nine-tails as his personal property. He was supposed to be honoured, supposed to bow and say, 'God bless,' and to make other servile utterances. Charles had submitted – hence his promotion.

August became curious about Nancy's privileged position on the Estate, and asked whether she liked living here on the Cove.

'Of course. It's my home. I was born here, I'll die here, and them will bury me here, too.'

'How come yu get to work in the house?'

'Boy, how you get so nosey, all of a sudden. You come all the way up here and ask me all these questions and I don't even know you from Adam. I should just pull out your tongue for asking mi such questions.'

'Sorry.'

'Don't be. If you don't ask how will you know?' she laughed.

August enjoyed her response. Something about it reminded him of Ami.

So Nancy began to answer August's question. Five years ago, she told him, she was passing Massa's window on the way to the slave quarters, which were about four hundred yards from where she now stood. She had been weeding the burial grounds where Massa's forebears rested, behind the house. She had always accepted that plantation society deemed it Massa's right to have a nega woman for his sexual pleasure. As a late developer, she had put off worrying whether such a fate would befall her. Inevitably, in time it did, right here where they were standing, on the veranda of Bardanage house. She could remember the exact date, because it was the eve of her twentieth birthday.

'You know, Massa John him like negro woman like me,' she went on. Her clear, dark, radiant skin had not escaped August's gaze. She kept her hair cropped close to the scalp. He thought her nose a little on the European side, but her lips were full and succulent. The night she spoke of was, she said, the first of many times that Massa forced himself upon her. 'You must know that John and Catherine belong to him?'

'Yes, I know.' August scratched his head, although it wasn't itchy at all.

'The child inside me belongs to him as well.'

'Oh,' said August, lost for words and now seeking to ask the question consuming him. After a long pause he took the plunge: 'You know a woman called Ami?'

'What is she? White, black, coloured, what?'

'She is from my homeland.'

'Well, I never hear that name before. Anyway, who tell you that I might know?'

'Sis Bell.'

'What does Sister Bell have to say? Lord have mercy; she is going to get me in a whole heap of trouble with the things she tells people. Don't pay her any mind. Do you hear?'

'All right. If you hear about her . . . '

'Boy, jus' move and g'way quick, before Massa sees you.'

August turned. From this vantage point he looked down the hill on the slave village disappearing in the twilight. He could still just see the plantain trees, whose leaves, crispy like torn sheets, draped the hut roofs; and at the top of the hill they stretched up, looming like scarecrows against the moon. The huts seemed to huddle closer together, shying away from the big house. The darkness would hide slave activity; small gatherings of people talking about the passing day and what the morrow might bring, and people singing and dancing – evoking spirits. Quarter of a mile or so beyond the village there was the flickering of torches where two gangs of field labourers, about thirty in each, were toiling – they would do so until nearly midnight. They were picking out brushwood or dry cow-dung for fuel to cook their supper and next morning's breakfast.

August watched the lights of the slave village, which never stayed on for more than forty minutes. A few hundred yards up the road following the coast, he saw a mule-drawn cart, its lamp glowing. He drew Nancy's attention to it, and she instantly turned and rushed into the big house.

'Massa, Massa, quick!' she called as she ran. 'They're here, they're here. The new guineabirds are here, Massa.' She darted through the central hall, calling to the other domestic slaves, and August could just make her out running through the east side entrance, sailing through to the west, leaping the steps to the dusty ground.

'Massa!' she called once more.

'All right, all right, I heard you the first time,' came the impatient response.

August moved to the threshold and heard Massa John dragging his feet lazily along the wooden floor of the office upstairs. August stepped backwards a few paces, then down to the bottom of the stone stairs: it would not be good for him to be seen to enter the house uninvited.

'Nancy, where are my shoes?' yelled Massa.

'Massa, they are under the bed!' she yelled back.

In less than a minute, he appeared at the bottom of the stairs, fighting with his trousers, trying to secure them with a thick black leather belt that he'd worn for many years. Massa John's colossal belly had forced it down to the level of his pubic bone, the belt screaming for some slack. He was eager to inspect his latest purchase. He stumbled down the staircase, then bundled through the doorway, tripping down the steps before thudding to the ground as he collapsed to his hands and knees.

August knelt to help him up.

Massa John slapped his hand away, then shrugged. 'What are you doing up here?'

'Mi just come to—'

'If I find you up here again I'll hang you in iron frames from a tree. Now clear out of my sight.'

August turned hastily and set off down the path, but he had not gone far when Massa John called him back. He told August to accompany him to the cart in case there was a task that needed doing. Massa John ambled down the hill towards the road to meet the approaching cart. August followed two steps behind, amused by the fat man's stride. Massa John was perspiring profusely by the time he reached the cart. August lost sight of him briefly as he

54

ducked behind the bullocks. On moving around, August saw a white hand appear on the other side. Massa John stood up on his toes to peer wildly before examining his five new acquisitions more closely.

Frazer spoke first: 'Evening, Master John.'

'Frazer,' he returned, tugging at the chains that led to the iron ring around an African man's neck. 'Not bad, Mr Frazer, not bad at all. Presumably the scramble went well?'

'Yes, it was all right. Had to give that Captain Knibb a piece of my mind, though. They looked rubbish when I saw 'em first. I had 'im clean 'em up nicely. You'd think he would've learnt by now.'

'Yes, I can see. Very good.' Massa John moved round to the other side of the cart.

'That one over there has the makings of a good strong field labourer, but he's going to need a lot of work to season him. I had trouble with him, and he may try to run in the next few days,' Frazer commented.

'Well, I pay you to see that doesn't happen, so make sure it doesn't. I'll say no more, and let you get on.'

'Don't worry, I have it all under control.'

'Be sure you have. What about the others? That boy looks like a weakling.'

'Nothing that a good feed won't take care of. All that yam, cow foot, and rubbish these negroes have for their own delicacies will do the trick in no time.'

Master John reached out, gripped the boy by the jaw and squeezed, opening his mouth like a dog. Master John inspected his mouth, scratching his teeth with his thumbnail. The boy recoiled when the grip loosened.

Master John smiled broadly at Frazer and asked, 'Did you hear anything in town about what happened at the Dickson plantation?'

'What? Do you mean Richard Dickson, our neighbour?'

'No, no – I mean yes. I'm talking about the property they have over in Trelawny.'

'No, I've heard nothing. Should I have?'

'I thought you might have seen William Dickson down at the harbour?'

'No, I didn't. Just as well because I had a run-in with Reverend Rose yet again. I don't know what they see in 'im. He has the makings of one of them abolitionists.'

'Quite. Anyway, that is not my concern,' said Master John. 'I heard a gang of escaped slaves raided the plantation and burnt Richard's house to the ground. It seems they were trying to create a disturbance. It is worrying. Very, very worrying.'

'But niggers have been doing that since the beginning of time, sir.'

'Yes, yes. But this happened in April. Since then I've heard of other disturbances – in one, two white men were severely wounded and a third was killed.'

'Where did you hear that?'

'I can't say, for sure.' Master John shifted awkwardly on the balls of his feet; he took a handkerchief from his back pocket, flapped it and wiped perspiration away from his face.

'The rebels – all guineas, I trust?' asked Frazer.

'I expect so. What would the island be coming to if creoles were involved? Be vigilant, because the idea of slaves running their masters ragged and taking over the island, like they did in St Domingue, is last thing we need. It's one that we – and especially you – should be on the watch for,' he warned, thumbing Frazer in the arm to impress upon him the seriousness of what was at stake.

'Ha. That couldn't possibly happen in Jamaica. I can't see it happening. Our slaves love our King. They wouldn't go to such lengths – for what? I don't know. There's always going to be the bad apples, but . . .' He trailed off.

'Just be vigilant, Frazer, that's all.'

# Chapter 7

# Maroon

CANE-CUTTING, OR CROP season, was always insufferable. The mills churned from sun-up until sundown, and all too often through the night. Each season seemed worse than the previous; because everybody felt the current one would be their last. The older folk had every reason to believe it would: five or six, sometimes as many as nine, never saw the next season.

'Boy, I don't t'ink Samson is going to make it through another crop season. It's like him ready to run,' Allick confided one day to August. Samson had never adjusted. He was like a gun ready to explode.

'What are you doing over there? You're both idle!' Frazer shouted. 'Allick, a horse needs shoeing, and Cambridge needs help building a shelter for the bakery. August, I want you to go and help Roger cut copper wood. The supplies are running low and more is needed to fire the boiling-house. I want at least sixty cartloads stored over there by dawn. I don't want that boiler to stop running. Allick, you, August and Samson will help Marky in the boiling-house at least for the next couple of weeks. You'll finish the shifts at about three in the morning; and you'll report back in the fields by eight.'

'Yes, Massa Frazer.' And when Frazer left, Allick muttered under his breath, 'Bastard.'

It was late during the midday break when August arrived at the gully just outside the village. He expected to find Allick praying. Instead he found him surrounded by at least ten men, mainly Africans although there were also a few creoles.

Allick was conducting a lively debate. August knew that, whenever break-time gatherings such as this took place, many things were discussed; the talk was often frivolous and mundane to begin with, but Allick liked to provoke discussion about more delicate matters.

This time, however, Allick had drunk too much rum and so went too far in criticising creoles: the only thing that made the guineabird different from them, he said, was that the creole man's sole ambition in life was to serve Massa. They badly wanted to be Massa's unwelcome guests in the big house on the hill. Creoles wanted to be sat at the table, sipping coffee, just like their white Massas. And if creoles, by some quirk of fate, got their wish, they would probably sit and drool at the prospect of filling their guts with the leftovers from Massa's table – they would even fight among themselves for such scraps. Creoles were a gutless, ignorant breed of African. They were too ashamed to call themselves what they would see so clearly with one glance in a looking-glass: African.

Everyone's attention locked on to Richard White, a tall, gangling, pale-skinned man, who had convulsed in fits of laughter. This stopped as soon as he realised nobody else was laughing. Born a slave, he was classified a quadroon. His father was a white man, his grandmother on his mother's side was a negress. In Massa's eyes, and indeed that of white society, he was not white enough to be set free. Allick turned to Richard and said that quadroons were the worst when it came to having that nigger mentality. Quadroons were the ones who ate leftovers from the great table.

The best was yet to come. Allick started talking about the Africans. Africans, he said, were proud. They were scholars, skilled in art and in hunting. Africans were stargazers. Africans were conquerors and not the conquered.

58

Africans would not indulge the white man's humour by letting him see them fight for scraps from his table.

The creoles instantly launched into an offensive of their own. Insults flew. August couldn't resist throwing some jibes in to help Allick out. But the creoles turned on him and he backed away.

August noticed a mulatto standing silently behind Allick. It was Nancy's son, John; he didn't appear to see the funny side of anything being said. Mulatto John was tall. His eyes were bright hazel and he had dark brown freckles, features that combined to make him look both unusual and attractive. August circled the men and clicked his fingers to get Mulatto John's attention.

'It is the first time I see you so serious. What's wrong with you?' asked August.

'Nothing,' replied Mulatto John.

'What is this I hear about you and your Papa?'

'Who tell yu?'

'Your mother.'

Mulatto John looked sharply at August and then away. He kissed his teeth and hissed. 'She always encourage me fe pattern myself after Massa John's ways. Massa was even t'inking of sending me and Catherine to America to school.'

'That is good.'

'Yes, but dat was until dis morning.'

'Oh?'

'Me and Massa catch up in one big argument 'bout t'ing and t'ings.'

'T'ing and t'ings?'

Mulatto John said his mother had always warned that his mouth would get him into trouble. She counselled him to stay clear of engaging with villagers in any deep conversation about the way things were between slave and master. She specifically warned him not to broach the subject with his father. And he hadn't, until two days ago. His mother's words had led him to think long and hard about his privileged position in the big house. His father harboured no malice, treated him well, usually asked him humanly to do things – though of course leaving out the 'please' and 'thank you'. He had lulled himself into believing that theirs was a good father–son relationship. So, while setting the table for breakfast, he took the plunge. He asked his father how white people got the land and why black folks were slaves. It ended with Mulatto John advocating support for men like Mr Wilberforce.

'What? You say that to Massa? I was born to hear how one boy could be so foolish. What Massa say to you?'

'Not'ing, at first. But den, dis morning, I was cleaning him boots on di veranda, Massa call me from his bedroom. He say, "Boy, don't bother set foot in this house again." He say, "You, you no have no privileges. Report to Frazer, make him find you work out in the fields with the dogs." He say, "Run, before I have you placed in stocks. Now be gone with you."'

August followed Allick back into the village to talk some more.

'Allick, dat was good. I liked how you criticise the black man back dere. I don't always understand everyt'ing you say. But it sounds good, all the same.'

Allick stopped, looked over his shoulder to check there was no one close by, then clutched August's wrist tightly. 'Yu ever hear the word "proclamation"?' he asked.

'No.'

'Yu ever hear the word "emancipation"?'

'No.'

'"Liberty"? "Freedom"?'

'Yes, I hear 'bout freedom, slave talk 'bout dat all the while.'

'Well, a righteous man always want him freedom; so him can sit at him own table and eat whatever him wants, when him wants to. One day, buckra isn't going to tell you what yu can eat, from what yu can't eat. Dat I know.'

He winced as he spoke, then clutched his stomach. August had seen Allick grimace earlier on, but thought nothing of it. But now Allick tucked his hand under his shirt and rubbed his stomach.

'Allick, yu no look like yu feeling well?'

'Me all right. Don't worry yuself. Now, what mi was saying? Oh yes. One day you will come to understand everyt'ing – everyt'ing dat is wrong with our people.'

'Our people? Yu mean back in Africa?'

'No, man, our people here in Jamaica – you can call wi creole, black man, mulatto or sambo. We is one people and we is all in trouble.'

'Trouble?'

'Yes, trouble.'

They had arrived outside Sis Bell's. Allick leant heavily against the corner post of the cabin. August put his hand on his shoulder, pressed gently and suggested, 'Sit down, man. Let us talk some more.'

They both sat, Allick on his knees, August crossed-legged.

Allick continued. 'Yu see, my brother, more and more I get to hear dese words, and always when people talking 'bout freedom. Is always de negro dat have dis wish upon dem minds. Nowadays, I hear people dat go to church speak 'bout liberty and equal rights and justice for all. The African man speak 'bout freedom all de while, and how him want burn the white man's house. The coloured man don't really want talk 'bout such things – some you will hear join in, but not all.'

'Keep talking. Mek me hear what you have to say.'

'Once, it was only Africans talking freedom, now t'ings changing. Yu must get to know dese words, understand dem, den repeat dem so others can hear.'

61

'Yes, mi will do that.' August glossed his nails against the growth on his cheek.

Allick winced and clutched his stomach again. Wearily he turned towards his cabin. He aimed a friendly mock punch at August's stomach, then went inside.

At dinner-time break the next day, August decided he would pass by the mill house to see if Allick was better. On the way he met Nancy, who greeted him as she passed, went a few yards on, then unexpectedly stopped and turned.

'August,' she called, 'come here. I want to talk to you for a moment – I won't keep you long.'

'Yes, Sis Nancy.' August trotted over.

When August reached her, she stood very straight and stiff, barely looking at him.

'You asked me while ago to see if I could find out 'bout a woman called Ami,' she said.

August could hardly believe his ears.

'Well, I ask the one Elvin Barker to see what he could find out when he was taking corn over to the Brown property up past Cocoon. He said they have a woman there called Annie, or Ami, or Amy – I'm not sure which. You think is her? Yu sure you gave me the right name?'

'Ami is her name. But what you say . . . mi don't know if it's her,' August replied, not wishing to sound ungrateful.

'Oh, well I jus' ask anyway. I will ask some more people to look out for you, and I let you know if I hear anything. That Ami is a very unusual name around here. If that is her name, I mus' hear something soon.'

'Thank you, but mi not sure if she still alive.'

'You never know. You never—Lord Jesus, what is happening over there?' She stared over August's head.

He turned and saw one of the village brethren running towards Charles, who was at the edge of the dinner-grounds, uprooting peas. The man was shouting, agitated. Charles paid no attention at first; he was fighting with an old hoe, stabbing at the bone-dry dirt and obviously cursing his blunt tool. He tried his cutlass but made no better progress, so he settled for the bill, which was shorter, sharper, easier to manipulate and more suited to stabbing furiously at the dirt.

August and Nancy moved closer and heard the man tell Charles that Samson had been caught running away.

As the news spread, August put himself about, trying to find out what had happened. He decided to wait until the bell rang for the labourers to go off into the hills to collect grass for the cattle. Then he saw Hopey, who told him Samson had run during the night. He had got as far as the maroon village, a village specifically for runaway slaves. The maroons arrested him and brought him back.

'Di maroon is a different set of people,' Hopey explained. 'Dem betray runaways all the time.' He told August that an agreement had existed between the Massas and runaway slaves for over a hundred years. The maroons lived in the mountains and came down in sporadic bursts to wreak havoc and breed fear on the plantations all over the island. The Massas could not overcome them in the rough hilly terrain, so they were declared free, provided they returned all runaways to the Massas. And they did so unhesitatingly. 'Mi tell you dat Samson never hear when people talk to him. Him think he know it all. Him is going wish dem did finish him off in the hills. You mark my word.'

It was true. Samson spent the next day in the stocks; for the rest of the crops season he would be worked in irons. Furthermore, he would have thirty-nine lashes upon his bare buttocks on the first Monday of every month.

From the pastures, August saw Allick and McFarlane approaching. He bowed his head and continued weeding Franky's dinner-ground. He was not in any mood to talk.

'How come yu see me and yu don't even say good day?' Allick called out.

August didn't reply immediately. He paused in his

digging while Allick approached, then began again with fury.

'Mi can't stop thinking 'bout Samson,' he muttered.

'Yu is not the only one,' said Allick.

'Franky say him would not conform, and now look at him. Might as well say him is dead already,' said August.

'True,' McFarlane put in.

'So what do yu think, Boy?' asked Allick.

'I think I am a coward.'

Allick ignored the comment. He said, 'Mi think Samson was hard-ears. Look how many times mi sit down and talk with him, and look what he end up doing. Him ears too hard. Mi showed you that from the first day, remember?'

August wasn't sure that he liked what Allick said about Samson, or Mensah, as he preferred to remember him, the mighty Ashanti warrior. Yet he detected misery in Allick's voice and realised that he had his own way of coming to terms with Samson's inevitable demise.

'Come, Allick,' said McFarlane, 'wi can't stand up here all day talking. We have too many things to do.'

'Yes, soon come,' Allick said.

'When my turn come,' August announced, 'Massa will never catch me. Me, mi will run as far and as fast as mi can.'

The men were amazed at August's bravado.

'Allick, talk to him nuh man. The bwoy nuh have no sense,' advised McFarlane.

Allick stood in silence for a while, watching the villagers cutting cane nearby. They usually cut from the edges in towards the centre, the idea being to drive the rats running rampant through the tall cane pieces to a central point where the bookkeepers were ready with forks and most slaves were armed with spears of sorts or sticks. They prepared for the rapid cutting down of the last clump in the cane piece, which would make the rats rush out in all directions, to be ambushed, slaughtered in their hundreds, stacked in a corner of the field and fed to the John Crow, a tattered parasitic bird that August loathed. Once, one of the women had grabbed an escaping rat, which promptly sank its long incisors into her hand. Her arm swelled up to the shoulder and she had to be sent to hospital. She had lockjaw.

Allick said, 'Samson run, and him was the fastest man mi ever did see. Samson show me dat we is all cornered rats. Running won't help us. But when a rat cornered, what it do? Attack. Because dat is its nature. Fighting is Samson's nature. Like the rat, him never have much up here.' Allick pointed to his head. 'A rat don't have sense to realise that it is no match 'gainst a man wit' a gun. The rat don't think before it attack. Yu is a cornered rat, yu have brain, so yu must spend time using it. Busha man won't pull the trigger while you stay put in the corner and behave yuself – not so quickly. Boy, you must t'ink again. You have a whole life fi t'ink 'bout other options. T'ink again.'

# Chapter 8

# Songs of Freedom

'BWOY, GET YUH backside outta bed. Don't mek bad spirits come torment me this morning.' Franky was in full voice. 'Mi will beat yuh, if yuh don't leave now. You are seventeen years old, you is a big man now! Boy, get your arse out of bed.'

August felt stale and smelly, having had neither time nor strength to wash the night before. Franky's bellowing was still ringing in his ears when he ran out half naked to catch the last gang of slaves going to the fields. He hadn't eaten anything the night before and didn't have time for breakfast either. He was worried because he knew that food is fuel – for a slave, the main substance of life. Furthermore, it was his day to work under Quaco. So he was not only tired and hungry but fretful when he joined the other fieldhands.

Eleven o'clock, time for the first break. August found Hopey and they went and sat down by a wall that separated the fields from the cattle pens. They drank water and ate fresh snapper with roasted plantains.

'Man, you heard di news?' Hopey asked.

'What news?' August was weary.

'Dat di black people in St Domingue – slaves – beat up Napoleon.'

'Remind me who him be.'

'Napoleon? Him is a likkle bad breed from a place dem call France, mi no lie.'

'So what dat have to do wit' me?'

'What wrong wit' yu, man? You no see dat mean slaves

66

is now free? Dem is free. Dem no longer have to answer to buckra, no more jumping to di sound of di morning bell. Free to sleep to dem heart content, yes, man.'

'How dem manage dat?'

'How you expect? By fighting, of course. Dat is the only way slaves gwan get dem freedom. Blood have to spill. Dat I know.'

'Tell mi somet'ing. Nancy always talk 'bout a gentleman dem call William Wilberforce. What him have to do with dis?'

'He . . . mi t'ink him did tell them fi rise up and take arms. Him will soon tell us fi do the same, watch and see if mi lie.'

'You really t'ink him going tell us to pick up gun and fight?'

'Yes, man. When dat day come, all hell going break loose. You know how Jamaica is already, is true?'

Freedom . . . the thought filled August's mind. He looked forward eagerly to Nancy's next bulletin about the revolution. She had followed events for the past eight years: Massa John often talked about such things at breakfast, and she then talked about them in the village. The name that cropped up time and time again was Napoleon, some great white demon trying to crush other white folk in the place they called Europe. But Nancy wanted to see Napoleon crushed as much as any buckra on the island.

The bell rang again at two o'clock, and the slaves went back to work. August's belly churned with hunger. When time came to collect grass for the cattle, he found that he was unable to gather his usual quota. He returned to have his bundles checked by Quaco.

'Yu normally collec' more dan dis,' said Quaco angrily. 'Yu is trying to pull a fas' one 'pon me? Yu have been attaching yuself to di wrong negroes and you mus' learn.'

Quaco knocked the bundle out of August's hand, and it landed in a heap on the ground. August moved to pick it up, but a blow to his side sent him reeling. He blew hard, trying to empty his lungs. Then he held his breath and made an effort to stand.

'Stupid!' Quaco yelled.

'De only stupid one 'round here is you. You see you — you is a shit!' wailed August.

Quaco backhanded him to the ground. August rose to his knees and, forgetting himself, dived at Quaco's midriff and bowled him over. August tried to deliver a volley of punches, but Quaco smothered him.

Frazer quickly intervened, ordering two bookkeepers to drag the boy off. Frazer paced backward and forward. August stood quietly waiting for judgement.

'Quaco,' said Frazer, 'lay him down and give him ten.'

Quaco enlisted another black man to help secure August. His hands were tied to the spokes of a cartwheel leant against a tree nearby, and two other slaves were ordered to yank his ankles apart and sit on them. August cried out as his legs twisted, giving way under the men's weight.

Quaco looked to the overseer for his next instruction. Frazer licked his top lip, then wiped his mouth with the back of his hand. It was time. A quick glance in Quaco's direction, and two quick nods.

That evening, August lay on the floor in Franky's cabin. Franky took a damp cloth and dabbed each cut. His back was a rugged landscape, like the mountainous Cockpit Country south of Trelawny.

'It's my fault, it's my fault,' she kept repeating when August told her of his hunger and that it had given him dizzy spells all day.

Many thoughts went through August's mind. When the first lash landed, the pain was blazing within seconds. Then there was the shock of seeing pieces of flesh lying around him while he was trying to recover from the tenth blow. He

68

cursed himself, wondering why he had bothered to strike out at Quaco in the first place. He thought crazy thoughts of escape. Then the image of Ami entered his head, for no particular reason. He tried to put her out of his mind. He considered the possibility of running to the hills to join the maroons. But he knew the maroons would not accept him into the community. There was another way, about which August thought long and hard: he could mix a deadly concoction of bush herbs and swallow it.

'What yu t'inking 'bout, bwoy?' asked Franky.

'Nothing.'

'You are, mi can tell.'

August felt obliged to say something, so he searched for a thought he could tell her about. Eventually, he found one. 'Ami.'

A whole minute's silence ensued, until Franky asked, 'Who she?'

'Mi never tell you 'bout her?'

'No.'

'I did!' he cried in disbelief.

'Bwoy, mi say yu didn't. Don't call me a liar.' Franky pressed the cloth hard on one of his wounds.

'Sorry! Mi sorry! Beg you, don't do dat, please!' August shrieked. When the stinging died away, he went on, 'Mi swear mi see someone who looked like Ami. Mi was at Massa Brown's property, delivering some corn with Massa Frazer; it was just the other day.'

'Yu call to her?'

'No, mi didn't t'ink it was her at the time. Mi see di side of her face, and she was far away. Ami is dead.'

'Yuh shoulda call her name.'

'But what if it was not she?'

'It no matter. All yu would have to do is say sorry.'

August wasn't in the habit of hailing people when he wasn't sure who they were.

'What yu t'inking 'bout now?'

'Not'ing . . .' he began, but then felt he must tell the truth. 'Mi was t'inking 'bout running. But mi no know where mi would run.'

'There is nowhere. Mus' stay put.'

August stared at his hands, picking the dirt out from under his fingernails. 'Is true?' he asked.

'True 'bout what?'

'Dat a runaway was found in the cave, down by the Cove, and dem kill him, and dem chop off him head and leave it in the cave?'

'Is true. Duppy live dere now.'

'Mi would never run dere.'

'No. Better yu stay.'

Escape was clearly impossible, so August's thoughts turned to revenge. 'One day, mi will kill Quaco for what him do to our people. No negro should do to another what him do to me. I hate him more than I do any busha man.'

'Hate.' Franky sighed, as though she could not bear to hear the word once more. 'Dat is somet'ing mi never know until mi come to this land. Hate is somet'ing buried deep in the white man heart. Because dem have too much fear bottled up inside dem – dem fear anyt'ing dem don't understand. Dem fear us.'

March 1807
Lord God, me good friend, Mr Wilberforce, make me free!
God Almighty thank you, God Almighty make me free!
Buckra in this country no make we free . . .

Everyone had been talking of the possibility for years; the rumour had been building for months; and for weeks expectation had been rife among the villagers. Nancy couldn't contain her excitement. Tapping out a tune in the thin air, she danced down the path towards the curing-house, her hips swivelling and her arms aloft, spreading the news that the white gentlemen across the sea had set all the slaves free. August was the first person she met. He was overjoyed at the news, though his joy was momentarily diminished by Nancy planting a loud kiss on his ear. When she told the people working in the curing-house, she turned round and danced all the way back up the hill to Bardanage, there to carry on with her housework. She was convinced that this would be one of the last times she would perform these duties for Massa as his house slave.

Later August met Sis Bell in the village. She was singing and dancing an ecstatic jig.

Allick appeared from behind a row of plantain trees and asked in surprise, 'Sis Bell, what on earth wrong wit' you? Why yu making such a damn fool of yuself?'

'We free! Mr Wilberforce set us free!'

'What?' Allick's jaw dropped. The reality was too enormous to grasp. 'Who told you dat wi free?'

'Nancy. We is free!'

'Is lie!'

Allick turned to August. 'Man, put down the cane and come mek me and yu go celebrate.'

'So what is it?' demanded Sis Bell, insulted. 'Am I not good enough to be seen with the both of you?'

'Sorry, Sis Bell. I mean you too.' August laid his hand upon her back, gently guiding her towards the village.

The news was spreading rapidly, Allick thought it was like water pouring through a drainage system, swishing through all the ducts, then finding its own level. Soon most of the fieldhands had downed their tools and were flocking to the bottom of the hill. They wanted Nancy out of the house again, so they could hear more details. August decided he would round up a few more villagers before heading up to the big house.

'Go get her and mek she tell wi everyt'ing,' someone said.

'Mi not going up to de house. Massa is a madman. Me don't want him sling gunshot after me.'

'Massa wouldn't do dat.'

'Dat's what you think. Dem say action tell who is friend or devil.'

August decided he must fetch Nancy out, so he went up the hill and spoke to her. She confirmed what she had heard said.

When he got back to the village, he found the villagers preparing for all-night festivities. Some of them absconded to neighbouring estates to find out what other celebrations were being planned. As the afternoon turned to evening, singing and the sound of drums permeated the village. August was amused to hear the word 'free' over and over again from the lips of a little girl who was throwing stones at a lizard with other children.

'Massas set we free today, but you no go free unless I say,' she giggled. Casting a big stone, she hit the lizard square on the head and killed it instantly. The girl was four years old, and equipped with many words belonging to an adult world.

'Today Mother say William Wilberforce has set we free and everyone go celebrate tonight.'

August, too, repeated 'free, free, free' incessantly in his mind. But he still couldn't embrace a vision of freedom. It would probably involve no more than everyone being summoned to Bardanage for a dinner-time gathering. And Massa would stand leaning on the balustrade, ruefully reading proclamations. How would Massa endure the scene of ex-slaves jumping up and down, slapping him on the back and wishing him the very best for the future, one equal to another? August felt empty, like a chief who had come home from a victorious battle, only to find that his village had been plundered. He made a quick dash to Franky's hut to look for his *goombay* drum, but he couldn't find it.

Hopey poked his head through the door, asking August to hurry. August gave up looking for his *goombay* and they ran out together. They found a spot by a plantain tree where two young girls, Beckie and Fibra, were performing traditional dances, surrounded by an admiring crowd.

Sis Bell moved out from the crowd and into the ring, and moved the two girls aside. She pointed at Allick, and then winked at him, summoning him to join her. The casual smile on his face said he was confident but not quite ready. She shimmied around him tantalisingly. A broad smile appeared on Allick's face; he seemed ready. She closed her eyes and flicked her head away in the opposite direction. Allick stiffened his upper body as he shuffled towards centre stage. Then he surprised his audience with a series of cartwheels and a back-flip, which left him unsteady but drew great applause.

'The next time you will break your neck,' said August. 'Must stop that.' Although he spoke teasingly, he meant it in all seriousness: at forty-five Allick was too old to be attempting such acrobatics.

Allick pulled his handkerchief out and fanned Sis Bell. August had never thought of the two of them together, but then Allick never talked about what he was up to with the women in the village.

The crowd began to impinge on the dance area and Charles made it his duty to keep the space clear. He backed up with outstretched arms, and said, 'Back off. Come on, everybody, back off. Give the people room.'

The dancing continued. Every so often, men skipped into the ring and stuffed coins down the best dancer's cleavage. Sis Bell was the main recipient of these gifts; she didn't seem to mind that the ryals were almost worthless.

August peered across at Richard White banging away on his comba, and moved over to talk to him.

He couldn't help bursting out excitedly, 'Eboe, mi know you are Eboe. Mi can see it.'

'What di . . .?' said Richard. 'Me is a Jamaican – Ja-mai-can.'

'Who give you your drum?' asked August.

'My mother's mother give it to my mother. Just before my mother come to work the Cove.'

'Your mother's mother must have been Eboe.'

'So what you trying to say? You telling me mi is a damn guineabird? Is that what you are trying to say?' Richard shook his fist. 'Don't tell me 'bout any ratted guineabirds.' Richard realised people were staring, so he quietened, gave August a polite yet superficial smile, then carried on drumming, as if nothing had been said.

August was astonished that his excitement about the Eboe and curiosity about the drum could be found offensive.

Richard was still angry. 'If mi hear you say that again, me will brok' you up.'

August realised that Richard had been conditioned to think in terms of class and colour. He never saw himself as white – how could he when he was a slave? And he certainly didn't see himself as black; he was just Richard the quadroon.

There was nothing more to be gained from asking about Richard's ancestry, so August moved back towards the plantain tree. The festivities were reaching a climax, and he would not let the quarrel spoil his enjoyment.

The sound of gunfire tore through the celebrations. Everyone ducked instinctively, then looked up and around to see where it was coming from. August tried to see over the top of the heads of people blocking his view. He caught a glimpse of Massa John coming down the path with dogs and about ten militiamen.

In tow were his headmen, Quaco among them. The villagers were rooted to the spot, watchful, fearful. The troop moved forward, their guns cocked. They circled the slaves and five more soldiers came out from the shadows between the village cabins.

August's mind darted back to the time when he had fought for his life during the scramble, now nine years gone. A flash of perspiration washed him.

Allick was the first to break the silence, moving slowly to the front, gesturing to the villagers to let him through.

Respectfully, he addressed Massa John. 'We hear that Mr Wilberforce set all of wi free, true? Massa, I beg you, please tell us.'

Massa John looked at him, stupefied. 'Over my dead body,' he said.

'But Massa, we is free. True?'

'No.'

'But—'

'All of you get back to work! And anybody who starts acting like they damn well please will be sent to the work-house – unless I decide to bury the lot of you up to your heads out by the Cove, pour honey over you and let the red ants eat you to pulp.'

Massa John signalled Lieutenant Dickson, of Davis Cove Estate, to take centre stage. The lieutenant held an official-looking scroll of paper, tied with in red ribbon. He unrolled it, and read out an article explaining that the trade in Africans had ceased to be legal and that there would be no more shipments of Africans from over the sea. But, he stressed, looking up at the slaves, that did not mean slavery had been abolished. All Africans and creoles already in bondage were to remain so.

Sis Bell pinched August's hand, directing his attention to Nancy, who was edging away, back toward Bardanage. The villagers began to disperse among the trees, fields and huts. Back to their bondage.

# Chapter 9

# Allick

AT MIDNIGHT AUGUST made his way to Allick's hut. Several men had gathered there and were talking in low, sombre voices, trying to make sense of the day's events; Sister Bell was there, too, warming chicken soup over a fire. Although they as usual all talked at the same time, the exchange centred on Allick and Charles. General bewilderment was suffused with anger and frustration, a swirling feeling of defeat – defeat for liberty, for equal rights and justice for all. The atmosphere stirred August. It was the first time he could remember seeing creoles and Africans coming together in a common quest. The earlier taste of freedom had been as sweet as the taste now was bitter: in no time at all, freedom had slipped away.

Creation first started with a thought – whatever the mind was capable of thinking would always come to pass. August had been told this by a village elder, back home, but had not been able to understand it then. Now it made more sense. He concentrated on what Allick was saying, for Allick seemed to reach a turning-point.

'Today I feel a higher spirit go through me. And let me tell yu that when the rain comes, it will sweep away everyt'ing. I believe that forty days and forty nights must pass before things get better – dat is what the Bible says. Fire and brimstone soon come for the wicked.' He paused, searching the heavens. 'The Lord try to reach out to us, but the devil try to block him. Praise be to the Almighty for he has sent a great angel Mr Wilberforce to us as our saviour in this time. Hallelujah!'

'Hallelujah!' Charles cried.

'Me feel me want to kill the next white man me see tonight,' someone said.

Sis Bell initiated a chorus of approval with her 'Amen'.

The murmurs were interrupted by Charles stamping his feet. 'Mi no want to hear any talk of mischief-making. All of you can forget it. Do yu hear me?'

August added, 'Reverend Rose always says dat the Lord will help those who help themselfs. All we have to do is ask, and we shall receive. True, Brother Charles?'

'True,' Charles replied. 'Patience. Let us wait for another sign from Mr Wilberforce before doing anything that might spill our precious blood.' He closed his eyes, raised his head to the sky and linked hands with Sis Bell and Allick. All those present followed suit, some bowing their heads, while others sank to their knees.

Charles raised his voice and prayed, 'Gawd, you say we the poor mus'n't judge unjustly, and accept the ways of the wicked persons over the righteous, dat we should defend the poor and faderless, dat we mus' do justice to the afflicted and needy.

'You ask us to deliver the poor and needy an' lead them out of the hands of the wicked for they know not, neider will they understand, they walk on in darkness, all the foundations of the eart' is gone.

'You are God, and we are all children of the most high.

'But we shall die like men. And fall like one of the Princes.

'But we are powerless, poor, weak an' ignorant. Gawd, I ask you to arise.

'O Gawd. Judge the earth, for you shall inherit all Nations.'

In the weeks that followed, August became aware of marked changes in Allick. He spent much time in Charles's company, regularly attending prayer meetings.

Something about buckra's religion had gripped him. Knowing how shrewd Allick could be, August thought cynically that it might be something to do with the privileges Massa and his overseer had extended to the few slaves who had made the change. Baptised slaves got passes to leave the estate much more easily than the others. Massa even allowed them to attend Reverend Rose's services, where they seized every opportunity to sing and clap, and – much to Frazer's annoyance – to dance and drum. August had heard, however, that this indulgence was gradually being restricted as the religion took hold in slave villages across the island. He thought it improbable that Allick could ever take seriously the notion of becoming a Christian. Allick kept asking August to go with him, and August was willing to do anything that would make life more bearable. He decided to attend a service or two, for if Allick thought it was a good thing it couldn't be bad.

Not only Allick but Charles and Sis Bell went to Reverend Rose's prayer meetings. They were held on Sunday mornings and were poorly attended, mostly just the hard core from the village and sometimes a few others from Haughton and Spring Valley. The regulars had reserved benches at the front.

Over the weeks, August grew to admire the Reverend's tenacity. His services were punctuated by snoring and grunting, but he carried on, apparently oblivious of the fact that the sapping heat, his monotonous voice and the week's toil combined to put his congregation to sleep. They had no desire to respond vigorously to his call to prayer. His words bounced off their tough shells, and they stared blankly at the wall behind him. Things changed like the rush of the wind, though, when it was time to sing; drums of all descriptions were brought out, and Sis Bell's voice sounded clear and loud on top of the chants, as if she were leading the verse.

August attended the services regularly. He listened carefully to what Rose said about the power of the lord. How could one god have so much power over all things? When Rose said pray, August prayed. At first he did so simply because the Reverend said he should, but the more he heard about Jesus and the miracles, the tighter he shut his eyes, praying for Jesus to deliver him. Rose's god was now his only chance of the miracle of better life. He believed the miracles Rose talked about were not happening to him because he didn't believe strongly enough. As time passed, he found himself praying harder, mixing prayer with tears when he had had a particularly hard day in the fields. Although the message gave him hope at times of trouble, August failed to see what Allick found inspiring about the Reverend. Allick explained that it was a good thing for Frazer to see them lapping up religious instruction from the white priest's table like yard dogs.

He also said that a handful of black pastors had recently come from America. One, a free man called Moses Baker, occasionally visited neighbouring plantations late in the evening, on the first Saturday of every month. That was the only time he could get a licence to preach; on other occasions he did so illegally. Allick talked at length about Pastor Moses' style of preaching. He encouraged his congregations to let the spirit run through; song and dance were central ingredients of worship.

'The spirit of Africa fill me every time mi hear him,' said Allick. 'Yu don't feel that when yu go to Reverend Rose's church, do you?'

'No, I don't.'

'Aha. Yu see? Rose preach a very good message – mi no say otherwise. But him like to talk and talk and talk. Yu suppose to sit there and listen, until him tell you to get up and sing, or get down and pray, whatever. And when time come to go home, that's when yu realise yu never listen to half of what him say. Now' – he paused for breath – 'when yu go to Pastor Baker, is a different t'ing altogether. When

Pastor Baker calls, yu respond. You don't haffi wait for him to call, either, just tell him, tell everyone, and tell the Lord what you feel within your heart. Cry out as if someone drop a horseshoe on your big toe. Jump up and say Hallelujah if you feel the Lord drop a powerful message on you – mek Him know yu hear Him.' Allick's excitement conjured up in August a feeling of release, of a place where he could escape unbearable thoughts of hopelessness.

'Why you never tell mi 'bout this man before? You have me wasting my time going to Reverend's church when mi could have been going there instead.'

'Because how you t'ink it look to Massa if yu catch religion and yu don't go to Reverend's church?'

'True. Mi never t'ink of—'

'Mi know you never t'ink – dat is why mi have to do so much t'inking fi you. Furthermore, the Pastor say many things Massa wouldn't like hear.'

'Like what?' said August, leaning closer.

'Oh . . . a lot of t'ings. One day mi will invite yu to a gathering so yu can hear for yuself. Mi will let you know when him going preach next.'

The Reverend Rose used to stand in the fields, observing the regime and making notes – a curious sight. Of late he had taken to arriving in the cane pieces just after the two o'clock bell, when the field labourers had finished tending to their provision grounds and were making their way to the hills. The labourers brought back guineagrass as fodder for the livestock, the animals' dung being used as manure in the freshly dug cane holes.

August did not know what the Reverend was up to and didn't really care. Frazer told the villagers he was gathering information so that he and other raving Baptists could sit in meetings, ranting about the suffering of slaves. And in their piety they would make a name for themselves within the abolitionist movement.

August shook his head, trying hard not to believe that there might be some truth in Frazer's words. August thought Frazer's actions only encouraged Rose in his convictions. The last time Frazer had hurled abuse at the Reverend in front of August, he had said that all missionaries and Baptists seemed to be outcasts, as if they thought themselves in the mould of Jesus Christ. Blasphemy! Frazer spat on the ground by his boot. He said he worried not in the slightest about all Rose's note-taking. After all, no one in his right mind would take a shred of notice of him and his kind? The Assembly was almighty; it was not in their interest to give voice to a few idiosyncratic, insignificant pests. In any case, if moral indignation about slavery were justified, it would surely have come from the Anglican Church a long time ago. August wondered why the Church was so slow to speak out against slavery; he felt some Christians even favoured it. What about the Rector of St Ann, the Reverend G. W. Bridges, whom Frazer knew well? He was renowned for the severity with which he punished his slaves.

The day after his conversation with Allick about religion, August was on his knees weeding, when he heard the cane stems rattle behind him and Reverend Rose emerged. Missing his footing on the last step, he tripped, then fell to the ground and into the clearing. 'Drat,' he pronounced, either unaware or not caring that the word was derived from 'God rot'. August laughed, for the Reverend was clearly not used to seeing slave work at such close quarters, and had not mastered the balance required for treading the uneven ground.

August dropped his hoe and helped the Reverend to his feet. He dusted him down, paying particular attention to a patch of dirt on his right knee. The Reverend bent to pick up his notebook.

'Massa, what you writing in that book all day?' asked August.

'Oh, it's something that I am writing for a friend of mine in England. Mr Clarkson's his name.'

'Ah,' August offered, still curious.

Out of the cane thicket came Sis Bell. She looked moody as she trudged along, her hoe in her hand.

'Hello, Sis Bell,' said Reverend Rose.

'Oh, mi never see you there, Oh Lord, forgive me. Mi sorry. 'Ello, Reverend, 'ello.'

August signalled her to perk up. It was not good that the Reverend should see her downcast.

'Is everything good with you?' asked the Reverend.

'Yes, everything is fine, thank you.'

'How is Allick?'

'Me don't know wedda him turning mad or what.' Sis Bell kissed her teeth and her sullen expression returned.

'What do you mean?' asked the Reverend.

'Massa John asked him to go into town with him to go find a worker to take care of his gardens.'

'Did he find one?'

'Yes, him find one.'

'Oh?' said the Reverend.

'Come, mek I quickly show you where he is,' Sis Bell urged.

August was intrigued by her expression and ominous tone of voice.

She led the two men back through the cane field to a clearing from where the main road could be seen.

'See him over there,' and she pointed to a stone wall which marked the outer boundary. Nearby, Allick and some other men were loading a cart with barrels of rum.

August recognised every man in the group. 'Where?' he asked, puzzled. 'I can't see the man.'

'See him there,' Sis Bell repeated. 'Are you blind?'

Not far from the labourers, a frail-looking old man was sitting on the wall. His head had grey-speckled hair with a bald spot on top that gleamed in the sun. He was decrepit, dirty and uncared-for, like a vagrant, and his dirty cotton trousers were shot through with holes. His shirt obviously hadn't been washed for months. August could imagine its stench; he thought it might come alive and extricate itself.

Allick stopped loading and went over to the old man. He lifted him cradle-fashion off the wall and laid him down in the protective shade of a banana tree.

August and the Reverend looked at each other, bemused.

'What on earth Massa going to do with that old man?' asked August.

'Why did Mr Crooks purchase him?' wondered Reverend Rose.

'The old man called Sussex,' Sis Bell said, plunging her hoe firmly into the dirt. 'Allick tell Massa John that him should buy him, 'cause him would cost likkle or not'ing. Massa John don't have money fi buy a whole heap of slaves these days. That's what I hear, anyway.'

'But even so . . .'

'Everytime I question Allick, he turn on me and tell me to mind mi own business. He get vex, so me jus' decide to lose myself. I don't know why he told Massa fi do it.'

'He gets angry when anyone asks?' said the Reverend.

'Yes. All him say to me is that only good works and mercy shall follow him to his death. Reverend, is you teach him that.'

They were indeed words Reverend Rose had uttered many times, though August nevertheless continued to think that it was peculiar behaviour.

When Allick had finished his chores he headed off back to the village, leading the old man by a thin rope tied round his waist.

# Chapter 10

# Better Mus' Come

ONE SATURDAY NIGHT, Pastor Moses Baker was due to give a sermon over at Haughton Court Estate. It was a risky, even foolhardy, plan, for the Estate was owned by the Hon. Simon Taylor, Custos of St Thomas in the east, a man who faithfully and ably filled the highest office of civil and military duty on the island. He thought black Baptists and lay preachers were ill-disposed, illiterate, ignorant enthusiasts, and instigated the acts of Assembly, preventing preaching by persons not qualified by law, persons like Pastor Baker.

Allick, John Smith and Sis Bell were going, and August decided to tag along. The four of them stole over from Crooks' Cove into the Estate, knowing that the bookkeepers would be tucked up for the night, either reading a book or with a slave woman warming their beds. On the way over, Allick and John talked about the services at Haughton and how lively they were. Sis Bell said it was where everyone went to feel a healing spirit, and that buckra's God loved black people the way He loved buckra.

Services had formerly been held at Sister Grant's place, but it was within sight of the new extension to the boiling-house, built as a base for the overseer to keep an eye on the comings and goings of black folk. So the venue for the services had shifted to an empty trash-house. This was a stone shed, comfortably large enough for the expected forty people. It was separated from the works, and had been emptied of trash that afternoon; the trash had been transferred to the boiling-house, to be used as fuel. Sheaths of crushed cane littered the trash-house floor.

The Pastor was usually punctual and made a point of letting his congregations know that he had no respect for people who arrived late. The villagers filed in in twos and threes, in good time and in a relaxed, orderly fashion. Some sat down in the middle while a few, mostly men, leant against the long wall.

August looked around and met the eyes of two acquaintances, Molly and Amelia, who laboured on different plantations not far away. Standing behind them, he saw with pleasure, was Samuel, a dark creole from the Golden Grove Estate at least twenty miles away. Samuel had been born and raised on the Cove, but had been sent to the Golden Grove two years before, having been hired to repair the roads there, so that they were in a fit state at the end of crop season for puncheons of rum molasses to be transferred to the port for export. Samuel was later sold to the Estate; Massa Crooks obtained a handsome price for him. One of Massa Crooks's fieldslaves, Hellina Crooks, bore Samuel five children before they married. He saw Hellina once in a while, when she was given leave to go and see him on her days off. The children he hadn't seen for almost a year.

'How did you manage to get over to this side, Brother Samuel?' asked August.

'The usual, me get a ride from anybody who will give it. August, is good to see you again.'

'You too. You look well, considering.'

'Me still keep the faith, thanks,' said Samuel. 'Have you seen Hellina or any of my children lately?'

'Yes, all the while. They still pray that one day the Lord will bring the whole family together under one roof.'

'That's what I pray for, too. I think very much about an anointing in the hope that the Lord will think me worthy and shower me with a blessing.'

'So, how are they treating black folk over at the Grove?' asked August.

'Man, I don't have to tell you, very bad. Very very bad. I hear that everybody in the big house is getting ready for plenty trouble.'

'Why?'

'Well, me hear that Massa don't want to obey the laws Mr Wilberforce put down to stop buckra from trading in Africans,' said Samuel.

'True?'

'Yes, man. But jus' the other day I see two half-naked Africans arrive new to the Estate. Them have marks on their faces and some of their teeth were filed – you know what I mean. Them couldn't speak a word of English.' He stopped short, realising that August matched the physical description. 'Sorry, August, but you hear what I trying to say. They are Africans and they shouldn't be here – not in shackles, anyway. The law prohibits it.'

August wasn't in the least offended. He was used to such remarks and accepted the creole mentality. As far as he was concerned they were ignorant souls, but he never blamed them for their shortcomings; he understood well that this was how creoles were taught to think of Africans.

He said, 'But the question I have on my mind is how the mother country going know who should be a slave and who shouldn't. I hear dem is still bringing in Africans to Spring Valley. Massa Crooks know is going to cost him to look after slaves that can't work no more. Is going to be expensive to replace all of we when we dead and gone. Wait till him find out that some of the women killing their babies before dem born. He going have to hire labourers from all over the place during crop season – or do something else.'

'My brother, there will be whole heap a trouble if people find out say buckra in the foreign land trying to free we poor blacks, an' that the Jamaican Assembly is trying to

86

stop them. You know how nega mentality stay. Them can get really ignorant when them ready.'

'It better do soon, otherwise, yes, all hell going break loose.'

They were interrupted by a voice announcing, 'Pastor Baker come!'

All heads turned. As the Pastor approached, people greeted him with hugs and handshakes. Then he asked for a pail to be lodged in the door. This was customary, for it was believed that any sound escaping the trash-house would go into the pail, and thus be prevented from reaching the ears of busha. As an extra precaution, someone was nominated to go outside every so often and check that no busha lurked nearby.

The service finished at two o'clock in the morning. Instead of setting off back to the Cove, August decided to look for Peggy Crooks, hoping to renew an acquaintance made two years earlier, before she was sold to Haughton Court. He was curious to know whether she still had any feelings for him. That night he didn't return to the Cove at all.

When dawn broke, he rose, crept out of Peggy's cabin and began trudging across the Haughton provision pastures. He saw a boy running across the cattle pens, over the last barrier into Crooks' Cove – probably one of the villagers stealing fowl from the poultry shed. Curious to know who would be so bold as to risk his backside for the sake of a few provisions, August gave chase. He caught the boy without breaking sweat and quickly wrestled him to the ground. He recognised him as one of the new slaves on the Estate. When he lifted the boy up by the scruff of his neck, his suspicion was confirmed: viscous egg, crushed in the fall, was dripping from the boy's hand.

'Boy, what you think you doing?' August demanded. 'You damn fool, how many times you think you can do this before Massa catch you?'

The boy bore the look of one about to be castigated. His teeth chattered.

August took pity on him, and calmed himself. 'Boy, what you name?'

'Andries.'

'Andries. Yes, mi remember you face. You arrive 'pon Crooks' Cove not so long ago. So who looking after you?'

'Nobody.'

'How you mean?'

'Since me come to this plantation, Massa give me a plot of land to farm and ask Massa Frazer to look after me, an' make sure mi all right, but he don't do that.'

'Yes. Sometimes we have it hard, but that don't mean is all right for you to bring trouble into everybody backyard.'

Andries remorsefully bowed his head.

'Boy, our people will always catch fire in this land if we don't pull together. Thieving will only bring problem,' said August, waving his finger at Andries. 'The last man caught thieving was an African called Harry. The book-keeper did know exactly how much eggs him suppose to have. When nobody own up to thieving from him, him jus' go tell Massa Frazer.'

Frazer, he told the boy, had called a black woman called Jennet to his house and informed her she would be beaten on the first Monday of every month, until the real thief owned up. No one did, and when Monday came she was flogged in front of all the villagers. Harry was among the onlookers. After the third stroke he began to cry and gave himself up. He was sent to the workhouse, but not before Frazer had slit his nose and chopped off the thumb on his left hand.

'What me should do?' Andries asked anxiously.

'Don't do a thing. Jus' come with me. If you hungry, all you have to do is bring your plate to one of the women and jus' beg them for a likkle food. The longer you live, the more you learn.' With that, he dusted himself down and led the boy back to the slave quarters.

The following day August made his way over to the pens at the edge of the Crooks' Cove estate, near the borders with Blenheim and Haughton. He strutted down the dirt path admiring the view of Spring Estate. Near the pastures' edge, beyond the lazy plantain walk, he saw Mulatto John struggling with the horrible task of stripping and cutting through the knife-edged blades of matured cane stalks.

August continued up the path past a few smallholdings on the way to the outer pastures. He noticed that the roofs of many of the huts along the way were made of new corrugated iron. These were the huts belonging to the quadroons – some female descendants on Massa John's side.

When he arrived at the cattle pens, he saw a few black men, Africans, huddled together outside a disused barn. They had lit a fire and were roasting plantain and what smelt like fish – probably crab. They were talking in the low voices reserved for important discussions, so he moved closer. No one noticed him as he crept around the back of the barn; through its window he glimpsed some large black Jack Spaniard wasp combs under the roof.

He edged round the side of the barn and, when he was as near as he could reasonably get, shouted, 'Buckra a come! Buckra a come!'

It wasn't a particularly well-executed prank. The men – Sam, Hopey, Marky and Harry – looked up quickly and then casually acknowledged August's presence, though none was at all amused.

'Stop the fooling, you damn fool,' Sam barked.

At this point Ben arrived. Greeting them with an almost curt flick of the head, he took up a central position. It was typical of him. Ben was a solid man who kept himself to himself; he never shared his feelings or his dreams, his life or his loves. He had friends, but none he could call close; more respected than loved, he was yet not disliked. He had an aura about him: it was said that his capture was the result of betrayal by his brother, an Ashanti general, but no one knew for sure; what everyone did know was that Ben had vowed to return to his homeland and take revenge upon whoever had betrayed him.

'You people look like yu going to take over the island,' August joked.

Ben cut a sharp look at him and said, 'Stupid boy. Did Hopey tell you about the meeting tonight?'

'No.'

'Well, you better find yourself down at Marky's hut tonight.'

'No problem,' August murmured casually.

'And you better not tell a soul,' Ben added. 'Anyhow buckra get to hear, is you that me going kill, personally.'

'No problem,' repeated August, though now feeling less assured. He understood from Ben's tone that only Africans were invited to the meeting.

'Make sure you tell Allick to come. Mi like that man. Him talk a whole heap of sense. Mi could well get used to a man like that,' said Ben. He seemed to sense August's discomfort, for he laid a reassuring hand on his shoulder and gave him a smile.

The six o'clock bell called the fieldhands to down tools. August knew what would happen next. Marky discreetly signalled across the field to another man. In the distance, the blacksmith beat out a solid rhythm as he worked, a code to all who were invited to the meeting. As the workers made their way to their huts, Ben and his men filtered off towards the meeting-point.

August wondered how many such meetings were being sparked off all over the island. The rumbling of discontent could be heard everywhere. Conspiracy was in the air. Were there enough rebels to make a difference? Was anyone brave enough to ignite the powder keg? It occurred to August that there were increasing numbers of mulattos among the malcontents; Mulatto John was just one. But there was more to it than this. It was said that the buckra gentleman in the mother country wanted to free the slaves. The planters feared that the mother country would try to force the Assembly's hand. For the slaves, it followed that the mother country would endorse or determine struggle by the slaves themselves.

As August hurried to the meeting-point, second thoughts were beginning to weigh him down. Hopey caught him up, and they shook hands and moved on together.

'Where is Allick?' asked Hopey.

'He wanted was to come, but him not feeling well at all – him feel dizzy in his head.'

'Mi sorry to hear that, no lie.'

August tugged Hopey's sleeve warningly. They paused for a few moments, while two creoles went by.

'When was the first meeting?' August caught Hopey firmly by the wrist. 'How long has this been going on?'

'Only one meeting before this one, truly.'

'So how come you never tell me?'

'The men never sure whether to invite you and Allick because . . .' He paused, searching August's eyes for permission to confide what others had said about him.

'Go on, talk,' urged August.

'Because . . . you both love the buckra's religion . . . too much, tell me if is a lie,' Hopey eventually managed. 'You are lucky that is me who tell them that you have good character.'

'Lucky! Is that what you people think?'

August failed to see how physical strength could win them the freedom they all wanted so much. He tried to persuade Hopey that it was buckra's God that had made slaves of the Africans because negroes were heathens – Reverend Rose had told him so. By August's reckoning, if black people would only get down on their knees and pray hard enough, the Lord might be persuaded to change

91

things for the benefit of black folk – of that he was convinced. He said, 'It is a sin to think you can serve two masters. The Lord ready to pass judgement upon the busha for the wickedness him inflict 'pon we poor negroes. All we haffi do is ask fi His help and strength.'

Hopey's eyes glazed over and August knew it was time to change the subject. He said, 'Tell me something, Hopey. What you really think them going achieve tonight?'

'Them don't really know, but that is why we all mus' meet, you understand mi.'

'Then tell me something else. How many other people involved?'

'All the Africans.'

'From where?'

'From here.'

'You mean no nega from other plantations involved?'

'Should there be?'

'Of course! But what kind of trouble you trying get me involved in? And tell me, where on this damn island you going run when the whole military and them vicious Cuban dogs come looking for you?'

'Me will run anywhere, me no care – the hills most probably, or me can get in a canoe an' go to Cuba. Me here say is a better chance of freedom there, truly.' But Hopey's confidence was beginning to wane.

'Anywhere! Anywhere – to the hills so that the maroons can catch you?' August turned and walked off to his hut, leaving Hopey wondering whether to implore him to go to the meeting or to follow his lead and not to turn up.

The next morning, Hopey went to the mill-house, where August was helping Allick put cane through the rollers. Hopey signalled to August to come over and talk outside. August gave Allick a nod to say that he would not be more than a few minutes.

'Them did ask for you last night, and me tell them you not feeling well,' said Hopey.

August kissed his teeth in disbelief and relief. 'Everything go all right?' He really did want to know.

'Yes, man, everything set, but them ask me to get you fi take an oath to say you swear to secrecy.'

August took Hopey's hand and Hopey swore him to allegiance.

'Did you say anything to Allick?' asked August.

'No, sir.'

'So who was there?'

'Everybody except Allick and you, yeah, man.'

'It went well, then?'

'Yes, man. Everything went smooth. Oh, there was one black man there.'

'Who?'

'A runaway. Him name Jack.'

'Mi never hear of him. Who harbouring him?'

'Dallas.'

'I shoulda guessed is her,' August said. Dallas was well known for harbouring runaways. 'Look, mi talk to you later. Massa Frazer watching us.'

# Chapter 11

# Play with Fire

AUGUST'S STOMACH WAS rumbling by the time he reached his hut. It had been a day he would prefer to forget. Franky put in front of him a plate of ackee and saltfish, and cornmeal dumplings – five of them – then piled it high with sliced baked plantain and a cut of yam. He said a quick prayer before taking a sniff at the plate; the strong aroma of saltfish and hot pepper made him forget any graces Franky had taught him. He dug his fingers in and came up with the ackee, which he 'gwapsed', his cheeks puffed. He rinsed his fingers in the calabash of drinking water and dried them on a red cloth that Franky had readied for him. Then he picked up his spoon, meticulously placed it beside the plate and began to scoop the rest of the food into his mouth.

'Nanny, beg you for a drink, please?'

Franky kissed her teeth and emptied the calabash. 'Go make it yuself. And anyway, look how yu put the food away so fast. Yu going get sick. Yu mus' eat slower.'

He grunted an acknowledgement, his mouth too full to speak.

While August ate, Franky went to the kitchen garden to gather provisions for the next day. Revelling in his meal, he allowed his thoughts to turn to Hopey and the others. Would the next day be the day of reckoning? He thought how edgy Hopey had been out in the fields earlier, working doubly hard cutting the cane and digging holes; he seemed flustered, and looked as if he was cracking. At times he lashed his cutlass at the cane with alarming frenzy. Ben went to try to calm him, but Hopey continued working

94

that way, so Ben sent Sam over. Sam's words were highly effective. When August asked Ben what Sam had said, he was not surprised to hear that Hopey had been told his throat would be cut during the night if he didn't immediately calm down.

August wondered what he himself would do if he were planning an insurrection. What day would he choose? Who would be involved? He would certainly avoid Christmas – it seemed that every report of any major uprising he'd ever heard about was quelled on Boxing Day. Even if Massa John thought relatively well of his negroes, he always prepared for the possibility of rebellion during the festive week. Several times in recent years he had asked his neighbour, Colonel Richard Dickson, to send a company of militia to guard Crooks' Cove. About ten men would be positioned at the border ready to shoot any suspect negro on sight, at the sound of the alarm bell. However, there had been no guard the previous year. All the plantations in Hanover had wanted protection and there weren't enough men to go round. Nevertheless, Christmas and New Year had passed and there were still militiamen milling around.

August jumped violently when Franky shouted, 'August, eat up, man.'

His thoughts had preoccupied him so much that he had left three of the tough cornmeal dumplings on his plate.

'Eat up, man,' Franky repeated. 'You need the strength.'

The following Sunday was August's chance to sit down with Hopey to find out about the meeting at Marky's. Hopey looked around guardedly before embarking on his tale. Although a conspiracy had been planned, he said, it was aborted. The plan had been to prepare to set fire to the cow pen at dawn, then go over to Frazer and cut him to pieces before setting the trash-houses alight. That was to be the signal to the negroes on Spring Valley and Haughton estates to join the uprising; then the Harding Hall

Estate field gangs would be brought in. Hopey would then take to the hills and set up a settlement away from the maroons. He felt that a gang of slaves three hundred strong would be able to protect themselves against the black gendarmes.

Hopey was on edge as he spoke, his fists clenched throughout.

'Hopey, I need to speak to you, now,' Frazer said, materialising beside them like a duppy by day.

'Massa, any time. Yu know me always available, whether Sunday, Boxing Day, Christmas or any time, jus' call and me will come,' replied Hopey, subtly reminding Frazer that it was supposed to be a rest day for the villagers. The two of them went off.

August sighed with relief: Frazer obviously hadn't over-heard the conversation. Nevertheless, the tone he had used to call Hopey away made August feel that things were not as they should be.

Two hours passed and there was no sign of Hopey. August decided he would go up to the house on the pretext of helping Sussex, who was planting seeds in Massa's kitchen garden. He took Sussex's hoe, and asked him to sit down and watch for any sign of busha approaching. August kept an eye on the house while he worked. Eventually, the door swung open and out into the sun came Frazer, Richard Dickson, Hopey and another man, pale, with a double chin. The four moved towards a mule and cart waiting to drive them away.

Sussex tossed a pebble: busha approaching.

August neatly passed the hoe back to Sussex, 'You see how I show you to do it. Make sure you continue to do it that way,' he said loudly. 'I am going back to do my own work.'

August took off down the hill. He tracked the mule and carts to the main road and watched it disappear out of sight, then raced back to the village to share the news with the others.

Hopey returned the next day. He was immediately surrounded by people eager to know what had happened.

'That damn bookkeeper. Him tell Massa John that we gather by the bridge the other night, whispering. Them take me to the magistrate fi answer questions.'

'What you tell them?' Marky enquired, wide-eyed.

A wry smile came over Hopey's face. 'Exactly what we plan to tell, of course. Yes, man. Truly.'

Every contingency had been covered. He told the magistrates that Ben had asked them to become clerk to their gambling syndicate. He said it was all new to him, that he had no idea of what would be involved and that he'd refused to go along with it. The authorities heard about a regulation made among the slaves: when one slave cursed another, the offender had to pay a fine of five shillings' worth of rum; also, any man fined would hold a drinking party at his house. This provided a cover for the meetings. The house where drink was to be had would be known as the courthouse. When asked to explain certain statements about the kings and governors being involved, Hopey had told them that Ben came to drink and said that he would be king and Marky would be the governor, but that it was all a joke. Hopey embellished the plot when he mentioned that he was offered the post of second governor and was so offended that he walked out of the drinking session. That is what busha had overheard. It was nothing serious.

'You think them did believe you?' asked August.

'Well, good enough to let me go.' Still grinning, Hopey turned to Ben and Harry and said, 'Them still want to see the two of yu before the matter can rest. All yu haffi do is keep calm and answer all questions them, as we agreed. No worry yuself 'bout it.'

This was exactly what the other conspirators needed and wanted to hear. They rehearsed their stories countless times. August was asked to pose some difficult questions, so that they could be satisfied that they were adequately prepared.

Ben and Harry were summoned for questioning the following day. The magistrate could find no evidence of a plot and let them go, doubtless concluding that they were too stupid to organise a rum party in the workhouse, let alone conceive of such a conspiracy. And when the men came together one last time to drink rum, they joked about how they stammered through the courthouse proceedings, regurgitating the docile caricatures that buckra had fed them.

A few days later, August was washing some mackerel he had got from the fishermen down by Davis Cove, preparing it for the evening dinner, when Missy Stewart appeared before him, as if in a vision. He flinched. She could have been there for ages for all he knew; he really had no idea. She was bedraggled, her long fair hair piled untidily on top of her head, secured only by a few pins.

August took no notice of her at first. He thought she must be looking for someone else, and that when she realised whoever it was she was looking for wasn't there, she would go on her way. He stayed crouched, head down, for a while longer. But Missy stood there, not saying a word, and he could feel her eyes penetrating him – it felt as though she was piercing a hole in his mind. Politeness prevented her from interrupting him; she presumed that it would be only a short wait before he looked up from his task and acknowledged her presence.

Missy's presence was off-putting, so August tossed a scowl in her direction, a churlish reminder that he wasn't at all enamoured of her, even if others were. He had been bold enough to tell her some time ago, without malice, that he disapproved of intimate liaisons with buckra, that when it came to men and women it should be each to his or her own. The advice was of little use to her, for she had already given birth to a boy by one of the bookkeepers – she wasn't sure which one. She was expecting her second by a busha man over at Davis Cove Estate.

Many of the young black men in the village readily engaged in conversation about what it would be like to put their dark skins in contact with the softness of her delicious honey-coloured skin. That sort of talk made August curse. 'What's wrong with the negro woman?' he grumbled to whoever was courageous enough to say such things in his presence.

However, Missy had as much white blood coursing through her as she did black. And she sought a better life for her and her son; after all they were unmistakably white negroes.

'Can I help you, Missy?' August eventually offered.

'I don't know,' she replied softly.

From her downcast tone August guessed that she was troubled. 'Yu don't know?' he said.

'Jeany said I should come and see you.'

'Oh yes. What about?'

'Well, I did witness one Massa mash up a slave woman, so bad. Him almost kill her. The law change an' I hear say Reverend Rose going to press charges. Them going to take him to court.'

'So?'

'Reverend ask me to testify – to be a witness.'

August froze for a moment, then carried on scrubbing the fish with his hands and nails, apparently indifferent to her words. 'So what you want me to do?'

'Mi no know. I mean, mi no know what to do.' She seemed helpless, vulnerable, and kept twiddling her fingers and nervously looking around as if she feared she'd made a terrible mistake approaching him in the first place.

'Wait one moment.' August glanced across at Sussex, who had been watching him clean the fish. August disappeared round the back to the kitchen garden. Missy hesitated, but after a few moments she and Sussex traipsed after

99

him. They found him standing over a *bankra* basket, looking for a small piece of meat to put with the mackerel. He had enough fish for Franky and himself; the meat was needed to make up the portions so he could feed Sussex as well. Some of the brambles had flaked off the basket and he pinched off some thin strands which had fallen on to the meat.

'I thought I did ask Franky to make another basket. How she expect me to keep the meat if we don't have a basket to smoke it?' He was irritable, preoccupied with his own problems.

'It doesn't matter. I'll come back later if you're busy,' said Missy. She turned to leave, but August told her to wait until he had fed Sussex.

When the old man had finished eating, August wiped Sussex's mouth with a clean part of his shirtsleeve. 'Is there anything else we can get you, old man?'

Sussex cupped his hands. August got a cup of water, squeezed lime into it and offered it to him. Sussex drank it quickly and gave it back. August put it down, then turned and said to Missy, 'Allick tell me off if mi no look after this man. Him fuss over him too much.'

'You think I don't know? But anyway, you are good to do as him says,' said Missy.

'Well, mi no know what that say about me – except that mi is a damn fool.' August smiled, but then his frown returned. 'If you know what is good for you, stay clear of the courthouse. Slaves not supposed to go to them places and testify 'gainst no buckra.'

'But Reverend say that we fi go and testify 'gainst busha man if them too severe with slaves.'

'Yes, mi hear that, but mi never hear of any Massa go a gaol on the basis of mulatto testimony. Have you?'

'No.'

'No. Well, my advice to you is stay well clear. The law don't allow negro to witness 'gainst buckra. The law is not there to protect we. Them say, "See an' blind, hear an' deaf." Just because the law allow mulattos to testify don't necessarily mean buckra want you fi testify. People like you too quick to exercise these little privileges that them give you. You will get yourself in whole heap of trouble if you no watch out. Them will not take your word for anything. Yu better watch out.'

Suddenly, a voice called, 'August, Marky want talk to you. Come quick! Nega going to be arrested.'

# Chapter 12

# Thirty Pieces of Silver

IT WAS TRUE: a slave had been arrested, though nobody knew why. Dallas volunteered to go up to the house and find out the details from Nancy. She soon came scurrying back down to the village, with Nancy following, and stationed herself in the middle of the slave quarters, near Sis Bell's hut. Everyone gathered round.

'One nigger going to dead, if him no watch himself,' she whispered.

In a low voice, she said that the arrested man was a runaway called Jack. He had run from Haughton with no idea of where to run to or how he was going to survive. When he heard that the insurrection had been aborted, he had returned to the Estate, scared that it would be only a matter of time until he was traced to Crooks' Cove.

Nancy took up the story. Jack had immediately been put in the stocks while his Massa made up his mind what to do with him. After two days, Jack broke his silence. He told his Massa that while on the run he had heard a conspiracy was to take place on a neighbouring plantation and Massa should beware. At first, he said he didn't know who was behind it, but he had said enough for his Massa to set him free.

'Did he name names?' someone asked.

'Wait,' said Nancy, 'let me finish. Chu.' Jack's Massa, she said, had sent word to his neighbours to be on the lookout for any unusual movements in and out of the estates, or of any slaves congregating. But that evening Jack was seen going back to the great house on Haughton to make another deal. In return for his manumission papers, he had named the leader of the conspiracy.

'Is who?' asked one of the creoles.

'Mi not supposed to say anyt'ing, so you all mus' promise to say not'ing.'

Everyone nodded in eager anticipation.

Nancy leant forward, raised her eyebrows and whispered, 'It was Ben.'

When darkness fell August returned to his hut to prepare for sleep. He could hear drums playing faintly in the distance. The sound came from the north, and was too far away to be heard by anyone up at the big house – he could only just make it out. It mingled with the swish of the waves as the tide came into the cove and the chatter of crickets in the fields, and was carried through the cabin by a warm breeze swirling in at the door and out of the window. The music faded away altogether every now and then, and it was difficult to detect a recognisable rhythm. It eventually dawned on him that it was the pattern of a particular ceremonial rhythm, similar to the one he associated with imminent sacrifice.

Now Franky heard it, too; it was accompanied by equally faint singing. She was halfway through plaiting her hair. She wedged the comb in the uncombed side of her silvery hair and went to the hut door, picking up her walking-stick on the way. Holding a lamp high in her right hand, she went outside to try and pinpoint where the ceremony was taking place.

August followed her. 'Yu think is duppy out there?' he asked. He was afraid it might be the bad spirit that was said to walk the cove at night.

'Shh! No duppy out dere.'

They moved further to the edge of the village. Squinting, they could make out graceful figures dancing about a fire.

'Obeah,' said Franky.

There had not been a ceremony on the plantation for quite a while. Obeah and other Myalist spiritual practices originating from the motherland had been banned for as long as August could remember, but he knew they were happening everywhere. He remembered Frazer once telling a new bookkeeper he was showing around the slave village that he had more important things to worry about than policing the spiritual practices of slaves at night: that was Reverend Rose's job.

Franky was getting excited. She passed the lamp to August, grabbed his arm and, using him for support, urged him to hurry back to the hut. Leaving him at the door, she made for a stack of clothes. She pulled out one of her white linen shawls and made ready to join the ceremony.

August tried to restrain her. 'Where yu think yu going?' he asked. 'You know that this mean pure trouble!'

The fury in Franky's eyes unnerved him. She tugged herself free of him, grabbed her looking-glass and stole a quick glance in it, a last-minute formality; without so much as a sideways look at August, she trudged off. He bowed his head momentarily and then shot off after her.

By the time they got to the cove the Obeah ceremony was in full swing and the drums were beating faster. About fifty village people, all dressed in white linen, were gyrating round a bonfire. Most of the women were swaying from side to side, entranced, their eyes closed. Every now and again they cried out and flung their hands into the air, their bodies all a-shiver. There in the middle of it all was Dallas, trembling with the spirit that had entered her. Franky joined in the chanting. Perspiration flowed.

As the ceremony grew more intense, August's discomfort changed to disgust. His attempts at shouting his disapproval were lost in the shrieking. The last straw was when Dallas collapsed on the ground, trembling as if overwhelmed by a violent fit. She yelled and screamed in strange tongues. August could bear it no longer and left.

He knew there would be consequences. And the next day at noon, at the boiling-house, there were.

'August, may I take some of your time to discuss an important matter?' It was Reverend Rose.

'Yes, Reverend, what is it?'

'Did you hear that the runaway, Jack, died this morning?'

'No, Massa, m-me no hear. How it h-happen?' August stuttered in shock.

'Nobody knows for sure. They say it was from a sudden seizure – apoplexy, I imagine.' The Reverend was keenly aware of August's agitation. 'Is there something you want to tell me?' he asked.

'Me never have not'ing to do with it.'

'To do with what?'

'I mean me never have anyt'ing to do with Jack death.'

'No one said you did. Do you feel guilty? Because there's no reason why you should – is there?'

'You are right, Reverend, for I would never get involved in Obeah.'

'But what would Obeah have to do with this? It is a wicked heathen practice and it is banned.'

'Mi know, Massa.'

'If you know anything that you feel would be counter to our struggle against the evil forces, I urge you, August, to speak and let me know.'

'Me no know not'ing. Not one thing.'

Reverend Rose marched off, plainly displeased.

August ducked behind a hut when he saw the Reverend Rose coming the next day. He now attended the Reverend's Sunday sermons less regularly, because he found Pastor Baker's services much more uplifting. Life was solemn enough throughout the slaving week without having to listen to the Reverend drone on about what the Lord was doing for white folk, and what the Lord would do for negroes one day, or in the afterlife.

But on Boxing Day August decided to attend Reverend Rose's service, because Allick had told him that the Reverend would be announcing something special to the congregation. The announcement was that Allick was to be baptised on New Year's Day.

When the service ended, Allick nudged August and suggested that they go over to Haughton to celebrate. This would also give them the opportunity to hear Moses Baker preaching. While wanting to show some loyalty to Reverend Rose, they both found Pastor Baker more inspiring.

The service had just started when they got to the meeting-place in the slave quarters up in the hills. Soon after praying together, the whole congregation began speaking in tongues. This was the highlight for August, far more intoxicating than drinking rum. But the aftereffect of Sunday worship was simply a return to the reality of enslavement. This so depressed August's church brethren that on Monday mornings children felt the need to make themselves scarce from their parents. Prayer and rum seemed to him to have at least one thing in common: neither was a panacea for the burden of slavery.

After the service August and Allick walked back through the night to the Cove. On reaching the village, they passed Sussex's cabin, saw that the old man was asleep, and decided to go their separate ways, agreeing to meet the next morning.

August set off towards his hut. He had travelled only a few paces when he heard a voice: 'Like as Christ was raised up from the dead by the glory of the father, even so we also should walk in the newness of life.'

'Allick?' he asked into the darkness, with a sideways flick of his head. There was no sign of him. He walked the few steps back to Sussex's shack and put his head and torch through the window. Allick was sitting beside Sussex.

'What you just say to me?' August asked.

'Nothing. Sussex wake up and tell me him is uncomfortable. So, mi jus' tell him that him could take my bed and sleep for the night. Mi going to sleep here. Mi will get some more plantain leaf to fill this mattress tomorrow. Make it more comfortable for him.'

'Yes, a good idea,' said August, wondering where the voice had come from. He turned to leave.

'August,' Allick called.

'Yes, Brother Allick?'

'Yuh don't forget the story of Samuel? Do you?'

'No, sir.'

'Well, when yu is called, you mus' come. New Year's Day, yuh hear? New Year's Day.'

'Yes, Brother Allick.' Then August left.

New Year's Day came. Allick and August were baptised.

The next day it rained hatefully. Frazer told August that he had been summoned to Bardanage. He was to be there by eight o'clock in the evening, before starting work at the mill-house.

August made sure he rapped on the door a couple of minutes early. Nancy appeared at the door to let him in.

Massa John sat at the table in the dining-room. 'I'll talk to you in a minute, August – there's an errand I want you to do for me tomorrow. But first I need my supper.'

August and Nancy stood and watched as he said grace, ate all his food, and burped loudly. Massa John had not lifted his glass of wine to his lips; instead he pushed it to one side, clinking it against a bottle of rum from which he had been swigging insatiably while waiting for August.

He seemed troubled when he spoke. 'Nancy, you have served me in this house for many years. I believe you to be my most trusted servant. And you, August – John Alexander Crooks – Christian. Frazer believes you have rebuked the devil?'

'Yes, Massa.'

'Puh. Frazer's gullible. He's turning soft on me,' slurred

Massa John. 'Do you still attend Reverend Rose's church gatherings?'

'Yes, Massa.'

'You attend no other gatherings?'

'Oh no, Massa.'

'No night gatherings? Are you sure you're telling me the truth?'

'No night meetings. August telling the truth, Massa.'

'You had better be.'

'I don't know whether baptism is a good or bad thing for negroes, but it seems to have been good for you and Allick.' Master John spoke less like one in authority, more as though he was about to bare his soul to them. 'Frazer tells me my negroes have heavy hearts. All this talk of free papers, it's inciting negroes all over to cause mischief, to want to run away.'

'But, Massa,' August interrupted, 'negroes will always talk 'bout freedom, but them is too idle and too stupid to know what the word mean. Them have nowhere to go, them too comfortable with this life. Them have food, clothes, a house, everything. What them want that Massa can't give? Them are happy being miserable. That is all.'

As August spoke, Massa John slid his finger around the rim of his crystal glass. Expressionless, he directed his gaze at Nancy.

'Nancy,' he said, 'I want you to sup from my glass.'

'Me, Massa, me? Oh no. Me is a negro woman. What Massa go do if me do it? Massa going to beat me?'

'Nancy.' Massa John pushed the glass towards her, his eyes probing hers. Nancy clasped it, drank half and set the glass down carefully, bemused.

'Go now, and leave me be,' he said. 'Both of you.'

'Yes, Massa.' Nancy dipped her head, then disappeared out of sight.

August slipped out the door. The errand Massa John required of him had not been mentioned again.

108

# Chapter 13

# Cousins' Cove

WITH EACH PASSING day, Massa John became increasingly restless. During dinner-time breaks he would walk with Frazer towards the out-offices, talking about developments not only up and down the island but throughout the West Indies. Notices of runaways were taking up more and more space in the journals, and reports of minor insurrection were on the increase. Property owners were leaving for the mother country. It was well known that sugar cane was under threat from beet-sugar production in Brazil.

Once and sometimes twice a week, August would see a dim light emanate from Massa John's bedroom, the only sign that he was in residence. When he appeared on the veranda, he was unkempt; a bottle of rum invariably lay on his lap. He would walk around the plantation for two or three hours and then disappear. There was a sense of change in the air. Everyone from Frazer to the most ignorant field slave knew that Massa John was not well.

Nancy said he was nervous being about them, all the villagers, particularly when he saw black men talking together in groups of more than three. Frazer had orders to disperse such gatherings and to find out what they were talking about. Massa John was leaving more and more of the business to Frazer; it caused further comment that Colonel Dickson, a frequent visitor, took long walks with Frazer. There was even a rumour that this very Colonel Dickson, proprietor of the Davis Cove Estate, churchwarden, probably a future Assemblyman and already extremely wealthy, was preparing to acquire Crooks' Cove Estate.

The rumour proved to be true. He saw it as a natural extension of his plantation at Davis Cove, which shared the border to the south just over the hill, beyond the great house overlooking both estates. A military man by career, full of nationalistic pride, he insisted that the Union Jack flew at half-mast when he was away from Davis Cove.

The new owner's first act was to rename the plantation Cousins' Cove Estate. His second was to sack two drunken bookkeepers he thought were not loyal to God and to the mother country. Any white member of staff caught taking the Lord's name in vain was instantly dismissed; slaves went straight to the workhouse for a term of hard labour.

As a parting gesture to Massa John, Richard Dickson made sure his favourite mulatto and quadroon slaves were suitably rewarded by being given generous land allocations. When negroes died, their land was carved up and distributed among the coloureds.

In every other respect, slave life became even more austere and laborious. Evening hours of work where extended. At crop season the mill kept going late into the night until there was no more sugar to churn.

Massa Dickson seemed to August to be obsessed with creating slaves of good character. This, he understood, could be ratified through association with the Reverend Rose. Massa Dickson had laid down clear rules about this: the Reverend was not to incite slaves to rebel. August thought Dickson had had more than enough problems with trouble-making preachers and mischief-making missionaries, while Reverend Rose came the closest to obeying Dickson's strictures. For all his eccentricities, Rose had always done what the Massas wanted, keeping slaves in check, civilising them a little while also attending to their spiritual needs.

One scorching day in February 1814, August was in the

cane field, leading the chant as the slaves sang songs of labour. Every now and again he looked longingly at enticing shady areas. Sweat ran into his eyes and down his cheeks, occasionally touching his lips so that he could taste the salt. Had it tasted sour, he would have spat. He grabbed his makeshift handkerchief, torn from a ripped shirt, and tried to dry himself – an impossible prospect in this type of heat.

Frazer ordered August to go and help remove the trash that remained after the sugar cane had been crushed and the juice expressed. When he reached the mill-house he found the yard a mess. He bundled up as much trash as he could, as best he could, and tied the bundle with rope. He dragged it away to be stored under cover, later to be laid in the sun to dry, and then used as fuel for boiling the cane juice.

Having finished this task, he saw a black woman called Charlotte emerge from the trash-house, her hands tearing at her bushy hair. She was wailing. She gathered her plain red cotton dress and swept past August, who skipped out of the way.

'Mind yourself!' he barked.

Hopey rushed over from the boiling-house to find out what was happening. The Reverend Rose had also noticed Charlotte's distress, and the three men went in hot pursuit of her. Cautiously entering her hut, they found her slumped against the wall.

The Reverend was the first to speak, asking softly, 'What is the matter?'

She looked up at them, her eyes full of tears. 'Them sell mi husband – them sell Thomas. Massa sell mi children away too. Them take away mi heart. Lord Jesus, what mi going do?'

Hopey and August relied on the Reverend to respond in his own particular style of buckra speak.

'Was there a reason?' the Reverend asked.

'Yeh! What in God name them do to yu?' said Hopey.

Revenue Rose turned and glared at him. 'May the Lord take out your tongue for using his name in vain. Shame on you!'

Hopey glared straight back. 'Thomas was harbouring a runaway from Harding Hall. It was only going to be for one night. Mi tell him that him would get me in trouble.'

'Who would?' asked August.

'The runaway, Joseph Samuel,' Charlotte replied. 'Thomas think it would be all right, and he would go tell Massa Dickson how badly dem treating Joseph. Him said Massa Dickson might help Joseph back to the Estate the next day and get him better treatment. But Massa him get on very well with them Harding Hall people and him don't want make trouble over nega man. So when Frazer ketch sight of Joseph sneaking out of the hut, the first thing him do is get angry and call me and Thomas over to the big house. This was before Thomas could get a chance to go see Massa and explain everyt'ing.'

'But what did you expect to happen?' said the Reverend. 'Harbouring runaways is very serious. You broke the law. Surely you knew that what you did was wrong?'

'Broke the law . . . Ah, what de . . .' growled Hopey.

'What is the matter with yu, man? Just calm yourself,' cautioned August.

'It's all right, August. I'll call another time,' Reverend Rose said quietly. He gave Charlotte a gentle, consoling pat on the shoulder as he left.

'Mi hear that man going to turn us all to buckra religion, try make wi into one of him,' Hopey snorted. 'You think is joke?'

'Yes, mi hear that too,' said August.

'So when yu think that going happen?'

'In a few weeks.' August had heard that masters up and down the parish were having Reverend Rose conduct mass baptisms of slaves, as many as three hundred at a time.

'Him going baptise all of we?'

'Yes, every last one. And some for the Brown property.'

'How much that going cost?'

'Nothing. Reverend Rose don't charge slaves, unlike some of the others running up and down the island making money off we poor negro. Nancy says this new Massa want all him slaves baptised. You know how him is – a church-warden already. It no look good when him stand up in church before him Reverend and him can't say that all of him slaves done bathe in the blood.' He grinned at Hopey. 'You have no choice.'

'Mi no really care, as long as them don't expect me to go to them church on mi rest days. If the baptism is on Sunday mi will be vexed. Massa Richard can do it any other time.'

'Mi no think him going to go that far and insist that everybody go church. Him is just doing it for show. Him going pattern himself on the vestry man – the ones with slaves.'

'When it going happen?'

'On the third of March, all one hundred and eighty odd of yu.'

When the ceremony took place, the twenty-four slaves belonging to Mr William Brown waded into the cove one by one, Rose said a few words, then they thrust themselves backward into the waiting arms of Charles and August, who dipped them briefly, then raised them back on to their feet. Most seemed invigorated, clearing their nostrils as they indulged in the triumph of having been sweetly saved. It was just as August had predicted.

October came, and the rainy season loomed. Dark grey clouds sat menacingly on top of the hills. They gradually sank lower, seeming to chew up the hills as they came, cursing with thunderous roars of anger, firing shots of lightning. Oddly, the clouds were broken in places by blue sky.

When the rain came, it was unrelenting, beating down on the bare backs of the field labourers. The storm made August much cooler than he had felt for the last three weeks. He was weeding in the cane fields; his skin gleamed as the rain intermingled with the sweat. As if perfectly waxed, rounded droplets slid off his body. Occasionally he would look up, and watch Frazer showing the new bookkeeper, Busha Ritchie, how he wanted slaves thrashed on the Cove. He gritted his teeth hard as a whip whirled.

'Work harder, nigger!' Frazer shouted.

He lashed a woman with the same force he would lash the strongest man, adding yet more scars to one bearing the marks of many years' toil. In the adjacent field a woman and a man, both shackled, were being dragged across the ground stumbling from time to time, falling then bouncing up again. They were trying desperately to keep up with a busha man.

On the third day of the rains, August crossed the village towards Franky's cabin to repair some damage caused by the wind. He saw a little light-skinned girl, probably eight or nine years old, her plaited hair drooping over her shoulders. She was sitting outside the hut that used to belong to a frail old man called James, who had died a few days ago in his sleep.

He decided to introduce himself. 'What is your name?' he asked.

'Sarah,' she replied sharply.

August planted his hoe firmly in the ground. With his hands clasped round the handle for support, he bent slowly and rested his chin on top of his hands. He peered down at the girl, saying nothing for a few seconds, pretending to size her up. Then he squinted at her, trying to get a reaction. 'Where is yu mother, Sarah?'

She turned her head towards the hut and answered in a sad drawl, 'In the house, a wash and a clean.'

114

Sarah obviously had no interest in making conversation. August understood this, so he decided to try a different way of befriending her. He straightened up and moved to one side, directly in her line of vision. She moved her head in the opposite direction. This turned into a game, repeated three times, after which she cracked and offered a bashful smile.

'Leave me!' she said, fighting back another smile.

August tickled her under the arms and poked her ribs gently. She giggled uncontrollably, hiding her face in her hands.

August's tried tugging her hands away, but that only made her force her head down between her knees, still hiding her face. August looked around for something, anything, that he could give her as a peace offering. He ran across to old Silvia's house, and without so much as a 'please' or 'may I?' whisked away a handful of guinep, juicy green fruit with a tinge of yellow, which grew in clusters like grapes, only three times larger. They were piled in one corner of Silvia's kitchen garden, and some stones lay a few inches away, evidence that Silvia or someone else had already been at them.

'Bwoy, you no have no manners!' Silvia shouted as he blew past her.

'Mi will give you this back later,' he promised.

'It's all right. Mi would rather wait 'pon you to come again so mi can take my machete and chop off your hand, yu ugly wretch.'

August paid her no heed: Silvia was always threatening to do something or other. He quickly returned to Sarah, and put the guinep down at her feet. She was even more pleased than he had hoped. She sprang towards the door clutching a fistful of fruit, pressing it against her stomach so she didn't drop any.

'Mother, we have fruit fi nyam tonight,' she called. 'We have fruit fi nyam.'

115

August was thrilled to have broken down her barrier of shyness. 'Where is your father?' he asked.

'Me no have no father.'

He didn't pursue that line of questioning, deducing from her pale skin colour that her blood father must have been one Massa William Brown. He was about to invite himself in, to meet her mother, when he saw Silvia chasing down the way, waving a cutlass at him. August instantly took flight. Sarah giggled again, amused by the sight of the old woman waddling after the man, plainly with no chance of catching him.

The following day, August decided to pass back round the hut to see how things were with the pair, perhaps welcome them, as it was unlikely that anyone else had done so already.

Mother and child were sitting outside the hut. Sarah was nestled between her mother's thighs, having her hair plaited and listening to a story which was reaching its end. August walked up and sat down beside them to listen to the next tale.

The woman vaguely acknowledged August's presence, lethargically raising her hand. Children playing nearby rushed to sit at her side. She cleared her throat as she made ready to tell the story. The children waited. One boy, a toddler in his older sister's arms, was picking his nose and wiping the snot on his patchwork cut-downs. They were bursting to join in the songs and respond when called to do so. Spurred on by the small gathering around her, Sarah's mother got up and started to perform. She opened her eyes wide, sure to make contact with each child. The instant she began the story, August knew that it was going to be performed in the style he had been used to hearing as a very young child.

She animated the story, bringing each character to life. She flailed her hands as she told of Johnny Do Good. She told them of the slave master who went to Africa to buy some slaves and was given the one called Johnny Do Good. Before Johnny was taken, he declared that he wasn't going to work for anybody, but the master did not want to hear this. He was taken to Jamaica, to the master's home. The morning they were called to work, Johnny Do Good took his drum with him and beat it when he was supposed to be working: 'Johnny Do Good. Do Good, Do Good, Do Good, Do Good' was the song he sang. When he was called to eat, he said no because he was doing his work – beating the drum and singing 'Johnny Do Good, Do Good'.

One day a black man decided that he would beat Johnny. He called some other men to help him, and they stretched Johnny out and started whipping him. But the man's wife cried out for she was feeling every stroke that they gave to Johnny. She complained to her husband, asking him to stop beating Johnny. The next morning the slave master decided that he was going to beat Johnny. He was so vexed that Johnny would not do work that he was ready to beat him to death. He, too, stretched Johnny out with the help of some men and started to strike him. But as he did so his wife called out to say that he should stop, for the master would kill her if he kept beating Johnny. From the remoteness of the house she, too, felt every blow the master laid on Johnny. When the husband got upstairs, he saw his wife bleeding all over. He went back downstairs and pulled Johnny Do Good to his feet, telling him that he was going to send him back home – to Africa. To get back they must pass through a forest on the way to the seashore.

The slave master's wife decided that she wasn't going to let the wild beasts kill Johnny – she would. She made journey cakes with poisoned flour, filled a bottle of water and gave them to the maid to give to Johnny. Then Johnny set off into the forest. The slave master's wife had two boys, who had gone out into the forest to hunt. They had been gone since Monday and it was now Friday. They were lost. As Johnny travelled he beat his drum. The boys heard the drum and thought they must be near home. They followed the sound for three days, moving further and further away from home. When they caught up with Johnny they were half starved. He took pity on them and gave them his journey cakes and water – he told them their mother made the cakes with her own hands. He told them to follow the path with the drops of green leaves on, and it would take them home.

They did so, but on the way one of the brothers died. The other went on. When he got home he told his mother that his brother had died. He said if it wasn't for Johnny he would never have made it back; Johnny had given them food to eat. His mother asked him what food Johnny had given him and he told her it was the cakes she had made. She cried out that she had lost both her sons. The maid said to her, 'Do good. Johnny says by his drum, "Do Good."' The husband turned on her in futility and despair. He chopped off her head and shot himself dead. All four died not understanding what a man had said about doing good. It was a message to anyone who decides to do bad.

Now she was tired, but the children begged her for more. Barbary, Nancy's fourth child, egged them on to plead even harder. Sarah sat beside Barbary, holding hands. But Sarah's mother said no and it was final, so Barbary let go Sarah's hand, promising to be her friend, and went off with other children to play hide and seek.

Pleased, Sarah told her mother of Barbary's promise.

'That is nice,' her mother responded, wiping the perspiration from her forehead.

August sat gazing at the woman, looking her up and down. There was something haunting about her, something strangely familiar about the way she spoke. He shifted slightly to view her face from different angles, while maintaining a respectful distance.

'Why yu looking at me? Why yu can't keep your backside still? G'way from me!' the woman said, flicking her hand. Moments of silence passed, with August unable to do more than fix his stare on her.

'Mi know you,' he said. 'It will come to mi.'

He thought back to the day of his arrival in Jamaica as a small boy . . . the deck of the schooner. The woman on the boat. She was without doubt the person he remembered. Almost unrecognisable, now that she was so haggard and forlorn, this woman struck a chord.

'Lord Jesus, merciful Jesus. It can't be you, but it is! Please to tell me your name?' he begged.

'My name is Ami Djaba, but I am always called Ami, all the while.'

From caged memories a bridge sprang between the two of them.

Ami said, 'You remind me of the ship that brought me here, and of a boy who did have fear in his heart. Boy, is you that? Praise be, is really you? But see here . . . oh, oh, oh.' Her eyes flooded and she wailed as if her daughter had died. She touched August's face, running her hands every bump, every impression, feeling for Boy. The two embraced tightly, not wanting to let go. As they hugged, she gave more thanks. They felt touched by a shaft of blessedness straight from the heavens.

August loosened his hug and brought his head from Ami's shoulder up to her ear. As he did so, the scarf around her head came loose and he felt a roughness. He pulled away slightly and stared at her savaged ear.

Sarah looked at her mother, bemused. She sprang up and darted round the back to the kitchen garden. 'Pupa, Pupa,' they heard her call, 'a man is making Mother laugh and cry. Come and see.'

Sarah reappeared from behind the hut, hand-in-hand with a dark, stout bow-legged man. His goatee distinguished him – three locks of knitted hair of varying length. Ami introduced him as her friend Sharper, a creole from the Brown plantation. August recognised him as the

119

man who had been dragged through the fields three days earlier; the woman must have been Ami.

'Hello, sir,' he said warmly. They shook hands, and the three of them talked for a while before they had to return to the fields, there to work into the night.

# Chapter 14

# Last Chance

THE NIGHT FOLLOWING their reunion August returned to Ami's hut, taking with him Franky and Allick, who were both eager to meet the new arrivals. Sussex, who was never more than a few paces behind, was equally curious. August introduced Ami as his older sister from guinealand. They sat down on the ground outside the cabin. Sarah cuddled up beside her mother, catching every word as Ami began to tell of her separation from August all those years ago.

Ami had emerged from the bottom of the heap of bodies, bruised and dazed but in one piece. The Hausa man was shot in a violent struggle to capture a gun from one of the shipmates. Ami was taken to a coffee and pimento estate owned by Massa William Brown. There she lived in the hills, rarely leaving the plantation except to farm her dinner-time ground.

Massa Brown stole her innocence on her first night and tossed her out the door when he'd finished, with no clothing to hide her nakedness, only her hands covering her face to mask her shame. She ran confused and disoriented out of the house, heading for the hills and beyond — to run away, never to return. She had got no further than the slave quarters when Sharper ran her down and offered a comforting embrace. He did for Ami what Ami had done for August all those years ago, saved her from going overboard; and they had stayed close ever since.

Within a few weeks she began to suffer the sickness that she recognised as the beginning of new life within her. She

121

wanted to end it, before a baby was born, one that would look her in the eye and lay claim to eternal maternal love. But she was too ashamed to ask the womenfolk how to do what she felt she must. When Sarah was born, she claimed all the love Ami had left to give.

Massa Brown took her many times thereafter, but she found a strength from ancestral spirits to overcome the shame when she asked the other women what to do if she fell pregnant again.

'You mean to say you destroyed the unborn?' August asked in disbelief.

Holding her head high, she admitted that she had. Massa Brown wanted to breed from her five, maybe six piccaninnies – that was why he had bought her in the first place. As they would be born as creoles, Massa could sell each one for a far higher price than he had paid for Ami. But Ami had lost her value – and lost Massa Brown much more in the process.

She told them of her master's drunkenness and his mal-treatment of her once he had discovered that she would bear him no more children. She had become a worthless nigger woman, yet, as the domestic slave, she was closest to him. He had violent fits of rage, and often beat her. Once, when she spilt a few drops of water on Massa Brown's food while pouring a glass of water for him during his evening meal, he clubbed her with a coco macao stick, a heavy-jointed cane over two feet long. He broke her arm, and capped the punishment by nailing her earlobe to the wall. She spent the whole night looking at the side of the frame of an English landscape.

August had difficulty taking in everything that Ami had endured. She looked hardy, like no other house slave he'd seen before, drawn in the face, puffed about the eyes. In its own way, her face told of the most miserable life in bondage.

Ami continued. Her only thought that night was of killing Massa Brown with a concoction of arsenic and root

122

herbs. And she would have done her utmost to do so had the Massa not decided to sell her away – she had got as far as acquiring a bottle of arsenic.

August was not only saddened and shocked to hear this, but surprised: he had thought Massas treated their domestic slaves reasonably well. But Ami's rebelliousness touched him deeply.

Franky could have been reading August's mind, for she asked Ami, 'Yu used to run plenty, don't it?'

'All the while.' Ami went on to tell of working as a hired hand on the coffee and pimento plantation not far from Brown's. She was one of several women who tended the ratoons and weeded the garden. Two lame women knew of her determination to run. They implored her to stay; she ran nevertheless and was caught the next day. The busha men secured her legs in bilboes, a long iron bar with two sliding shackles, through which the ankles were secured and locked with padlocks. But the locks were not secured properly; and after the evening shift she ran again. This time she made it as far as Industry Estate before being found. She was chained and collared.

Eventually, attention turned to Sarah.

'What a lovely-looking chile. Is true she free?' Franky asked.

'Yes, Muma.'

'How come?'

'Massa Brown conscience burn him, I guess. He free her the day she born.'

'So why him let her come with yu?'

'Him couldn't stop her. She determined to be with me. Anyway, he never want pay to maintain her. When him free her, me make sure mi hold 'pon the free-paper so she don't lose it.'

'Well, yu don't need to worry on this place, mark my word. She already friendly with Barbary, Massa Crooks's coloured daughter. She won't have no problems.'

'Yes, mi know how coloured people think already. Them think them is buckra. But mi never bring up my daughter to love their ways. After she see what happen to me, she would never let herself have buckra baby. She know better than that.'

'Yu better make sure yu don't keep talking like that around here,' Franky warned her. 'Them say that is not every fire everybody want to fan. That child is mulatto, derefore only good can come.'

'Ah, so you think. If she want to be white, mi will send her straight back to Massa Brown.'

'Mummy, why yu want to send me away?'

'Hush, chile, big people talking.'

At the sound of the bell the next morning, August rose and set to work hoisting the last hogshead of sugar on to a cart. As he was making it ready to be sent to Lucea, he heard Andries calling him, breathless with urgency. Andries got closer and lowered his voice to impart his news: 'They put one beating on Mother Brown, you see, and me can't find Brother Sharper anywhere.'

August asked Allick to finish off for him and raced out to the pens with Andries. There was Frazer marching towards the village with Quaco close behind. Ami, who was being supported by Charles and another fieldhand, followed them. Both her eyes were swollen, as was her right cheek. She staggered past, making a noble attempt to hide what must have been excruciating pain with a twisted smile at August. August could do no more than cry out for strength, 'Oh Lord. Merciful father.' He then prayed to his ancestors in his native tongue.

'Sister Bell say that if them catch you talking like that, them will send you away,' said Andries.

Later August swapped with one of the other field labourers, so that he could work in the same cane piece as Charles. He wanted to find out what had happened. When

124

he got near Charles he took his bill and hit it against his cutlass; two quick clinks followed by three was a code which meant they must talk.

August looked sternly at Charles as he approached. 'Mother Ami?' he whispered.

Charles winked, acknowledging August's purpose, and said loudly, 'You see you, you damn black boy, I going to beat you like Quaco beat that guinea woman this morning.' He hit August, with his macca stick, pulling the blow at the moment of impact. 'If you think that you can try and chop me in me head with rock stone like that stupid guinea woman, you making a sad mistake.'

Hearing this August stopped working for a few uncomfortably long seconds.

Charles got worried. 'August, August start working,' he growled, passing the stick from hand to hand, peering anxiously over his shoulder.

'Charles! What's the problem?' The bookkeeper sounded angry.

Charles grinned 'Nothing. Watch.' He turned and whacked August twice.

'Ahhh! Jesus have mercy!' yelled August.

'Mus' work!' Charles hit him again for good measure.

Charles had August's full attention and seething animosity; August felt there was no need to have hit him that hard. August couldn't imagine what he could do to help Ami. It did sound as if Frazer had been provoking her all along, uttering threats to sell her to a plantation far away, interspersed with abuse about her dishevelled appearance. What Charles told him in the field was that Ami and Frazer had traded insults, culminating in Ami's violent reaction.

August decided to seek Reverend Rose's advice. That evening he ate his plate of food as quickly as possible and got Massa Dickson's driver, Elvin, to give him an ox-cart to ride over to Reverend Rose's house. He didn't have a pass to leave the Estate but he didn't care; he would find some excuse if a problem arose.

The Reverend saw August straight away, and August implored him to intervene. While the relationship between Frazer and Rose remained malicious, the Reverend had blessings for Massa Dickson. He told August that he was likely to see Massa Dickson in town. A big meeting was being held for the Custos of Hanover in Lucea the next day, and Dickson had mentioned in passing his keenness to talk to Rose about a number of issues and to hear how the religious instruction of the Cove slaves was going. Dickson had learnt that the Haughton Tower Estate was thinking about a mass baptism of slaves such as he himself had sanctioned previously. Reverend Rose told August that the attorney for the estate had already approached him and that the Haughton slaves would be crossing Dickson's land to the Cove, where the ceremony was to be conducted. The Reverend said he would seize this opportunity to discuss the treatment of Ami.

Two days later, Reverend Rose met Dickson and Frazer at Bardanage. The Reverend arrived at four o'clock and didn't emerge until two hours later. Then he visited August at the mill-house.

'So what is going to happen, Massa?' August asked.

'Ami will be given one more chance. Both Frazer and Mr Dickson agreed with me when I put it to them that the woman was not properly seasoned and that what had happened was unfortunate. I emphasised that it would be a great test of Frazer's skill and reputation if he were to break this woman's demon spirit.' He paused and his expression changed. 'You never told me that she was a suspected myal woman.'

August bowed his head, embarrassed. He had indeed heard this said about Ami, usually by creoles, who considered her strange and remote. He chose not to defend her, for he knew that the Reverend would disapprove of any religious practice other than Christianity.

Returning to his usual line of argument, the Reverend said firmly, 'She will need intense religious instruction. Can I rely on you to help?'

'Oh yes, Massa. Don't you worry, mi will instruct her in all that you done teach about our saviour Jesus Christ. Mi already have his picture ready to give her.' August pulled from his Bible the image of Christ given to him by the Reverend. It was a drawing of a beautiful man, with long curly blond locks swept over the shoulders.

'Make sure she gets down on her knees and asks the Lord's forgiveness.'

'Yes, Massa.' August put the picture back in his trouser pocket, taking care not to crease it. 'Thank you, Reverend, thank you.' If protocol had permitted, August would have acknowledged his indebtedness with a simple handshake. But he bowed and that was enough.

'Oh, one other thing. The woman Ami will be at Frazer's beck and call. He has accepted the challenge she presents – and in good spirit, too.'

'Sorry, Reverend. When you say "beck and call", what do you mean?'

'Well, she's effectively his to do with as he wishes.'

'For how long?' There was a slight quiver in August's voice.

'For the rest of her days on this plantation.'

August's head dropped.

In a reassuring tone Rose said, 'It was the best I could do, August. She'll be all right. I'll see to it, and Dickson will see to it. In a few weeks Frazer will have his mind set on other matters. He has a grudge with everybody; this one will soon pale into insignificance.'

With sadness August acknowledged the Reverend's efforts. 'Yes, Massa, thank you. May the Lord continue to heap a blessing upon your kind soul.'

*

127

The following Sunday, August hitched a ride to Lucea market, again with Elvin. When they reached the market at noon, it was busy. Much of the buying, selling and bartering went on in a row where skilled people had work-shops in the working week. There were men and women clustered along the row, their wares laid out on top of flannel carriers on the ground. August wondered at times how hard-working labourers found time to grow enough food to feed themselves as well as go to market to sell. How was it possible, between toiling and the few hours that were allocated for sleep? He used his rest time for resting; others used it for cultivating provision grounds – which in August's view was a short route to an early grave.

August moved through the row, hopping and stepping over rotting fruit fallen from the stacks and strewn every-where in the dust. The sight of a squashed, fly-infested mango made him think of Samson and then of other run-away slaves who had escaped: any hope of survival a decay-ing afterthought. Most who went on the run returned to the plantations in time, begging their Massa for forgive-ness and for some food. Some, though, were never heard of again. He had heard stories of maroons returning the heads of runaways to plantation owners as proof that the hundred-year treaty was as robust as ever.

August stopped to haggle with a woman selling yams in the street. He pulled from his back pocket three ivory-textured shell bracelets which Franky had strung the week before. He was to exchange them for as many yams as he could. August offered one for five. The woman told him to 'remove himself' with the prescribed measure of ferocity. She picked two bracelets from August's hand, and her angry expression was transformed into a charming smile. She slid two yams towards him with her foot. August picked them up and a third for good measure – the largest he could lay hands on. They argued for almost a minute before the woman picked up her machete and chopped the third in half. August accepted the offer because he was eager to move swiftly on to his favourite haunt along the way, where many men and women gathered.

He wanted to hear Edward, the Lucea town jester, telling stories about himself which he swore on his mother's grave were true. He told of being a soldier in the Black Dragoons, one of the West Indian regiments, and of journeys to other islands avowing the interests of the mother country. But it was well known that he had spent all his life in the parish of St Thomas, working in the fields, and have never set foot off the island. He had recently been baptised into the Christian faith, and changed his name from the Ashanti name Yaw.

Edward was odd in appearance and manner; his silvery beard delightfully matched his eccentric behaviour: he wore his trousers back to front, he scratched his head all the time, he had a habit of walking about fifty yards before crouching down and springing back on to his feet, then continuing on his way. He entertained August no end. He always wore the same off-white shirt. It was said that he always looked raggedy and smelt, as though he hadn't washed ears for days, because he had no woman to look after him. August himself was already eyeing a few young females back at the Cove.

A man burst through the crowd. 'Yaw, where the hell is my cutlass and machete, the one I did lend you last crop season?' he demanded. 'I know you jus' a try to avoid me, and me no want to hear no shit from you. Now go and get it before I really get vexed.'

Edward looked nervous. He didn't have the said tools; they had been lost within a week of his having borrowed them. He became even more agitated when the man told him that without them he couldn't farm his provision grounds.

A brassy grin crept over Edward's face. 'Sir,' he ventured,

'you keep referring to me as Yaw. You don't know that I get baptised jus' last month?'

'Yes, but me don't care whedda your name is Edward, Puss, Dawg . . . jus' gimme the cutlass and machete, before me and you come to some serious blows.'

'I can't, 'cause me is somebody else now. Yu cannot expec' Edward to pay Yaw's debts.'

This made the people around him collapse in fits of laughter, which only served to fuel the man's anger. He lurched forwards to grab Edward, but was prevented from doing so by men in the crowd who knew Edward and did not wish to see him harmed. August retreated out of danger's way. As he did, his attention was caught by another group of men and women, eleven or twelve of them, talking intensely a few yards away. One of them, who was dressed in blue striped trousers and a waistcoat, was speaking with a rage that attracted several more people. He was pacing backwards and forwards, eyes wild with excitement.

'Me tell you say freedom soon come!'

'How you know?' asked an onlooker.

'Because me hear say them a make a register for all slaves 'pon every plantation.'

'So what that mean?' asked another.

'It mean that they need to make it official.'

'You should be careful what you tell people,' August cautioned. 'Mi done hear 'bout some registers that say we were freed a long time ago. An' nothing go so. There was a whole heap of trouble over this in one of the other islands last year and—'

'Kibba yu mouth, man. You don't know what you talking about!'

August took exception to the man's tone. 'Don't tell me to shut up. You don't know who you dealing with. Is your master tell you this?'

'My master don't have to tell me nothing. Yu expect him to tell a slave that him going lose everything him have?

130

No, sir. He would rather hang himself. Mi see the book the Massas going use to record all the names of all free slaves.'

'Well, mi no see no book where I am from.'

'Well, you want to open your eyes and look.'

'You better be right. My brethren.'

'Don't rely on Massa. As I said, him not going to tell you nothing. Not at all!'

'Well, I going make sure before I fly my mouth.'

Time was moving on, so August set off hurriedly back to the ox-cart. He almost forgot that another reason for having gone to the market was to buy maize, peas and British oil, which Franky needed to remedy her aching joints. When he had everything, he returned to the cart. On the way home, he told Elvin all that had happened and of his desire to find out what the registers really meant; without causing problems for the villagers.

# Chapter 15

# Changing Times

SITTING ON A rock on the beach, August watched Sis Bell and Dallas wade into the sea on the other side of the cove. The women were going to show Dallas's two girls how to wash clothes properly. Occasionally Sis Bell – who, for all her gentleness, was a strict disciplinarian – chastised them for not getting out every bit of dirt, grease and grime.

'What wrong with you? You must have two left hand,' she joked.

August moved from his rock to bathe in the shallows. He floated on his back, feeling an inner peace. Two boys from the village, both in their late teens, arrived on the beach nearby. They had finished the morning shift in the pastures and, exhausted, were eager to plunge into the cool, refreshing water.

'Do you see that,' said August, 'how Sister Bell is teaching the children the right way? You should learn. Back home we say it takes a village to raise a child.'

They laughed. 'Yeah, man. Back home, back home. When last did you reach back home?' said one of them. They stripped naked and joined August in the water, submerging themselves beneath the incoming waves.

'Chu! You people are too ignorant. Because you raise here in Babylon, you think you know so much.'

As August left the water, he felt sand scouring between his toes, and pebbles brushing his feet. He kicked and splashed his way out, then sat down and absorbed the power of the sun as it dried the few remaining droplets on his back. He could feel his back being toasted, so he moved into the shade of the mangroves that hid the mouth of a cave where, it was said, the skulls of runaways or Arawak Indians lay. August faced the sun, closed his eyes, and became lost in meditation.

Allick appeared and quietly sat down beside him. Sensing that someone was there, August opened his eyes. He waited to hear what Allick wanted, but there was silence – August felt he could have counted to a hundred and still Allick stared out over the sea, not uttering a word.

'What wrong with you?' asked August impatiently.

'Not'ing,' came the weary response.

August saw that Allick's unblinking eyes were wet; he thought it must be because of the breeze blowing into them. He said, 'Mi notice for a long time now. Things not right with you.'

'Man, I sick in my stomach.'

'Mi know that from long time. Every minute, I see you rubbing it. Mi always wonder what the problem is.'

'The other day Sis Bell found me on the floor. Mi done passed out.'

'Oh, Lord.'

'Yes, man. The Lord calling me. Him telling me that my time soon come.'

August and Allick sat in contemplation for a while. Then, inevitably, they began to reminisce. Allick agreed that life had become a whole lot harder during the last five years, since Richard Dickson had bought the land from Massa Crooks. It was like the bad old days when noses were slit and ears cut for the slightest misdemeanour. The Jamaican Assembly had reluctantly passed a law restricting more severe punishments, and slave life was supposed to have become more bearable, but with Massa Dickson there was no change at all. Indeed, the only respite the slaves had was when Colonel Dickson and his overseer went to church on Sundays.

The few landowners taken to court had been acquitted.

Richard Dickson seemed exempt from being summoned. His close friends held high positions; his eldest son was a regular juror.

The following evening August and Allick met at the same spot. They watched the sun floating on the horizon, its light spread out before them like flame. The sky's fire was matched by the ocean's; it was as magnificent as it was disturbing. They enjoyed the sun at evening, but by day it scourged them.

August reflected on the many slaves who talked constantly of setting fire to the landscape. He thought Hopey was the one most likely to invite the terrible wrath of buckra upon the village. Hopey had been absconding to Haughton Court nightly, to meet a negro called Robert and twenty-four slaves belonging to small neighbouring plantations.

Robert had been arrested and convicted of attending the meetings. Hopey and the others were also arrested, but discharged with a reprimand. Wherever there was talk of rebellion, the villagers knew that Hopey was connected in some way. He even had August engage in a fantasy about how the villagers might assert themselves in a struggle for freedom. It was never serious, just comforting to think about; another release, it helped pass the day in the fields.

August began, 'You know, sometimes my head tells me that I could do some wicked things to change how life is. But I give thanks and praise that Jesus teaches us to have love within our hearts and to submit patiently to our lot upon this earth, so that we may be blessed in the Kingdom of Heaven.'

'Where does it say that in the Scripture?' Allick sounded sceptical.

'I . . . I am not sure.'

'Mi know you not sure. Buckra have a word, "interpretation". Yu know what that means?'

'Yes, it—'

'It means,' Allick interrupted, 'yu mustn't follow every damn thing yu hear. Yu must listen and find a deeper understanding. Learn to read – read and find the deeper meaning. Look at the sky, look how the Lord put the light to it tonight. Can yu remember when it looked so beautiful and yet at the same time looked like hell?'

'No.'

'Well, then, that is a sign, the Lord trying to tell us something. Yu must open your eyes and read the signs. Look 'round yu. Nature tell yu everything yu need to know because is God-given. Look 'round you, the Garden of Eden. We have to make this fi wi paradise too, like buckra make it fi him.'

August agreed, childlike in his humility.

'The Lord help those that help themselves,' Allick went on. 'The scripture no tell you that, but is my interpretation of what the Reverend tell me. And when the time comes, when yu see the sign, you must not be afraid to help yourself. Black people in hell but we have to go out of slavery to find heaven. No white man going to give yu the pass – him too busy keeping it for himself. The only thing him giving yu is the dream of a nicer place in the sky, when he done with yu.'

'Allick, you right.' August sat up straight.

'Of course mi right. You remember Samson? Him dead trying to help himself. Mi try tell him that he should take time. The trouble with him is that him never read the signs properly. You tell me that slaves in Barbados try to help themselves plenty; the white man start fret right now. Yu must read the signs!' Allick wagged his finger in August's face. 'And another thing. Reverend Rose is not God. The Reverend no know what God is thinking any more than you or me.'

The two men talked until it was almost time to start the night shift in the sugary, a shift that would continue until the cock crowed.

135

Sussex appeared out of the trees. 'Brother Allick, excuse me. Massa Dickson want you. You better come now.'

'Mi soon come,' Allick replied. He picked up a guava and gave it to Sussex. Sussex thanked him and, with his broken stride, set off back to the village.

'Mi say mi no have much time, but when the Lord come for me mi want yu to look after that old man. Yu hear me?'

August had often wondered why Allick bestowed so much attention on Sussex. Allick never said; he just avoided the question.

Now August felt the need to try again. 'Why do you keep doing that?'

'Doing what?'

'That. Feeding Sussex. Yu no see that him good for nothing?'

'But yu no see the man hungry?'

'Yes, but yu always give him feed when yu no have to give.'

'Man, mi will always have food. Is not the same for him.'

'Allick, yu always lay him 'pon yu bed, and yu sleep on the floor. Yu let him drink from the one cup yu have in yu yard. Mi even see you carry him into the sunshine when him cold. And when him hot, you put down your tools to carry him into the shade of the coconut trees. Now your body getting old, too, and yu still doing the same things. Yu lucky Busha Frazer let yu get away with it for so long. If yu were anybody else, him would have beaten you.'

'A true.'

'He must think yu mad. Tell me, is Sussex your father?'

Allick was silent, but his expression said no.

August persisted. 'Uncle? Or some other relation?'

'No, him is not my kindred or even a friend.'

'Den who is he?' August was getting exasperated.

Eventually, Allick said, 'According to the Holy Scripture, when your enemy hunger, feed him; and when he thirst, give him drink – for in doing so you shall heap coals of fire on his head.' He chewed his lip. 'August, yu want to know who him be? Him my enemy, that's who. My enemy.'

Sussex was the very man who had sold Allick to the white slave traders in the motherland. Allick had been astounded to see him on sale in the market, and had persuaded Massa to buy him.

The conversation petered out after that revelation, and the two men set off back to the village. August could not help thinking about Allick: about the way his mind raced, about how he was sometimes confused and sometimes restless, and about his frequent headaches. At night Allick couldn't sleep, and one night Frazer had found him wandering naked in the rain while Sussex slept in his bed. His stomach pains were getting worse, and there were days when he seemed dull and vague.

On his way back to his hut, August saw some women talking loudly by the curing-house. One of them, Susan James, a woman with a body as large as her mouth, hailed him and told him that Massa Dickson had instructed his overseer to prepare a register of slaves. She pointed at Frazer's house, where people were already gathering to volunteer the required information. He walked briskly over to them. There were two things on his mind now.

Frazer sat at a table in a makeshift office outside his house, wearing poorly fitting spectacles and with his pen at the ready. August moved round to the side to gain a better view. Nancy was bending over the table, supporting herself on her hands.

Frazer said officiously, 'Old name?'

'Nancy.'

'Christian and surnames?'

'Nancy, Nancy Crooks.'

'Colour, nigger,' he sneered under his breath, and he wrote 'negro' in a column headed 'Colour'.

Nancy heard him. She lifted her head, pursed her lips

and said, 'Yu can't tempt man with something for which him have no desire. Me don't business what you have to say, all me interested in is getting what is coming to me.'

'Oh? And what do you think that might be?'

'Never you mind, jus' get on with what you have to do and let me go 'bout me business.'

So he proceeded: 'Age?'

'Forty-five.'

'African or creole?'

'Creole,' Nancy replied curtly. She kissed her teeth at Frazer, turned her back on him and headed for Bardanage.

August followed her. He was none the wiser as to what all the fuss was about – he would come back and ask later, when there were fewer people about and Frazer was less agitated. His thoughts turned to Allick, and then to Franky. He would ask Nancy what could be done about getting them proper medical attention. She stopped as soon as he called to her. She looked dishevelled after having the crowd pulling her about.

'Nancy, thank God I catch you at this time. Brother Allick is sick, Mother Franky is sick, and mi don't know what to do. What you think mi must do? You think doctor will come and have a look at them?'

'Me and Franky have the same problem with the heart. Doctor say is nothing.' She sounded unsympathetic but there wasn't any more to be said. The wind blew her hair across her face, and she caught a tuft between her fingers and smoothed it back. 'Franky is seventy years old. As for Allick, it sound like him have the King's Fever. They are old. Better you go and get bush herbs from Dallas.'

August didn't have to keep his promise to look after Sussex. The old man died quietly one day while listening to August and Allick debating whether God was black or white and whether it mattered anyway.

Allick's symptoms worsened. He got severe abdominal

pains, then fever followed by weakness. One evening, a year after Sussex's death, he was out by the Cove when he fell into a coma and died. He was buried in the negro cemetery. His last request was that the festivities be held two miles away from his grave – he said mockingly that he didn't want to be woken from his sleep – and his wish was respected.

Franky held on to life for one more crop season. When she died, she was given the largest funeral the Cove had ever seen: seven hundred slaves, some from as far afield as Lucea, attended it. Massa Dickson even allowed the villagers the day off. Her body was wrapped in white linen, and all the beaded trinkets she had made over the years were laid in the coffin. She was buried in her kitchen garden, beside the spot she had kept uncultivated. It seemed as if everyone present was drumming, or blowing a cowhorn and singing songs; everyone except August, who slipped away from the din, and went far up into the hills to be alone, to remember her. He would miss her terribly; he shed selfish tears.

There were other deaths in the ensuing years. But everyone was shocked when Massa Richard Dickson died soon after being elected Assemblyman for the parish. Many suspected Dallas, now a fully fledged Obeah woman. William Dickson then stepped into his father's shoes. He had come through the army ranks, following more or less the same route as his father. Under him, the death rate among villagers rose because he demanded more productivity and a stricter regime.

1820

It was midnight; Reverend Rose had just finished preaching to what was left of his congregation. He saw August moving towards the door, and called out to ask whether everything was well. August assured him that it was. The Reverend still looked enquiring, so August suddenly

139

decided to snatch this opportunity to disentangle the confusion surrounding the issue of freedom papers. Were slaves or were they not about to be freed, for ever? He knew how difficult Massas could and would make the Reverend's life if he were thought to be turning the minds of slaves against their masters. Even mentioning the prospect of freedom would be construed as incitement to rebel, for which the Reverend could be severely punished.

'Reverend,' he said hesitantly, 'I hear rumours that we will soon be free. Is this true?'

'No, it isn't.' Rose flapped at a mosquito. 'There's much talk at home in England that slaves ought to be free, but it isn't going to happen overnight. You, I'm afraid, must tell your friends and family to be patient. Do you understand what I'm saying?'

August nodded. Something about the apologetic way in which the Reverend spoke eased his mind slightly. August saw Rose as a man for the people, but not of them. Rose, for his part, didn't seem in the least perturbed by August's question. He laid his hand on August's shoulder, which gave August the courage to go on.

'But the register Massa put together three years ago. I hear that next week he will have to do it all over again. What does this mean?'

'Ah, so that's what this is all about, the registers. August, my friend, the trade was stopped some years ago, but slaves are still being smuggled in from Africa, and the mother country knows it. I'm sorry, but the register is to help the mother country ensure that property owners can account for every single slave on the island. If any white man is found in possession of new saltwater negroes, the mother country will want to know about it. The slave trade is illegal. Do you know what that means?'

August nodded.

'Good. If a slave dies, the mother country will want to know when. If one is sold, the government will want to know when and where. If one is born, they will want to know to whom, when and where. That's all the registers are – nothing more, nothing less. The register will no doubt be sent across the sea to the mother country, with all the other records produced by planters all over the island. They'll be looked at by some bureaucrats somewhere, then filed and promptly forgotten – that is, until the next census of slaves is carried out. That is to be done every three years, so the next one will be three years from now, in 1823. Does that answer your question, August?'

August braced himself and asked an even bigger question: 'So when do you think freedom will come?'

The Reverend sighed. 'I don't know. What I do know is that it will require a lot of faith and plenty of prayer. One thing is certain: it won't be tomorrow.' He turned and picked up his Bible. 'However, let's turn to a happier subject. It's some time since we last talked. I trust that you've thought about becoming a deacon?'

The question came out of the blue, and all August could think of to say was 'Reverend, I think 'bout it and pray every day that the Almighty will show me a sign.'

'Well, I believe the time has come. Allick always spoke well of you and you should consider it seriously.'

'Yes, Reverend, I see what you trying to say.'

August still felt frustrated by his ignorance, by his reliance on the misleading information others were selling as the truth. He asked, 'May I look in your Bible, Reverend?'

'Of course you may.'

August flicked through the pages but the black print made no sense to him. 'Will you teach me to read? I only want live my life according to God's word. Allick once tell me that the Bible is the written word of the creator of all 'pon earth. I want to read to have His word revealed.'

The Reverend paused.

'Please, Massa?'

The Reverend stroked his chin, wondering how best to

141

frame his reply. Eventually he said, 'Of course I'll teach you, but there are two conditions. One, that you attend my prayer meetings regularly. Two, that you do not tell a single soul – you know why. You must swear.'

'I swear I won't. Let the Lord strike me down if I do.'

'We'll make a deacon out of you yet,' laughed the Reverend. The two men embraced in shared delight.

## 1823

August wandered out to the spot by the sea where he and Allick used to go. It was noon and the bell for a late dinner-time break had not long sounded. He wanted to practise his reading before visiting Reverend Rose later in the evening. He was convinced that Allick's spirit came to look for him here, and between spells of reading practice he talked freely, confiding to the wind the things that played most heavily on his mind and all that he wished fate would bestow on him.

Today, he was thinking of Franky. He still missed her, her warmth, the cooking, her dependence. He thought of the years that had passed since his arrival on the island and of all the friends he'd lost. August cherished the time he had spent with Allick debating, challenging and receiving some wonderful insights from a man who understood so much more than he did.

'Bredda August.'

Startled, August swung round. He saw Sarah Brown coming towards him. His heart lifted. She had grown up into a tall, graceful twenty-one-year-old, in a process so slow he hadn't been aware of it. Today she was wearing some cast-offs of her mother's and looked delightful. She was different from most other young women, too, because she made no distinction between coloured people and negroes.

He asked, 'How did yu find out where I am?'

'Hopey tell me where me can find you. So talk, Bredda August. Let me hear what you have to say.'

'Oh. I have so many t'ings on my mind I don't even want to talk about it.' August felt shy and fiddled with his hair, twisting some short dry strands into fine locks. 'How is your mother?'

'The same, still giving Massa plenty headaches.'

'She should stop that.'

'That's how she is, and not'ing goin' to change that.'

August asked Sarah to sit down beside him. She sat away from him at first but then, at his request, moved closer, though she was careful to remain an arm's length short of intimate.

'So,' said August, 'what someone like you want with a man like me?'

'Me jus' come to tell yu that my madda want you fi come fix her roof. She say yu mus' bring all the others with yu, to help.'

'Who? Yu mean Hopey as well?'

'No bother bring him – that man have no manners.'

'All right, then, I ask old James Dickson and his son Thomas. The two of them can build anything with their hand.' August rose, ready to go back to the village. As he did so he noticed that Sarah's right shoulder was bare.

'You are playing with fire if you don't wear your blue cross. Where is it? What are you going to do if bushamen somewhere take you for a slave? That would be very dangerous for you.'

'But yu can't see that me is a slave jus like you. Me depend 'pon Massa for everyt'ing me have. Me feel even poorer than you. See how me always have to come beg you fi a little food to eat, to live.' Sarah had no rights or privileges distinguishable from August's. And it was true; she was a slave in her very essence. Sarah also rose. She pecked August on the cheek. 'Yuh look like yu not eating right. Me will cook for you tonight.'

'What? Yu mean when we finish the work to your

madda's roof?' August was not sure how to take the offer.

'Who's we?'

'James, Thomas and myself.'

'Mek them go home when them finish.'

'Do you want me to bring anything to the house – a fowl, or a something?'

'Who said yu be bringing anything? It is I who will be bringing the fowl over to you.'

'Oh?'

'Oh.' With that, she turned and strode off.

August called to her to wait, and accompanied her back to the Cove. It was Friday before the harvest, and all the villagers had been given a half-day to farm their provision grounds in readiness for Sunday market.

All, that is, except Ami. They found her hoeing and weeding a cane piece alone; Frazer's orders. She was to make ready for manure and the planting of new cane. Busha Ritchie had been assigned to watch over her. Sarah was allowed to give her mother a drink of coconut water as sustenance.

Looking idly around, August saw Reverend Rose coming down the road. He decided not to go over to him, for he had heard that the Reverend was severely displeased to have received a written warning from the vestry that his licence would be taken away if he continued to run his newly established day services. He had already been prohibited from setting foot on some of the plantations over the border into Westmoreland, and there was even talk of his being sent to another island. He had told August that the property owners realised the notes he took in the field up and down the parish and across the island were being passed to the Society for the Gradual Abolition of Slavery in England. Public opinion in the mother country was changing. Pressure was mounting for Britain to intervene in the affairs of property owners in the West Indies. The

Reverend was one of a few people accused of stoking up antagonism between the Jamaican Assembly and the British government.

Reverend Rose changed course and stamped across the field towards Busha Ritchie. An argument soon flared between them. Although it was inaudible, it was clearly about the way Ami was being treated. August told Sarah to stay with her mother, and, keeping at a safe distance, he followed the Reverend as he set off towards Bardanage.

Frazer was outside the big house, talking to Nancy and some slaves hired from Harding Hall. The Reverend marched up and launched a vitriolic attack on Frazer, who clenched his fists and gritted his teeth – strangely, however, he showed little other reaction. August moved close enough to make out Dickson standing at a first-floor window, peering down on the furore. Frazer looked fleetingly up at him. It was illegal for him to vent his temper on hired slaves. He dispersed them, slashing at them with his whip, which infuriated the Reverend even more. Then he brushed past the Reverend and went off in the direction of the wooded pastures to the rear of the house.

# Chapter 16

# British Apprehension

THE CHIMES OF Big Ben announced that it was three o'clock in the morning. The wind was howling and a thin frost had formed on the ground. It was freezing but clear. The moon was particularly bright, making a halo around the dome of St Paul's Cathedral. It was mid-week; most of the people of London were fast asleep, their nightcaps keeping their heads warm.

This was not the case for three high-ranking politicians in a chamber deep in the recesses of the House of Commons. They had been talking almost all night over a bottle of the finest port.

Mr Wilberforce was dozing in a chair by the bookshelves, in a dark corner of the wooden-panelled room. He had withdrawn from the debate for a few moments, and fatigue had got the better of him: he nodded off every now and again. After about half an hour the jerk as his head dropped to his chest woke him, at which point he got up, bade farewell to his friends and slipped out the door. He coughed and spluttered as he closed the door behind him.

After a moment's silence to ensure that he was out of earshot, the discussion resumed.

'William looked very tired, didn't he?' noted Mr Canning, taking a sip of port.

'Yes indeed, Prime Minister. His health is of major concern to all of us who work in the cause of abolition,' said Lord Buxton.

Buxton leant back in his chair, rubbing his eyes and yawning. Like Wilberforce, he yearned for some solace

146

from the previous day's events in the Commons. It wasn't so long ago, only ten hours, that he had made his most important speech on the subject of abolition, a speech to which the Prime Minister had had to respond. It was ironic that these two men, who sat on opposite sides of the House, should have spent the last four hours in each other's company. Serious analysis of their earlier confrontation had had to be held back, because both men had a high regard for the ailing Wilberforce. Now that he had left, however, they reverted to grappling with the question of how and when slavery in the West Indies should be abolished. They were no nearer convincing each other of their points of view than they had been when the slave trade was abolished in 1807. Here they were, sixteen years later, and still no progress had been made.

'The Society, as you well know, believes that the country would back the compromises that we have proposed,' argued Buxton. Pointing an accusing finger at Canning, he went on, 'To put it candidly, I am vexed that the members of your government see fit to protract the process. Slavery must end.'

'Of that I am assured. I do not intend labouring that point.' The Prime Minister inhaled deeply. 'The mood of the nation is such that there is more to be gained than lost from its abolition. I am aware of that.' Although he was tired, and his mood relatively conciliatory, he paused to let his argument sink in.

Buxton, however, did not let the silence last long. 'You decry slavery, yet your Government obstructs the natural course of the emancipation cause.'

'Pray be calm, my lord. Allow me to give you a little more port.' Canning replenished Buxton's glass, then went over to the window, and stared out at a street lamp across the road near Westminster Abbey, enjoying the way in which the light seemed to fragment as it sprayed the cobble stones in the road. Refreshed, he was ready to resume

147

the exchange. 'Lord Buxton, you say that the children are the greatest victims of slavery?'

'That's right. I made the point in my speech, and I will repeat it as long as necessary: the slaves have been made captives by robbery. I say they have more of a right to their bodies than the masters, certainly.' Canning tried to interject, but Buxton continued, 'Let me finish. Children are the greatest victim of this cruel system. They are born to a state from which there is no escape. Piracy, I say. Piracy.'

'And we should relieve them of every vestige of servitude?'

'That's right,' repeated Buxton. It was a point he'd made often enough in parliamentary debates.

'You also feel that by taking upon ourselves for a season the whole burden of their maintenance, education and religious instruction, we may raise them into a happy, contented, enlightened, free peasantry.'

'Yes, you are right once more – I respectfully conclude that the Prime Minister has listened to what I have said so many times. I am duly surprised, as I am impressed. What is your point?' Buxton's impatience was mounting.

'My dear Buxton, it is this. Our constitution and the Christian religion are in their spirit unfavourable to slavery, and naturally hostile to it. Yet neither constitution nor religion prohibited slavery. Do not forget that we are dealing with beings possessed of the form and strength of a man, but the intellect only of a child.'

'But, Prime Minister, that is a matter of opinion. You, my right honourable friend, claim to sympathise with the Society's aims, yet you block our attempts to see even that the children of slaves born after a certain date are given their freedom. This is a solution to the problem of keeping the West Indies planters reasonably assured that we care for their interests, too. This truly is the ultimate compromise. The Society firmly advocates it. The gradual phasing out of slavery over decades rather than years is the perfect answer.

It will at best appeal to the country as a whole, at worst upset a few of our subjects in the colonies of the West Indies. I am confident that a significant majority will not worry very much because they will not live to see the transition completed. The pain for the government is imaginary.'

'I agree, but—'

'The gradual phasing out, without danger to the common interest.'

'Yes, but to have the children free while many adults remain slaves is neither sensible nor practicable.' The Prime Minister kept to himself his next thought: 'How in God's name can free people live on this earth while slavery continues to exist?' It seemed preposterous that Buxton would venture such a proposal on the Society's behalf. The two men broke off.

More tired than ever, Buxton bent forward, hunching over the pristine oak table. Despite his dwindling energy, he forced himself to turn to another topic. 'And what, Prime Minister, of the Jamaican Assembly? What say you about the band of mischief-makers on the other side of the world who see fit to take no notice whatsoever of your government's directives?'

'Yes, I understand you.'

'I know full well that you do. What did you say the directives would do? Improve the conditions of slaves? Huh!'

'The Jamaican Assembly, like all the other assemblies of the West Indies, are stubborn – I know that, too. There are three possible ways in which Parliament might deal with the people of Jamaica. The first, as I said in the Commons, is to crush them by the application of direct force; the second is to harass them by fiscal regulations and an enactment restraining their navigation; and third is to pursue the slow and silent course of temperate but authoritative admonition.'

'Yes, yes,' retorted Buxton. 'Doing nothing is always this government's favoured course.'

'I do not believe that in trying the third mode Parliament would be doing nothing. I hope we shall never be driven to the second; and with respect to the first I will say only that nothing but brute force would encourage me to use the power of Parliament over dependencies of the British Crown. The power is a secret of the Empire, which ought to be kept within the shadows of the constitution. It should be brought forward only in the utmost extremity of the state, when other remedies have failed to stay the raging of some moral or political pestilence.'

'Bravo, Mr Canning. I've never heard such a long-winded description of doing nothing.'

'You know, my lord, I believe we are not really at odds about the need to secure the end of slavery, for we – the country – are friends of slaves. It comes down to a question of how their due rights, moral improvement and general happiness are to be communicated to the great multitude of slaves, without endangering the safety, the lives and the security and interest of the white population, our fellow subjects and fellow citizens.'

'Hence our proposal.'

'I understand, but how long would it take to implement? How soon shall the end of slavery come?'

'It is clear . . .' Buxton hesitated, knowing he was repeating himself. 'It is clear that it may take decades to prepare the slaves for responsibility of liberty.'

Canning decided to bring the conversation to a close; they could continue tomorrow. 'In order to diminish both the danger and the burden to be incurred, I am disposed to the gradual approach.'

# Chapter 17

# Cacoon

1824

IT WAS A blazing day. August was stooped low, batching some newly cut canes. The next day they would be gathered and taken to the boiling-house, where they would be used to make rum. He was idly thinking that he would need more help doing it, and looking forward to the Easter Sunday break in five days' time, when he saw Sarah coming towards him.

It was clear from her expression that she had important news, but August was wholly unprepared when she happily told him she was expecting his child. He quaked with disbelief at first, then felt terrified of the responsibility that would be his. He accused himself – and found himself guilty – of selfishness, of inflicting the burden of slave life on the unborn child, thereby condemning it to perpetual bondage and misery. The sentence he pronounced on himself was to lighten that burden as best he could, and his conscience pledged to honour his obligation.

Memories of the uprising on St Domingue were revived, and an uprising in East Demerara, British Guiana, in August the previous year was endlessly discussed; the name of the slave Jack Gladstone was on everybody's lips. August had read about slave rebellions on other islands in the West Indies. The news of how, when, who and what happened followed the usual route – from the assembly to the newspapers to Massa to Nancy and then to the slaves. There was now a distinct militancy in the air, different from anything before; there was anger, even rage, among the villagers.

There were reports of outbreaks all over the island. And people, slaves, were eagerly discussing the possibility of a struggle for freedom in Jamaica.

The Massas were on their guard. The number of men convicted of attending the nightly mutiny meetings caused serious concern. On the Cove, there was much talk of a twenty-nine-year-old creole named Davie, of Harding Hall: he had been sentenced by the slave court in April 1822 and transported from the island for life.

It was in this atmosphere, in November, that Sarah bore her first child, John.

August had a secret dream that John would one day lead the slaves out of bondage, charging into battle in military uniform. He had reason to dream. A new type of slave was emerging, far less compliant than the older slaves. The young creoles, in particular, made light of being feisty with buckra. They dressed it up as good old slave humour; nevertheless, it made the likes of Frazer cringe. Angry whispers reverberated round the village, reflecting the discontent among coloured and blacks alike – the change from early times was tangible.

Furthermore, Ami Brown's behaviour towards the busha men was becoming a catalyst, stirring the villagers' repressed desire for vengeance on buckra. It was now her ninth year under Frazer's supervision, and she remained resolutely unseasoned, though seasoning should have taken no more than two years. She refused to answer to her new name of Judy. She often flung curses directly in his face.

August knew Frazer had only to give her fifty lashes and she would die – that would have been simple enough. But he also knew Massa William Dickson was following the situation carefully, and had given Frazer strict orders not to martyr her. Instead, Frazer resorted to putting her in the stocks, but this never broke her indomitable spirit. Frazer had been shown to be impotent, a failure; and all the other slaves knew it.

August accompanied Hellina and Becky, her shy young daughter, who were making an urgent delivery of food to Elizabeth Smith. Then it was out into the fields, to plant more ratoons in the new holes dug the day before. A girl called Fanny was tying dried cane in bundles, to be taken for processing. They had to be dragged by hand to the mill-house two hundred yards way, because the cart that was usually used was needed elsewhere for a few hours. The mill was still churning, as William Dickson insisted it should be. Frazer ordered that some negroes stop the weeding and instead carry the heavy bundles of cane until the cart was returned. Among those selected were August and Hopey.

They first helped Fanny heap the bundles in one spot, and she took the opportunity of saying to August: 'When you have time you had better go and talk to your mother-in-law.' Her knowing look warned him that Ami was planning to run again. August dragged his bundles of cane to the mill-house, then picked up some crushed cane and took it over to the trash-house, where he knew he would find Ami. She was outside, laying out crushed cane to dry. August saw that there was already enough dry trash in stock to keep the mill-house furnace working non-stop for the next two days.

'Mother,' August began, 'people talking 'bout you.'

'What they saying?'

'I hear you going run again,' he said worriedly.

She told him that it was true and that she had nothing to hide. Speaking in a fast and frantic whisper, she blurted out a plan to abscond to Blenheim before making for the hills, to a settlement still undetected by the maroons. She was fired up and determined to free her spirit. A shaft of pain shot though her, and she convulsed and almost lost her balance. Sarah had told August a few days ago that Ami was ill, but this was worse than he had expected. Ami, though, carried on telling him her plan.

153

'Mi will help you,' August promised, interrupting her incoherent flow.

Ami was so startled by the offer that she became relatively calm. August advised her against trying to live like a maroon. She should go to Montego Bay, once he'd spoken to Dallas and a few other people. There she could lose herself among town folk; many successful runaways were already hiding out there. A slave called Elliston made regular trips to Montego Bay. When she was well enough, she should find him and he would pass the word as to her whereabouts. In the meantime, August would devise a plan for her to get to Kingston. He would send Sarah, because she was free to come and go as she chose.

It took August almost a week to work out the details of his plan, and he kept it secret from everyone, even Sarah. Once everything was in place, he went to see Ami and told her what she must do. First, she should complain of illness to Massa Ritchie. Then, in a show of sympathy for her discomfort, August would return with keys to loosen the padlocks securing the chains round her ankles. Charles would supply the keys, although August would take care not to implicate him. That night Ami would run. By the time Massa found out, she would be long gone.

The following evening, he visited Ami again and gave her a kitchen knife and a pass. The pass was one that he had used himself a few days before, when he was over at Haughton to deliver a chest of rice and a barrel of rye flour to the villagers. As he turned to leave, Sarah came pushing through the half-shut door; behind her was their loyal friend Barbary.

'You up to something. Is what?' Sarah demanded.

Ami couldn't look her daughter in the eye. August hoped Ami would speak, but Sarah instantly realised what was going on, and became frantic.

'You running, aren't yu? Oh no, please don't, I beg you, don't.' She turned on August and hissed, 'What yu have to say for yuself? Yu helping her, aren't yu?' He could not reply. She kicked him and screamed, 'Bastard! Stay out of we lifes. Get out, stay away from wi. The one mother mi have and yu trying to kill her off!'

August caught her wrists and looked deep into her eyes. 'No. I would never do a t'ing like that. I can't stop her – you can't stop her, either.'

The violence had exhausted Sarah, who lunged towards her mother, burying her face in Ami's lap, begging her not to run. She wept and begged for a full ten minutes, then slumped despairingly to the floor. Ami went painfully over to her and lifted her up as if she were still a child. She stroked her hair and said gently, 'Is the will of the ancestors. They calling me. They no want me to be a slave for any white man no more.'

August knew that if he had only had Ami's spirit, he would gladly have gone before. But running didn't make sense. 'Allick once told me that we no going be slaves for ever. The day soon come. I didn't feel it then. But I feel it now. The time coming when we won't be slaves no more. Mother, I think you feel it too. I beg you stay. Please, stay?'

'Allick dead waiting for his free-paper! What am I supposed to do? Chu, man, just tell me your plan, so I can go 'bout my business.'

Sarah listened solemnly as August gave Ami her final instructions. He warned Ami again to avoid the main routes to Montego Bay and go straight to Bower Hill Estate, staying within the woodlands that circled the main estate. She was to head due west into the hills towards Haughton Tower; she would then be able to follow the Cacoon River to her destination. On arrival at Bower Hill she was to look out for the doctor-man, Quashee. He would be watching for her. Quashee had trained beside a white doctor for many years and was often called upon by black folk from neighbouring estates to tend their sick. He would provide her with food and somewhere to sleep

155

for the night, and would tell her how she could make her way further into the hills and then down to Montego Bay.

Ami was to lie low for at least five days while the main search party would be out looking for her. Given her illness and frailty, it would take her a day to reach Bower Hill; it was not far, but it was a climb. When she reached the surrounding woodland, she should bed down on the western side of the property. Quashee would find her, if she did not see him first.

From his pocket he took some coins wrapped in a clean handkerchief. 'Here.' He moved closer to Ami, as if to conceal the gift. 'Nancy say I must give you this.'

Ami took the handkerchief from him, her rough, dry hands touching his, lingering for a few moments. 'Dat head of yours, always thinking something, it take a clever man to come up with a plan like that. You know, if you did have a plan to take us all to freedom I would follow you, I would.'

'God be with you.'

'And may the spirits of the ancestors watch over you.'

The next morning, while August was labouring in the fields, bending for hours to cut the cane, he felt a sharp pain in his back. He stood up, trying to ease his spine by first stretching tall and then bending to touch his toes. For the first time in his life, he could not reach his toes. This made him think ahead to a time when he might be joining the older folk sitting at the openings of the thatched huts gazing out as the sky tip-toed by, or wistfully engaged in idle banter at midnight. He chopped a length of cane in half, then in quarters, and then threw the pieces aside. He stood upright, feeling the aching stiffness in his back. I can't take this no more, he thought.

From near the tall cane chutes, Frazer called to August that Massa Dickson would be entertaining a visitor from Scotland that evening; also that August must drop some

156

freshly cut cane over to Nancy. Frazer waited for August's acknowledgement, before strolling off towards the pastures.

The mention of Nancy seemed to echo in his mind, and her image formed before his eyes. He was overcome with anxiety about things he had been trying to repress all morning. Had Ami got away on time? No one had yet mentioned that she was missing – that was a good sign. She might have reached the river by now. He offered a prayer for her deliverance, then bundled some prime cuts of cane together and trudged wearily towards Bardanage.

August silently repeated what he and Quashee had meticulously planned for Ami. If she had got away soon after the last lamp went out in the village, at about two o'clock in the morning, by dawn she should have reached the wooded provision grounds at the bottom of the hill two and a half miles away. From there she should have followed a stream that flowed westwards. Although Ami did not know the area, she had nodded enthusiastically, agreeing to everything, even when August knew he was relaying the directions less than precisely. He prayed once more for her deliverance.

Nancy was at the door when August arrived at the house. He quickly took his cane inside. She swayed when she walked, and she gave him a dreary smile, an attempt, he supposed, to cloak sickness. He asked whether he could get her some water mixed with lime and ginger, to make her feel better.

'Um, I just had some coconut water. I still have plenty more coconut inside. I feel so tired. I feel like I going pass out. Come, pass me the chair.' Nancy gestured to the spot where she wanted it set. August whisked an old chair from under the table nearby and helped her to it.

'Have you seen the doctor?' he asked.

'Yes. He tell Massa that I can continue to do work 'bout the house but that I should get plenty of rest. He can't find not'ing wrong with me. But I feel so terrible, so weak.'

Nancy leant forwards in her chair, trying to find a comfortable position. August rubbed her back gently, hoping to ease her pain, but his thoughts had again turned to Ami. Quashee had said that it would be a miracle if she got much beyond the Cove. It was Quashee's idea that Ami should be sent in his direction, to the Cacoon Estate. And August had devised a story for her to tell if she was caught either before or after she reached Cacoon: she was to say that the reason for absconding was that she needed medicine; she could not wait until she got permission. In these circumstances Frazer might be relatively lenient. Ami was, after all, manifestly ill. Quashee had been primed to persuade Ami to stay at Cacoon for a short while, at least until she recovered her strength. If Frazer caught up with her, she should tell the same story. If she made it beyond Cacoon, the same applied, but she should also say she had decided not to return; then she would be on her own, fending for herself.

August was nervous about the risky role he was to play. He was to tell Frazer of Ami's absence soon after noon, before Frazer discovered for himself that she was missing. Ami had August's pass, and he would soon be needing it himself: the time to talk was overdue. He would say that Ami had begged him for it and that he had taken pity on her. He knew he would be punished, but not as severely as if he had been suspected of helping her to run away. The alternative was to say nothing of Ami's disappearance. Unthinkable.

'August, yu look like yu have plenty t'ings on yu mind. Yu better go,' said Nancy.

'I have one or two things, but I can stay a while longer. You sure you don't want me to fetch you anything?'

'No, no. I am sure. I will ask one of the girls, if there's anything I need. You go. Go on with you.'

On his way back to the cane piece, August saw Frazer approaching from the pastures, gesticulating wildly. He was with Quaco and four other black men whom August did not know – probably fieldhands from a property nearby. As they drew near, August sensed danger.

Frazer lunged forward, grabbed August by the arms, shook him viciously and yelled, 'What did she say to you, before she left? Tell me!'

'She who, Massa?'

'Ami! Jabba! Judy! Brown! You fool!' Saliva sprayed from his mouth. 'I'll kill that flaming nigger woman!' He looked and sounded more menacing than ever before.

'Massa?' August was still staggering from the assault.

'Massa!' Frazer mocked. 'The dogs won't be fed until that woman is found. The longer they take, the less they'll bring back!'

'No, Massa, beg you. Ami say that I must tell you her whereabouts. I should really did tell you this morning, but I did have so much to do for Busha Ritchie. Ami gone to Cacoon to look for some herbs to heal her sick belly. She no gone long. If Massa no believe me, Massa must send Quaco to go look for her. He will find her in Cacoon.'

'Does she have a pass?'

'Yes, Massa.'

'Yours?'

'Yes, Massa. She say she be back by now, before anyone even know she gone.'

Frazer's mouth twisted, a sign that his rage was beginning to subside. He took his hat off and wiped the sweat from his forehead. He looked more at ease, more assured that August was telling the truth. He handed Quaco his cat-o'-nine-tails and said, 'I'm going to Cacoon myself. If I'm not back before the afternoon break, cat him. Give him five stripes on the hour for every hour it takes me to find the woman.' He turned back to August. 'Nigger, you're more foolish than you'll ever be able to understand.'

# Chapter 18

# Goodbye

THREE HOURS AFTER the afternoon break, with uncertain steps August began walking to the hothouse. Hopey and Andries were on either side, supporting him; without them he would have fallen. The clear sky had turned pink, softening the scene just outside the village where a shock of red marked the place where August had lain after each flogging.

The blurred shape of a man with a wide-rimmed hat came into view. Andries confirmed August's blurred impression that it was Frazer, and Hopey said that Ami had been found. When he heard that, August collapsed. Hopey and Andries carried him to the hothouse as gently as they could manage, and laid him down on the floor.

The first thing August saw when he came to was the figure of Ami lying across the small room. Her eyes were vacant, apparently staring up at the roof. She was shivering and muttering, as if rehearsing her death. Her hardy bare feet, cut in places, and her filth-ridden clothes were testaments to her ordeal. Her hands were clasped together, covering her chest. They said she was forty-seven but it was hard to believe. Suddenly she turned her head to face August. Bravely she pulled a smile, revealing bright pink gums where her bottom teeth were missing.

August sat up, his head pounding, the wounds on his back a little less painful than they had been. Beside him was a small table on which stood a basin of water. There was a bloodstained cloth hanging over the side of the basin: someone had tended him. He pulled the basin towards him and squeezed the reddened water from the cloth, dragged his damaged body over to Ami and gently wiped her forehead.

'Mi reach Cacoon?' she asked.

'Almost, Ami, almost.'

Her eyes narrowed, as if she was disgusted at her failure. 'How come yu is here?' she asked hesitantly.

August could not bring himself to explain that he had risked his life for her. Why didn't I just leave the damn woman for dead? he wondered. It would have been easier for all. Aloud he said simply, 'Rest yourself.'

He sat down beside her and eased her head on to his lap. She was as frail as a fallen leaf. Browned by the unforgiving sun, like a leaf she might be ready to disintegrate at any moment. Was this the same Ami who had once mothered him? At the memory of her in those times, he felt tears sting his eyes.

'Oh, Mother Ami,' he said sadly, 'you going get us into a lot of trouble. Look at the example you setting the young people. What you want them to see? Just suppose we all follow you, what you think going happen to us all?'

She smiled sweetly up at him. 'Boy, you don't stop crying since the first time I see you. Stop the crying now.' She swallowed, then added, 'If you follow me, you going to yu grave. But see me, mi never lie down for too long. Mi is just the kind of person that will climb out the grave and kill Massa. You think death going keep this black woman down? No, sir!'

August nodded respectfully, admiring her defiance. Though he looked forward to rising up and meeting his creator, death didn't figure in his plan; death was still a few crop seasons away. At least he and Ami were both still alive, and for that he gave thanks.

'Why don't you accept that name Massa give you?' he asked. 'Judy is a good name. God would bless you.'

Ami responded with a look of contempt. 'Tell me,' she

161

said, flinging the cloth off her head, 'what yu take me for? Is that a question you would ever ask a bird, a creature born to be free? Massa keep you in him yard like dog. What life is that? Anyway, how can Massa keep a dog unless dog is stupid an' obedient? Sometimes, I don't know whether is Massa's dog mi talking to or you.'

'Father, have mercy!' August's patience was running out. 'My Bible tell me that the Lord will rescue his people when he see their strength gone. He will have mercy on those who serve him. When he see how helpless they are, he will ask where are those mighty gods you put all your faith in. Make them come and rescue you now. He know who is the enemy, and he waiting for the right time to punish them.'

Ami said nothing. August waited a while, then, when there was still no reply, went over to the table and used the cloth to dab cool water on his raw wounds. In this new quiet, Ami turned on her side to face him and sombrely began to describe how she had been caught.

She had reached the hills, where she was greeted by the sight of boundless rock mingled with arid soil. She did not know which way to turn, so hid under a bush and slept, not waking until the sun rose. She nearly panicked then, for she realised that she had not gone far. And she began to worry about whether the alarm had been raised. Her mind was warring with her body: her mind wanted to drive her onwards, but her body refused to go further than a hard stone's throw at a time before demanding rest. While she rested, her mind sided with her body: no more. But then something deep within her would raise her to her feet: onwards.

Soon after she came within sight of Haughton Tower, she saw the river flowing into Davis Cove. She followed it for about half a mile, keeping hidden in the woods, then, exhausted, she leant against a tree to catch her breath. But its trunk was entwined in creeping cowitch; stung by the stinging hairs on its branches she dived to the ground, rubbing her arms frantically to try to relieve the intense itching.

When she was able to move on, she soon came to an abrupt halt on the edge of a precipice. She was awed: she could look over what she thought must be the whole island, lying at her feet like a vast garden. Her mind soon forced her on again, and she got within sight of Cacoon – she remembered that. But then she must have passed out, for she remembered no more, not even being brought back to the Cove.

'So, you never reach Quashee.'

She shook her head slightly. She reached out to August, and he took her hand.

'Boy, beg you ask Sarah to come get me.'

'Yes, Ami.'

'In the morning?'

'Yes, Ami.'

'You promise?'

'Promise.'

It was dark, and Ami had fallen asleep, by the time Sarah and Andries arrived to help August back to his cabin.

Next morning they returned to take Ami home. She was in a bad state, and drifted in and out of consciousness all through the day. Massa William Dickson and Frazer made a surprising and peculiarly uneasy visit to her in the evening.

Dickson was the first to speak. 'How is she?'

'Poorly,' Sarah replied.

'Hmm. So why isn't she back at the hothouse, getting attention?'

'She say is here she want to rest,' Sarah said defensively.

Dickson's eyes wandered round the hut. He produced a handkerchief from his pocket and held it up. 'Can any of you tell me how Ami got hold of this?'

'No, Massa,' lied August fluently. 'Yu sure it is not Mother Ami's?'

'Oh, I'm quite sure. But thank you. I shall make enquiries elsewhere.' He turned to go.

'Sir,' said Frazer, 'aren't you going to question Ami? I'm sure she's only pretending to be asleep. I'll bet my wages that if I put her in the stocks you'll see a miraculous awakening.'

Massa Dickson gazed at Ami while he addressed Frazer. 'If I were you, and I wanted to continue as overseer on this plantation, I would leave her be. Your job is to work the negroes, not to be their executioner. Make sure she gets what medicine she may need. Make sure she's well – and ready to come back to the fields – soon.'

'Aye, sir.' Frazer was uncharacteristically subdued.

Later that day, the whole village was astonished to hear about the misfortune that had befallen Nancy. The talk was that Massa Dickson had questioned her about the handkerchief. Nancy had sworn blind that she had not given it to Ami, but Dickson accused her of lying and said he would send her children away unless she explained how it had been removed from the house. At that threat, she threw herself to the floor, scraping at his feet and begging forgiveness for what she had done. The outcome was that she was to serve a week's sentence in the stock.

August was guilt-stricken that he had not prepared a story for Nancy's protection – it was a bad oversight. He decided to take Andries with him to see her. Nancy's head and hands hung limp, sticking out between the wooden planks. Her three daughters sat nearby, wailing spiritual songs, and Mulatto John was crouched beside her, quiet and morose. The only one who so much as stirred when August and Andries joined them was Nancy, who raised her head a fraction and waggled her fingers sluggishly, a greeting of sorts. To August, her hand looked like a humming-bird's claw outstretched. Nancy clenched it into a fist, tight, as if to will away a tremor of pain. Catherine stroked it. The hand went limp, and Nancy's head also sagged.

Mulatto John took his machete and made a hole in a coconut. He held it so that the milk trickled down the side of her face towards her mouth. Nancy poked her tongue out and managed to lap up a little, though most fell on the ground. August wondered what it could be like to do nothing all day but think. Thinking about pain, about this miserable life, about the Massas' disregard for their slaves' suffering – that would surely lead to a longing for death.

The girls began another spiritual.

> Come down
> Come down, my Lord
> Come down
> Way down in Egypt land
>
> Jesus Christ, He died for me
> Way down in Egypt land
> Jesus Christ, He set me free
> Way down in Egypt land
>
> Born of God I know I am
> Way down in Egypt land
> I'm purchased by the dying Lamb
> Way down in Egypt land
>
> Peter walked upon the sea
> Way down in Egypt land
> And Jesus told him, 'Come to me'
> Way down in Egypt land.

When they ran out of verses, they repeated an earlier one. Eventually Mulatto John had had enough. He bent towards Nancy, took her head between tender hands and kissed her goodbye. As he left, Nancy's hand fluttered a farewell.

The next morning August was on his way to the workhouse when he heard Sarah cry out in distress. He immediately set off towards her hut. Forcing his way through the people congregated outside, he peered over their heads and through the open door. Eventually he saw her, sitting on the makeshift bed; next to her, Ami Brown lay motionless. Sis Bell was sitting by the bed, rocking to and fro, holding Ami's limp hand.

August fought his way inside to comfort Sarah. They could do little more than hold each other tight. Sharper was another source of concern. He had lost the woman who had been his companion for over two decades. August drew him into the embrace with Sarah, and the three of them wept together. When August felt strong enough, he turned his attention to Ami. He barely recognised the statuesque figure lying there, and he grappled with the thought of her spirit divorced from this empty vessel. Her eyes were partly open: she cast death's vacant look upon him. August and Sis Bell, together, gently shut Ami's eyes for the last time.

'She smiling. Look, she smiling,' Sis Bell said in her softest voice. After further silence, she began a hymn familiar to all who attended Reverend Rose's services.

> Swing low, sweet chariot
> Coming for to carry me home.
>
> I looked over Jordan and what did I see
> Coming for to carry me home
> A band of angels coming after me
> Coming for to carry me home.
>
> If you get there before I do
> Coming for to carry me home
> Tell all my friends I'm coming too.
> Coming for to carry me home.

Those who did not know the words hummed quietly. It was true: Ami was smiling. Her resistance had ended; the spirit had broken free.

August led Sarah to the door and out of the hut, leaving

Sis Bell and some of the old women to prepare Ami's body for burial. Praying began as soon as the couple left.

August thought it his duty to be at Sarah's side as much as possible for what remained of the day. He asked Barbary to look out for her, too. Barbary had thought of making a special plea for Sarah to stand in for Nancy at Bardanage, a suggestion to which Massa Dickson agreed readily.

All too soon, it was Sarah's turn to offer comfort and sympathy to Barbary. The next day Nancy, having completed her week's punishment in the stocks, retired to her cabin complaining of dizziness. She went to sleep and never awoke. The shocked and grieving village had to prepare for a double funeral.

Sarah bore particularly heavy responsibilities. August asked Sis Bell to go with him to help her. On reaching Sarah's hut, they saw three young women setting down some freshly picked lime wrapped in a good-sized cloth. Sis Bell asked for some ginger to make the juice, but it had not yet arrived from Mama Cecelia's. Mangoes were expected from Silvia and salt beef from Barbary. One of Sarah's hogs was killed in preparation for the evening ceremony. She had a friend make sure that the entrails were buried, and from the flesh and bones Sarah made soup.

Ami's body lay beautifully adorned in her kitchen garden. She was covered by a linen shroud; trinkets, including necklaces and bracelets made with beads, wood, shells, copper and gold, were laid neatly around her; and she was surrounded by flowers.

At dusk, the whole community gathered around the garden and hut. The sounds of drumming and horn-blowing began to build. Massa Dickson had banned loud music when he took over the Estate, and he made sure that his staff rigorously enforced his rules. However, on this occasion he told his workers to keep their distance, and he ordered Frazer to take leave of absence.

Massa Dickson preferred to avoid situations which

might inflame the slaves' passion. The ceremony, being Ga in origin, would entail Ami's body being put in a coffin and carried around the village before burial. The villagers saw Frazer as responsible for her death, and Dickson feared that they might carry the coffin to Frazer's house and refuse to move on. This practice was common when other slaves were felt to be responsible, but these were changing times and the manner of Ami's death might bring about something unprecedented. Frazer would not have tolerated a gathering outside his house. He would have disrupted the ceremony, possibly triggering a confrontation with far-reaching consequences.

As more and more people joined in the singing and dancing, a carnival atmosphere began to take over. Many slaves crossed over from neighbouring states; some had never met Ami but had heard about her and wanted to pay their respects. The burial was planned to take place well into the evening, so that as many people as possible could attend.

At last the time came for Sarah to begin the ceremony. Beniba waved a calabash that Sarah had prepared three times, and put it down. Sharper, Hopey and three others laid Ami's body in the ground. As they began to cover her with soil, the villagers united in a terrific scream. The sound of drums, rattles and tambourines filled the air.

Mulatto John looked bewildered.

'Her spirit won't rest until forty sunsets,' August explained. 'You see, she has to travel on a long journey and she will need food. That is why they are laying food by her head and rum by her feet.'

'They still believe that her spirit will go back to Africa?'

'So they say. I don't really want to see Ami turn duppy around here, no sir!' August broke off. He didn't mean to be as disrespectful as he sounded. 'It would be nice to think that God will find a place for her in His Kingdom. That would be very nice.'

'Amen, Bredda August,' said Mulatto John.

While they were talking, August saw Hopey take up a position a few feet away. He was exchanging squinted looks with six men loitering on the edges of the ceremony. August knew them to be from Haughton Estate. He knew also that Hopey was plotting again. After Mulatto John moved to observe the ceremony more closely, Hopey slipped over to August. He put an arm around August's waist and whispered in his ear, 'Brother August, come make mi tell you something. Come, follow.'

August obeyed, and they headed in the direction of the six men.

However, they were intercepted by Sarah, who grabbed August's shirt from behind and demanded, 'So where the hell you think you going, both of you?' Hands on hips, she looked August up and down, scowled at Hopey, and then stormed off, kissing her teeth.

'Them rebels look like they going get you in a lot of trouble, Hopey,' August said.

'So what make yu think black people not in trouble now?'

'You know what I mean.'

'My bredda, we have two hundred and fifty so far.'

'What? Guineamen?'

'Guineamen – I hate when yu have to talk their way. Yu sound too much like buckra. I can't stand when you talk them foolish talk. Chu! There's even one man from St Domingue them call Blacka Fenucane.'

'But the black people of St Domingue free, they fought for their freedom long-time now. A long, long time ago. What the hell such a man doing 'pon this island?'

'Mi no know. Mi not even sure if him is a slave, but him know a whole heap of people in Kingston, and we have guns ready to shoot buckra if them try to stop we.'

The size of Hopey's band of would-be rebels encouraged August, but rebellion carried with it many burdens. Men suspected of conspiracy were transported away from the island, never to see their kith or kin again.

'Is who leading things?' August asked.

'Virgil, from Harding Hall. Every night me go over there to hear what him have to say. Him talk all the while 'bout a Baptist who organising everything, but nobody know who him be. Him go by the name Ruler. If ever you lucky to see him, that is what you mus' call him. You mus' never ask him name unless he tells you himself. That way he doesn't end up like Ben – dead – and have no use to anybody.'

'Where you get money to pay for guns?'

'For three years now, Virgil been going all over the place. Him tell everybody him is collecting money for the church.'

'I did wonder why he keep asking me for money. Only the other day him ask me for a money. The man take it and never tell me what him doing with it.'

'Yes, man, well that is money fi buy guns and powder.'

'What? And the money that come from the prayer meetings over by Retreat?'

'Yes, man, all that as well. All for guns.'

'My God.'

'Yu not to tell a soul.'

'So, tell me, when the *t'ing* going to happen?'

'Christmas time.'

'Wrong time.'

'There is never a right time!'

# Chapter 19

# Hopey

HOPEY INTRODUCED AUGUST to Blacka the following week in the hills bordering Davis Cove Estate. The meeting-place was in an area thickly grown with trees and shrubs. Hopey chose it because it was unlikely that any busha men could sneak up on them unheard. As he and August pushed and chopped their way through the undergrowth, they heard someone call out.

Hopey recognised the voice as Blacka's and called back, 'It's me, Hopey. See here. I bring a friend with me. Me did tell you about him already. Him name August.'

From the thicket emerged the Goliath-like figure of Blacka, all of six feet eight inches in height. He had a smile on his face and a small crucifix around his neck.

'Why him smile so much? I don't trust anybody who smile so much,' August muttered, his hand over his mouth so that only Hopey could hear.

'Hush, man. This man will kill yuh if him decide him don't like yu.'

Blacka talked a lot, mostly about the best time for him to pass on guns to Hopey, guns that he acquired in Kingston. It was to be a delicate operation, fraught with danger. Every now and again he would break into St Domingan French patois.

'So what will happen Christmas Day?' asked August, excited.

Blacka stopped his incessant smiling and growled, 'Who want to know?'

Hopey had been sworn to secrecy – by no less a person

than Blacka himself – because a leak of information might jeopardise the conspiracy, and he immediately reassured Blacka that August could be trusted. Blacka whipped a blade out of a sheath at his belt and, with the speed of a lizard's tongue, grabbed August's wrist. The edge of the blade slid across his forearm, making him cry out. In the same movement Blacka cut his own arm and mingled his blood with August's. Thus August, too, was sworn.

Taking turns talking, Blacka and Hopey explained that the intention was to set fire to the trash-houses and works on Prospect and Harding Hall estates. When the white people came to put out the fire, rebels would set upon them with their guns and cutlasses. They would then begin burning all the estates west of Orange Bay beyond Cousins' Cove as far down as Negril. If the border to the south were defended, the militia advancing north would encounter the marsh land and the mosquitoes of Negril. Blacka said that trees would be cut down and put in position as barricades; deep trenches would be cut into the road. Any army of white men new to the island would soon be weakened by disease. Hopey took over to describe a planned onslaught from the hills led by a free mulatto, one result of which would be the capture of many more weapons. There would also be a battalion of slaves defending the road down from the north of Cousins' Cove. All white people would be killed.

August became increasingly uncomfortable as he listened. 'White people you want kill?' he asked.

'No, August. It is white people *we* going kill,' said Hopey.

'Remember is your children's future that *we* fighting for.'

'If you think is 'fraid me 'fraid to fight, you wrong. Mi always dream that this day would come. But I want to make that this thing plan properly. I see too many of these things come to nothing but a little fussing and fighting on some property. I want to be part of it, but not one stone must be left unturned in the plan. When the first white man dies, that is it. There will be no way back for anybody; for me, or my family.'

The topic of August's involvement was abandoned. There were more urgent issues at stake. Hopey needed to organise the transfer from his end.

Later – after midnight – Hopey and a few of his men from Harding completed the task of collecting the guns and hiding them in the hills near the provision grounds under the palm trees. Hopey set off back to the village, taking the route that took him past Frazer's cabin. He went that way because he was tired, and with his fatigue he got careless, hence capable of doing stupid things.

He had a pistol in his trousers and some powder and ball bullets wrapped in a handkerchief. He was taking them back to his cabin purely to satisfy his own vanity, nothing more. He had been caressing the pistol ever since Blacka put it in his hands. Blacka's parting words had been that Hopey must ensure that the weapons were concealed at all times; he must do nothing that would betray the fact that an insurrection was being planned. But this was different: the pistol was his property; it wasn't even loaded.

'Who goes there?' called Frazer.

Hopey froze in panic. What was Frazer doing up so late? Why was he patrolling the area at this hour?

'I know someone's out there,' Frazer insisted.

Hopey ran. He saw a light go on in Frazer's house, and then Frazer coming after him, a lamp in his hand. When Hopey reached the village, he hid behind the hut.

'Whoever you are, you're here somewhere. And if you're here, I'll find you!' Frazer bellowed.

Hopey drew his pistol. He could hear where Frazer was better than he could see. His mind was racing. He heard Frazer go inside the cabin belonging to a black woman called Susan James. This gave him an opportunity to collect his thoughts. As his own cabin was next to Susan James's, that would most likely be Frazer's next port of call. So Hopey moved fast but silently to Mary Anne's hut, less than a hundred yards away. Mary Anne had no children, which was good from the rebel's viewpoint.

When Hopey shoved open the door, Mary Anne was startled awake and opened her mouth to scream. Hopey dived on top of her and covered her mouth with his hand. She couldn't see a thing.

'Shhh!' he hissed. 'Is me, Hopey.'

'What you want? You try rape me. Dirty nega, get off before I kick you!'

'Mi can explain. Frazer chasing me. You mus' help. Beg you please keep quiet.' He ripped his clothes off as he spoke, and as soon as he was bare he started trying to strip Mary Anne, too. She fought him for a moment, but then she heard Frazer's voice coming towards the cabin, and she obligingly slipped out of her nightdress. Hopey pressed the hard metal surface of the pistol and the powder balls against her stomach as he mounted her. She raised her knees as he rested between her thighs. Hopey heard the door creak open as Frazer entered the cabin, but could see nothing until Frazer held the lamp up. He saw his shadow rise up the wall; his and Mary Anne's soon engulfed the room as Frazer held the lamp closer to them. Hopey stretched his hand behind his back and pulled up the thin sheet to cover their nakedness. He turned his head to see where Frazer was.

'Excuse me,' Frazer said, faintly embarrassed, hence uncharacteristically polite. As he turned to walk away, he glanced back at them. He was, after all, still looking for somebody. 'Why do you need a sheet in this hot weather? Where are your trousers?'

Without waiting for an answer, he strode over to the bed and pulled the sheet back. Hopey pressed himself against

Mary Anne, making sure that there was no space for the gun to be seen. Frazer held his lamp directly over the couple. Hopey's fear overwhelmed his embarrassment at revealing his ebony buttocks. He prayed that Mary Ann's bounteous breasts, squeezed against his chest, and the sight of his trousers down round his ankles would convince Frazer that he was not the man Frazer wanted.

'Hmm. I was looking for someone,' Frazer said, 'but it wasn't either of you.'

When Frazer had gone, Hopey heaved a sign of relief. Still glued to Mary Anne, he subtly registered considerable discomfort: his phallus was like stone, resting on the hard metal of the pistol. He slipped down off the metal. Looking anew at Mary Anne, he felt the heat of her soft melanin-enriched body. The smell of a natural body aroma sparked a feeling of raw attraction. The thought of pressing home his advantageous position crossed his mind, mixed with all too recent fears of the precariousness of his situation. He made as if to dismount.

'Where think you going?' she said, grabbing him low down and gripping him tight.

Hopey looked at her, surprised. 'Nowhere,' he said in a delighted whisper.

The next morning Hopey returned to his cabin to discover his few possessions scattered on the floor. His table was overturned; his dirty linen on the ground and covered with the dust. The hut had been ransacked.

A voice behind him said, 'I didn't want to disturb you last night so I decided to return to your cabin this morning to ask after you. And on the floor I found this.'

It was Frazer, of course. Between his index finger and thumb he held a powder ball. Horror flushed across Hopey's face. His mind raced back to the early hours of the morning. He remembered asking a young man named Philip Anglin to pick up a box hidden in the cabin and

175

take it to the secret place to be buried with the rest. Philip must have dropped one bullet.

'Me did find that at market. Ah the truth, Massa, Hopey no lie. Yu know me is a good negro.'

'It doesn't matter to me. What matters is whether this stands up in the courthouse.' Frazer's signalled to two bookkeepers standing outside to escort Hopey to Bardanage.

It was the millwright who brought August the news that Hopey had been arrested. The word was that one of the slaves on Harding Hall Estate had told his fifteen-year-old son of the planned rebellion. It transpired that the boy had realised something was up even before his father had told him: he had twice seen negroes assembled in a secluded spot by Orange Bay, and he had heard them speak not only of rising up but of killing all white people. Massa Robert Allwood, overseer on a nearby property, was suspicious and questioned the boy. Allwood was warned that he would have a bad Christmas and that if he wished to be saved, he should go to the Jerusalem Estate, in the hills towards the Westmoreland border.

This had happened early the previous day. Allwood had alerted all the other estates' overseers, naturally including Frazer, who had therefore spent most of the early hours patrolling. The boy had given the names of five slaves who he'd seen talking to his father, and had also said that two others had been standing close enough to hear. One of them was soon identified as Hopey, whose name was given to Frazer in the early morning, as the cock crowed.

Hopey sat trembling throughout the courthouse hearing, which lasted a whole day. During the proceedings, five other rebels were tried and sentenced to a life of hard labour in the workhouse. Virgil was caught red-handed with his pistol hidden in his hut. Ironically, his wife appeared in court and confided to the judge that her husband frequently went out after dark and didn't tell her where he went. She thought he was out seeing other women. Virgil was sentenced to transportation and sent away on a ship bound for Nova Scotia. It was said that such a sentence was death itself. Rebels sent there never returned.

The judge could find no evidence linking Hopey's bullet to a possible insurrection, because no firearm had been found. Nevertheless, he was declared guilty of possession and punished accordingly; his previous association with planned mutinies also went against him. He wept as his sentence was pronounced. August patted his back. Still hunched over, Hopey removed a beaded necklace from round his neck and buried it in August's hand.

During his testimony August said he had gone to Massa Dickson and volunteered the information that he had seen Hopey finding the bullet at the market. This risk was great: he was gambling away his reputation as a good negro and Christian. Although he knew there was little chance anything he could say would make the slightest difference to Hopey's fate, he was prepared to lie for Hopey's sake.

# Chapter 20

# Daddy

July 1830

DRIVING THE OX-CART out to where the labourers were working was a task August didn't mind. He would help them load cane and then bring the bundles to the work-house for processing. He was trying to conserve energy by moving slowly yet surely across the fields. He passed a gang of slaves singing as they set about the land, digging holes and laying dung in the holes ready for the new cane.

> Guinea Corn, I long to see you
> Guinea Corn, I long to plant you
> Guinea Corn, I long to mould you
> Guinea Corn, I long to weed you
> Guinea Corn, I long to hoe you
> Guinea Corn, I long to cut you
> Guinea Corn, I long to dry you
> Guinea Corn, I long to beat you
> Guinea Corn, I long to trash you
> Guinea Corn, I long to parch you
> Guinea Corn, I long to grind you
> Guinea Corn, I long to turn you
> Guinea Corn, I long to eat you.

And so it went on until the words seemed to blur as he put distance between himself and the labourers and he came within sight of Bardanage. His eye was caught by one of the chairs on the veranda, the rickety brown rocking-chair that used to belong to William Dickson. Whatever happened to that man? he wondered. Massa William was many things to many people: a military man, a juror, a church-warden, a parish gentleman. August thought that he must have got bored with being William the sugar planter.

From that broken old chair, Frazer had told the slaves that William's longstanding friend, Alexander McCullum, was going to take over the Estate. He was a feeble-looking man who had served with Dickson as a juror. August knew him to be a junior merchant, too, but not as wealthy as Dickson. Fearful of the discontent shown by many black men towards Massas up and down the parish, he started paying the head men wages, thinking it would make slaves more pliant; friends told him it wasn't a good idea, but he did it anyway. But Massa Alexander soon died, and he was succeeded by his brother Neil, who cared little about the running of the Estate; he was more concerned with bal-ancing the books. August saw Neil McCullum only once, and that was when he came to the house to discuss business with the new attorney, John Lee.

August looked up at the big house and cursed – that damn Massa John Lee. The worst thing that could happen to any slave on any estate was to see the ownership put into the hands of an attorney. The villagers grumbled that he was the worst attorney that could possibly have been set on them. In fact, it was from the old rocking-chair that Neil McCallum gave Massa Lee the job. And from that chair he got rid of Frazer.

John Lee had heard about Frazer's failure with Ami before she died, now almost six years ago; he wondered why Frazer hadn't been sacked long before then. He considered it dangerous to have an overseer whom the slaves no longer feared. Dismissing him was the first thing he did to make his mark. A washed-up overseer was as much use as a broken slave; he just didn't have it in him any more. August often heard white people say that what goes around comes around, and that certainly applied to Frazer. As it was, Lee brought in a new overseer, a young protégé of his called Ned Jones.

Massa Jones derived his experience from the infamous Golden Grove Estate. The workhouses in the western parishes had had their fill of slaves from that plantation over the years. Golden Grove was the sewer of Hanover.

The first time August met Jones they had a conversation about the prayer meetings that August was now holding.

'Well, August, I am told you preach to many negroes, around here and on neighbouring property. Is that so?'

August was surprised that the new busha man should know anything about him so soon – this was the day after Jones started on the Cove – but he was more concerned at being singled out as a preacher. He had no licence to preach, and preaching without a licence was against the law, though some Massas were more lenient about this than others. So he replied, 'I hope I am a praying man, sir. Perhaps that's what you mean, as white folk always calling praying preaching.'

'No, I mean that you take a book and preach to people out of it.'

'Massa, how can I preach from a book when I can't read? How can Massa think that I could take a book and preach when all the people know I can't read?'

'Well, I don't know what you call it. Don't you say prayers to people?

'Yes, I talk to my neighbour and friend, truly, I am not ashamed of it. Religion makes me happy, and I want my fellow creatures to be happy, too.'

'Well, then, you must be a preacher, surely?'

'Massa can call me what him like but I must always pray and talk to God. As long as I have a breath, I would do it continually.'

'Oh, I see. Perhaps you could preach to us, although you don't know a letter of the book? Who betrayed Jesus

Christ? For you are preacher and you must know,' Jones mocked.

August stood his ground. 'Judas,' he replied, 'for thirty pieces of silver.'

'Hmm. Who disobeyed Joshua?' Jones scowled.

'Achan, from the tribe of Judah.'

'What did he do?'

'He stole gold and silver from Jericho and hid it.'

'How can that be, when Achan was slain?'

'Beg Massa pardon, but Achan was put to death after Joshua found out that he was a thief.'

'Was Moses a good man?'

'Yes. A man after God's own heart.'

'What! After God forbade him to enter the Promised Land?'

'Ah, Massa! You read God's word and you don't realise that when Moses doubted the Lord, he fell. Massa say he read the Bible. Suppose Massa was to look in him Bible, him would know that God tell Moses to speak to the rock. Instead Moses hit the rock because him feel a certain anger within him heart. God's judgement was swift, but Him never stopped loving His servant. Why should He? The Lord don't stop loving all who try to do His works.'

'I didn't realise you were so knowledgeable,' Jones said. 'You had better not fill the villagers' heads with these things. They begin to know too much already, and it's a bad thing when niggers know too much.'

'But, Massa, God's word is good, and I been telling my fellow creatures what good religion has done for me; if is good for me, it must also be good for them. And God's word is that I must not let my brother and sister alone, but must try and bring them all to Jesus Christ, so that their blood don't rest 'pon my head in the last day.'

At that point, the conversation had come to an abrupt end. Now, August was equally abruptly brought back to the present by Lee's harsh voice threatening to beat him unless he hurried up.

'Yes, Massa, I'm moving, I'm moving fast.' August gave his ox a pang with a short whip and he continued his journey. He had gone as far as the plantain walk when he heard his name being called. He turned and was relieved to find that this time it was Reverend Rose.

'Massa, it is always good to see you.'

'You flatter me. How are Sarah and the baby?'

'Barbary? She not long standing now. She have two front teeth in her head.'

'They don't stay babies for long, do they?'

'No, sir, they don't. Sarah is so happy, even though she sometimes still talks about the baby Sam we did lose – must be three years now, I think? Yes, born 1826, died 1826. We no forget. But God done bless us again with baby Barbary and I give humble praises.'

'You're a good man, but you must get John and Barbary baptised soon. It doesn't cost you anything but your time. I'll say no more.'

'I will. Have you heard anything more about what happened to Barbary, Sister Nancy's daughter, the one them did sell off?'

'No, but I've not been getting around as much as I used to,' said Rose. He began treading a stone into the dust, and, looking down at it, said, 'Listen, August, I want to ask your advice about something.'

'What we can do for you, Massa?'

'Stop calling me Massa for one thing. You know there's only one Massa and He is our Lord God.'

'Yes, Massa – I mean Reverend. You teach that we should serve only one Massa, that Holy Spirit in the sky. I don't forget that. You is a teacher and we slaves too stupid to learn everything you teach.'

'I haven't time to dwell on that now, as I said.'

'Me can offer you advice?'

'Yes. There are few people attending services these days, as you well know. How do you think I can increase negro attendance?'

August was only too happy to answer this question, for it was an easy one. 'Invite the lay Baptist minister Sam Sharpe to give a sermon. That will sure bring them in.'

'Sam Sharpe?'

'Yes, Reverend.'

'The negro?'

'Yes, Reverend.'

August knew well that his suggestion would not meet with Lee's approval and that the Reverend would worry about this. Some negro Baptists were spreading the word that freedom was imminent, which was creating tension all over the island. Seeing that the Reverend was indeed perturbed, August went on to reassure him that Sharpe was an excellent preacher and was bound to attract a large congregation.

'Very well, then. Please arrange to invite him. But please ensure that he does not bring any unsavoury politics about freedom struggles to the church. Church is for worship. The Lord will decide if and when slaves will be set free and we must await guidance. Am I understood?'

The service was duly planned for the following Sunday, at midnight. August got there ten minutes beforehand. There were already some fifty negroes crowded round the church, and more arrived with every minute. He was nervous: he had persuaded the Reverend not to inform local property owners of his intention to let Sharpe preach here. He was also delighted: the church was going to be full to overflowing. The black folk always arrived late, after their long days in the fields. Many people were dressed in white, and the women, as usual, had covered their heads with fresh white scarves. All arrived barefoot, while those who could afford shoes did not put them on until reaching the church. The contrasts between the dark night, the white linen and the black skins were spectacular.

August went over to the Reverend, who was unlocking the doors of the rickety church.

'Good evening, Reverend,' he said.

Rose looked at him wearily. 'August, it's good to see you.' He was pale, his eyes deeply shadowed.

'You don't look well at all, Reverend,' said August with concern.

'I'm not feeling very well. I've had a runny belly all day.'

'You want to go home and take lime-water. You should mix it with rum and salt. Drink it and it will make you feel better.' August was sure.

'Thank you, but I think I'll be all right.' With that he hauled the door open, and the people rushed in.

August had already reserved seats at the front for himself and his family. Ensuring that Sarah, Barbary and John were comfortable, even if the children were restless, he looked around to see who he didn't know. He took delight in extending his hands to greet people, occasionally springing up from his seat to do so. For him, this occasion embodied a great feeling of community, of people gathering together for harmonious worship; it was the best of what he remembered about his motherland. He remembered his position as a deacon, and went to join Reverend Rose, who was welcoming people at the door. More wagons arrived after midnight. The church was full and overflowing. There were between eighty and a hundred people crammed inside, many standing; some of the late-comers were even trying to get in at the windows. Men plucked handkerchiefs from their back pockets to wipe away their sweat. Reverend Rose had lost his handkerchief earlier, and felt worse for it.

In the expectant hush, Sam Sharpe stepped out of the crowd. He made his way to the tables and chairs at the front of the church, and introduced himself to Reverend Rose with a firm handshake.

184

'See him there, that mus' be Daddy Sharpe, see him,' Sarah nudged August hard. She had already made it clear that the main reason for her presence was to see and hear the preacher.

Daddy Sharpe stood about five feet nine inches, had a fine, sinewy frame and perfect jet-black skin. He was not yet thirty, yet had considerable bearing. His forehead was broad, his nose and lips were full; when he smiled he displayed brilliant white teeth, contrasting beautifully with his skin. He looked round the crowded church.

'Greetings in the name of our Lord and Saviour Jesus Christ,' he intoned in a medium pitch.

'Hallelujah!' the crowd responded. 'Glory in Jesus' name!'

Sharpe coughed in a mock attempt to clear his throat, important to the style of preaching for which he was renowned. He opened his mouth to continue, but was interrupted by the sudden wailing of a baby. He waited a few moments for silence to resume, but the baby's mother's efforts to calm her child had little effect. Daddy asked her if the baby was a boy or a girl.

'A boy,' she replied meekly.

'My dear, the child needs food so that it may grow and protect you. He needs his mother's breast so that he can nourish himself; let the child suckle. You are within the house of the Lord and He has given this child unto you to feed and nurture. Feed your child, please.'

Embarrassed, she pulled out her left breast, to warm applause from the crowd.

Daddy Sharpe was not yet ready to start his sermon proper. 'And where, if you don't mind me asking, is the child's father?'

'Massa sell him a few weeks ago. Him never tell me that he was going to do such a thing. Me don't know where him gone,' she replied.

Everyone was mesmerised by this unexpected exchange. Everyone understood the mother's plight.

'One day, brothers and sisters,' said Daddy Sharpe, 'one day things will get better. Put your trust in the Lord. Amen.'

'Amen' came a subdued response from the congregation.

Rose suddenly rose from his chair, his hands pressed against his stomach; he raised an apologetic eyebrow at August. August looked across at Daddy Sharpe, who was watching the Reverend move towards the door. August waved at Daddy to catch his attention, and rubbed his stomach, indicating the problem.

When the Reverend had gone out, Daddy said, 'For those of you who have Bibles, will you turn to Deuteronomy, chapter twenty-eight, verse six, please.' He waited while a handful of people rummaged through the pages. 'It doesn't matter if you do not possess a Bible or have no understanding of the written word. The Lord has charged me with the duty to tell you all of His teaching.' Daddy held up his own Bible for all to see. The gesture signified that the words he was about to speak were not his but the words which the Lord had inspired.

He said softly, 'The Lord will praise everything you do. Hallelujah.'

The congregation rose to their feet saying, 'Amen, hallelujah, thank you, Jesus.'

Then Daddy launched into his sermon. He spoke quietly and soothingly at first, but soon raised his voice and began pacing back and forth to increase the intensity of his delivery, slapping his Bible after every few words. 'If you obey the Lord your God and do everything he commands, He will make you His own people, as He has promised.'

'Hallelujah!' August exulted in Daddy's words. Daddy approached August and, placing a hand on baby Barbary's head, told him that the Lord would give him an abundance of crops in the land that He promised his ancestors. And that he would one day be independent. An older man sitting in the row behind said, 'Amen.'

'Preach, Minister, preach. Make we hear!' someone called from the back.

Daddy flicked through his Bible, reciting verse after verse, occasionally glancing down for prompts. Short of breath and sounding parched, Daddy paused and asked if there was any water anywhere. Sarah stepped up to him and offered her goung goung, a container used to carry water which when split in two was used as a calabash. He removed the cork and sipped a little. When he finished he fiddled around trying to put the cork back in. Sarah obligingly took it from him and replaced it. Daddy Sharpe thanked her.

Then a woman started to sing and the whole congregation stood and followed the verse. The church filled with clapping, singing, swaying and the beating of drums.

A man leapt up and down shouting, 'Glory! Glory! Glory hallelujah!' Then he spoke in tongues before jumping into the air and collapsing to the floor, shaking as if struck with fever. Some men and women, still praying loudly, immediately surrounded him, and a silver-haired man gave him a shoulder for support.

'Cover his ears. Quickly, so master and busha don't hear, otherwise we'll all be in trouble!'

A woman bent quickly and covered the man's ears. This was done, August knew, in the belief that it would stop the sound going any further than the church doors.

On the thought, August stood up and began to sing loudly and defiantly.

> We will be slaves no more,
> Since Christ has made us free,
> Has nailed our tyrants to the cross
> And bought our liberty.

The whole congregation joined in. The men by the rear windows stopped singing after the verse had been repeated twice, and gazed out into the night.

One of them called to August, 'Oh Lord. The Reverend a come and him look vex.'

Reverend Rose forced his way through the door with renewed energy. 'Stop this,' he said firmly. 'You must all leave now. Please! Go!'

The congregation fell silent, then gradually drifted out through the door.

August waited with Daddy, who was thanking people for coming. He made sure almost everyone – barring Sarah and the children – was safely out and on their way, then turned and looked expressionlessly at the Reverend.

'Reverend,' said Daddy, 'we didn't mean anything by what transpired. You know as well as I that slaves will always pour out what they feel inside through song and dance. There is only so much Massa can suppress. The Lord protects good men. You have nothing to fear.' He said goodbye to August and left quickly.

'I am not sure how to take what he has just said,' said Rose. 'Is it true what he said, August? Is this how slaves behave at these services?'

'Reverend, you know all slaves want is the freedom to say what we feel and do what is right. That is all.'

'Hmm.' Rose pondered, not knowing what to make of what had happened. 'I cannot think clearly at the moment. I need rest – and some of that concoction you mentioned earlier. Lock up for me, will you.' He handed August the key and padlock, then dragged himself wearily out the door.

Sarah lit a lamp and gathered the children close, and they all left. Several paces into the dark, August heard a metallic clicking; it was difficult to tell where the sound came from. Then, from behind him, a voice shouted, 'Catch!' As he whirled round, a tiny ball, almost invisible in the dim lamplight, arced towards him. Instinctively, he shot his right hand out and caught it. It was a powder ball, a bullet for a gun. He peered into the darkness, and made out the shape of a man leaning against a tree trunk.

The man stepped forward and his face became visible as he moved into the lamplight. He said, 'Two years, that is all it takes for you to forget a face? That is not good. Bonjour, mon ami.'

'My God, look who it is – Blacka!' August was astonished.

'Oui, it is me.' They clasped each other's hands in the warmest of handshakes.

'I never saw yu inside,' said August. 'Where were you?'

'I just reach here.'

'Sarah, come meet a friend of mine, Blacka Fenucane.'

August introduced his family to Blacka. Sarah was cautious. She had never heard Blacka's name mentioned, nor ever seen him. What kind of friend could he be? When August explained, she was appalled.

'So you're the one that get John Hope in trouble. What's wrong with you – you don't have no remorse? You should feel shame. Look how you just skin up your teeth.'

Blacka's broad smile vanished and he turned to August. 'I did hear about what you did try to do for Hopey in the courthouse. It was stupid. But that kind of courage is why we need men like you.'

'Hopey was my friend. But if me did stop to think about death me would have stayed right in my yard. Death and me no friends. You understand what mi trying to say?'

'Well, I respect you all the same.'

'So what bring you here tonight? I expect you to be out there burning a few property and things.'

'No no. I only chop the wood. It is for people like you who must ignite it and fan the flames.'

'What you mean?' asked August.

'Now is not the time. Do you know Miss Jane Crooks?'

'The quadroon woman that buy her freedom and the

189

freedom of some old folk at Retreat? Yes, man, I know Miss Jane well.'

'Good. Everybody heading over there as we speak. So let us not waste time.'

'Who is "everybody"?'

'Daddy Sharpe and some others you wouldn't know. Come, let's go.'


When they got there an hour later, they found Daddy Sharpe and Jane sitting outside round a fire, talking. Jane had only three stools, so the men sat crossed-legged on the ground. Lime drinks were offered from an earthen jar.

Daddy was particularly taken with John, and searched in his bag for something that would entertain him. He found a conch shell; conches were used by the maroons to send messages across long distances. He demonstrated by blowing into it a couple of times, and John at once stretched his hand out for the shell, eager to try it himself. Satisfied that the boy would be occupied for some time, Daddy directed him to the edge of the front of the garden, out of earshot.

Jane mentioned that she expected nine or ten other visitors, who were coming from Golden Grove, Miller, Richmond, Blenheim, Batchelor Hall, Harding Hall, Baulk, Eton and Caldwell estates. All these were sugar plantations except Miller, a small coffee and pimento estate. To Sarah it sounded as if the whole of Hanover had been invited.

It was some time before the other visitors arrived.

Relieved, Daddy said, 'Ah, here they come, a little late, but that is only to be expected.'

'What's happening, Ruler?' a tall dark man asked him.

'Come, we do not have much time,' he replied.

'You're the one they call Ruler?' asked August.

'So I'm told.'

'So what must I call you?'

'Anything you want, so long as it is something that you

wouldn't mind calling yourself. I normally answer to the name Daddy.'

'Do you remember a man called Hopey, John Hope, from Cousins' Cove?'

'I know the name. I talk through some people – not to all people.'

'But you knew him?'

'Yes, I did.'

'Do you know what happened to him?'

'I know what becomes of all those who rise to the call of the one they call Ruler.'

'Is he alive?'

'He was committed to the workhouse in Westmoreland, there to do hard labour. I wouldn't have expected him to last long.'

August gripped his hands tightly together. Although he badly wanted to know more about Hopey, he leant back and gestured to Daddy to start the proceedings. This was as Hopey would have wished.

Everybody hushed as Daddy prepared himself for the meeting. He put some more wood on the fire, to give a little more light, and stared into the flames as if into another dimension. Then he screwed up his mouth and pressed his hands into the dust, making two shallow handprints. He buffed them clean and looked around at each person present. Addressing the group as his beloved brothers and sisters, he began, 'I would rather die than be a slave.'

This set the tone for the rest of the meeting. He spoke slowly and in even tones; each word, each syllable, was chosen with supreme care.

'The time has come and the Almighty has said He will lead us to the Promised Land. Many of you already know the struggle that has been played out by the plantocracy and the British government persuaded by William Wilberforce. Soon we will have to take our rightful place in the

191

struggle for freedom against the forces of oppression. It will be an historic struggle between the oppressed and those who seek to oppress. I am talking about the master and the slave. The *thing* is now determined upon – no time to be lost. Our friend the King of England and his parliament have given Jamaica freedom, and it is held back by the whites we call our masters. We must take it at once.'

August was spellbound by Daddy's eloquence. He spoke of the wickedness and injustice of slavery, impressing upon all those present that the future of the next generation was in their hands. There was only so much that white men thousands of miles away in the mother country could do. Whatever Mr Wilberforce couldn't do, Daddy said, he willed the slaves to do for themselves.

'Whether you be black, mulatto, quadroon, mustee, sambo, white, African or creole, however far removed from Africa you are, or think you are, we all have one destiny: freedom. This *thing* is about the right to sell our labour at a fair and just price, without punishment as the main motivator for our work. This is the will of the Lord and Saviour; and we will fight for what's right. Amen.'

'Amen, Ruler. Hallelujah,' came the response.

'Men like Neil Malcolm, John Campbell and John Edward Payne, to name but a few, meet regularly behind the closed doors at the courthouse in Lucea. The convenor is none other than the Honourable Robert Allwood, Custos of Hanover and a justice of the court. They drink claret and eat yule cake and plan to break from the mother country and align themselves with the Americans. If that happens, our freedom will be lost. It is their intention to kill all black men, and to save all black women and children, keeping them in slavery. If the black man does not stand up for himself and take freedom, white people will put us at the muzzles of their guns and shoot us like pigeons.'

Daddy's message was clear. Everyone must make a stand.

192

An agent would be sent with detailed instructions on how to prepare for the struggle.

August was prepared; a glance at Sarah, though, and he could see she had mixed feelings. Daddy raised his Bible and had each man and woman take an oath of allegiance to the cause. Everyone kissed the Bible.

# Chapter 21

# The Baptist Sam Sharpe

July 1830

AUGUST CALLED A dinner-time prayer meeting at Sarah's hut. Charles agreed to lead the meeting. Little John was excused, for he had the all-important task of watching out for Lee or any of the bookkeepers: Richard Dickson had banned unauthorised prayer meetings during the dinner-time break, and the ban continued to apply after his death. August had cut the number of prayer meetings from three a day to two.

Charles began with a prayer. 'Oh, great and blessed God, we thank and bless Thy holy name, that Thou give we anodder opportunity of meeting together in the place where we pray, we acknowledge with shame and confusion of face we great unworthiness to approach Thy sacred foot-stool, and much less to handle Thy sacred name between we polluted lip. We have not done one t'ing right nor fitting in Thy sight ever since we born up to this present hour.'

'Busha come, busha come!' Little John shouted.

Everyone except August, Charles and Sarah ran out of the hut and through the kitchen garden to disperse among the trees at the back.

Charles stood outside the door and confronted the busha. 'Ah, Massa Jones. Massa, is there anything Charles can do for you?'

'Yes. Answer me this. How often is a church held in this house?'

'A church? Massa, no, not here,' replied Charles.

'Oh yes it is,' Jones asserted.

'Please, Massa, what Massa mean?'

'Mean!' Jones pointed at the hut, the threat in his voice increasing. 'Why, that you are in the habit of preaching in a church you have in that house, are you not?'

August and Sarah peered anxiously out of the window, listening to every word. August wanted to go to Charles's aid, but Sarah, well aware of Charles's ability to talk himself out of trouble, restrained him with a tug at his trousers. She knew that it would add to Jones's suspicions if August suddenly appeared. The two of them should sit quietly and pretend nothing was going on outside.

Jones fixed his venomous stare on the knees of Charles's trousers, which were thick with muck and showed signs of wear and tear. 'I have often noticed that my drivers go through many pairs of trousers. Isn't it funny that the ones who go through the most are always the preachers? I've never seen a driver go through so many pairs of trousers as you. You're a driver. You're supposed to stay on your feet chasing gangs of field slaves all over the place. How comes your trousers are dirty and so worn at the knees?'

Charles dealt neatly with the awkward question by explaining that the trousers belonged to August. He said he had lost his own while bathing down at the Cove.

'How often do you preach?'

Charles looked Jones in the eyes and said earnestly, 'Preach, Massa? Me poor ignorant man. Me no able to preach, me no able to speak much less. Me be quite glad if me could preach.'

'Come, come, don't play me for a fool, or I'll have you thrashed. I know you preach in there.'

'No, Massa. Me praise some time in me house, that is all.'

'Well, what do you call that but preaching and holding a church in your house?'

'Well, then, if that make me have a church in the house,

195

that Massa himself mus' have a church in his house as well. Not true?'

'I have a church? Certainly not!' Jones's annoyance was mounting.

'Please, Massa, but don't Massa belonged to the church in England?'

'That, yes.'

'Massa is a Christian, and a belonged to the Church of England, Massa have morning and evening prayers with his family?'

'Yes, yes.' Jones hesitated, not liking the direction this exchange was taking.

'Well, then, what that make me, sir, if me have church in the house, and Massa have church in him house?' Charles's wiles were working and he knew it, so he dropped his eyes and stared at a bit of manure wedged between the heel and ball of Jones's boot.

'But people come to you from considerable distances, and I understand you preach to them,' said Jones.

'I, Massa? Sometimes, when me friend and brother Christian come down from the country to market and call for me, we discourse 'pon different things 'bout religion, and then bow down on our knees together – that's all.' Charles again turned the question on Jones: 'When Massa friend come in to see him from the country, Massa no discourse upon different things too, and then bow down the knee together in the same fashion?'

'I don't know about that,' said Jones, 'but what I do know is that an affidavit may well be filed against you by the Peace Office, for preaching.'

'Well, as for that, me is a quiet man, me never do nobody no harm; but there is many of them in this country that don't like religion, and that's the truth.'

'I promise you you will do yourself harm if you persist in this attitude. After all, you are the head driver. I strongly advise you to leave off the praying.'

'Well, Massa, me can't help that because me can't leave off the praying. Me no trouble what person say 'bout me, me don't trouble 'bout that at all. Good words don't do me much credit, and them bad words is no disgrace.'

Over Charles's shoulder Jones saw August and Sarah looking out of the window. 'Have you two nothing better to do with your time?' he said. 'There's work over at the boiling-house which needs doing.'

August was late to bed that night; Sarah and the children had long since gone to sleep. He lay on his back, looking up at the moon through the window and thinking about the day's events. He was beginning to drift into sleep when he saw the flicker of a flame torch outside and heard his name called. He snarled with irritation at having his sleep disturbed, but went outside to find out what was going on.

He could just make out the figure of Andries in a group of about fifteen men and women. Andries held his torch a little higher so that August could see more clearly. August looked around; he was satisfied that no one was close enough to overhear them.

'What you people want this time of night?' he asked.

'I bring the people to hear what you have to say 'bout the meeting with Daddy Sharpe. We all want to hear more. I beg you, please tell us more.'

August could see that a lot of villagers were losing sleep in these tense times, and realised that it was time to tell people some details of his conversation. Feeling that it would be safer to talk further away from the village, he made everyone follow him to a clearing in the cane piece.

When they got there, everyone sat down. August took a deep breath, wondering where to begin. There was a respectful silence, and one or two people settled themselves more comfortably. In a calm voice, he began describing the wondrous spirit that moved him. He went to great lengths to express his regard for the Baptist preacher. But the

197

group was getting impatient, eager to hear details of what Daddy Sharpe had said. August found it difficult to pick out the things the villagers needed to know.

'Bredda August, who is Daddy Sharpe?' Andries asked.

August rubbed his eyes. Yawning, he replied, 'He is the man they call Ruler. He has come to deliver us into the Promised Land.' Suddenly less tired, he began to express himself with clarity. Everyone had heard about the man known as Ruler. They had believed him to be one of the Eboe kings, but now it began to sink in that he was in fact the lay Baptist preacher. This meant that it was the Baptists who were imbuing thoughts of freedom.

'And Daddy say slavery is an evil and unjust system.' August was speaking fluently now, his confidence regained. 'He show us that the white man have no more right to hold us black people in bondage than we have to enslave them. The King make us free but the white man meeting secretly in the great houses all over Jamaica. Them is plotting hard how to kill all black men, and save the women and children, to keep us in slavery. Me can tell you that if the black man no stand up for we selves, the white man going shoot us like we is fowl.'

'We mus' fight!'

'Yes, we mus', but if the white man want us to work, him mus' pay we. If them try force we to work as slaves, we must fight for our freedom. Big things going happen on the island 'round October to December and we must prepare weself. This is what Daddy said.' August was done, at least for the time being. 'We must go back to our huts and tomorrow we talk more.'

'But wait one minute. What him want you fi do?' Andries asked.

'Mi must check on Davis Cove and Spring properties, to see that everybody is preparing, and let the generals know.' August allowed himself to say that much, but he knew that it was important not to divulge too much; what little he knew must not in any circumstances be repeated yet. He urged everyone to have courage for what was to happen.

September 1830

There were several weeks in which to prepare for the uprising. First, a tall, brown-skinned man with a reddish tinge to his colouring visited August. He said his name was Linton, and he was the head slave on Hermitage Estate. Like Daddy, he had high status. In the eyes of his busha, he was therefore loyal to the establishment.

August met him several times by night in one of the trash-houses – the prayer meeting was the usual cover. Afterwards, they always discussed the main issue, freedom. Linton kept August informed of how many were being signed up across the western parishes of the island. The white men had guns but the blacks had the numbers. For every white man on the plantation there were at least thirty slaves. August believed that the slaves had an even greater weapon on their side: the Lord.

So as not to arouse suspicion, August received his orders from other conspirators. For example, one evening the excitable Richard Trail came from Shuttlewood Estate, accompanied by Deacon Thomas Haughton, also from Shuttlewood. Thomas held a large Bible in his hand. There were two other men: Andrew Llewellyn, a carpenter from Silver Grove, and the regimental-looking John Martin. Thomas did most of the talking. He knew his Bible well, but his coarse sense of humour did not appeal to August, who found all four men rather odd. He would not have followed them had Linton and Daddy not instructed him to do so.

At the beginning of September, August asked some of the Cove people, Alexander Crooks, Elvin Barker and Robert Anderson, to a meeting in the hope that they would be persuaded to join the movement. They were among the few villagers still undecided about taking the oath. By the time the meeting drew to a close, they were keen to join but feared the potential backlash from Lee. Alexander, in particular, was reluctant to give a firm commitment.

Suddenly, John Martin came alive: he had been standing stiffly to attention, remaining silent throughout. Without warning he produced a gun from his trouser pocket and aimed it at the three potential enlistees. The reckless precision of his aim, as it moved from right to left, held all three motionless.

'Eeee Hin. Eeee Hin. Do you people know exactly what is going to happen if you don't take the oath?' he threatened, the gun pointing at Alexander.

Andrew Llewellyn leant across the meeting table and pulled his gun from under his shirt. He rested it on the table with his finger curled around the trigger. And then Richard Trail pulled one from his small carrying-bag and, eyes ablaze, aimed it at Alexander's head.

He said, 'If you don't take the oath I will shoot.'

And Deacon Haughton snarled, 'This is not the time to make fun. Do what is right and the Lord will be pleased. The wicked are doomed by their own violence.' He was no longer the happy, chanting preacher, but had adopted the attitude of his men. 'Now take the Bible, and take the oath, weak hearts!'


September was nearly over. In the last week of the month, August was to meet Linton for the last time, to check that everything was still on course. August, Charles and eight other men waited for Andries under a tree at the centre of the village. Eventually Andries appeared from behind one of their huts, walking briskly towards them. Missy Stewart was behind running to keep up with him.

'Is where she think she's going?'

'You think you can stop her? She is the reason why mi late,' Andries said.

August looked at Missy, ready to upbraid her, but he

200

held back when he saw her face. An overseer at Harding Hall had hit her days earlier, and her face was still swollen and puffy. Lee had considered making it a court issue, but had decided against it. Missy had accused a busha man who claimed that he had been in Montego Bay at the time of the incident. He had blamed it on a coloured slave with whom Missy had been seen. Lee chose to believe the white man and that was the end of the matter, at least as far as he was concerned. In Missy, however, the lack of justice had awakened a new determination. August realised that it would be futile to waste precious time arguing with her against joining the delegation. Her refusal to be crushed reminded him of Ami; this combined presence would bring him strength whenever he needed it.

The group headed for the provision grounds. Most had brought drums and other musical instruments for cover.

'Come, Christmas, you going set down your tools.'

'How you mean? We mus' stop work?' asked Archie McIntyre, a thirty-three-year-old creole.

'Yes. You going set down? We mustn't trouble anybody, not one person or thing must be hurt. We must sit peaceable.'

Charles looked puzzled, Missy confused and unhappy. Andries gave a sigh that could be construed as plain relief. He himself had never been a man capable of damaging people.

'You mean we no kill buckra?' Andries asked for confirmation.

'You must not burn anything or fight, unless violence is used against you. And if violence is used against you, you will eradicate it with all the power the Almighty send you. But I hope that, with God's guidance, it will not come to that.'

# Chapter 22

# Rumours

CHRISTMAS DAY 1830 was a rare opportunity for the Cove community to relax. The time was spent dancing, singing, talking and, of course, drumming everywhere. It was one of the only three holidays during the year that Lee felt he must endure; in order to do so, he had no alternative but to stay within the confines of Bardanage, entertaining guests.

The drink was plentiful: the distillers had kept a couple of rum puncheons from the distillery the night before, and this was in addition to the quota Lee had allowed. Some villagers poured rum down others' throats. Spouses and friends poked fun as merriment spilt out of the huts into the village. The festivities were fast turning into a carnival.

Smoke billowed from fires on which hogs were roasting outside some of the huts, and the air was full of the aromas of roasting meat and spicy chicken. From the yard in front of the trash-house Charles and August watched the celebrations, taking a tipple of rum every now and again.

Archie McIntyre called to Charles, 'Hey, Christian, I thought you people don't supposed to drink the strong drink!'

Charles shrieked back, 'Wine is a mocker when strong drink is raging, and this drink no rage in me, now go away!' He had had a little more than he should have. Their spirits were, however, in need of lifting. What had become of the much-discussed revolution? To them it seemed to have been talked to death. Was it really now dying a slow death? Everybody was waiting for the next person to make the first move, with the result that nobody moved. People seemed more concerned about the sanctions if the insurrection went wrong.

'Look at everybody, jus' enjoying themselves. Weak hearts,' said Charles.

'True, true. But the weaknesses is not in their hearts,' August replied.

Sarah came and joined them; she put her arm round August's waist and led him to a quieter place. For them, Christmas was a time to enjoy each other's company as well as the village celebrations.

Feeling how tense he was, she moved round to face him, her face full of concern and devotion. They sat down on a bench. He gazed at her intently, loving her full lips, her spread nose, the brown eyes and her freckled cheeks. He ran his fingers through her finely plaited cane row, before gently squeezing her arm.

'Mi going for a walk,' he said after a while.

'Where?'

'Out by the cove.'

Sarah made a move as if to go with him but he laid his hand on her shoulder, gently restraining her.

'I want to go alone.' He smiled crookedly, as if gallantly hiding inner pain.

'Don't be too long. Anyt'ing could happen to you out there, and me wouldn't know what to do. Huh, don't let me go out there later and find you with another woman,' she added trying to introduce a lighter tone.

He nodded, and by the time Sarah had cast an eye towards the festivities and back again he was gone.

August went to a spot just outside the village. It was dark, though the village threw light out just far enough for him to cast a vague shadow. He sat down for few minutes. It had rained earlier, and the moisture accentuated the raw smells of grasses and soil. He closed his eyes and let nature pamper him with a cool breeze. Lost in meditation for what seemed like hours, he decided to give thanks for the things that were God-given, for the space to contemplate, for the mind that had nurtured hope, for better things to come. He recited the Lord's Prayer. At the words 'deliver us from evil', he stopped. They brought to mind a psalm, one he'd often repeated parrot-fashion but had never taken the time to understand; the one beginning 'The Lord is my shepherd.' He had started to recite it, slowly, quietly, when he heard footsteps approaching. He was less afraid than annoyed that someone was about to impinge on a deeply private moment.

'Good evening, August. I heard you praying. I didn't mean to interrupt.'

August stood up. 'Good evening, Reverend Rose. Is strange, mi was just thinking about the Holy Scripture and wanted to ask you 'bout it.'

'Oh, really? How odd. I saw you leave the slave quarters and thought I would come and have a word with you.'

'Massa, "Yeah though I walk through the valley of death, I shall fear no evil": what does that really mean?'

The way August asked the question made the Reverend uncomfortable. He felt as if he were being addressed by an equal or, worse, being schooled.

'What has prompted you to ask me that?'

'If men was created equal and do another a wicked thing, is he possessed of the Devil?' Question upon question in response.

'Well, it depends.'

'And what does it mean, then, if is busha men who do wicked things to we poor people?'

'August, we shouldn't be having this conversation.'

'And when you tell us to pray to the Lord to deliver us from evil, what do you mean? And if I walk through the valley of death, the Lord going with me with His rod and his staff?' August was treading on the line that marked the limit of their friendship.

'The Lord in His great wisdom decided that this is the way things are, and in His great wisdom He will decide if it will change. And we must patiently submit. Do I have to say it more clearly than that?'

'No, Massa.'

Dread struck August as he came to his senses. Recovering from his momentary lapse, he bowed his head, took a step backwards and apologised profusely.

The Reverend wagged a finger at him. 'I'm well aware that some wicked persons have persuaded slaves that the King has made you free. What you have been told is false – as false as hell can make it, do you hear? You must go back to the village and pray for forgiveness for letting demon spirits into your heart. If you have any love for Jesus Christ, for me, for those kind friends in England who have given money to help us build our chapels, you must not be led by wicked men.'

August bowed his head again. He said goodnight to the Reverend and set off back to the village. He wondered what had possessed him to address the Reverend in such controversial terms – Rose was white, after all. Their exchange had confirmed something he had always known deep down: that men like Rose craved familiarity with black folk only on a superficial level; and there were reasons why it should remain so.

Reverend Rose watched August move away. The heaviness of August's heart weighed heavily on Rose, still taken aback by the demonstration of one slave's power of reasoning. You call them, they come; you tell them, they know; they even believe, but never are they truly enlightened. Negroes – slaves – were supposed to be incapable of grasping things of an intellectually rigorous nature. Rose had heard this so often, and from so many sources, that he hadn't realised how deeply it had become entrenched in his own thinking. The ghostly wind of negro enlightenment had touched him briefly. August was but one negro on a fundamentally placid plantation. Yet if he was having these thoughts, how many others were, too? It struck him that gaining the freedom of the blacks meant more than a humanitarian act of good will. One seed of negro enlightenment was budding right before his eyes. August was a friend.

'August, wait!' he called. But August was too far away to hear.

Summer 1831

August read all he could about events in the mother country months earlier. According to one issue of the *Royal Gazette*, an agreement pertaining to slavery had been reached in May of that year. The article struck him as a rather vague rendition of a proclamation discussed within the edifices of the British government. It was full of incomprehensible long words, but he had long since learnt to put a value on interpretation, so interpret he did. What he told those who wanted to know was that slavery had indeed been abolished.

A later article reported that the British government was doing much in the name of a gradual abolition. When Lee found out that the Society for the Gradual Abolition had become the Society for the Immediate Abolition of Slavery, he smashed his hand against a coffee table so hard that it needed medical attention. The news of his outburst spread quickly through the Cove, for some of the house slaves had heard him vent his fury. It maddened him that Mr Wilberforce had been given one inch and was pressing for a mile. If the wrong trigger were pressed, the government would cave in.

The information didn't altogether tally with what August was telling everyone, but nobody cared. Freedom time was now.

At the end of October, the hurricane season was fast

approaching. Sweeping in with it came a feeling of change throughout the island. The increasingly frequent comings and goings of the militia made it much more difficult for slaves to cross to neighbouring estates. Questions – always questions. Where are you going? Why? Where is your pass? When do you expect to return? Which other negroes will you be in contact with? Where? The answers invariably needed checking with the Massa.

Lee had ordered that as few slaves as possible went to the Sunday road market at Orange Bay. Instead, a small market was set up for them between the Cove and Haughton Tower. It was closely supervised, and the bookkeepers intervened whenever they saw slaves congregating in any numbers. Conch shells were confiscated, because they had been recognised as a means of communicating over long distances. The time was right to strike.

One Sunday at the end of the month, August, Sarah, Andries and Missy absconded to Spring Estate for a night prayer meeting. They were greeted by Linton, and there were delegates from a number of surrounding plantations. Linton said that on 27 December all slaves in Hanover, St James and parts of other parishes would refuse to work. Every man and woman was expected to take up machetes, cutlasses – any tool that could be used as a weapon. 'If them try to coerce us back to work, we will take up arms and take lives if necessary.'

Missy asked what this meant for the Cousins' Cove Estate. In particular, she wanted to know what arrangements have been made for the quota of guns to arrive. Linton said that it was too risky to get guns to the west coast because of the military build-up around Davis Cove and even further south. The rebellion would start in St James and spread west towards Hanover; more regiments would be making their way south through Westmoreland towards St Elizabeth. After each successful engagement with the military, the rebels would stop, replenish their supplies, then move on to the next.

Linton issued orders that the villagers were not to kill anybody except in self-defence. Also that they should burn the trash-houses as beacons for the slave regiments forming on neighbouring plantations. This would ignite a revolution, which would develop its own momentum. The burning trash-houses would give the impression of a village on fire, of war being waged, a Baptist war. He gave specific instructions that the other workhouses were not to be touched.

'Why not burn the whole place down?' Missy asked.

'Because we need them to build a future for ourselves. You understand me?'

Missy understood. 'But what about training?'

'Do you know how much that would take to organise? What you think Massa going say if him see a whole heap of slaves playing soldiers in him backyard? Talk sense, woman.'

'We don't stand a chance,' Sarah said.

'We have numbers,' said Linton encouragingly. 'If there are weak hearts out there, they going gain strength when them see the beacons burning.'

'What about the big houses like Bardanage?' asked Missy.

'Me no care 'bout them. Burn them. If we don't, them will provide cover for the whites,' Linton replied.

'Me going to make sure me kill Massa Lee and the dirty whore him call his wife.'

'Daddy say yu must leave them alone. Yu not to touch them unless them try to stop you. This *thing* is 'bout freedom, not death. My sister, me no want you becoming my problem – yu understand me?'

Missy's militancy worried August. He remembered Daddy's view that it was the minds not the hearts of the people that might prove the undoing of the rebellion. Once begun, it must proceed; he would pray for a successful outcome.

A week passed, two weeks, and there had been no further news. Sarah told August that he should go to Bardanage to find out what he could from Missy.

August went cautiously up to the side of the house. He was nervous and felt he looked suspicious. Missy came out of the house with a pail and threw the water out, narrowly missing August. He whispered her name loudly. She looked around to make sure no one from the house was watching, and then leant with ostentatious tiredness on the veranda balustrade.

'Talk,' she urged.

'Why has Massa Lee put all these restrictions 'pon us?'

'Don't tell a soul, but mi hear that all the buckra worrying 'bout negroes laying down tools and striking on Boxing Day when everyone supposed to go back to work.'

'So how him find out?'

'Mi no know.'

'Him know 'bout us?'

'If him know, him no say not'ing.'

'You think him know?'

'Mi don't think so.'

'Mi going go tell the others.'

'Yes, but be careful. Mi hear say that things going to get even harder for people to come and go from the plantation.'

'How you mean?'

'Anybody who leave the estate better make sure them have a damn good reason, your Miss Sarah included.'

'Miss Sarah all right. She not going have no problem.'

'Stay there think so. The Bible say that sensible people see trouble coming and get out of the way, but people who no think go right into it and regret it later. You mark my words.'

Lee shouted from inside, demanding to know why Missy was taking so long to empty a pail of water.

'Massa, me soon come!' she replied. She told August to leave at once, and scurried back inside.

That evening, August sat crossed-legged outside his hut with Sarah, watching the hills gradually disappear into the low hanging clouds. Sarah was sewing clothes. He saw someone leave Bardanage and walk down the hill towards the village. He lost sight of the figure behind the works, but a few minutes later a man emerged in the row, apparently coming towards them. It was Jones, staggering along the way, with papers in his hand.

'Oh Lord, Sarah, it look like him coming for us,' said August.

'Sweet Jesus, I wonder what him wants of we poor people. Why him don't leave we alone?'

'Where the children?'

'Them is gallivanting out in the fields somewhere.'

'Go find them. Tell them it is time for bed. Mi don't want them out playing. It look like strong drink raging.'

Sarah eased herself out of her chair and slipped away round the back of the cabin.

When she returned with John and Barbary, Jones had already left. August told her Jones had wanted to know whether August would give up his religion in return for his manumission. The free-papers had already been drawn up and were in his hands. August told her that they planned to set August and his children free.

'What you tell him?' Sarah had difficulty in absorbing the import of this news.

'Mi never pay him any mind whatsoever. Mi just tell him that mi want fi free, but mi could not deny the Lord.'

'What him do?'

'Tear it up in front of me and throw it to the ground. Then he went, gone 'bout his business.'

By the middle of December the atmosphere was so highly charged that any spark might ignite the tinder of

210

insurrection. The slaves gave their masters sidelong hostile looks; whispering and rumour-mongering increased the tension.

Lee watched the Cove workers even more closely; he knew something was brewing. He thought he had found it when, as he was crossing the fields one day, he saw August talking casually with other field labourers and with Charles. Lee's jaw tightened: what was a head driver, whose job was to make the labourers' work hard, doing chatting to them as if they were best of friends? Then he saw George, a young boy who had just started working in the fields, running past. Here was an opportunity.

'Mr Wallace, go and fetch that boy!' Lee shouted to the bookkeeper in the field.

Wallace whisked George up under his arm, carried him over and set him down in front of Lee, who produced the sharp knife he used for stripping cane. Lee checked that everyone was paying attention, then raised his knife. He held it tight, pressing his thumb against the blunted edge.

'This is what happens when niggers get too familiar with each other,' Lee pronounced.

He put the knifeblade behind George's ear and sliced it off with the coolness of a butcher dissecting a hog. George screamed in agony, and blood spurted, covering Wallace's hands.

Wallace winced; he was only two days into the job, and it was the first time he'd witnessed so cruel a mutilation. But he dared not let go: he held on to George's jaw so that he could not break loose, and watched as the blood flowed down the boy's neck and on to his chest.

August ran to George's side. He stared at the severed ear, mangled like a piece of offal, and quickly kicked dust over it, a miniature burial. Then he calmly moved Wallace aside and picked George up.

Only too well aware of the point Lee had wanted to

make, he was careful to keep his voice steady. 'Why you have to do this to the child, Massa? Why?'

Lee didn't answer. He turned his back and walked away, merely saying indifferently, 'Mr Wallace, get that boy seen to and return him to the fields, at once.'

As soon as possible August went to tell George's mother, Sister Jane, what had happened. He had hardly begun when someone knocked at the door. August opened it and found Wallace standing there, wringing his cap in his hands, his head bowed.

'I . . . I came to—' He broke off. His eyes were filled with remorse.

There was a long silence.

'Yu want to come in?' asked August.

'No,' said Wallace. 'It's the boy's mother I really wanted to see. Will she come to the door?'

Sister Jane heard him and moved to the door. Delicately, she eased August to one side.

She said, 'Massa, you come to the wrong house to beg for forgiveness. If you believe in the Lord you go to His house and ask for Him.' She closed the door without another word.

That evening, August called a prayer meeting of a few of his most trusted men. The rendezvous was a clearing out in the pastures.

Missy was in belligerent mood. She pointed at August and said scornfully, 'What wrong with you people? None of you have any fight left in you?'

'Stop your noise, and where's your manners?' said McFarlane.

'She right,' Andries said.

It was a bad start to the meeting. People began speaking at the same time, without listening to each other. In the end, August calmed everyone down with a few choice words about what would happen if Massa heard them. He sat picking yesterday's soil out of his over-grown fingernails while the others talked in low voices, saying over and over again that Boxing Day was only a couple of weeks away and the strike would soon begin.

Eventually his silence drew everyone's attention.

He looked up and said, 'There will be no violence on the day of the strike because there will be no strike on this plantation.'

'What you mean?' demanded Elvin.

'No strike.'

'But what did we all agree?' someone asked.

August clasped his hands and brought them up to his chin. He described an earlier incident. He had been standing on an ox-cart trying to tie down the cut cane. He sang a song about how Mr Wilberforce was supposed to have set the slaves free. Quaco overheard and reported him to Lee. Lee summoned August, Sarah and the children, reminding them that August was the only black man of advancing years who was still part of a family unit, uncommon in most parts. August hadn't appreciated this at the time but it was true. Lee told August that if he did whatever he could to prevent trouble, he would be rewarded. On the other hand, for every man who refused to work a child would be flogged every hour, on the hour, until everyone had returned to work.

August pointed in the direction of the beacon poised high up on the hill towards the east, now veiled by darkness. His voice a little shaky, he continued, 'So when you go back to your huts, make sure you tell everybody one thing. Make sure that every man, woman and child knows that there will be no action on Boxing Day.' Squaring up to Charles, he said in a lower but still urgent voice, 'But when the trash-house at Haughton starts to burn, Massa Jones and Massa Lee will lose them life. Them don't have no place in the new Jamaica we going build for our people, just as the Devil don't have no place at God's right hand.'

'You know this will bring prosecution on a Church?' Charles whispered in August's ear.

August nodded slightly.

Charles took the Bible, kissed it and put it down by his bare feet. He whipped out a knife and slit his finger. He took a basin, let the blood seep into it and mixed in a quart of rum with some grave dirt. Everyone swore to fight. Everyone took the oath to drive the white people out of Jamaica.

'Drink,' he told them.

One by one they all supped from the basin.

# Chapter 23

# More Rumours

'COME, AUGUST, YOUR turn to play,' urged Andries.

'Wait, man,' August replied. Andries was impatient to continue their game of Oware, but his own mind was elsewhere.

Twelve holes had been dug in the dust outside August's cabin. Four peas were placed in each at the beginning of the game. Each player had emptied most of the peas from one hole into the adjacent holes, moving counterclockwise. The aim was to place the last pea in an opponent's hole containing one or two peas, thus capturing not only the peas but any of the opponent's adjacent holes that still contained two or three peas. The game was close, with August just one pea ahead. August's day-dreaming only increased Andries's impatience.

August was supposed to take his time casting his peas in the village challenge. He had strategically laid his plan two moves ago and he sensed victory was in the offing. He dropped his peas and smiled. 'You must bow to your master, boy!' he said.

'Hey. You don't see me start win some games of late? Won't be long before the master is mastered,' Andries quipped – but without a morsel of truth.

A large detachment of militiamen galloped by on the old road, heading north. As Christmas approached, soldiers had been seen more and more often.

'Do yu see that?' said August. 'You know what that means, don't you?'

'What it mean?'

'Is a sure sign say things getting hot out there. The people, them must be raising hell all over.'

'Look how many! I never see so much soldiers on horseback in all my life.'

'Neither have I.'

'So what we going do? We can't just sit 'pon we backside and play games.'

'We must wait, as planned,' August urged.

'But look, we can't just stand here and wait. Is action me want.' Andries shook his fist combatively in the direction of the militia.

'Oh, so you ready to lose your life. You really ready now, huh?' said August. The recent change in Andries's attitude was marked; he only hoped it wouldn't lead to foolishness.

'Me ready to take freedom right now. The time is now.'

'Quiet! Mi say you must wait. Wait until you see our people march 'pon the Cove. Mi expect no less than one thousand militant black men to arrive and burn Haughton Tower. Then, you no have to wait 'pon me to say anything. You just have to do.'

At that point they saw Lee rush out of the house and shout to the militiamen. One of them – August recognised him: Colonel Grignon – stopped briefly to talk to him, then rejoined the detachment. Within hours more soldiers arrived. Half of them stationed their heavy guns in the quarters up by Bardanage; the rest went on and out of the Cove. By evening more had left, heading in the direction of Lucea, leaving six men behind to guard the big house.

The next morning, after watching the guard-shift change, August left for the fields to load a cart with copper wood. Several cartloads had to be delivered to the boiling-house promptly. He saw that the guards were moving into the village and rifling the ramshackle huts, scattering the villagers' clothes and strewing their few possessions outside. Most upsetting of all, they dug up the kitchen gardens, destroying both the slaves' ability to feed themselves

216

and their main means making a little money. Fortunately, though, the militia didn't dig too deeply. They knew that these grounds were also the slaves' sacred burial grounds, and they were secretly afraid of the Obeah men's curse.

At about two o'clock August trotted the mules out with a cartload of boards, shingles and nails; extensive work was needed to repair a cattle pen damaged by wind during the hurricane season. He saw a militiaman on horseback galloping towards him, and recognised Colonel Grignon, the man who had talked to Lee the day before.

The Colonel drew up alongside him and looked him up and down, twice. 'Massa Lee tells me you are a praying man.'

'Yes, sir,' replied August.

The Colonel spat. 'When we go on detachment I will put you at the front; I will take good care of you.'

'Massa, thank you very much for your kind words. But the back would be just as fine for me, sir. Is not good for a negro to tread a in front of Massa. Massa always lead we poor ignorant negaman.' August was feeling bold.

'Well, how about if I take you to blow all these ministers' brains out? How would that make you feel?'

'Sorry, Massa? I never know say the ministers guilty of something.'

'To be sure they are.'

'But don't the law of this country say every man is innocent until them find him guilty? If them try and condemn already, then it will be time enough to blow them brains out. You persecute the minister because you don't like we to get no learning.'

'Oh, oh! But, as an honest man, answer me one question. Don't these ministers teach people to rob their owners? Answer me at once.'

'No, sir. If them did, we would say it not right, and we would have not'ing to do with them.'

217

'I am told you like to pray,' the Colonel said mockingly. 'What makes you pray?'

'Mi pray because mi is a sinner.'

'I suppose you found that out when you were converted?'

'Mi was a sinner before mi was converted, sir, and then mi pray to God.'

'What do you mean by sin?'

'There is two kinds of sin, original sin and actual sin. Me myself did break God's law and therefore mi pray to God for forgiveness through Jesus Christ.'

'What do you mean by original sin?'

'The sin of our first parents. But please to let me ask you, don't you pray to God?'

The Colonel pinched the bridge of his nose. 'Yes; but you pray too much.'

'No, sir. God tells us to pray always. But please let me ask you another question. Don't you call God "the Father"? What ungrateful children we is if we don't obey our Father's command. And if we acknowledge Him to be a King, how shameful not to be loyal to Him. But mi can account for it.'

'Can you indeed? How?'

'Because the scripture say the carnal mind is enemy against God, not subject to the law of God, neither can it be. And if the spirit of God don't teach us, we is dark and ignorant people, though we know plenty things else.'

'What do you mean by the spirit? The spirit of rum?'

'O fie, sir,' August was flippant in his imitation of buckra language. 'You call yourself a Christian, and make a mockery of spiritual things?'

'What else do you mean by the spirit? Have you ever seen it?'

'Mi feel it, sir, but mi no see it.'

'How do you know there is such a thing if you've never seen it?'

'Don't you say, sir, that man has a good spirit if him do

218

anything worthy of praise? Yet you don't see that spirit. You believe you have a soul, but you never see that soul. And, sir, would a blind man say he couldn't eat because he wasn't able to see the turkey.'

The Colonel was intrigued. He had actually enjoyed this cut-and-thrust of ideas. But now he was distracted by the distant sight of one of his men galloping at top speed towards Bardanage. There was evidently a problem.


Three days before Christmas, Lee made an announcement: the rest days would be reduced from three to one over the festive season, as was the practice on most other Jamaican estates. Then he promptly left Cousins' Cove for business in Trelawny, leaving the overseer and bookkeepers to deal with the disgruntled villagers.

On the following Sunday, Jones burst into August's hut, interrupting his morning prayers, and ordered him to go to Bardanage. Lee had returned and was preparing to make another announcement. August hurried off up the hill.

Lee came out on to the veranda, frowning sternly. He moved toward the steps and stood there for a while, his legs splayed, his fists nestled in the hollow of his hips. He looked around to check that all his staff and most of the villagers were there, then took from his pocket an important-looking document. Loudly, he said that what he was about to read was a proclamation in the name of King William IV which had been issued on 3 June 1831.

*'Whereas it has been represented to us that the slaves in some of our West-India colonies and of our possessions on the continent of South America, have been erroneously led to believe that orders have been sent out by us for their emancipation.*

*'And whereas such belief has produced acts of insubordination, which have excited our highest displeasure We do hereby declare and make known that the slave population in*

*our said colonies and possessions will forfeit all claim on our protection, if they shall fail to render entire submission to the laws, as well as dutiful obedience to their Master.'*

The proclamation went on at great length. The slaves listened in intent silence.

August stared down at the ground, at a loss to think what the next move should be. 'Buckra is really trying to vex me now,' he muttered. He bit his tongue and felt a trickle of warm blood in his mouth. Raising his chin, he tasted the blood slipping down this throat; it was good. He wiped his forehead and drew his hand down his face, soaking his hand with perspiration.

Suddenly, anger flared in him. He shoved his way though the crowd until he found Sarah, and snarled, 'Where the hell is my cutlass? Me going to cut one big hole in that man's backside.'

Sarah was taken aback, and frightened by his ferocity: was he really ready to turn even on her?

Charles and Brother Sharper helped her restrain him, but a number of people had heard what he said.

'Freedom now, freedom now, we want freedom now!' they cried, beginning to surge forward and shaking their fists in defiance.

Lee jumped backward when he saw a missile – a half-eaten unripe mango – heading for him. 'Who threw that?' he yelled. 'I want the mill-house running all day and night on Boxing Day – there will be no rest. Any slave caught resting that day will be flogged, and I will deliver the flogging personally!'

He grabbed a whip from Busha Ritchie, and a gun from Jones. Holding both above his head, he fired two shots, and the slaves fled in all directions. He whirled the whip round his head, then slashed it against the ground. Slowly he backed up, again leaving his workers to bring some order to the Estate.

'Niggers,' he said contemptuously, 'they're like barking dogs. Once they're tamed, you just have to shoo them away. One thing you may be sure of: there won't be any dogs biting their Massas here.' Lee went back inside the house to calm himself with a bottle of rum.

The New Year, 1832, had a grim beginning. On 2 January, Lee gathered the slaves together and read out a printed warning from Major Willoughby Cotton, Major-General Commanding. It said:

### To the Rebellious Slaves

*Negroes,*
*You have taken up arms against your Masters and have burnt and plundered their houses and buildings. Some wicked person has told you that the King has made you free, and that your Master withholds your freedom from you. In the name of the King I come among you to tell you that you have been misled.*

*I bring with me numerous forces to punish the guilty, and all who are found with rebels will be put to death without mercy. You cannot resist the King's troops; surrender yourself and beg that your crime may be pardoned. All who yield themselves up at any military post immediately, provided they are not principals and chiefs in the burnings that have been committed, will receive his Majesty's pardon; all who hold out will meet certain death.*

A young man cried out, 'Fire a go burn the wicked!' and others echoed his words. August had no idea what he should do next. He became an observer. He felt the chain that had kept slaves manacled to a wall of passiveness that stood like a headstone, a taboo to centuries of enslavement. There wasn't going to be any blood spilt on the Cove that day, even though he contemplated giving a signal to take up arms, to put an end to the lives of Lee and Jones. The ever-present military were among the trees. His instinct was to continue to wait for the burning beacon and the flag of liberty. If it were meant to happen there and then, it wouldn't need prompting from him.

'No watchman now,' August heard as in a distant dream, 'no watchman now. Nigger man burn the house, burn Buckra house! Brimstone comes. Burn Massa house!' August's eyes opened in a flash and he sprang up. Sarah, too, woke, wondering what had disturbed him.

He felt around in the darkness for his trousers, accidentally brushing his hand across Barbary's face. The child stirred, cried out briefly, but was deeply asleep again almost immediately. August crawled across the dusty floor. He pulled himself upright, using the post, and felt around for his lamp.

'Who out there?' he called softly.

There was silence. August became wary, and decided not to light the lamp yet.

'Don't bother go out there,' said Sarah anxiously. 'Yu going find yourself inna whole heap trouble.'

There was a thud which sounded like someone falling. It was followed by the sounds of a fight, fists pounding on a chest or back.

'You see, Sarah, mi no lie,' said August. 'Someone is out there. Let me go out and see what is going on.'

'No.'

August heard Quaco say vindictively, 'Me catch you, you little wretch!' Quaco was assigned to root out any conspirators by night. August found a half-full bottle of Kerosene and stuffed a piece of cloth in the neck for a wick. He lit it.

'August, come back!'

Ignoring her, he slipped out of the door. He could still hear fighting and cursing, and with due caution he crept

222

towards the sounds. Before long he saw two men: Quaco was holding the fallen man down, beating him relentlessly.

'That's enough!' August put down his lamp and dived on top of Quaco. Quaco was very strong, but August got him off balance and wrestled him to the ground, grunting to his victim to get on Quaco's back. The young man tried but was too weak. August was not strong enough to handle Quaco on his own, and he soon began to tire. Suddenly out of the night came Elvin Barker, Elliston and Brother Bigga, who not only lived up to his name but was the toughest man for miles around. They clubbed Quaco with their fists and sticks until August told them to stop. They did so, but Bigga put a headlock on Quaco and held him still.

August put his lips to Quaco's ear. 'Mi hear say the rebellion to end rebellions done start and it soon reach us. The gentleman in England have decreed that we are free. Is only a matter of time before the Assembly clean the wax out of them ears and hear what them supposed to do. When it happen, there going be a lot of nega man like you who going eat judgement. And let me tell you that when it happen you better pray that you is not one of them. Anyhow, this boy gets so much as one lash 'pon him back, me going make sure that you get thirty 'pon yours – that is, if we don't cut you from top to bottom. You understand me, bwoy?'

Quaco went limp. Brother Bigga loosened his grip ever so slowly until he was sure there would not be another surge of violence.

A week passed, and still they had no news of the uprising elsewhere on the island.

Eliza Douglas was the only person August could think of who might know what was happening outside the Cove. He had orders to collect grass before his last shift before late-night worship; he would go and see her then.

Andries and another young man joined him. They passed through a thicket of woodland and made their way down the slight incline towards Eliza's hut. They found her outside with her two helpers, coaxing the chickens into their roost. She greeted them and offered them some rice and pork, which they gladly accepted. She also offered to prepare some vegetables – callaloo and cucumbers – but August did not want to put her to the trouble and encouraged her to relax. Eliza sat on the one chair she owned, while everyone else, including her helpers, sat on benches and on the floor.

With needle and thread in hand, Eliza set to work on some clothes that needed mending, and she told them what she knew. At noon that day she had seen a driver by the roadside. The driver said that he and his Massa – at that moment deep in the bushes because of a runny belly – had been going to Trelawny to look at some land the Massa wanted to buy, but they had turned back on hearing from the military that the rebels were digging up roads; the soldiers also said rebels had set fire to Kensington Estate and killed a white man. His Massa had already begun to talk about leaving. In England there were already many absentee proprietors: more and more slave-owners had been leaving Jamaica in recent years.

Though the news was sketchy, it was certainly better than no news at all. Eliza added, 'The fire at Kensington did start in the evening on Boxing Day. Me hear, too, that Daddy Sharpe going appoint a governor in every parish, if him wins.'

One of her helpers interjected with the information that high-ranking slaves – slaves who were known to have the complete confidence of their Massas – had joined the struggle. 'Free coloureds, too,' said another.

Eliza suddenly remembered that she had a newspaper for August. It lay on a small cabinet nearby, still folded neatly. August felt like a child unwrapping a gift as he quickly unfolded it; it was the latest edition of the *Watchman*. He shuffled through the pages, looking for relevant stories. On page four he found something, and he began reading it aloud. It was an officer's report on the fires raging in the western interior of Jamaica. On New Year's Eve, slaves on most of the plantations in the western parishes had begun imprisoning their Massas and burning the trash-houses – in places the whole sky had been illuminated. Incredibly, in some cases high-ranking military officers had withdrawn their troops without firing a shot, because they did not wish to involve them in a contest to which they were not equal. Overleaf there was an article extremely critical of the Hanover companies stationed at Round Hill and led by Colonel Grignon.

There were five hundred rebel warriors involved in the attacks and the numbers were growing all the time. Furthermore, St James and Hanover were singled out as particularly active areas. Some of the strikes had been accompanied by violence – but then nobody believed that there would be no casualties on the other side. Jamaica was in turmoil. Civil war had come; it was real and taking place on an unimaginable scale.

It was getting late. August asked everyone to form a circle and join hands in prayer.

# Chapter 24

# The Thing

WHEN AUGUST ARRIVED at the church the following Sunday, an agitated Reverend Rose met him outside.

'August, we must talk before we go into the service.'

'I am not stopping really. Mary Anne asked me to pass by with some attoo. She said one of the children is crying for them belly-ache.' He held up six thin strands of the dark root for the Reverend to see. He was chewing another strand; cleaning his back teeth with it. Reverend Rose was shifting agitatedly from foot to foot, so August asked, 'What is it, Reverend?'

'I entreat you not to believe all that you have heard about freedom. You should urge the villagers for their own sake to go about their work as usual and not harbour any thoughts of making mischief.'

August turned his head awkwardly, squinting, making an effort to keep his voice steady. 'August no hear of anybody talking 'bout making mischief, Reverend.'

'For the love of Jesus Christ, do not be led toward a false promise of salvation.'

Rose sounded desperate, so August was relieved to be able to cut the conversation short: 'Mi think Reverend Stones looking for you.' He pointed to where two roads met near a clearing in the field. 'See him over there. You must excuse me. I have plenty to do over by Davis Cove. Them want me to help lift some heavy load and my back is not really up to it; so I might as well say good day to you, Reverend.' He waved as a king might acknowledge a thousand loyal subjects, then strolled off.

226

On his way to Davis Cove, August met Sam McFarlane, who asked for recent news about 'things'. August had been making every effort to play down anything he'd heard about the turmoil in Cornwall. There was still no sign that the campaign was succeeding. He wanted to be certain that it would, otherwise the only certainty would be seeing Haughton go up in flames.

'Brother August, you know that the youth are ready to take up arms against buckra? You know that them talk 'bout it every day? When you think it going happen? When are you going to give the order, sir?'

'You people really start to get on my nerves. You know, it is one man that is leading this thing, that is Ruler. Wait for the signal. Be patient, man.'

'Me did watch you and Reverend Rose stand and chat. What him say?'

'Nothing but pure foolishness. Him come ask me 'bout who and who is mischief-making. You must be careful when you talk to the Reverend. Massa could be using him to find out information. I only tell you because mi already know how much you and your brethren can chat.'

'No, sir. Me swear 'pon the Holy Bible that me wouldn't say a thing to any buckra.' McFarlane held his right hand up as if swearing. 'Them is hunting Ruler. Them put reward 'pon him head.'

'Where you hear that?' August asked, bending a little to look McFarlane in the eye.

'Missy tell me. Them issue proclamation. Them say any slave who know where him be will be set free. Massa, that is a whole heap of temptation for one man.'

'The same fire which turn papa to ashes harden brick,' August said.

January was almost over. The rebellion was continuing, but success seemed no nearer than it had weeks ago.

In an effort to escape the tension for a while, at dusk one

evening Sarah and August went out to the pastures to relax and watch the fireflies emitting their mysterious light. As it grew darker, the insects provided a blanket of mystical beauty as they shimmered in the cane fields. Sarah sat for the best part of the evening watching them create their universe of pretend stars and meteors: they seemed at times to vibrate along indeterminate axes. August tried to count them, but it was impossible because they darted about all the time. Instead, he decided to catch as many as he could and take them home in a glass jar. Sarah helped by pointing out places where a lot of them had settled, sometimes an island of tall fern trees soaring out of the pastures. The insects were elusive, dispersing as soon as August swooped, but nevertheless it wasn't long before he had enough blinky flies in his jar to illuminate the cabin.

When they got back to the village, they saw a group of men standing chatting by one of the huts.

Charles emerged from the group and, with a look of raw inquiry, asked, 'Sarah, did you see anything?'

'No, nothing at all,' Sarah replied apologetically.

'Not even a little smoke anywhere?'

'No, nothing,' said August.

The rest of the group had listened intently to Sarah and August. Now they started mumbling among themselves, some just kissing their teeth. Charles picked up a rock and hurled it into the ditch. The resultant ripple widened and soon vanished, seeming to symbolise all that was happening to the revolution. August felt sullen. Another day and still no sign, still no action, no change, still no sign of the beacon. The villagers' talk of burning Bardanage had become less a threat than a dream.

August could no longer bear to go up into the hills to watch for the beacon, so Sarah took Missy with her instead. As the days and weeks went by, they still had nothing to report: no blowing of shells, no slaves marching in their hundreds, no shouting, no weapons of destruction disguised as farming implements, no gunshots, no singing. August found himself growing slightly resentful of the time Sarah was spending away from the family.

One day, while chatting to Brother Bigga and a few other men, he saw her coming back from the hills and decided to confront her about it, although he hadn't taken time to think of where the argument might lead.

'What you doing up in the hills all day long?' he grumbled. 'You don't see the children waiting for their mother?'

'So where the pickny then? What yu do with Barbary?' Sarah replied. Until now she had been as calm as the cows grazing in the fields, but she felt a blood rush. She put her hands on her hips, a minatory sign.

'She with Silvia,' he responded, already wishing he had not raised the topic.

'Why man love argument so?'

'Well, what you expect me to do when you are out just lazing in the hills?'

'Empty barrel always mek the most noise.'

It was a continuation of many arguments that they had had about August palming the children off on the older villagers, whenever she went off by herself.

'I work hard for you. I raise the pickny, I raise plenty of stock and take them to market to sell. I work in your dinner-time ground. I work sometimes till the second cock crows,' she said fiercely.

August turned away to rejoin his friends.

Sarah was furious. 'No turn your back on me,' she shouted. 'Me talking to you!'

'Man, you should have fist her in her face for talking to you like that in front of we. Box her down, man!' said a tall muscular man called George Kerr.

August responded by knocking George to the ground with a short sharp hook that swung in fast, crashing against his temple. 'Don't to tell me how to deal with my woman, fool. You think my name is Willie?'

This was a reference to a negro, Willie Gardner, who had been tried for the murder of Rachel, a woman belonging to Flint River Estate. He was found guilty but given mercy because he was then only twenty-three. He had been freed a year ago. The fact that the judge freed him had been the talk of the Cove for many months; it wouldn't have happened had Rachel been white.

The other men held August back. George sprang to his feet, flashing a small blade, and roared, 'Nigger, mi going cut you.'

'Enough!' shouted Brother Bigga, tackling George from behind. Confusion reigned about who needed more restraint.

The fight ended when busha men were spotted approaching from the workhouse complex. The fact that they were being watched closely was the best sign that there was still action of some kind on the battlefront.

# Chapter 25

# Ebb Tide

THE UNCERTAINTY CONTINUED all through February; they heard nothing but vague rumours, occasionally spiced with news of a burning or a riot.

One evening in March, August came back from the fields one evening with a new treasure, a two-week-old edition of the *Royal Gazette*, hidden inside his shirt. Sarah had prepared his favourite, pea soup in a Dutch pot brimming with yam, green bananas, meat off the bone and cornmeal dumplings; she liked to see him eat well and was quick to criticise him for looking scrawny. Tonight, though, the meal would have to wait.

August headed straight for the table, fished the newspaper out of his shirt and smoothed it out on the table-top. He switched back and forth between pages, skipped the middle and eventually turned to the back page, to the section with notices about runaway slaves. Where was the news about the rebellion? He searched a little more slowly and found that he had missed a full-page article about the events of January. He read it slowly, then went back outside and asked Sarah to serve the food. She obliged.

He took a couple of slurps of the soup and sucked the goodness from the bone marrow. He bit into the cassava bread, left over from the day before and rushed it down his throat. He sipped water.

But his mind was on a vivid account of how the rebellion had spread rapidly over the parish of Trelawny; scores of slaves had taken refuge in the mountains. The maroons had gone to retrieve the situation. As a result, many of the

Trelawny rebels had been returned to their plantations to face certain punishment. With bitter resignation, he realised he would have to accept the knowledge that yet another attempt at rebellion had failed.

'What yu reading?' asked Sarah.

'The rebellion look like it done,' he said. He opened the paper again and read her a paragraph describing how the Council of War had decreed a state of martial law for the month of February. A whole month of martial law was unheard-of; no rebellion had ever warranted being taken so seriously. The curfew, the massas' curb on the comings and goings from the Estate, it all made sense, it all tied in with the war raging elsewhere in the western parishes. The fuse was lit for an explosion of slave anger that threatened the sovereignty of the island. The tranquillity of the western parishes had erupted, but the rebellion had been put down before it could reach the Cove.

'It look like we not going to hear from Daddy,' August said despondently.

'It looks so,' said Sarah.

During the next five or six weeks, a number of other newspapers turned up on the plantation, circumventing Lee's ban. But it was not until May, when the curfew had officially been lifted, that August learnt the true extent of the destruction that had been wreaked elsewhere, while Cove people slept quietly in their beds. A hundred and one plantations had been completely destroyed – their loss had affected the whole island. August read accounts of rebels put on trial, of the seven hundred and more field workers, livestock workers, tradesmen, drivers and house slaves who had been convicted and sentenced to death. One man was sentenced to five hundred lashes and another to two hundred with hard labour. Of Daddy Sharpe there was no word, except that he was being held in Montego Bay gaol awaiting trial. The outcome seemed inevitable.

On his day off, August decided to take advantage of the lifting of restraints and venture out to the road market at Orange Bay. His intention was to seek out the craftwork stalls, where he could exchange some provisions for ornaments for Sarah and maracas for John and Barbary. Hoping to hitch a lift, he was glad to see in the distance two large light brown oxen drawing a cart; he could not see who the driver was, so he carried on walking. Soon he could hear hard wooden wheels grinding over the dusty road. When the cart was within hailing distance, he looked up, ready to beg a lift. To his astonishment, the driver was Mulatto John, whom he hadn't seen since the week following Nancy's burial because he had been sold away to Mount Pleasant. They were delighted to see each other. Both had changed considerably since their last meeting. Mulatto John had lost his fresh looks; he had creased somewhat about the eyes; his hair had thinned considerably and there was little to speak of on top. August now had grey-speckled hair and had lost three teeth, one upper and two lower incisors.

August jumped up on to the cart and made himself comfortable on top of a stack of rum puncheons. Having exchanged news about their families, they went on to talk at great length about the curfew. Neither had a clear picture of what was going on. Both had heard that the rebellion had taken place, but neither was sure how it had ended. Since August's run-in with Quaco, he had kept well out of Lee's way.

In time, they reverted to more light-hearted topics. August laughed at Mulatto John's stories; the more he did, the more stories John told. One was about the time he'd fallen asleep under a guava tree; it was in the middle of the day and he was supposed to be working. One of the other slaves woke him to warn that the overseer was angrily looking for him. Mulatto John appeared before the overseer and told him straight, 'Sleep no have Massa.' If it hadn't been

233

for the fact that he'd made the overseer laugh so often, he would surely have had his back torn off him by now.

Inevitably, however, the conversation wavered from the personal to touch on the subject dear to their hearts, that of freedom.

'Mi never tell you say Sarah with child again.'

'Man, congratulations.'

'If it is a boy me going name him William.'

'What? Wilberforce?'

'No, just William Crooks.'

'But yu going name him after William Wilberforce.'

'Yes, for Mr Wilberforce is going to liberate us. Tell me if a lie.'

'Wilberforce,' Mulatto John smiled. 'Wilberforce – dat man is a good buckra; him wan' mek wi free. And if him can't get us free no oder way, we jus' have to do fi weselves – only we *Will By Force.*'

They both roared with laughter, and August tipped back so far that Mulatto John had to reach out and stop him rolling off the rum puncheons.

When they were calm again, Mulatto John said, 'Did I tell you that Massa beat fifteen of us the oder day jus' for arriving back in de fields five minutes late?'

'No.'

'Yes – five minutes. And him take the stick him have in him hand and start to beat we.'

'Oh no!'

'Oh yes.'

'That is terrible.'

'But me no finish yet; as soon as Massa turn him back, we start sing: we don't give a damn, oh! We don't give a damn. A head driver tell us to do dat. Mount Pleasant slaves, yu know, don't mess around. But you know how we stay already.'

As they crossed the spring into Pimentos Valley, August's spotted Reverend Rose heading in the opposite direction. August thought Rose might say more about the unrest, so he asked Mulatto John to stop the cart. He jumped down, exchanged a few niceties, then began to question the preacher, who leant against the wheel, accepting a drink of water from a calabash Mulatto John offered him.

'Massa,' said August, 'so tell me what did really happen that other day over in St James. You is the only one that know for sure.'

'Well, I understand that discontent among the slaves at Salt Spring Estate in St James was where the first strike was reported. There was no fire but the Western Interior Regiment was sent to deal with any problem. On Boxing Day the rebels burnt the trash-house at the York Estate. The regiment stationed at York apparently withdrew. There were also the five hundred men at Lapland who, I'm told, had bound the York slaves by a solemn oath to obtain their freedom or die in the attempt. Strange, because it wasn't as if property owners didn't know that something was about to happen, but I suppose nobody took it seriously – I don't know for sure.'

As if talking of fire made him thirsty, the Reverend held up the calabash for Mulatto John to replenish. He went on to tell them of the torching of Kensington and Belvedere estates, where white men were put to death. There had been fires all over Westmoreland, and rebel numbers grew by the hour. The maroons were called in to help the whites. Remarkably, there was a report of a white man who had helped negro Baptist preachers escape arrest.

The rebels weren't all men; there were women too. They marched to the sound of *abeng*s; wind instruments made of eight or nine inches of the small horn of the cow, with a pea-sized hole in the tip. When many were blown at once, they could be heard for miles.

'So they were coming this way?' August asked.

In his excitement he took the calabash from the

Reverend's hand, drank from it and gave it back. The Reverend looked astonished. He wiped the opening of the container and returned it to Mulatto John, looking sharply at August. Realising that drinking from the same vessel had caused offence, August apologised. The Reverend continued. He told them that the rebels had headed towards the western tip of the island and would have reached the Cove had they not inexplicably changed course at Hazelymph. They had thought they could defeat the St James militia; they were wrong.

'Reverend,' said August, 'you said that the rebellion was heading this way, then change direction. Why?'

'That I don't know.'

'No?'

'Is it important?'

'No,' August said, withdrawing a couple of steps. 'And what about the maroons? Did them help capture any rebels?'

'Yes, they did. A party of Accompong maroons captured nineteen rebels somewhere along the Great River between Unity Hall and Eldersley. That same day they brought the ears of eight negroes and another twenty-seven prisoners in addition to the nineteen. And they travelled to other towns to help quell the rebellion. I don't know the details.' He paused to think what other news he could tell them. 'Oh yes. The rebel they called Captain Dehany – he was a rebel sent from hell, I have heard it said. He shot the overseer of one of the estates in the neck and kept him prisoner in a cave for several days. The overseer's brother had his head chopped off before the overseer's very eyes. The overseer died soon after he was found by the militia. Dehany was executed, like many of the leaders. Then there was Patrick Ellis. The militia apparently surrounded him. They say he stepped up, bared his breast and told them, "Give me your best volley. Fire, for I will never again be a slave." '

'So how many negro man did get executed?'

'I can't say for sure. I can only talk about Hanover, for it is my parish. What I do know is that ninety-six of one hundred and thirty-eight were sentenced to death. I know that one person got three months' imprisonment with three hundred lashes at the beginning and two hundred at the end. Others sentences were variations on this. I can also tell you that outbreaks occurred all over the island. Heads were exhibited in parts of another parish, Portland, I think. In the public square in the centre of Montego Bay, I myself witnessed the sight of gibbets and the bodies of executed men suspended, stiff in the still air. Their necks were contorted and stretched by gravity's force – ghastly. Many of those being taken to their execution remained as calm as if they were going to their daily toil in the fields. Incredible. That negro Dehany I told you about, he refused to incriminate his Baptist missionary friend Burchell – you might have heard of him, August?'

August knew the name but had never met him. 'No.' He nodded to keep the Reverend flowing.

'When they tried to execute Dehany, they found it as difficult as trying to capture him in the first place. His powerful frame broke the rope as he almost died. Would you believe that they had to revive him before bringing another rope to complete his execution?'

'What of the preacher Samuel Sharpe?'

'Executed. He was defiant to the end. My friend and Methodist missionary Henry Bleby was with him to the end and thought him extremely courageous though, to some extent, naive.'

'Did he say anything before he died?' Mulatto John asked.

'Chu, man,' chided August, 'how Reverend Rose supposed to know that?'

'Actually, I do,' the Reverend said, his voice jittery. 'Bleby told me. I made a note of it somewhere.' He opened his Bible and a folded piece of paper fell from it. He picked

237

it up and read, 'Sharpe said, "I depend on salvation, upon the Redeemer, who shed His blood upon Calvary for sinners."' Rose paused, then slipped the note back into the Bible. 'Sharpe could have been a great man, but surely he knew that what he did went against God and the laws of this land, that it was wrong?' The Reverend had lost the thread of what he was saying. He looked down, his face full of sadness.

Mulatto John and August exchanged glances.

August ventured to offer what he felt – and what he believed Rose knew deep in his heart. 'Daddy was capable of noble things. If he had been set free, he would have commanded another struggle for freedom. He wouldn't have stopped until we poor could earn a little money for ourselves, until we could look white folk in the eye as one equal to another without fear of the whip, without fear of losing everything we have: our family, our lives. Sharpe, he a great man – and I don't care what anybody says.'

Rose did not dissent but smiled and nodded absently.

August sensed that the Reverend wanted to be on his way. He had just one question left. 'So what do you think is going to happen now?'

'I don't really know. What I can tell you is that Hanover and St James have been largely destroyed.'

# Chapter 26

# New Order

LEE AND JONES sat grim-faced on the veranda of Bardanage with their feet up on the balustrade. Barely a word passed between them for a whole hour; they stared dispiritedly out at the specks of dark – labourers – sprinkled randomly among the cane pieces. Lee had just returned from Kingston, from a meeting with Neil McCullum to discuss the mortgage on the Estate. 'Absenteeism' was the word that preoccupied the lenders. It referred to the landlords who were fleeing the island in droves. Attorneys like Lee now ran an ever-increasing number of estates, and they were being blamed for the high proportion of sugar plantations that had gone into receivership. Planters up and down the country were talking about bleak prospects for an island economy in recession.

Lee shifted despondently in his chair. 'Westmoreland, Hanover, St James, St Elizabeth, Trelawny – the damage done runs into millions of pounds,' he told Jones. He reached for a jug of cane juice and refilled their glasses.

'Were they all field negroes?' Jones asked.

'Mostly. They say just over half of them.'

'Just over half?'

'That's right. They say there were more than twenty thousand of them on the rampage – and that's just a conservative guess. The other half was made up of every kind of slave, from watchmen to cartmen to house slaves and even skilled tradesmen.'

'It's more serious than we thought, then.'

'Yes, much more.'

'They should bloody well hang every last one of 'em,' said Jones.

There was an uncharacteristic air of resignation about Lee as he pondered the implications of such a move: 'So where do you think that would put us?'

'We could import men from England,' said Jones.

'What, and pay them? We're already losing the price war, and that's with free labour. I don't think so.'

'Hmm. Maybe not, then.'

There was another long silence until Lee finished his drink. It was Jones's turn to top up the glasses. He was about to do so when Missy came along from the side of the house. She turned to go up the stairs and inside. Lee put out his hand to stop Jones pouring the drinks, and called Missy back to do it. He saw, as if in a nightmare, the time when she would perform the task of her own free will, not as subjugated slave. He gestured to her to place the drinks in their hands. Once she had done so, he sent her away.

Turning back to Jones, Lee said, 'In the beginning there was the white indentured servant, now there are none. Those days will never return.'

'Oh, this will pass. Let's not forget how quiet the western parishes were before all this started.' Jones seemed desperate for a seed of optimism.

'It won't pass. This is just the beginning.'

Jones looked at him questioningly.

'You see, there were serious outbreaks all over. All the way down to the two parishes farthest from the fighting.'

'What, Portland and St Thomas?'

'Yes. It was full civil war.'

'Heavens!'

Lee got up and shook his head. With his hands on his hips, he stared out towards a group of field labourers moving wagons in and out of the fields, 'We're in a right bloody mess.' He was gripping the balustrade so tightly that his knuckles were white. Then he swung around to face Jones. 'Maybe we should think seriously about following all the other absentee proprietors back to England.'

They both knew, though, that in England it would be difficult to maintain the standard of living to which they were accustomed, and reflected further on the possibility of return.

Jones toyed with the sharp bristles on his face; he hadn't shaved for a week. 'You're right, it's a bloody mess. It's up to the Assembly to make sure that this never happens again.'

'Huh! They've been trying for half a century, and they'll be trying for another century – of that I'm sure.'

'Why do you say that?'

Lee sat down again and stared westward towards the village, which brought the slave burial grounds to mind. He saw Mr Ritchie leaving the village, and said, 'Did I ever tell you why I got rid of Frazer?'

'Remind me.'

'Well, yes, but Mr Ritchie will recall better than I.' Lee summoned the distant figure with a wave. While they waited for Ritchie, Lee found himself thinking of Sarah Brown's mother. He said, 'Ami Brown was Frazer's personal project. He was supposed to tame the beast that dwelt within her. He failed – badly. But it wasn't just that. Ritchie told me of days when he would pass Frazer and Ami in the fields – go on, Mr Ritchie, tell us what you used to see.'

'Oh. She was the Devil incarnate, that one. Something evil lurked beneath that skin of hers, as it does with all the Obeah witches. You could see her body getting weak, but it was as if the evil was transferring away from her into the other blackies who would stand around observing the two of them – that's Frazer and her I mean. He was under her curse. Whatever he did to her served to make her witchcraft more powerful. That's how it seemed, anyway. There were times when we – Mr Lee and I – used to stand on the

241

veranda here, watching the slaves watching Frazer at work. Then the negroes would talk among themselves.'

'That's right,' said Lee. 'You see, Jones, Frazer provided all the evidence I needed to show that, even if we had an island full of hardy overseers like him, we still could not turn back the tidal wave of change. I learnt that from Reverend Rose. I hated him for saying it – even stopped attending his church – but it was true. Frazer was sacked for being too bloody committed. He was of no further use.'

'In Frazer's time,' said Ritchie, 'severe punishment was the only deterrent we had at our disposal. Nowadays it's a catalyst; it fuels negro rage. In the time it took him to break one inferior field slave, he bred ten more young rebels. He had to go, right, Mr Lee?'

'That's right, Mr Ritchie.'

'So why me, Mr Lee?' asked Jones. 'I have, and always will have, great respect for the methods used by men like Mr Frazer.'

'Well, you see, when Frazer left discipline on the Estate went to rack and ruin. The slaves became slack, given to disobedience – much more so than usual. I have a reputation to uphold, you know. It would be an overstatement to say that I was wrong getting rid of Frazer. But, as I said, we needed some fresh blood around here. People like your good self bring modern ideas about negro control.'

It was a hazy September day. August stood cradling his new son, William, in one arm while he tried to read the *Royal Gazette*. It had come from Reverend Rose by way of Hellina a quarter of an hour earlier. She had told him, in a manner befitting a wild hog and out of tune with her character, to 'read it'. Not liking her tone one bit, he folded it up, looked her up and down and sniffed at her before sauntering off. He turned his head enough to steal a look at her. Seeing her smirk, he realised there was something she had not told him. But his mood was such that he was not to be played with. Ever since the previous May he had been thinking about the news that he'd heard from Missy, who had heard it from McFarlane, who had heard it straight from Charles, that the buckra gentlemen in England were passing new laws to end slavery. The word was that it was only a matter of time before slaves would wipe out all the plantations and leave nothing in their wake. The talk among black folk everywhere was that the Assembly had handled things so badly that the British government was planning to force their hand.

Right now, these thoughts were intermingled with attending to his children. Barbary entertained herself, her only desire to see her baby brother smile. She performed a somersault and then a cartwheel. She laughed and the baby kicked and giggled. Barbary was encouraged to repeat her feat. She kept the child entertained. All the time their father was performing the delicate act of turning the newspaper pages with one hand, while keeping his son absolutely still in the crook of his other arm. He thought he'd perfected the act with Barbary and Little John, but today it wasn't working quite so well. Baby William reached upward as if trying to touch a few of the tightly curled hairs on his father's chest.

And then August found it: an article that said everything he had ever wanted to hear. It said that slavery had been abolished; that Prime Minister Lord Grenville had said it was contrary to the principles of justice, humanity and sound policy; that plantation owners faced ruin; that freedom had come – freedom at long last. Moved beyond measure, August dropped slowly to his knees and buried his face in the dust. When he straightened up, there were tears of joy in his eyes. He gave praise. He felt the warmth of his son's compact body against his ribs and kissed him twice. 'Freedom come, freedom come, Hallelujah, freedom come. Boy, you are a free child now. Thank God you don't

243

have to go through what we have gone through. Son, you are free.'

Later, August went over to Bardanage. When he arrived, Lee was just coming out of the front door, with Charles behind him. August told them the news and showed them the article.

As he read it Charles turned to Lee with a big smile. 'Is it true that we are free?'

'Bloody hell, news travels fast around here!' said Lee. 'Not free exactly.'

'What you mean?' Charles's smile widened.

'Well, the law doesn't change until April next year. You still have to work like a good nigger until then.'

'I know that, but thank you all the same.'

'Why?' asked Lee, puzzled.

'Is the first time me ever hear you say the words that freedom soon come. It sound so sweet, coming from you.'

'If you know that, you also know that you're all going to have to serve as apprentices for six years after that.'

'So?' The smile disappeared.

'Well, as far as I'm concerned you're all still slaves. You'll labour as such for six years – until around 1840, by my reckoning,' said Lee.

'Why?'

'Why? Because blackies need preparation to go it alone, by their reckoning.'


The day felt much like any other. The work was as hard as ever: holes to be dug and fields to be weeded. Little had changed on the surface. But this was the apprenticeship period, a time of real change, and of painful adjustment, for white society.

In the heat of the day, August sat on a fence out by the pens, watching the cattle grazing in the fields. He was chewing a piece of grass and swung a long stick in his hand like a pendulum. Every now and again he used it to take a swipe at mosquitoes as they hovered about him. His throat felt full, so he hawked up a viscous ball of phlegm and spat it all of five yards into the growth of grass and weed. The transparent globule hung for a while until it dripped slowly, waiting to be dried out by the sun.

August was minded of changes that were taking place in villagers' attitudes. He was amused at the sight of book-keepers making doubly sure that the labour was intense. The new laws required that the whip be banned from the plantation, and this was perhaps the most symbolic gesture. It was noticeable how withdrawn Quaco had become. He had been stripped of any vestige of power and was now an outcast, ineffective in discharging his duties as a driver. Any attempt to tell anyone what to do was met with the kissing of teeth; young men feigned backhand slaps towards him. Labourers seemed relaxed and in reasonably good spirits.

Then a number of less agreeable changes were introduced. First, Lee decreed that the villagers would no longer have Friday afternoons free, which meant they found it even more difficult to devote time to their provision grounds. Next, it was announced that they would lose their weekly entitlement to saltfish, as they were no longer slaves in the eyes of their masters. These measures were the last straw. Slaves once again talked of the possibility of insurrection. Once more, feelings ran high: the air was tense with the rumours of yet more outbreaks; masters and attorneys slept with their eyes open and their guns beside their beds.

August saw a bookkeeper approaching. It was Ritchie.

'August, what are you doing lazing around out here by yourself? I thought I told you to go and help Cuffee finish thatching the mill-house. Cuffee needs help, boy.' Richie scowled.

Turning away, August explained that his back was aching.

'Boy, get out and do some work. Now!'

'Who are you calling "bwoy"?' For a split second August saw Ami's face.

Ritchie flushed and raised his fist. August beat him to the punch, banging his knuckles square into the bookkeeper's face. Ritchie went down, crashing his head against the ground. Dazed fear registered in his face. August looked defiantly down on him.

Blood trickled from the bridge of Ritchie's nose down on to his lips, his chin and his white shirt; his nose was broken. August was excited and wanted a good reason to dish out more. But it was not to be.

Ritchie slid back to a safe distance a few feet away, and slowly got up. 'You've just made the worst mistake of your life. You'll pay for this, blacky.'

Sarah was surprised to see the magistrate entering the village in his horse-drawn cart and going towards Bardanage; she was shocked when Missy told her that he had come for August; and she cried when she heard what August had done.

'Mother,' she begged silently, 'don't let them do it. Don't let them take him away from me like they did you.'

She ran to him as fast as she dared, mindful that baby William was wrapped tightly on her back. Andries followed her. They reached the cart and Sarah went to the front and stood there, begging that August not be harmed. She panicked when she saw the vacant expression on his face. For the first time, all his years of bondage were etched on his brow.

'Take the child back to the hut,' he said impassively, as if resigned to his fate. 'Don't worry, slavery days done. Them can't do me any wrong. Mi soon come. Andries, make sure you look out for the older boy. Make sure him don't get into trouble. Make sure him listen to his mother.

'Sarah, I want you to ask Reverend Stones to baptise the

children in his church. Mi no want to keep bothering Reverend Rose. You think that's a good idea?'

Sarah nodded in silence, then moved to one side to let the magistrate's men continue their journey.

As the days went by and there was no word of August's fate, Sarah worked herself to a standstill, from stress, baby-minding and endless domestic chores. While doing the washing one morning, she realised that she was close to exhaustion. She couldn't think clearly; her mind kept drifting.

There was a sudden wail from Barbary: 'Gimme it back!'

Sarah looked up and saw Little John run round the side of the hut, waving a half-eaten mango over his head. Barbary was in hot and tearful pursuit.

'John,' called Sarah, 'behave yourself and give the pickny back her mango – chu!'

John ignored her and kept running. Sarah ripped off her headscarf, unveiling her matted crown of dark brown hair. She whirled one end of the cloth through the air; holding on tightly to the other end, she brought it down in a stinging slap across John's back. He skidded to a halt and the mango squeezed out of his hand and landed in the dust. There was a pause while Barbary gazed down at her soother, now uneatable, then renewed wails.

'Lord Jesus, pickny, stop the crying!' said Sarah wearily. She told John to go and pick another mango for the child. 'Make sure that it is as sweet as the last, otherwise me going break your backside.'

John set off at a run, not looking where he was going, and almost bumped into Sis Bell as she came through the garden.

'So what?' she said, grabbing his arm and clipping him across the head. 'You don't have any manners? Say excuse.'

'Excuse me,' and John ran off.

Sis Bell turned to Sarah. 'Lord, child, you look terrible.'

247

'Is these children. Me can't tek them no more.'

'Sarah, why yu don't go look for your man?' Sis Bell picked William out of his crib and held him to her breast.

'Me no know fi sure whether him is alive; anyway, me not sure where him is. And the children . . .'

'No worry about the children. Me will take care of them for a few days. Anyway, Andries dying to be godfather to the likkle boy John. When him going get baptised? You have a date yet?'

'Yes. All three going get baptised together, on Christmas Day.'

'Good. Anyway, might as well the boy stay with Brother Andries for a likkle while? The boy turn so wayward.'

Sarah took Sis Bell's advice and decided to make the trip to the workhouse in Westmoreland. She cried all the way, for she knew she might not get to see August; she was, at best, hoping to find out whether he was alive.

When she arrived, she saw two black men standing to attention at the gate. She told them that she had come a long way and had food for the one called John Alexander Crooks, but they had orders not to let non-whites pass. Sarah pleaded with the taller of the two, but he did not know how flexibly he was allowed to interpret those orders, and merely referred her to the shorter, a man called Clarkey.

'Do you have any official pass?' Clarkey enquired.

'I am a free Miss.' Sarah showed them the blue cross on her left shoulder.

'Miss, where are your official papers of entry to the workhouse? That is what I asked you for. I didn't ask you to tell me of your status, Madam.' He turned to his colleague: 'Why do these people always think people must bow to them?'

'Listen, Mr Speakey Spokey, it mus' be because you have a uniform on that you think you can talk to people anyhow you like.'

An exchange of insults, and then a cursing-match, ensued. But she had failed in her mission. Sick at heart, she turned away.

Sarah hitched a lift on a cart for the last five miles of the journey back to the Cove. She got off half a mile from Cousins' Cove and dragged herself wearily over the west side of the hill, past Bardanage.

She noticed for the first time how run-down the great house looked. The grain in the woodwork showed where the paint had been stripped away, eroded by years of the salty ocean breeze blowing in. The house could easily have been mistaken for one of the sugar plantation workhouses. She ran her hand along the railing fence and felt the dry flecks of blue paint peel away under her hand, collecting in the creases of her skin. The wood itself had turned a greyish brown and the grain had separated, allowing the wind and rain to weaken it even more. The fence had not been painted or repaired since the hurricane of 1815, one of the fiercest in living memory.

'Jus' look how the place look mash up, merciful Jesus, what a way it look bad,' she said to herself. She stepped back a few paces until the house was in full view. The posts at the front were tilting slightly where the joins had weakened, and a thick covering of dirt masked the splendour of what it once had been. Lee didn't care. He owned property elsewhere and spent most of his time away, just as the previous few owners had done. He turned up only occasionally, during the working day, to see to the Estate's business affairs. Massa Neil McCullum was supposed to return and do something with the place but rarely did he set foot on the property. So rarely, in fact, that no one was sure whether he spent any time on the island at all. Jones was putting himself about in much the same way as Lee.

Sarah saw a big crack in the ground-floor window at the side of the house, one she hadn't noticed before. She went to take a closer look, and heard voices inside the house. 'Ah, this sounds promising,' she thought. To her astonishment, the first voice she recognised was that of Neil McCullum, executor for the Estate since the death of his brother almost ten years ago.

'Twenty-six pounds, fifteen shillings and tuppence three-farthings a head – for field labourers? That is utter nonsense! Go back and tell your boss, whoever he is, that I want an average price of eighty pounds a head. How dare you come on my land with such an uneducated proposal? And you want to give me four pounds, six and eightpence for my aged, diseased and non-effective slaves, even though they're completely worthless. Where is the method in your madness, man? Compensation – compensation, you call this! You clearly have no idea of what you're talking about. Bastard, get off my land. Away with you!'

McCullum sounded ill as well as angry. Overcome by curiosity, Sarah peeked through the broken window. McCullum was unhealthily flushed, and the other man, presumably a valuer, looked dumbfounded.

'What was that all about?'

Wallace's voice from behind made Sarah jump. He had sneaked up behind her so quietly that he had caught her completely unawares.

She drew a deep breath in fear of what might happen, and babbled, 'Please, Massa, mi was only inspecting the crack in this glass, me wasn't listening, really me wasn't, mi swear 'pon my madda's grave,' she babbled.

She needn't have worried, for Wallace was one for counting fowl rather than chasing workers around the Estate imploring them to do work.

He smiled kindly at her and said, 'I think not. So what are they talking about?'

'I t'ink them a talk 'bout slaves. Massa McCullum want a good money when the slaves walk free.'

'Oh yes, there's a lot of talk about compensation. Vulgar,' said Wallace.

'How yu mean?' Sarah asked.

'Oh, merely that in a decent and just world, it would be the slaves who received compensation. Don't you agree?'

Sarah stared uncertainly at him.

# Chapter 27

# A New Dawn

WHEN AUGUST RETURNED to Cousins' Cove he felt physically and mentally broken. He stood by the roadside, as forlorn as an abandoned cart dumped there for the elements to decide its fate. The sun was going down behind him and he stared blankly at his shadow stretching across the ground, then looked slowly along the course of the stream leading to the cattle mill wheel. He wore the same faraway expression as he had worn when taken away. Now, however, he also wore the workhouse chains with which the gaolers had seen fit to ornament him – a leaving present of sorts.

The first person to spot him was Sis Bell. 'My Lord Sweet Jesus!' she shrieked, covering her mouth with both hands. All the villagers within earshot instantly came running up.

'Quick, get Nero. Get him to cut off the chains,' someone shouted. Brother Bigga said he'd go, and would also tell Sarah that August was back. He raced off.

Nero the blacksmith soon came trundling up with his hacksaws, hammers and other tools. He cursed when he saw the state August was in, and set instantly to work. Within minutes the chains lay in the dirt, in pieces. Nero kicked them angrily aside with his bare feet.

Sarah arrived. When she saw August she stopped dead, horrified, on the edge of the group. Her eyes met August's and she moved tentatively towards him. He looked down; during his months of incarceration he had so longed to see her that her actual presence here in front of him was almost more than he could take. His rigidly controlled face gave no inkling at first that he had registered her presence; not until he was at home with his family and his closest friends would he be able to express, through smiles and tears, the joy he felt.

Sarah, too, was too overwhelmed to show her joy. August tracked her as she began circling him, looking him up and down. He wondered what she might be thinking of him standing there, his sweat-soaked shirt covered in grit and bloodied by unattended wounds. The breeze rose, ballooning his shirt like the sails of a schooner in the high winds and soothing his soreness – a rare relief from pain. Standing as still as a statue, he held his sodden shirt away from his skin until the breeze dropped. Sarah gently eased her hands under his armpits; her hands took the form of crow's claws turned towards the heavens. Exhausted, August collapsed into her arms.

This was the cue for the villagers to help Sarah take him home where he could heal.

August had more or less recovered within three weeks. He was set immediately to work, helping a young man named Richard Pierce bring in copper wood. This was less strenuous than the tasks he had spent most of his life doing; but now he was nearing forty-eight, old for a praedial labourer.

Richard bored him with talk about the first thing he would do when freed. He said he would go and look for his father, a negro sold away to a plantation somewhere in Westmoreland.

August's mind went straight to thoughts of villagers past. 'What happened to Charlotte's two little girls, Belinda and Mary, after they were sold to Massa Neil Malcolm?' he asked. 'Boy, that must be well over twenty years now.'

'What you say?' Richard said.

'Massa John just sold them – he punished Charlotte for her husband's wrongdoing. By now those girls have probably bred a whole heap of coloured pickny.'

253

They were having different conversations, Richard still rooted in thoughts of his own freedom. 'Me hear dat dere is a lot of talk 'bout setdown – a proper strike,' he said.

'Mi hear that, too,' said August.

'Yu think dem should fight?'

'What for? You no see that emancipation soon come?'

'Yes, but dat too far away, Bredda August.'

'Chu, you don't read the papers?' August turned his back on Richard.

'After me can't read. You know how many of us would like to be as fortunate as you.'

August kept quiet for a while, realising that his allusion to reading had been less than tactful. But when he had finished tying his bundle of wood, he volunteered, 'Brother Richard, I read the people are ready to fight. In St Kitt's, they are already refusing to work under apprenticeship. They have their own Daddy Sharpe down there. For these reasons, apprenticeship going finish much sooner than you expect. It not going finish in three years' time. Buckra is ready to free us so that we can go and earn a righteous pay. Emancipation will come next year. That is official.' He dwelt on each syllable of that last word, then added, 'You know, it wouldn't do any harm to let all the Massas know that the people are not afraid to give them some bother-ation, every now and then. Make them know that the black man don't joke.'

August bent to his work again, feeling his stiffened joints cry out for rest. He felt old and weary. He had done what he had done in the name of emancipation. The fire that had for so long raged inside him was now little more than a flicker.

1838

A procession of ox-drawn carts made slow progress along the narrow stony road, the procession stretching some hundred yards. In the carts were sugar hogsheads and a large consignment of rum puncheons. They were about a mile out of Cousins' Cove and moving towards Black River, the trade and business hub of the parish of St Elizabeth, to deposit a supply of port for export.

Leading the way with his oxen was a brown man called Thomas Dickson. The sleeves of his baggy linen shirt were rolled up past his elbows and his trouser-legs above his knees. He was tugging at two long ropes attached to the horns of his oxen, which had a long, thick stake laid across their necks to keep them together.

Parishioners lined the road. The leaves of the coconut trees on either side of the road met in the middle, forming a shady tunnel along which the labourers marched.

August walked at the back, nodding acknowledgement as he passed people along the road. Not that he knew them – most faces were unfamiliar; it was merely the usual courtesy and respect country folk accorded one another.

Further along they passed through some woodland. Through a break in the trees, August saw a number of people standing talking animatedly. He recognised them as his church brethren, and Reverend Rose was in their midst. He called out to them and they beckoned him over. August asked someone to cover for him while he took time out.

A dark man with a rasping lisp was the current centre of attention. His name was October. 'We jus' talking freedom talk,' he said excitedly.

August passed on to them something Lee had told the villagers a few days ago. He had said that the Cove people would be free to leave the property on the first day of August. He told them that they would all become waged. The head men would receive a small increase in their current allowance. The wage would be one pound, the rent eight pounds a year. Eviction notices had been served on Andries and Sis Bell's boys, because they told him that they would not work.

255

'The fact is, many of the estates were unviable, even with free labour,' said Reverend Rose.

'They are all robbers, thieves and liars,' scowled August. 'I can't take the Cove any more. It looks as if my eviction paper will soon come.'

'The Reverend say we don't have to worry about what buckra is offering,' someone commented.

Reverend Rose was excited. He explained how eager the planters all over the island were to sell their land and properties.

'So what good is that to we poor black people?' asked August.

'All you haffi do is partner with a few people,' said October.

He explained that the poor black folk were beginning to pool their money on a scale never before attempted – sometimes as many as fifty people were involved. August nodded: this was similar to what the village people did back in his homeland. Every week, October went on, after market people would contribute whatever they could afford to the partnership, and every week the pooled money would be given to a particular person, who would use it to buy land. That person would continue to contribute in the normal way and the next week someone else would buy a neighbouring plot of land. And so it would continue until everyone had a chance to acquire their own plot with their own house. The outcome would be the establishment of a new village. Partnerships were springing up everywhere.

'Massa hate we for doing it. You watch, them soon will stop we,' said a voice from the back.

'That can't work. Me hear that the new executor, William Gordon, wants to sell the land, all one thousand six hundred acres, all in one go. Which partner can afford that?'

'Missionary churches,' said Reverend Rose.

'How?'

'Our church is buying many of the small to medium-sized plantations and selling them to negroes for reasonable prices so that villages can be set up. We are dividing up the land and selling it in small lots.'

August looked disbelievingly at the him. 'I am nothing but a humble servant of the Lord – and negro slave at that. I don't have the education that you have, but even I can see that you can't buy up all the land in one go. And the church would be lucky if it could buy a tiny piece of land on the Cove.'

Rose's excitement diminished markedly, and he admitted that it would take months, even years, to happen.

'What will happen in a few months, when people get thrown off the land? Where will they go?' August asked.

'Squat, of course,' October replied.

That was not what August had expected to hear, and not an idea with which he felt comfortable. Reverend Rose simply pretended he hadn't heard.

'What else people doing?' asked August.

'A lotta people prepare to buil' a life for demselves far up into the hills,' said October. He chewed his bottom lip tensely for a moment, then went on in a quick, low voice. 'When yu t'ink 'bout it, it mek lotta sense. What if one day, soon, buckra decide fi change his mind? How we know dat we were not free a long time ago, and dat buckra changed them mind? Better, safer, to run to de hills. Dat way them can't find us easily. Dis is the plan of the masses. And I t'ink dat's what me going to do. Freedom no come every day. Take it and run.'

August liked the idea and wanted to hear more, but the procession was almost out of sight and he would have to hurry to catch it up. He said no more except that he hoped to speak to Reverend Rose again soon.

When August arrived back at the Cove he was tired. He passed Sarah outside the cabin relaxing with the children. She nodded to him as he slipped by. Inside the hut, he sat down on the floor and put his head between his hands. Endless possibilities crossed his mind. Being so close to freedom, yet so far from it, was torment. Although he felt a fragile attachment to the village, he was consumed by a desire to leave this part of his life behind for ever. He prayed for strength and guidance to have the courage to do God's will in taking his next step.

He closed his eyes and tried to clear his mind. Faces, some only hazily remembered, began to form in his imagination and memory: Samson; then Allick and Hopey; with a quiver, he remembered Franky's broken spirit and those of all the black men who had had their families torn away, of the women who had been torn from their menfolk.

*'Take Sarah and the children and go.'*

He put his hands behind his neck and caressed the craggy waxed scars on his shoulders.

'Mother Ami, I will do that.'

# Chapter 28

# Free-Paper Come

SARAH WAS UP early. The July sun would soon grow hot, and she had washing to do, the last before the celebrations began: it was the eve of emancipation. She removed dry clothes from the previous wash, folded them neatly and put them away in an old wooden chest.

August joined her, stretching and wiping the sleep out of his eyes. She asked him to get John and William up – Barbary had already been woken by barking dogs – and take them all down to the river to wash. August cheerfully agreed, clapping his hands as he went back inside.

'Mi no want to work in the fields today,' John protested, still more asleep than awake.

'Get up!' Sarah shouted, looking at him through the window.

'Why do you have to shout so much?' asked August.

'Because the children no hear when me talk.'

'Yes, but do you have to wake up the whole village? You're getting like Susan James. The two of you have mouths like horn. Chu!' His face contorted with annoyance.

August duly took the children to the creek to bathe. On their return they found clean linen and their best clothes laid out for them. As soon as they were dressed, they sat down and waited for Sarah to dish up the ackee and saltfish with piping hot breadfruit. August said grace before the family began their breakfast.

'What yu going do today, August?' Sarah asked.

'I'm going over to Harding to talk to some people to

259

work out plans for this evening. Lucea is going to be packed. We need to set off early. I'm going to see if I can get Brother Campbell to give us a ride in.'

'Don't forget to tell them that I still have some money to give him for the rice he did buy me the other day.'

'Don't worry 'bout that, I've taken care of it already.'

The celebrations were expected to go on into the next morning and even through to noon. They would return, sleep, and then go over to the church in Green Bay – an American Baptist was preaching there. Like many, August and Sarah planned to renew celebrations the following evening, so most of the day was taken up with preparing plenty of food. August helped gather what few possessions they had, so that they would be ready to leave the Cove the day after emancipation. Other villagers were performing similar tasks and were calling on each other for help. The animals, too, had to be looked after. The fields were deserted.

August had organised a party of some thirty people to go to Lucea. The roads were crowded, everybody criss-crossing and moving in different directions to the place where they would bring in the new dawn. When they came in sight of the town, children who had never seen it before screamed in excitment and awe at the night view of the harbour with its glinting reflections of lights from houses around the bay.

Halfway down the hill was the church. Rarely did black folk go there to worship, but this was a special night and the doors were flung open to all. The church was full, but people were still arriving for the service. Everyone was dressed in their best; everyone was courteous, with no pushing or shoving. There was a feeling of unity. Everything was surprisingly calm. There were only hours to go until emancipation.

August entered the church, clutching Sarah's hand. He looked around but didn't see anyone he recognised, so struck up a conversation with a young man who was sitting nearby with his wife and four children. The young man explained that he was a labourer on the Miller coffee and pimento plantation, where his Massa was trying to force him to stay and work. He said he had just now decided to stay, in the hope that things would get better. Sarah sensed that August wanted to persuade him to alter his views, and begged him not to interfere. August assured her that he had only one thing to say to the young man.

'Think about what freedom really means. You and your children's children will never release the bilboes if you decide to continue to work for Massa. You have been taught to depend on Massa and to do nothing for yourself. You will tell your children the same thing, I know. And they will tell their children what you told them. I am African, so I am already blessed with knowledge of a better way. My children won't depend on anybody for anything. God bless you and your family, and everything that you do.'

Out to sea the sky was bright with haze. August, Sarah and the children travelled back to the Cove in Campbell's wagon. They were silent and pensive.

August's mind was full of conflicting thoughts about the choices they had made and could have made, and he was sure Sarah's was, too. They would be leaving all security behind. If sickness should befall them in the hills, what would they do? They would be stranded. How would they find food when there was none? Who would help maintain the routes to other settlements? How would they get tools to work the land?

There were too many imponderables they couldn't bear to talk about in detail. When they did talk, it was about the hope of starting a new life and what it would mean for the children. Whatever happened to them all from here on was down to them. As the cart rumbled along, August noticed Sarah looking every so often at the hills and forests

261

on the horizon, the wilderness. He knew she believed him when he told her that after the celebrations were over life would be hard. They wouldn't have to rise at the sound of the bell, but they would still have to rise early each morning to cultivate the land, and they would work harder than they had ever done with a Massa standing over them with a whip. But, though life was hard, they would make it fruitful. One day, their children would know true freedom.

He smiled at Sarah and said, 'We should be back before evening.' He reflected for a couple of minutes on times past. 'Do you know, when I first came to this country I travelled this very same road. I just remembered that the first mill-house I ever saw was somewhere along this stretch. My head was hurting, and so were my back and my heart. Let this be the last time I travel this road.'

At noon on the day after emancipation day Reverend Rose rode over to the Cove, looking for August. He found many people making ready to move out. Everywhere there were carts stacked with a lifetime's possessions. The villagers' happiness at emancipation was mixed with sadness as people who were leaving said their goodbyes to those who were staying. Many of them would probably never see one another again. They hugged, shook hands and exchanged gifts, while children played as usual, blissfully unaware of the new epoch in their lives.

The Reverend found August's cabin deserted, and worried that he might have missed him. He saw Archie McIntyre looking out of his cabin next door, and called to him, 'Where are August and Sarah and the children?'

'Gone about fifteen minutes ago, after the prayer meeting.'

'Which way?'

'Them gone Savanna La Mar direction.'

The Reverend turned his horse and cantered off towards

262

the road. He soon came in sight of August, driving slowly along in an ox-cart Mr Wallace had sold him for next to nothing. Wallace was himself heading for Australia. The Reverend called out and August stopped.

A little out of breath, Rose panted, 'You didn't say goodbye.'

'I asked Reverend Stone to pass on our best wishes.'

'So where are you going?'

'Jerusalem Mountains. We're going to put those big mountains between us and this place. We're God-fearing and we never want to set eyes 'pon hell again.'

'Jerusalem Mountains,' echoed Rose. 'To do what?'

'To farm. They say buckra never did get deep into the hills to cultivate. They say there's a lot of land up there that doesn't belong to anybody. We're going to capture land, you know, make something for ourselves.'

'You'll be in a difficult position the day you're found with property you can't lay title to.'

'There will always be obstacles put in front of us to stop us moving forward. Nothing is going to change. We will just trust in the Lord. He will protect us.'

'He will, I'm sure. Good luck'

'Black people will never have that.'

Rose took a piece of paper from his pocket and scribbled a name on it. 'Here,' he said, handing it to August. 'The Reverend Henry Clarke is a missionary, a good friend of mine. He and some others from his mission have managed to acquire quite a bit of land up in the hills of Westmoreland, some of it not far from Jerusalem. Just mention his name to anybody in those parts. When you see him, say you're a friend of mine.'

'Thank you, Reverend. That's very kind of you.'

'Don't mention it. I shall remember you and your family in my prayers, always. God bless you.'

Reverend Rose stepped up on to the cart and kissed Sarah on the cheek, then each of the children in order of their age. August held his hand out to shake the Reverend's, but the Reverend moved across and hugged him. August held firm and wilted not. He smiled at Sarah briefly, holding the Reverend in a dignified embrace. The Reverend got down off the wagon and waved his handkerchief as August whipped up the ox and the Crooks family set off again.

August and Sarah locked up their memories of the Cove Estate and threw the key away. August recited a passage from Exodus that Rose had once taught him. The Promised Land lay ahead.

*And the children of Israel journeyed from Rameses to Succoth, about six hundred thousand on foot that were men, beside children.*

*And a mixed multitude went up also with them; and flocks, and herds, even very much cattle.*

*And they baked unleavened cakes of the dough which they brought forth out of Egypt, for it was not leavened; because they were thrust out of Egypt, and could not tarry, neither had they prepared for themselves any victual.*

*Now the sojourning of the children of Israel, who dwelt in Egypt, was four hundred and thirty years.*

*And it came to pass at the end of the four hundred and thirty years, even the selfsame day it came to pass, that all the hosts of the LORD went out from the land of Egypt.*

*It is a night to be much observed unto the LORD for bringing them out from the land of Egypt: this is that night of the LORD to be observed of all the children of Israel in their generations.*

## THE BEGINNING

# Appendix

# Family Tree

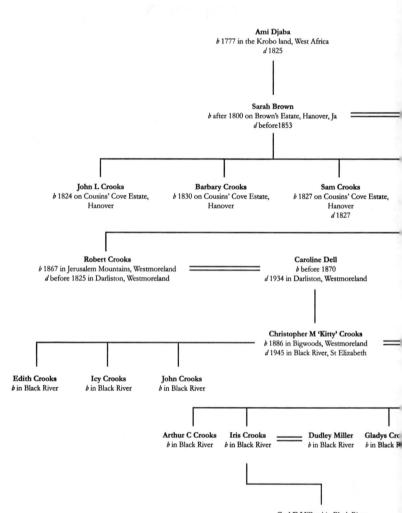

**Ami Djaba**
*b* 1777 in the Krobo land, West Africa
*d* 1825

**Sarah Brown**
*b* after 1800 on Brown's Estate, Hanover, Ja
*d* before1853

**John L Crooks**
*b* 1824 on Cousins' Cove Estate,
Hanover

**Barbary Crooks**
*b* 1830 on Cousins' Cove Estate,
Hanover

**Sam Crooks**
*b* 1827 on Cousins' Cove Estate,
Hanover
*d* 1827

**Robert Crooks**
*b* 1867 in Jerusalem Mountains, Westmoreland
*d* before 1825 in Darliston, Westmoreland

**Caroline Dell**
*b* before 1870
*d* 1934 in Darliston, Westmoreland

**Christopher M 'Kitty' Crooks**
*b* 1886 in Bigwoods, Westmoreland
*d* 1945 in Black River, St Elizabeth

**Edith Crooks**
*b* in Black River

**Icy Crooks**
*b* in Black River

**John Crooks**
*b* in Black River

**Arthur C Crooks**
*b* in Black River

**Iris Crooks**
*b* in Black River

**Dudley Miller**
*b* in Black River

**Gladys Cr**
*b* in Black R

**Carl E Miller** *b* in Black River
**Doreen M Miller** *b* in Black River
**Sheila Y Miller** *b* in Black River
**Sandra Miller** *b* in Black River

**ohn Alexander Crooks**
*b* 1787 in West Africa
*d* after 1840

**William Crooks**
*b* 1832 on Cousins' Cove Estate,
Hanover
═══════
**Ellen Crooks**
*b* after1824
*d* before 1932

**Charlotte M Dunkley**
1893 in Hilltop, St Elizabeth
*d* 1973

**Violet Letmond**

**Joseph Letmond**

**Ethlyn Crooks**
*b* in Black River

**Mogletta Crooks**
*b* in Black River

**Hyacinth V P Crooks**
*b* in Black River

**George M N Crooks**
*b* in Black River

**Doreen Fay Cousins**
*b* 1941 in Mount Pleasant,
Portland

**Lloyd Crooks** *b* 1963 London, England
**Paul Crooks** *b* 1964 London, England
**Mark Crooks** *b* 1973 London, England

# Afterword

I COULDN'T HAVE been older than five or six when a dreamy, unstructured thought sparked a curiosity that continues to rage. It was a bright Saturday morning in late spring, I think. I had been watching television. There were images of black and white – it must have been one of the old Pinewood Studios films. I wondered whether these actors were still alive. My mind drifted. I thought deeply of these images, and, at the same time, tried to make sense of the world around me. Then the question entered my mind: how did I get here, to England? I couldn't shake it.

Later, I remember asking Dad questions. Was the world black and white when you were young? Did black people come from England? Where were you born? Did you have a dad? Where is he? I learnt, too, that Dad came from a parish in Jamaica called St Elizabeth. His father died when he was six. His father was from the parish called Westmoreland.

'There is a whole heap of Crooks in Wezmoreland, loads of them,' he often said. 'We come from a place called Darliston.'

I pictured Westmoreland from a vantage point high up in the sky. I had thoughts of looking down on it, and seeing a sea of black people, a nation, like the Israelites. The way Dad said it made me think that no other people lived in Westmoreland. I thought about the name Crooks. How odd it sounded. I had begun to wonder why it was that some black people had African names and others had English names. I asked other questions. Did the Crooks

269

family appear in Westmoreland by magic? Did your dad's dad come from there, too? Who was the first Crooks who ever lived? Was he a white man? I asked my father the same things repeatedly, in the hope that he could and would elaborate. The best I ever got was that there were still people called Crooks in Westmoreland. Also his brother Arthur, almost twenty years older than Dad, often visited Darliston and knew them all. But Uncle Arthur lived in Jamaica and I didn't know him.

I yearned to understand the events leading up to my parents' marriage. Where, how and when had they met? What had preceded these events? They were both born in Jamaica. They had three sons: Lloyd, Mark and me. Why in London and not in Jamaica? I suppose it was inevitable that I should need to find out their paths, rather than expect anybody else to answer my questions.

I was seven and at primary school when I first became aware of the connection between black people and Africa. I had also watched enough Tarzan movies by that time to know that Africa and black folk went together in the common consciousness, like rice and peas. One morning our so-called teacher addressed the class.

'Children, do you know why Africa is called the dark continent?' I was all ears. 'Because nothing came from there – until the Europeans went there, of course.' A shiver of embarrassment ran through me. She didn't look at me specifically when she said it, but the bullet hit the intended target. I imagined a land, dark, empty and grim – a kind of nothingness. I pictured it being illuminated by the sudden appearance of white people. It didn't feel right. I was too young to articulate why I knew she was wrong, but I remember that she babbled on about there being no such thing as white lies, only black lies, black sheep, black comedies and a whole load of other negatives about the colour black. My later schooling taught me that black people came from Africa and that we were brought here – to

England, that is – as slaves, by white people; there was no mention of Jamaica or America. Nothing made sense. I knew that I had been born in England and that both my parents came from Jamaica; no mention of any African connection.

In 1973 my paternal grandmother died. Within days Dad had caught a flight to Jamaica for the funeral. He returned with an album full of family photos he had taken there. Among them was one taken in 1941, showing Dad as a toddler with my Uncle Arthur, my grandmother and my grandfather, Christopher 'Kitty' Crooks. He hung the framed picture on the wall in our living-room. Every so often I would get up on tip-toe and try peering into Grand-dad's eyes. They looked unusual, opaque, not dark like my grandmother's. Granddad looked too old to be a daddy. He was fifty-six when the photo was taken. I once asked Dad whether he was sure he was his father, not his grandfather.

I visited Black River, my father's place of birth, for the first time in 1977. It was as though time had stood still in parts of this little town. He and I walked into town each morning. Dad would use these walks to reminisce about his childhood, for example, going to the bread shop every morning to buy coca bread; that was among the experiences we repeated together. Whenever we passed it, he would point out the house where he was brought up. We visited his old playing grounds. We walked out to the bridge to see where he had made a name for himself climbing to the top and jumping into the river. I relished every moment of that three-week holiday.

My brother Lloyd discovered Radio One's John Peel in the late 1970s and I was introduced to roots reggae. Each night, in between the punky music, Peel would play two or three reggae tracks in succession. Lloyd would rush into my room to tell me when this was happening. I taped groups like Culture, Burning Spear, Prince Fari and more. I listened intensely to the lyrics. Burning Spear's 'Invasion'

271

and 'Black Soul' spoke to me. He sang to the sounds of dub music with the hypnotic *nya bingy* drum rhythms. His music was an ode to the history of black people in the Americas. And with the poetry of Linton Kwesi Johnson, I awoke from a deep sleep to the blur of my identity and to the struggle of black people in England. I needed to make more sense of it. I wanted to start by finding out about my slave ancestry.

In 1985, Dad handed me a book he had borrowed from the local library: it was called *Blacks in Bondage*, the first volume of Richard Hart's *Slaves Who Abolished Slavery*. He said it was a very important book for me to read. I scanned the pages and read first-hand accounts of the slaves' suffering at the hands of their masters. I hadn't known that such accounts existed. I believed that our past had been jettisoned with the passing of time. I was intrigued to find out where Mr Hart had got hold of these accounts. I found the sources at the back of the book and made a note of them, particularly the archives in England. I thought it might be of use, one day.

In the summer of 1988 my Dad's niece, Sheila Miller, came to visit us from America. Here was a member of the family who shared my desire to discover our history. Sheila undertook organising a family reunion. We talked excitedly of doing some research beforehand. She wrote to as many family members as she could, mentioning that she wanted to write a book which she would dedicate to our paternal grandmother, Charlotte Crooks (Modder). Her letter referred to her 'getting direction from somewhere' to do this. I felt this too.

We booked a trip to Jamaica, for the family reunion, the following year. Dad knew I was keen to do some research there, and said we should visit the Spanish Town archives; Uncle Arthur would take us there. I naively thought I'd be able to find out everything I needed to know in one visit to

Jamaica. In preparation for this, I visited the Jamaican High Commission in Prince Consort Street, London, hoping to get some advice. It seemed a good place to start. But I needed to find out what slave records existed in Jamaican repositories. I made no appointment. I just turned up on the door and was directed to a man who was kind enough to offer me a seat in his office before dropping a bombshell: almost all the records relating to plantations in Jamaica had been destroyed; they had been burnt around the time when slavery ended, when the rebellion took place and many of the 'great houses' were set on fire. Very few, if any, survive today. It would be an impossible task, he said.

The meeting didn't last long and he was soon wishing me the best of luck. My confidence was at a low ebb as I left the building. I had been there for only five minutes, and had nothing to show for my journey to the heart of Kensington. I felt I'd made a fool of myself, and dispiritedly walked the short distance to Exhibition Road, where my car was parked, and drove home.

The family reunion took place in 1990, as Sheila had planned. The main event was to get together at the church in Black River. We visited my Aunt Ethlyn after the service, and she showed Mark and me photos. I huddled beside her on the settee; Mark perched on the arm. Then we began to ask about the past. She took us through some of her most treasured photos, speaking in a low, tense voice as she introduced the people in each of the photos. There was a black-and-white one of a woman that captivated me. She was young and beautiful.

Aunt Ethlyn pushed it into my hands. 'Keep it,' she said.

This was unexpected. I felt as though I was begging – something I wasn't brought up to do. I pushed it back, but she wouldn't take it. I accepted. She went on to give me many others. She knew what she was doing. I later found out that she was suffering from a terminal illness. I realise now that she was actually willing them to both Mark and myself.

There was an elderly woman, probably in her late seventies, who sat quietly in the corner of the living-room. Aunt Ethlyn told us she was Aunt Violet (Vi) Letmond, a good person to talk to if we wanted to find out more about the family's history. Mark and I moved over to Aunt Vi. She had a good spirit. We asked her about those who had gone before. I don't think Aunt Ethlyn appreciated that Aunt Vi's memory had begun to fade; she had some difficulty recollecting the names and family ties, but I sketched out a tree while Mark scribbled notes on a pad. She told us that Grandma and Granddad met in Cuba, and that they later worked together in Black River. She also mentioned Dad's half-brother, Granddad's first child, whose name was John.

Soon after arriving back England, I started constructing a simple family tree. I wasn't sure what to do next, so I put it away for safekeeping.

A year on, a letter dropped through the door. It came from a family research agency, and contained information about the Crookses. Intrigued, I sent off for the 'Return if you're not satisfied' package. I had high expectations. When the package came, the first thing that dropped out was a picture of a white family. What a shock! The only members of the Crooks family that I knew were black – us. Never had heard of any Crookses originating from anywhere except Jamaica. There was also a list, which must have run into the hundreds, of people called Crooks in America, Germany, Switzerland, England and elsewhere. There was no listing for Jamaica. Worse still, my family didn't appear in the English list. I concluded that the African Caribbean had been excluded. There was a section on sources of genealogical information. Before I sent it back, something told me to make a list of the addresses, in case they proved useful one day. My wife, Sandra, found the list a few months later lying around the house. She picked it up and filed it away with other items I had been collecting along the way. Thank you, Sandra.

In February 1992, Sandra and I visited the Gambia. It was her choice; she always knows where my head and heart are. It was the first time we had been to Africa. The locals told us that we look like the Fante people. I liked the idea, but we dismissed it as the locals saying what they thought we wanted to hear, buttering us up for money. If only they had appreciated the extent to which my blood had been mingled with that of other West African nations. We visited St James Fort, where the slaves embarked on their journeys across the Middle Passage. I wondered all the time whether this was the place from which my ancestors had embarked. But in the end I didn't feel that it was.

On return to England, I bought a computer. Not long after that, I snapped up a family-tree software package I saw in the sales. I retrieved my sketch and started creating a proper family tree. I was corresponding with Sheila by e-mail. I rekindled the idea of research but sensed that Sheila had lost her spark. I found myself communicating regularly with her husband, Milton. He had a keen interest in family research, and had compiled a detailed database, which included Sheila's side. He sent me the file. I retrieved my grandfather's date of birth, Christopher Crooks. The file recorded it as 18 January 1886 – and I accepted this at the time, although I later discovered it was not wholly accurate. The name of my great-grandfather Robert Crooks was also included. Aunt Iris (Sheila's mum) was the source. It was a tremendous leap back in time. I calculated that I was perhaps two, maybe three, generations from my slave ancestors. The file revealed the name of one of my great-grandmothers – or so I thought. I was later to discover that this woman, Ellen, was Robert's mother. It was incredible. Milton had resurrected the stimulus I needed to continue my search. He supplied me with other sources of information held in England. One of the addresses was that of the Family History Centre, in Exhibition Road, London. It was at the Church of the Latter-Day Saints. I went there, with the purpose of tracing the Crooks lineage back as far as I could. The building was modern – not in keeping with the traditional image of a church. I thought it uncanny that it was a spit away from the Jamaican High Commission. On entering, I asked for the Family History Centre and was directed to the second floor. At the reception desk I was asked to sign in. I walked in, a little unsure of myself: all the attendants were busy helping others.

Then one asked, in a distinctly American accent, 'Can I help you, sir?'

I said politely that I wanted to look up the births, marriages and deaths for Westmoreland, Jamaica. They were extremely helpful, spending a few minutes explaining to me how to use the database. Then I was on my own. I typed Dad's name into the computer. He wasn't listed. I felt shy about asking the attendants for help. There were about a dozen visitors, each one intensely busy and looking as if they knew exactly what they were doing. After an hour of exploration I went home, mentally exhausted. I knew this was only the start.

I was more hopeful on the next visit and I ventured to ask an attendant for help. That night, I went home with a computer printout, which gave some references for the birth records in Darliston. I went back the following week to investigate the references. I was disappointed again on being told that the relevant files had not been archived in London. There was some comfort, but not much, in knowing that these records existed, albeit in the Spanish Town Archives in Jamaica. I wished I could scoop up the records and bring them to London so that I could search to my heart's content. I certainly could not easily entertain the idea of making several trips to Jamaica. I felt as though I'd bitten off more than I could chew. I gave up searching, yet again. I was sure I had.

A few months passed and something irrepressible kept urging me to go back to the Family History Centre. I answered the call and returned. I tried looking up my mother's father, although tracing my maternal ancestors was not what I originally had in mind. This was a detour. I was looking for something that would give me hope, perhaps lift my spirits. I thought it might be easier because I knew the year of his birth, if nothing else – 1916. I could have cried when I found listings for 1915 and 1917; but 1916, as far as I could see, was missing. This was evidently not the direction of my calling.

Within weeks the urge was back gnawing at me. I went back once again to the Centre, unsure of my purpose. When I got there, I found myself a place at a computer. I sat down and went through the motions of calling up menus, but found no useful leads. I prayed for inspiration; I asked the ancestors to provide a guiding light. I was sure I had arrived at the right place at the right time. I felt that all would be revealed to me sooner or later. Then a female attendant asked me how my search was going. Not so well, I confessed. She probed a little, and I told her exactly what I was looking for. My heart lifted when she told me that the Centre did hold some Jamaican records but they were not entered on the computer. I kept saying to myself, 'Everything happens for a reason.' I was learning to trust that *something* that had led me this far. The attendant referred me to one of her colleagues, who knew a little more about the West Indian records. She showed me cabinets that housed records of Jamaican births, marriages and deaths (book format) copied onto microfilm. There were numerous microfilms – too many to count. I hadn't a clue how to begin. A black woman, who seemed to be hovering, then intervened. Her name was Marcie Williams. She told me of the Centre's indexes, which the workers knew little about. She had become such an expert that attendants often referred to her for help. She said she was having great success tracing her family links around the world. She told me that the Centre had obtained microfilm of birth, marriage and death indexes held in Spanish Town Archives.

As I searched the indexes, I thought of the anonymous person who had painstakingly compiled all this by hand. I doubted that that clerical assistant could ever have appreciated the interest that their meticulous efforts would draw over a century later. I wanted to confirm Christopher Crooks's date of birth and then, if I could find his certificate, confirm that his father's name was indeed Robert. Frustratingly, there were no records after 1877. But that wasn't a good enough reason to put anything on hold. I could still look for Robert. I used to arrive at 6.30 p.m. when local parking became free, and scroll through metres of tape. Usually, just when I was getting into my stride and thought I was homing in on something, a voice would ring out: 'Ten minutes before closing time!' Time ran out more often than I could bear. Sometimes I felt ready to throw a tantrum, especially when the second call announced, 'Five minutes and we're closing!'

Then, one cold winter's evening in 1995, I found it. Robert Crooks was listed in the baptism records of 1868, the only one of that name listed in the Westmoreland index. I started compiling a list of everybody named Crooks. I found no mention of my family name before 1838. I built a database and did some analysis. I tried to group the names according to the birth dates to see if there were any obvious relationships or groupings. But something was emerging that I hadn't been prepared for: I had had a preconceived notion that all Westmoreland Crookses were in some way related by blood; this was proving not to be the case.

I found the marriage listing for one William Crooks to Ellen. This was for 1856, eleven years before Robert's birth (which, I discovered later from the baptism records, was in

1867). This must be where my Aunt Iris got the name Ellen from, I thought. Could Ellen really have been one of my great-grandmothers? Only a detailed record of Robert's birth would confirm it; but I couldn't find one. Never mind, I would press on regardless. There were still two problems: I had no documentary evidence that these were indeed Robert's parents; and I had yet to find a birth record for William – in Westmoreland. That William Crooks would have been born, say, twenty to thirty years before William and Ellen's marriage. My search had so far yielded nothing. Maybe this was as far as it went, I thought. Then I gave up. Yet again, I consoled myself that I had reached as far back as I was ever likely to.

A few months later, Dad reminded me of his uncle's names, Manny, Buddy and Jimmy. I remembered having found a James Crooks, a mulatto born in Westmoreland in 1825. I gravitated back to the Centre to check, hoping that there might be a connection. I was too ready to accept that there was. I looked up another record and was excited when I found the names Mary and Belinda, both baptised in Westmoreland in 1810. I assumed one to be the mother of James. But where were the records of their parents? It seemed implausible that they were the first slaves to carry the label Crooks. I couldn't confirm any links with my line, so I assumed them. This was turning into a marathon and I was wilting at the prospect of how far there was still to go. I was daunted by the thought of having to explore new avenues.

In the ensuing months, I lost sleep wondering about the significance of 1838. Why were there so few Crookses recorded before then? Something was urging me to find the answer. Yet the evidence suggested that my forebears had arrived in Westmoreland from somewhere else. I was beginning to feel that my search was in some way hindered by my ignorance of Jamaica's history. If I was going to solve this mystery, I had to address my ignorance. I would read any book about Jamaica that I could lay my hands on, searching for vital clues.

Eventually I discovered that slavery in Jamaica ended on 1 August 1838. Many ex-slaves left the plantations for the hills, hoping for a fresh start. It dawned on me that the Crookses must have been part of that mass exodus. What was the political, economic and social motivation for this flight to the hills? I reread Richard Hart's books, and made several trips to the British Library between visits to the Family History Centre. This knowledge was to prove invaluable in leading me to other sources. I rested for a while, hoping for a sign.

It turned out that a colleague of mine had a grand-mother by the name of Crooks from Hanover, though she didn't know which area. Even if she didn't come from Westmoreland, I felt certain that we must be related. I was somewhat confused at first, because no one had ever mentioned that we had distant relatives living in Hanover. Then I realised the significance. Black folk, I imagined, could travel only relatively short distances in the early nineteenth century. So, if I were looking for the property on which my forebears were held in bondage, it made sense to study a neighbouring parish as well. My despair evaporated in an instant. That evening I sped to the Centre and pulled out the Hanover records pre-dating 1838. To my great jubilation, I found listings for dozens more Crookses. I was fascinated to notice that there were many baptisms, marriages and deaths before 1838 but significantly fewer after that date.

The Hanover parish records moved me deeply: I felt connected to these people. I was a little doubtful that everyone named Crooks lived on the same plantation somewhere in Hanover. A disproportionate number were classified mulatto, or quadroon. Where were their black forebears? I had an information block. Something else took over at this point and I decided to force a link between the

Hanover slaves and my great-great-grandfather, William Crooks. I started with the premise that Christian names were handed down over time. I found a mulatto slave named James and an African woman by whom he had children in the 1770s and 1780s. My head was fighting with my heart, telling me to bring this to an end. My head won the battle and I proceeded to construct a flawed family tree, based on names common to the last three generations of Crookses. I planted all such names as James, Robert, Christopher and John as a branch in the tree. I even connected myself to the white plantation owner named Crooks, purely to establish a root.

My wife's patience was wearing thin, but she never really let on. I would bore her with the tales of what I found. One evening she commented that I never asked her how her day had been. I had become totally self-absorbed; I had lost regular contact with close friends and family. The need to bring this addictive quest to a right and proper end was like an all-consuming fire, burning every diversionary thought in its path. The daily visits to the Centre and the frequent disappointments wore me down. I was feeling physically, mentally and financially drained. Long hours at work didn't help. I was returning home from the Centre after my daughter had been put to bed. I had been missing her terribly. Then one day my wife told me that the rag-and-bone man had come to clear the garage and that my daughter – who was then two – skipped up to him and called him Daddy. I stopped going to the Centre.

Six, maybe seven months passed and I became increasingly restless. When I next went to the Centre, I did so without telling Sandra, fearful that she might try to persuade me not to go. I had to prove that Robert Crooks was indeed my great-grandfather. Aunt Iris's word was good enough, but I wanted to set eyes on documentary evidence. Finding my grandfather's birth certificate would identify his parents.

281

I learnt that I could order birth certificates for Jamaicans born after 1886. The microfilm I needed was filed in Salt Lake City Family History Center, Utah. It would prove costly as well as frustrating if the date of birth given to me was even one year out. As far as I was aware, there were no indexes created after 1877, which meant that I could not go straight to the document I needed. I ordered the microfilm for 1886. It arrived a month later. I couldn't find Christopher's birth certificate. I tried on two separate occasions, once when tired and once when I was fresh. I found nothing for 18 January. The microfilm had to be returned to Salt Lake City within a month. *Something* urged me to search one last time.

Three days before the microfilm was due to be sent back, I found my 'holy grail': the birth certificate of my grandfather Christopher Maitland Crooks revealed that he was born on 9 January 1886, and his birth was registered at a place called Bigwoods, just outside Darliston; furthermore, it confirmed Robert as my great-grandfather and Caroline Dell as my great-grandmother – not Ellen, as Aunt Iris had thought. Aunt Iris wasn't sure how she had come by the information. She didn't quite know how to take it when I told her that Ellen was in fact her great-grandmother. This was vital information. I headed home, driving through Hyde Park to the sounds of Buju Banton's 'Hills and Valleys', now charged with emotion. When I reached Paddington, I changed the music to the New York Restoration Choir's, 'Holy Lamb of God', and I wept for joy.

Marcie told me that Guy Grannum (author of *Tracing Your West Indian Ancestors at the Public Record Office*) was giving a talk at the Royal Genealogical Society. The day was sunny and bright with a slight chill. Sandra accompanied me, and treated it like an adventure, 'boldly going where we had never been before'. We arrived late, missing Mr Grannum's talk, but were in time to catch the second speaker, Steven Porter. One of the things that interested me was how few black people in London were tracing their roots; by contrast, many white folk were apparently researching their West Indian roots. During his lecture, Porter held up a book called *Monumental Inscriptions*, saying that the inscriptions discussed in it came from the tombstones of the most prominent people in Jamaica's past. After the meeting the book was placed on the desk for all to see. A woman got there before me. When my chance came, I browsed eagerly and found a James Crooks who died in 1743 in Lucea, Hanover. It occurred to me that he might well have been the owner of a large property. If so, it followed that he might well have owned a large number of slaves. I had found a location in Hanover where I could focus my search. I had the feeling that I was on to something big.

Next came an e-mail from Marcie informing me that the Royal Geographical Society, in Kensington Gore, held old maps of Jamaica. I went there, and told the attendant that I was looking for a slave plantation in a parish in Jamaica. I asked whether he had any maps that might be of use. He led me to a drawer and fumbled through some index cards. He showed me two that he thought might be relevant, giving details of maps of Jamaica dated 1768 and 1804. He disappeared for about ten minutes and returned with the 1768 map. It was cloth and about four feet by two. I recognised the place names as those of properties and plantations; in many cases the names were also those of the property owners. While the attendant went to find the second map, I scanned the parish of Portland in search of the name Cousins. Then I peered at Hanover, especially around the port of Lucea. Nothing particularly exciting sprang out of that area. I became increasingly apprehensive as I scanned the Kingston area, and all over St Elizabeth. Then I placed my hands over Westmoreland and imagined myself travelling back in time. This map was more than two hundred years old. I could feel my heart beating rapidly as I tried to *thread my mind that long ago*. Now here was something: my eyes had flashed past; I'm sure I saw Crooks. I concentrated on finding it. Those few seconds felt like an eternity. I spotted it: Crooks' Cove. I trembled with sheer excitement. I wanted to shout and punch the air. I wanted to share it with somebody. I wanted to thank God. I knew I had found my ancestral origins in Jamaica.

When the attendant returned with the 1804 map, I announced that I had found what I was looking for and pointed it out to him. Crooks' Cove was also on the later map. He seemed glad to have been of assistance, but he cannot not possibly have appreciated the significance of what I had found. He kindly offered to make copies for me, for which I remain grateful. I left the building walking tall, feeling euphoric. A whole new avenue of enquiry had opened up.

The following month I went to Jamaica. On that trip I talked over my findings with Aunt Iris and her husband, Uncle Dudley. I had my family tree with me and shared all I had found out.

One day, I travelled one hundred miles from the east of the island to the west, to visit Cousins' Cove. I had no game plan or any real expectation. My wife, Dad and my daughter came with me. We stopped at Lucea and found ourselves at a spot overlooking the cove. I had a vision of it in the days when it was a thriving eighteenth-century trading port. Looking out towards the horizon, I imagined a slave ship coming into port, the port where my ancestors entered the New World and a life of bondage. Passing through Lucea, I discovered the Hanover Museum. There I was given information about records held in the National Library of Jamaica. They told me of a man who lived in Cousins' Cove who would be worth meeting. We duly found him.

He told us that new houses had recently been built on the Cove. While the foundations were being laid, bones had been raised from shallow graves. My first thought was that this might have been a mass burial ground. The thought that my ancestors' resting-place might have been disturbed was distressing, but I was powerless to do anything about it. It was getting dark and we didn't have a chance to explore the area. I vowed to return another time.

On returning to London, I visited the Centre and met Marcie leaving. We brought each other up to date on the current state of our searches. I told her I had made lists of all the Crookses in Westmoreland and Hanover before 1877. She then told me that I hadn't delved as much as I could have done. She said that the indexes were merely signposts to more detailed information about birth, marriage and death records, including birth certificates. I was aghast. I realised that I still hadn't seen a detailed birth record of Robert. I had relied too much on the indexes alone. A whole new set of information opened up for me. I found the record confirming that Robert's father was William Crooks, a labourer. Robert's birth was registered in the Jerusalem Mountains. I went through the records, noting Robert's siblings. I wasn't surprised at all when I found that the eldest was named John – the name my grandfather had given his first child.

I set myself the objective of confirming William's birth. Referring back to the Hanover indexes, I found two Williams, one born between 1800 and 1825, the other born between 1828 and 1836. The date of 'my' William's marriage to Ellen gave me a pretty good idea of which could be discounted. Sure enough, it was the other William, a mulatto baptised in 1813; I later discovered he was seventeen at the time.

After a few more visits I found a more detailed record of 'my' William's baptism in 1834. He was baptised at the age of two, along with his two siblings. I was more pleased than surprised to learn that the eldest sibling was John, aged eight. They had a sister named Barbary, aged four.

Their parents were recorded as John Crooks and Sarah Brown. I was dizzy when the records showed that both parents were from Cousins' Cove Plantation. John was an unskilled labourer. The records also implied that the property had changed ownership between 1804 and 1834.

I was now ready for a trip to the Public Record Office. I was ready to research the slave registers of 1817–34. I knew the five names I would look for. I needed to be more tightly focused than I had been so far. It would take a day or so to familiarise myself with the PRO and its systems, and goodness knows how long to find what I was looking for. I therefore planned to take two weeks' leave from work. Again, I would have to shut out my friends, family and others in order to concentrate.

I would have to handle this delicately with Sandra. She greeted my token request for time out from family life with a loving smile, which eased my anxieties. I sensed that she knew it was better to let me off the leash to run wild for a few hours than to obstruct me and, in so doing, increase my frustration. But I felt also that she had begun to harbour an unspoken desire to research her own ancestors: we had the odd moment of light banter about which one of us could lay claim to maroon ancestry; prestige attached to the side of the family with the most rebellious individuals. What had the man at the High Commission said about records being destroyed? I was excited, on an unprecedented high.

On the second day, I hit a rich vein of information. Opening the Hanover slave register of 1817 was like pressing a button on a time machine and accelerating back two hundred years. I knew it made sense to look at Cousins' Cove Plantation first, but I wanted to savour the moment of looking for properties owned by Crookses. These were two or three smallholdings with no more than ten slaves on each. As I flipped the pages I spent some time looking at the style of writing of the day, appreciating the effort that went into compiling the registers. I found to my amazement that the slaves' ages were included. Even more interesting were statements of origin. I was astounded when I discovered that on each plantation at least one-third of the slaves were listed as African – I am not entirely sure why I was expecting a smaller proportion. The remaining two-thirds were listed as creole, meaning that they were born on the island. When I was satisfied that my ancestors did not labour on the small Crooks properties, I searched Cousins' Cove and found it listed under the ownership of Richard Dickson. There were 187 slaves on the property. I found John Alexander Crooks, aged thirty, a negro; his slave name was August, and he was African. I wondered where his name was taken from, and I suspected that it was also the name of the previous owner. There was so much more to be gleaned. The records were updated every three years to take account of the changes in the slave population on an individual's property. I searched for a record of John's death, but could find none. Instead, I found a record of his firstborn, John; his mother was Sarah Brown. Sam died twenty-eight days after birth; his mother, too, was Sarah Brown. Then I found a Barbary and William; their mother was Sarah Brown. It occurred to me that Sarah herself was not listed on the original slave register. Her children were recorded as sambos, a classification used for those of mulatto and negro parentage. I concluded that Sarah was a mulatto. Also that she had been manumitted, as some mulattos were. I discovered the names of the owners and their attorneys. I even found the compensation paid to the executor of the estate when the 187 Cousins' Cove slaves were emancipated. Interestingly, there was a record of John Hope, a man who had been convicted of a slave conspiracy. Tensions on the estate? Was he the leader of a planned rebellion? He would be the same age as John Alexander Crooks – African, too. Were they friends? How much would John Crooks have known? Would he have colluded with John Hope?

I wrote to the National Library of Jamaica requesting any information they had about Cousins' Cove. Within no time at all, they were able to provide me with a report and survey of the Cove Plantation dated 1820. The survey map had two things of interest: the location of the great house on the hill and that of the slave village, by the cove, where the villagers' final resting-place had been disturbed by the thrust of development. Later I learnt that slaves used to bury their dead in the kitchen gardens, a practice which continued when slavery ceased. I went back to the Family History Centre, searching for a record of John Alexander Crooks's baptism. I found that he had been baptised on 1 January 1813. He was one of the few slaves to have been baptised. Why? I went back a few times to try and link the slave registers with the baptisms. I stumbled across more records, which showed estates where mass baptisms took place, well over a hundred slaves at a time, but nothing for Cousins' Cove.

I analysed the slave register for hours under a dim light in my study. I worked hard at understanding relationships and matching families. In essence, I was trying to reconstruct life on the plantation. One night I was so tired that I found myself nodding off, and decided it was time to turn in. The last name I saw was Judy Brown, an entry in the register of 1826 that I had seen on numerous occasions. She died in 1825, aged forty-seven. I had often wondered about the circumstances of her premature death. She must have had a real rough time of it, I thought. I turned off the computer, my thoughts dwelling idly on Judy Brown, Judy Brown, *Brown*! Suddenly I was wide awake again. Until that point, I had concentrated on the name Crooks and, in particular, on John Alexander Crooks. Sarah Brown had slipped to the back of my mind. I reached for the register of 1817. I noticed her name under female listings, which I had passed over so many times: Jabba Brown (Christian Name), Ammie (Old Name), African, negro, aged forty. I

288

sat back in my chair and cursed myself for not having spotted this earlier. I had skipped past the name, misreading it as Annie. It was clearly written out as Ammie but I'd never heard of such a name. Maybe it was Amy. It had been staring at me for months. Sarah's mother. It was as if she had been crying out to me from the very pages – find me! I asked a Nigerian friend about the name Jabba. He told me it was a Muslim name, male. I couldn't accept that. Jabba Brown was clearly listed as a woman. I asked another friend, a Nigerian woman, whether Ammie (which I pronounced Amy) meant anything to her. It didn't. However, when I said Ammie (pronounced á-mee) it struck a chord. She said it was probably short for Amina, a name common in northern Nigeria among the Hausa people. But everything I'd read suggested that most African Jamaicans – something like 90 per cent – originated from Ghana. I asked a Ghanaian friend. He had never heard of Ammie but Amina was familiar; he thought it was common in the north but wasn't sure. I cautiously accepted Amina as the correct name, assuming that the slave masters had shortened it. I had begun harbouring hopes of finding her exact place of birth.

On a Friday, several months later, I woke and told Sandra that I needed to go back to the PRO. *Something* was telling me to do so and by now I had learnt not to ignore it. I told her that I wanted to find out more about Ammie. I wasn't sure that this was so, but I had to give a reason.

As many times before, I asked for the 1817 Hanover slave register. I was told that someone was using it. There must be some mistake, I felt sure. Who else would want that particular document on that particular day? The PRO has ninety miles of shelving and a 5,500-page guide. It was just another uncanny moment, I guessed. I asked the attendant to check again, which she did, twice. I asked if she could tell me who had it, but data-protection laws made that impermissible. She saw my quiet distress, then said that she would find out when the person would be finished with it. I went back and sat down at my table. I was watching the woman out of the corner of my eye. She didn't move for five minutes; then she entered the reading area and spoke to a black man, one of two in the reading room – I was the other. She had a brief word with him and returned to her post at the reception desk. About two minutes later, she approached me. She told me that I would have the document shortly. I was duly given it and found nothing of any use. I kept watching the man. Eventually, I could bear it no longer. I went across to him and asked whether he, too, was researching the Hanover Register. Yes, he was. He agreed to my request that we talk.

We went out of the reading area and introduced ourselves. We spoke a little about our respective projects. He said he was researching all the plantations in Hanover and hoping to write a book. He told me he had information on Cousins' Cove. We exchanged addresses and promised to talk further. He wrote to me the following week and sent me some information he had gathered about Cousins' Cove. He had found an article, on one of the microfilms at the Colindale Newspaper Library, of a notice placed in the *Gleaner* on 17 September 1792 by John Crooks of Cousins' Cove, who was hoping to trace the movements of four of his runaway slaves – all African. One was called George Crooks, but I knew enough by now not to claim him as my ancestor.

I visited the man. My wish was to exchange information with him, but when we got talking he plainly wasn't interested in what I had to offer. He was more interested in a general overview of Hanover. His research was extensive and his collection impressive. He had been engaged on full-time research for the last seven years. Like me he had no grant to support him; he, too, I guessed, was driven by the need for enlightenment. He had been to all the relevant repositories of information; he had a deep knowledge of

Hanover's pre-emancipation history. The small room he occupied was itself a repository. He had hardly any other possessions. He had written articles on every plantation and every event that he had ever found. Sometimes he had painstakingly typed out original handwritten documents, word for word. He had no computer, so he used the local library. He made his cardboard folders. From behind his bed he pulled out a number of maps measuring about four feet by two. He showed me surveyed property and the extent of plantations in the minutest detail. He seemed to enjoy having me around. I asked him what information he had on Cousins' Cove. I was astounded when he produced a letter from the Rev. D. W. Rose (the man who had baptised John Alexander Crooks) to the Custos, stating that, unlike many of his counterparts, he was not charging slaves for baptising them. The man had information about a mass baptism that took place on the Cove in 1814. I discovered that forty slaves, from a small coffee and pimento plantation, joined the Cove villagers. Mr William Brown owned the plantation located a few miles east, in the hills. I was given information detailing slave ships that had docked in Jamaica at the turn of the eighteenth century.

I am deeply indebted to that man. I believe our meeting was more than chance.


The task I thought would give me greatest difficulty was identifying my grandfather's siblings. Dad didn't know his uncles' Christian names, and I needed their real names in order to find out about them from the Centre. I knew that there was at least twenty years between my grandfather and his youngest brother. I had enough faith by now to know that this information would reveal itself in time. I hadn't realised that the process had started in 1990, when my elder brother, Lloyd, married and moved to Birmingham. I had been keeping him appraised of my work. During the mid-1990s, he informed me of discoveries he was making.

He told me of a number of Crookses he had come across in Birmingham, mainly through the church. Curious, I asked him to find out whether their parents originated from Darliston in Westmoreland. They did. Lloyd had discovered our second cousins. And one, Patrick, reunited us with the family we thought we had lost. By the time I completed the penultimate draft of this book, Dad had been united with his first cousins from Darliston whom he hadn't seen for almost a half century. They not only told us the Christian names of my grandfather's siblings, but filled us in on copious other details; such as my grandfather's relationship with Jimmy, the youngest of ten children born to Robert; they told me of Caroline Dell, of life in Darliston and visits to Black River to see my grandfather, affectionately known to them as Uncle Kit.

I completed *Ancestors* believing that my journey had gone as far as it was ever going to go. A few weeks after submitting the manuscript to my publisher, Lloyd called me. He said that he'd met a Ghanaian man at his local church. The man had told him that he knew the name Jabba and that it was unique to a particular area in Ghana. It was definitely not a Nigerian name – he was adamant about that. At first, I suspected that Lloyd tried to convince me of this because he had recently visited Ghana and had a particularly happy time there. However, I was also open to this being another sign. I spoke to the man. I treated his information with the caution it was due. I mulled over it for a couple of weeks. Then I picked up the phone, rang the Ghanaian High Commission and asked for help. I was put in touch with a woman called Georgette Jabba. She agreed to meet me. I told her of my latest quest to find out where in Ghana the Jabbas originated. She told me that Georgette was not her real name and that all the girls in her family were called Dede. Also that the name Jabba was Krobo; the Krobo occupy the south-eastern region of Ghana. I pulled from my briefcase a photocopy of the 1817 register and asked whether she recognised the name Ammie. She looked closely at the spelling. She took out a pen and corrected the spelling of Jabba to Djaba. I asked her to look at Ammie.

'The name means "Born on Saturday", she said, correcting the spelling to Ami.

'You know someone called Ami?' I asked.

'Yes. Me,' she said.

I now have vital information which I believe will lead me, in the end, to the place from which my ancestor Ami Djaba originally came. And I know I will find it because, throughout this journey, I have sensed the truly awesome presence of *something* guiding me – ancestral spirits, perhaps.

# NOTES

Page

27  Based on an eyewitness account of the Ashanti conquest of Dagomba (Dagbama), J. Ade Ajayi and Michael Crowder, *The History of West Africa* (New York, 1985), p. 498.

39, 70  Slave entertainment, using self-ridicule as a form of protest: Braithwaite, p. 211.

97  Adapted from an account given by a slave, Richard Montagnac, 26 December 1823: Hart, vol. 2, p. 231.

129  Based on an anecdote before slavery ended: Phillippo, p. 203.

137  Ibid., p. 367.

150  Based on views Buxton had put forward during parliamentary debates supporting movement toward the gradual abolition of slavery: Klingberg, p. 226.

176  Based on a record of a trial, PRO: CO 137/157: Hart, vol. 2, pp. 228–9.

178  Songs of slave entertainment sourced from *Colombian* magazine, vol. 2, May 1787, p. 766: Braithwaite, p. 222.

180  Adapted from accounts given to Phillippo before slavery ended: Phillippo, p. 316.

187  Moses Baker, a Baptist minister during the Maroon War, was arrested for quoting in a sermon a hymn from a Baptist hymn book. Originally from John Clarke, W. Dendy and J. Phillippo, *The Voice of Jubilee: A Narrative of the Baptist Mission, Jamaica, from its Commencement: With Biographical Notices of its Fathers and Founders* (London, 1865), p. 34: Braithwaite, p. 255.

194  Adapted from an account given to Phillippo: Phillippo, p. 351.

198 Based on accounts given by Henry Bleby, a Methodist missionary who saw Sharpe in gaol at Montego Bay, and on an account given to Bleby by Edward Hilton, one of Sharpe's fellow conspirators: Hart, vol. 2, pp. 250, 253.

205 Based on a warning issued by a Baptist minister William Knibb when opening a new church in St James: Hart, vol. 2, p. 271.

217 Adapted from accounts given by a missionary writing to Phillippo during the 1832 insurrection: Phillippo, p. 318.

219 Hart mentions that this proclamation was not made public in Jamaica until months after it was received: Hart, vol. 2, p. 246.

221 Hart notes that this was a printed warning from Major-General Sir Willoughby Cotton to Belmore, 2 January 1832: Hart, vol. 2, p. 293.

222 Based on an incident in Trelawny recorded by the Presbyterian minister Waddell: Hart, vol. 2, p. 266.

226 Accounts of the trial are available at the PRO: Hart, vol. 2, p. 333.

# BIBLIOGRAPHY

Ajayi, J. Ade, and Crowder, Michael, *The History of West Africa*, 3rd edition, 2 vols, New York, 1985

Braithwaite, Edward, *The Development of Creole Society in Jamaica 1770–1820*, Oxford, 1971

Conniff, Michael L., and Davis, Thomas, *Africans in the Americas: The History of Black Diaspora*, London, 1994

Dookhan, Isaac, *A Post-Emancipation History of the West Indies*, Kingston, Jamaica, 1975

Equiano, Olaudah, *The African*, Black Classics (and imprint of X Press), London, 1998 (first published in 1789)

Grannum, Guy, *Tracing Your West Indian Ancestors*, London, 1995

Hall, Douglas, *In Miserable Slavery: Thomas Thistlewood in Jamaica 1750–1786*, Jamaica, 1990

Hart, Richard, *Plantation Society*, Jamaica, 1985

Hart, Richard, *Slaves Who Abolished Slavery*: vol. 1: *Blacks in Bondage*, Jamaica, 1980; vol. 2: *Blacks in Rebellion*, Jamaica, 1985

Higman, B. W., *Jamaica Surveyed: Plantation Maps and Plans of the 18th and 19th Centuries*, Jamaica, 1988

Klingberg, F. J., *The Anti-Slavery Movement in England*, London, 1926

Phillippo, James M., *Jamaica, Its Past and Present*, Westport, Conn., 1843

Segal, Ronald, *The Black Diaspora*, London, 1995

Tanna, Laura, *Jamaican Folk Tales and Oral Histories* (pp. 65–8: 'Johnny Do Good', story told by Adina Henry, August Town, St Andrew, 15 May 1973), Jamaica, 1984; reprint Miami: DLT Associates Inc. 2000

Zinke, F. Barham, *Days of My Years*, Jamaica, 1892

296